A Case for the Yarn Maker

A Case for the Yarn Maker

An Ainsley McGregor Mystery

Candace Havens

TULE
PUBLISHING

A Case for the Yarn Maker

Tule Publishing First Printing, April 2020

The Tule Publishing, Inc.

First Publication by Tule Publishing 2020

Cover design by Sue Traynor

ISBN: 978-1-951786-97-7

Chapter One

"GEORGE CLOONEY, IF you don't get in here right now, I'm never speaking to you again." My throat was raw and my head hurt, but I refused to give in to the head cold I'd been battling for two days. This was a big day at Bless Your Art, and I had to get there fast. Nerves tightened into a ball in my stomach, and I shoved a hand through my messy hair.

Today has to be perfect.

Unfortunately, George's new friend Mr. Squirrel was running back and forth across the fence line, driving him mad. "No more *treats*—ever—if you don't come inside right now." George stopped his incessant barking. He glanced at me, and then at the squirrel, and then promptly trotted back into the house.

"Amazing what the word *treat* can do for a certain someone." I laughed, thinking that it was good this dog kept my feet on the ground. Otherwise, I'd be a giant pile of worry.

He sat, and then stared at me expectantly, as I opened the jar on the counter and pulled out a large chew for him. Gently, he took it into his mouth and gave me a weird smile around it that might be scary to some people, but for me, it was nothing short of heart-melting.

George, my harlequin Great Dane, was the best dog on

the planet—when he behaved, which was most of the time.

After running upstairs to change into dark jeans, my favorite boots, and a soft blue sweater, and taking some more cold medicine, I loaded him into the back seat of the Explorer.

He put his enormous head on my shoulder. "Do not drool on me. Today will be one of our biggest days ever. If everything goes as planned."

I glanced at George Clooney in the rearview mirror, and he cocked his head as if he were listening to every word. I'm pretty sure he knew exactly what I said.

A few minutes later I drove down Sweet River's picturesque Main Street. I loved this Texas town with its quaint buildings and friendly people. Warmth blossomed in my chest, easing the tightness there a bit. I'd been here two years and it felt like home.

My grandmother lived here, and some of my best memories from childhood were hanging out at her house. The very one I inherited from her. But it was the people here who made Sweet River special.

"Wow. Look at that, George."

He grunted.

There was no parking left on the street and there was a double line of people down the block to my friend Shannon's coffee shop. All of those people waited to get into my store, Bless Your Art. "Whoo-hoo!" I shouted, as I did a fist pump.

George woofed, as if he understood my excitement. The tight knot in my stomach loosened. And for the first time in weeks, I relaxed.

This might work. There'd been so much planning and the special guest of honor, Yarn Goddess, who would arrive in exactly an hour and a half, liked everything a specific way for her book signings and the classes she'd teach afterward.

But it was worth the headaches and working myself to death to see that line wrapping around the building. Yarn Goddess had lived up to her hype. I'd been told that she was the Jennifer Aniston of the world of knitting and crochet. I hadn't believed it. When her assistant first contacted me, I thought I was doing them a favor.

I was wrong. Turns out that she has a multibillion-dollar yarn empire.

No one was more surprised than me when they wanted to do a book signing here. I still didn't know why.

"But lucky us."

George grunted again.

I parked in back and led George through the break room. The store was bustling on the inside, with each booth filled to the brim with crafts and artisanal items. This was my happy place. Even today with a spring cold and a headache that would kill a cow, it brought a smile to my face.

"Morning, Ainsley," said Mike, my favorite winemaker and fiancé of my bestie, Shannon. I'd helped him a few months ago when he was accused of murder, and ever since he'd been my right-hand man, making sure the store was clean and always organized. He had a winery to run, and I kept telling him he didn't need to help out so much here, but he and Shannon had insisted.

Today, I was more than grateful. Sleeping in had helped with the cold, even though the jackhammer continued to pound in my head. “Hey, thank you for everything. I can’t believe how organized this place looks.” With a myriad of booths selling everything from wine to yarn, to fake medieval weapons, art, and antiques, the place sometimes looked a bit hodgepodge, but not today.

“No worries,” he said. “I’ve had a lot of help this morning. Everyone knew how bad you’ve been feeling, and they really pitched in.”

My little gang of crafters and artisans had become a cheery, if somewhat dysfunctional, family. With that came a lot of nosing around in my business, but it was worth it. I had a group of friends who never let me down.

“Oh, and fair warning…” Mike followed me to the front of the store. “Mrs. Whedon has been grumbling all morning about how she’s going to give Yarn Goddess a piece of her mind.”

I rolled my eyes. I loved Mrs. Whedon. She was a curmudgeon of the highest degree but had a heart of goodness and light under all that crustiness. The chicken soup she’d made me yesterday was the only reason I was able to get out of bed this morning.

She had a popular booth in the store where she sold yarns from all over the world, and some that she spun herself. People came from all over Texas to take her classes. But man, when she had something in her craw (they like to say that around here) she was like a badger on steroids—never letting go of her prey.

I was about to go have some words with her when my phone rang. I waved bye to Mike and headed behind the counter, which was slightly raised so I could see the whole store from there. I got George settled while I talked.

"Hi, Ainsley, it's Hilary." The shrill voice sent the muscles tightening in my shoulders. I'd had at least thirty calls from her in the last two days. Yarn Goddess was demanding in a way I'd never experienced before, and her assistant, Hilary, was the messenger.

Maybe all CEOs with multibillion-dollar businesses and best-selling books on knitting patterns were like this. It was our first book signing, so I wanted things to be perfect, but even I had my limits.

"Hi," I said quietly. *Is she going to ask for pink elephants and giraffes next?* Mrs. Whedon had said that yesterday and it made me smile. "Are you guys excited about today?"

Hilary chuckled but it wasn't a happy sound. "I just wanted to give you a heads-up that we'll be coming about an hour early. She wants to make sure everything is done exactly the way she wants."

"Oh." Thank goodness Mike had come in early to make sure it was all organized. We only had thirty minutes until she arrived.

"And were you able to get her special water? If it's not exactly a No. 3 alkaline, she'll refuse to sign anything."

Even though she couldn't see me, I stopped myself from rolling my eyes. Poor Hilary was kind and often embarrassed by her boss's many demands. None of this was her fault.

"I did. I have a case of it." I'd had to drive to Austin, which was about forty miles away, to find it. We'd also ordered special tablecloths because she had to have all-natural fabrics around her. There were two vases of peonies, in pink, sitting on the table, and special handwipes she liked to use that were scented with lavender.

Did I mention Yarn Goddess was high maintenance?

"Great. Okay, well, we'll see you soon. And, um, Ainsley?"

"Yes?"

"I apologize in advance," she whispered. "She's having one of her bad days."

Then she hung up.

Um. Great. What did that mean?

THIRTY MINUTES LATER, loud voices from the back of the store had George sitting up from his nap.

Mike's face was priceless. His eyes wide, and his eyebrows nearly disappearing into his hairline.

"Let me guess," I whispered as he neared the counter. "She's here."

"Um. Yep. And she's not happy," he said. "Something about the peonies not being large enough and it's messing up her feng shoo shoo something for the signing."

The woman was impossible. Who needed fêng shui for a book signing? She couldn't cancel the signing this late. All of those poor people were standing in line to see the woman. Surely, she wouldn't disappoint them.

I guessed this is what Hilary meant about her having a bad day.

I grabbed a sip of water to push down the knot of terror in my throat. We'd bought several hundred copies of her books, and they were nonreturnable. I'd be out all of that money.

"I guess, I should say hello," I croaked.

George followed me to the middle of the store where several of the booth owners worked to move things around.

Yarn Goddess, who was at least sixty but thanks to a great plastic surgeon, could pass for forty, wore a Chanel suit with pearls. Her dark hair had been styled into a chignon, giving the appearance of an elegant woman one might see shopping on Fifth Avenue in New York.

I'd watched her videos and she seemed so friendly on camera. But nothing could be further from the truth.

"I don't want my fans to see any other yarn than my own," she shrieked. "Do you have morons running this place? Why would you try to take away from my business when I'm doing you a favor?"

Maybe, I'd just go back to the checkout counter.

Sensing the tension, George barked.

"Ahhhhhhhh!" Yarn Goddess screamed. "What is that beast doing in here? It's contaminating my yarn."

"Hello," I said, forcing my voice to stay calm. No one called George a beast, except me. "I'm Ainsley, the owner of Bless Your Art. I wanted to thank you for being here," I said. "We're very honored to have you."

Her eyebrow lifted, not too high, as I'm sure there was a bunch of Botox keeping her from having many facial expressions.

I reached out a hand to shake, but she just stared at it.

"Why is your nose red? Do you have a cold?" She grabbed one of her wipes. "Did you touch anything in here? What is it with this place? Animals and sick people. Hilary," she shrieked as she waved toward me and George, "take care of this. Now. Or I'm leaving."

Nerves boiled deep in my belly.

"I'll take George for a walk," Mike said.

I took a deep breath. "Can you see if maybe Jake can watch him for me? Just until the signing and classes are over?"

Jake was the fire chief and a great friend. His place out in the country was next to mine, and he loved George.

"Got it," he said.

Hilary guided me back to the front of the store. "I'm so sorry. I know I keep saying that," she said. "I'd like to say she's just nervous. This is her first time in public since her—um, procedures. She's worried people will think she had work done, even though she did."

I bit my lip to keep from laughing.

"But she's never the most pleasant person to be around." Hilary was dressed in a black suit and white blouse. Her heels were sensible, and I had a feeling that, unlike Yarn Goddess, she was trying to look older than she actually was. She had a sweet smile but a stern appearance.

"Her fans seem to adore her," I said, as we neared the counter.

"Wait, you'll see. With them, she's an angel. That's why I'm glad she's getting back out in public again. She needs them—or her ego does. I know that sounds terrible, since she gave me a chance when few would. But she feeds off that adoration, and it's been months. It's why, when I saw your email, I jumped on it."

I pursed my lips together. "Is she maybe put out that

we're such a small town? I'm sure she's used to big signings all over the world."

Hilary nodded. "I convinced her this was a great way to get back in the limelight. Do people even say that anymore?" She laughed. "Anyway, it's all show. She's a diva to the nth degree but she'll do the signing. She's also a professional. Just, maybe, keep your dog away from her. And you may want to steer clear."

No. Problem.

"THE CROWD IS winding down," Mike said four hours later. "Finally."

Thank goodness. Now we just had to get through the demonstrations at the community center and I could send Yarn Goddess on her way. The woman was a tyrant. Hilary was right. While she was quite kind to her adoring public—and wow, did they fuss over her—behind the scenes, I was more than willing to strangle the woman.

That's not nice. She'd brought a lot of business to the store, but it came with a price. At the last minute, we had to rearrange the booths to make sure she had plenty of "breathing space," and find her a closed tumbler for her water so people couldn't spread their germs.

I'm pretty sure that was directed at me.

Oh, and making poor George stay with my friend Jake, because she "abhorred animals of any sort, and they didn't belong anywhere close to her yarn." That had been screeched so loudly when Mike brought George back to wait for Jake, that it was audible from the front of the store.

I was ready to send her packing. Ugh. I'd never met a more disagreeable woman.

"Shannon set up coffee and desserts at the community center," I said, "and I made sure with Hilary that we have the demo table just as Yarn Goddess likes it."

I may have said her name a bit more sharply than I'd meant to, and Mike smiled.

"Who changes their legal name to Yarn Goddess? I mean, for real."

He laughed. "She is…something."

"That she is."

She smiled and shook hands, and even took selfies with her fans.

And then she glanced up and gave me a death stare.

I turned away and gave Mike a tight smile. It was the best I could do. "I appreciate it." I coughed, which was another reason I'd been working the registers at the front of the store. About two hours ago, I'd gone to check on her. Yarn Goddess took in my red nose and pale complexion, and pointed a finger and just said, "Go. I told you I don't want you anywhere near me."

Which was fine by me, really. Alaska wasn't really far enough away from her.

A few more hours, and she'd be out of my hair.

I couldn't wait.

BEFORE SHE COULD get out the back door to head to her

hotel for a nap, Mrs. Whedon stepped in her path. The older woman crossed her arms and gave Yarn Goddess a hard stare.

I shivered.

More surprising was that the mean billionaire stopped to listen. I stepped down from the register and crossed the store quickly, prepared to tackle Mrs. Whedon if things became physical.

"You're hurting people," Mrs. Whedon said.

"I have no idea what you're talking about. Everything in my company is made in America, and we use top-of-the-line dyes."

Mrs. Whedon was in her eighties—at least—but she had a fancier cell phone than I did. She popped her phone in front of Yarn Goddess's face. "These are pictures of people who have had reactions to your new line of yarn. You're selling it at an idiotic price and you're hurting your customers. You used to stand for something. But people need to know the truth and I'm going to lead the charge."

"People are always trying to sue people who have money. It's nothing new. They could have touched poison ivy or any number of things. Doesn't mean it came from my yarn."

Mrs. Whedon's jaw tightened. "All I'm asking you is to do a bit of research. You know what something like this could do to your business. I realize you're probably richer than Oprah by now, but that doesn't mean you shouldn't put out a quality product."

Hilary came in from the back of the store, with a look of sheer panic. She'd probably been waiting for her boss.

"Ma'am," Hilary said to Mrs. Whedon, "I'm sorry but we have to keep moving." She'd moved around to put a hand on her boss's back.

The octogenarian—or perhaps nonagenarian—didn't budge. Part of me was proud of her, the other part mortified.

I was about to move forward but stopped when Mrs. Whedon held up a hand. "Promise me you'll look into it."

"I will," the billionaire said. "I promise."

I almost fainted.

TWO HOURS LATER, a crowd of nearly two hundred awaited Yarn Goddess at the community center for a VIP event. She'd insisted on resting for two hours before taking the crowd through some of her favorite knitting patterns from her latest book. I couldn't blame her for needing a nap. She'd signed books for four hours.

But when she didn't arrive on time, I sent Hilary to look for her. The young woman, whose prim suit and thick glasses gave her the appearance of a harried librarian, came back perplexed.

"I left her at the hotel to rest, but she's not there. I've gone into every shop, but I can't find her. This isn't like her. She's a pain in the—well—but she always shows up for her fans. I'm going to check the hotel again. Maybe I just missed her. I'll be back in just a minute." She rushed off.

That knot in my stomach came back and twisted so hard, it stole my breath.

"We're going to need a plan B," I said.

Yarn Goddess was missing.

Chapter Two

AS IF SHE could read my mind, Shannon ran up to the side of the stage with a giant cup of espresso with cream and sugar. "What's going on? I sensed you might need this." She wore her jeans and a soft sweater with her Coffee Klatch apron over her outfit. Her blond hair was in a high ponytail. She was my dearest friend in Sweet River and didn't judge my caffeine consumption.

"We can't find Yarn Goddess anywhere and all of these people are waiting for her," I said in a hushed tone.

"I thought it was *The* Yarn Goddess and do you want me to go look for her?"

"Thanks for this." I raised the cup. "She told us we could just call her Yarn Goddess. And, no, her assistant is running all over town. So is Mike and some of the rest of my crew."

My phone dinged four times in row. Texts from the gang but no one had found her.

Shannon snickered. "Who changes their name to something like that? Maybe I should be Coffee Goddess. You could be Art Goddess."

I laughed with her. I blew out a breath. I needed that.

Hilary rubbed the back of her neck as she ran back to the side of the stage. "I've looked everywhere for her. I think we're going to have to cancel. I can't believe she'd do something like this. When I left her, she was on her laptop at the B&B. She sent me out to get her a salad. I came back and she was gone. It's not like her to disappoint fans."

Had something happened? Worry niggled deep in my belly. Hilary knew her best, so maybe something was wrong.

"You kids need to get this show going," Mrs. Whedon said, as she walked up. Today she wore an avocado jumpsuit with a knitted vest—in the same color—over it. "The audience is restless." Her curly white hair was like a haphazard halo.

Tell me something I don't know.

"Yarn Goddess seems to be indisposed," I explained for what felt like the hundredth time that day.

"Harrumph." Mrs. Whedon shook her head. "It figures she wouldn't show up when she was supposed to and there's no way anyone else is going to please that audience. She's an awful woman."

I cleared my throat. If our local curmudgeon thought Yarn Goddess was bad, that had to mean something.

"I know what to do," Mrs. Whedon said. "Stall for ten minutes, and I'll be right back." For a woman in her eighties or nineties (no one had ever been brave enough to ask), she moved pretty fast.

What just happened?

"But…" It was too late. The older woman was gone.

"I know what we can do," I said to the crowd of booth owners who had gathered around on the side of the stage. I had no idea what Mrs. Whedon had planned but we could definitely stall. "Why don't each of you introduce yourself and you can tell the audience about your crafts or artisanal items. That should buy some time."

I'd nearly lost my voice, but I headed out onto the stage. I'm not afraid of crowds, even though this one might have hated me. Maybe it was my teaching experience.

I quieted down the crowd. "We want to thank you for coming out today. We know that some of you came from as far away as New York to see Yarn Goddess. We're so grateful she was here with us today, and we have some great surprises ahead for you. But first, I'd like to introduce some of our crafters from Bless Your Art, who are amazing artists."

Each of the crafters introduced themselves and the audience seemed to be taking it all in stride. As Mike finished up talking about his wines, Mrs. Whedon returned.

"I couldn't find my favorite needles, but we're going to give this a try," she said, and the old woman strode out on the stage like she owned it. Her avocado pantsuit was nearly blinding in the light.

"Welcome," she said. "I'm Livira Whedon and I've been knitting for nearly eighty-five years. Since Yarn Goddess is not feeling well, I'll show you how to do my special rose stitch." The audience grumbled. "I'm no Yarn Goddess but I hope you'll stick around because I think you're going to be surprised."

Everyone seemed to settle down and pay attention. Never in my life would I have thought Mrs. Whedon could hold an audience like that but she did. When the seminar ended, everyone gave her a standing ovation.

I walked out onto the stage again. "Let's give Mrs. Whedon a round of applause. Thank you so much," I said, giving her a stiff hug. "And that concludes our day of crafting. Thank you so much for joining us and we hope to see you again soon."

"We definitely need to get you set up on teaching some more classes," I said as we walked off the stage. Mrs. Whedon just nodded.

"If I ever see that Yarn Goddess again, I'm giving her a piece of my mind. Keeping those poor people waiting. What was she thinking?"

"I'm worried about her," I said. "What if she really is sick? Or if she's hurt herself? Hilary swore that she never disappointed her fans."

"All I know, is that woman only cares about money," Mrs. Whedon said. "Maybe she was mad because I confronted her."

I shrugged. I'd wondered the same thing. "Well, you did a great job filling in. Thank you."

She nodded and walked off with her basket of yarn.

After the gang helped me clean up the community center, I texted Jake and told him I was ready to get George. He texted back that they were just around the corner and I met him outside my shop. He took the boxes out of my hands without even asking and handed me George's leash.

That he looked like Chris Hemsworth wasn't the only reason my heart did a double beat. Jake was the whole package. Kindhearted. Thoughtful. And he loved George, almost as much as I did.

"Thank you so much for looking out for him today," I said.

"I heard you guys had a big crowd," Jake said. "It was no problem. George and I had a blast. He played tag football with me and the guys. By the way he's a really great receiver. Well, he pooped out after about four plays, but he totally understands how to get to the goal. The guys thought he was hilarious, and they want him to come back next Saturday. It might be a regular football date."

Lucky dog. He went out more than I did.

I laughed. And looked down at my furry friend. "You have all kinds of hidden talents." I scratched under his chin, which was his spot to be scratched, as his hind leg jiggled. Jake laughed.

"Are you done for the day? I was wondering if you and George might want to join me for a hamburger at the Dairy Queen." Jake gave me one of his devastating smiles. Understandably, I couldn't say no.

We'd been spending time together as friends. Would I like more? Probably. But I wasn't very good with relationships and this was a small town. If something happened between he and I, folks would have to take sides.

Nope, it was best to keep my feelings to myself in that regard. Besides, I think, probably because my brother is his best friend, he didn't see me as anything more than a kid sister.

"That sounds great. But George isn't allowed to have cheese on his burgers anymore. There are…um, aftereffects, at an atomic level. Last time I almost made him become an outside dog permanently."

"Good to know. He ate the heck out of some fried chicken earlier. And don't worry, I took it off the bone for him." Jake chuckled.

While food didn't sound super appealing, ice cream did.

My throat was so raw from talking all day and the cold meds were wearing off.

"I need to put that stuff inside." I pointed to the boxes in his arms. "And then we can go."

I held the door open for Jake as he followed me through. "Where do you want these?"

"On the counter is fine."

Jake's muscles were nothing short of arm porn.

Stop it.

I forced myself to look away but that didn't keep warmth from spreading through my body.

Just. A. Friend.

I had to keep reminding myself of that. Every woman in this town wanted to date him, and I wasn't going to be one of *those* women.

George pulled on his leash and whined. He probably wanted a treat from the break room.

"No. We're not staying. We're going to get hamburgers," I said.

His ears perked up, but he still pulled me toward the center of the store.

Maybe someone was in here. "Hello? Is somebody here?"

There was an eerie silence. The hair on my arms stood at attention, which was never a good sign. Someone or something was here.

George slipped from my grasp and charged away.

"What's going on?" Jake fell into step beside me.

"I hope we don't have mice or rats. We did before the renovations, but the pest control guys assured me we were all clear." But dread sat heavy on my chest, making it difficult to breathe. This wasn't vermin.

George's whine intensified.

We rounded the center booths and Jake caught my arm as I stumbled a bit over George's tail.

"No," I gasped.

Jake let go of me and rushed forward. He put two fingers to the woman's neck and shook his head.

Yarn Goddess was dead.

Chapter Three

TEN MINUTES LATER, I sat down on a chair in a booth across from the crime scene. My store buzzed with deputies and crime scene folks. I couldn't stop looking at the body. There was a note, a teacup, and some knitting needles. But something about the scene didn't feel right. It was the surprise on her face that creeped me out. Everything was set to look like a suicide. But if that was the case, why would she be surprised?

My brother Greg, the sheriff, stood at the edge of the booth where Yarn Goddess slumped over on the table. Our friend Kane, the coroner and medical examiner, did his thing. Greg glanced at me, and then the victim, and shook his head.

I shrugged. It's not like I wanted to find a dead body in my shop. Later, I'd talk to George about this terrible habit of his. At least the last time he'd found a dead body it'd been in the park. That had been bad enough. But inside my shop? Even though I wasn't guilty, nerves pooled tight in my stomach.

My hands shook and the jackhammer pounded in my brain again.

Greg's forensic team was all over the store putting stuff in evidence bags. For a small college town, Sweet River had a state-of-the-art police force and teams to handle just about anything. Well, technically, the sheriff's department was over the whole county.

Greg's officers were trying to keep things on the down low, but events like this tend to spread like wildfire in Sweet River. It didn't help that just about every police car in town surrounded the building.

Before I sat down, people were shoved up against the glass at the front of the store. Jake and the other firemen were out there trying to help keep the crowd under control.

"Any idea on the cause of death?" Greg asked Kane. "I didn't see any external wounds."

"I haven't found any." Kane bent down to look at the victim's hands. "You know how much I hate guessing, but from the discoloration in her eyes, and the odd pattern on her tongue, I'd say she was poisoned. I need to get her back to my lab to run toxicology. If the poison is what I think it is, I probably have twenty minutes to figure it out. Then it will have left the blood stream."

Greg sighed. "Do you think the tea was the delivery system?"

Kane sniffed the cup. "Maybe. I'm bagging the cup, and the contents, to test."

"So," Greg said as he rubbed his temple, "even though it looks like she was leaving a suicide letter, it's murder?"

Kane nodded. "I don't see why someone would poison themselves like this. From the discoloration on her face, the heart was involved. It had to hurt."

"Any idea on time of death?"

Kane shook his head. "Remember the thing I said about

guessing?"

My brother took a deep breath. Kane was one of his dearest friends but his need for exact facts sometimes frustrated my brother to the nth degree. "Just an estimation?"

"I'd say three hours, at the most."

So while we were all at the demonstration someone killed her in my store.

My stomach churned.

"We've got a mess on our hands." Greg shoved a hand through his hair. "Ainsley had hundreds of people through the store today. We'll have trouble weeding out prints. It's useless to even try. Once you know the kind of poison, that will help us out."

"I'll have an answer for you in a few hours," Kane said.

"Has someone contacted her family? If people here know she's dead, it will be all over the internet soon." And what a terrible way for her relatives to find out. She may not have been the nicest person in the world, but no one deserved this.

"I sent an officer in Dallas to let them know but no one was there," Greg said. "Her assistant has contacted them. They know what happened."

At least there was that.

Greg texted someone on his phone.

Why would someone make her leave a note? Especially one that didn't make sense. And why did it say, "I'm sorry, H, I didn't know"?

That was it. Had she been writing to Hilary? The note had been written in calligraphy and had the same signature that Yarn Goddess had been signing in her books all day.

I shivered. It was all too much.

"It doesn't make sense that she'd poison herself," I said. "And that isn't much of a suicide note. Maybe someone made her write it?"

"No." Greg gave me that look of his. The one where his eyebrow goes up and means do not even think about it.

"No?" I said. I might have been a bit tired and hangry. We'd had a long day with the signing and classes, and my head cold was not any better. I was so not in the mood for Greg's attitude.

My tone roused George, who'd been at my feet. He grumbled, probably hungry as well. It was way past our dinnertime.

"You're right, but you're not getting mixed up in this, Ains. This is your shop, and while I know you had nothing to do with it, we have to do all of this by the book. That means keeping you and your nosy friends as far away as possible from my case."

This time it was my eyebrow that went up. "Wasn't planning on it," I said sharply. But this was my store. The one place in the world where I felt like I belonged, and I wasn't going to let anyone destroy it.

But I didn't say any of that to my brother.

He was right, but I also wouldn't tell him that. This was my store, and he couldn't play favorites in any way or we'd both look bad.

"The crowd is contained," Jake said as he came around the booth. "Ains, I hope you don't mind. I'm having Chinese food delivered to your house in a half hour, so we need to get there. After hearing you talk, I thought maybe some wonton soup might be better on your throat."

I frowned. "What?"

Jake and Greg glanced at one another.

I sighed. "Let me guess, he wants you to be my babysitter," I said to Jake.

Jake gave me one of his devastating smiles. "Nope. He asked if I could take you home, but we'd already planned on food. I just changed the menu. Plus, I bet George is starving. We played hard today."

That man's smile—I couldn't say no. I'd like to see anyone try.

"I'm not leaving because you want me to," I said to my brother. "I'm tired and my head hurts like crazy. When you talk to the family, please tell them how sorry I am, and to let us know if there's anything we can do."

He nodded.

I pointed a finger at him. "Don't leave a mess and lock up when your team is done." I tossed my brother the keys and then waved goodbye to Kane, who also had a winning smile. But he was busy putting the victim in a giant black body bag.

Ugh.

"Oh, Ainsley," Greg said as I stood. "I'll be by later to take your statement with one of my deputies. Both doors had been locked when you came in, which means someone had the keys, so I'll need a list of everyone who has access to those."

I nodded.

I can't believe I'm going through this—again.

That sounds so selfish because a woman lost her life. But

this town, until the case a few months ago when a man was killed in the park behind my shop—George also found that body—hadn't had a murder in thirty years.

Ugly stuff happened in other towns in the county, but never here.

Until I arrived.

The toughest case my brother and his deputies usually covered was vandalism by college kids, or crowd control at university events.

This was not my problem—except that it had happened at my store. This time, I'd keep my nose out of my brother's investigation.

I glanced back at the body bag. The way she'd been positioned and the cup of tea—and that letter. What was that about?

No. You promised. Stay out of it and let Greg handle this one.

But I had so many questions.

Chapter Four

EVERY SUNDAY I grade papers. I teach popular fiction classes at the local university. Which, lucky for me, the students enjoy. So the dean keeps asking me back every semester.

After opening Bless Your Art, I thought I might stop teaching. But I enjoy talking about books with the students and, maybe, showing them a way of looking at literature that's a bit different. Each week we worked on a different genre or subgenre. For a generation who reads most of their books on their phone or tablet—not that there is anything wrong with that—my class this semester was incredibly bright and interesting.

After texting Hilary to see if she was okay, I sat down with a cup of coffee and my laptop, ready to grade papers, when my phone rang.

"Ains?" It was Maria from the store. She was one of the many artists at the shop who had become a great friend. That she was the mom of five kids and still ran her own business amazed me. I could barely keep up with George and me.

"What's up?"

There was a long pause, which was never a good thing.

Bile rose in the back of my throat.

"I'm guessing you haven't talked to your brother today?"

Nope. This was not good news.

"He arrested Mrs. Whedon—at church."

I gasped. What was he thinking?

I was going to kill him.

George's ears perked up.

"Why? Did she park on the sidewalk again? Or did she create some kind of protest at the church bake sale?" Mrs. Whedon might be in her eighties, but she wasn't afraid to speak her mind—ever. There'd been an incident at Christmas where she'd tossed baked goods donated by several members who had the nerve to buy them at the store.

It was actually a rule that the goods come packaged from a store to avoid any kind of contamination, but she didn't see it that way.

More than once she'd had a stern talking-to from my brother about disturbing the peace, but arresting her seemed a bit drastic.

Her avocado-colored wardrobe might get her arrested by the fashion police, but nothing more. She was as curmudgeonly as they came but had a heart of gold. She was the first to show up with chicken soup or flowers for those in need. She was known as much for her gardens, as she was the outfits she wore.

"No. They say she's accused of murdering Yarn Goddess."

I stood up and nearly knocked my laptop off the table. "That's ridiculous." I shooed George outside and then ran upstairs to change. I put Maria on speaker.

"I agree. She's wicked smart, but under that gruff exteri-

or she's a big fluffy bunny."

I don't know about fluffy bunnies, but she was definitely one of the good ones.

"Remember that day of the signing, she had some sort of beef with Yarn Goddess?" Maria asked.

"Yes, but it's a big jump to murder from there. Mrs. Whedon was upset about the yarn causing allergic reactions. And about the prices Yarn Goddess charges."

"Well, I heard they can place her at the scene of the crime."

"Of course they can—it was right next to her booth. Her fingerprints are probably everywhere. All of our fingerprints would be. We were running around like crazy trying to please that woman."

Be nice, Ainsley.

I played the day before back through my head. We'd been at the community center, and Mrs. Whedon had left to go get her yarn and knitting needles. Did she have a confrontation then? No way she'd have time to murder someone. She's spry for her age, but she hadn't been gone for more than ten minutes.

No. My brother had it wrong.

"I'm going to head down to the station. I promised Greg I wouldn't get involved, but this is crazy."

I had a soft spot for Mrs. Whedon. She was the first to sign up for a booth at my store. She'd been so pleased that someone was interested in sharing art with our community and possibly drawing tourists. Since the grumpiest, and pickiest, woman in town had signed on, others soon followed.

I owed her.

"Let me know what you find out."

We hung up.

After loading George in the SUV, I turned on the ignition. My phone dinged with a text from Hilary.

It's crazy. I'm at the Austin house with the family. Everyone is sad and on edge. Will call you soon. I have an idea.

I wondered what that meant. And it was odd that they were on edge. I could understand sad. I hoped Hilary called soon.

After backing out of the drive, I headed into town. Greg would not be happy with me, but I had to find out what was going on. My stomach churned with nerves, but poor Mrs. Whedon needed my help. I'm not sure what I thought I could do, but that woman was not guilty of murder.

Ten minutes later I pulled into a parking place in front of the station, which was on the first floor of the courthouse. I loved the old Gothic architecture of the buildings in Sweet River. It reminded me of the small towns in New England.

Though, our town was just as beautiful—and a lot warmer.

Kevin, who ran the front desk and was the biggest gossip in town, waved at me when George and I made our way to the reception desk. He was on the phone.

"No, ma'am. I'm not allowed to talk about ongoing cases," Kevin said into the phone. "Yes, ma'am, it was a misunderstanding. Uh." The caller must have hung up because Kevin stared at the phone.

It was all I could do not to snort. He was known for blabbing to anyone who would listen. My brother had chewed him out more than once for sharing information on cases. He wasn't a bad guy; he just liked to talk.

He hung up the phone.

"Hey, Ainsley, you and George out for a walk?" He smiled.

"Something like that. Was that call about the murder?"

"Yes. It was my grandma, Helen. She had some not so nice things to say about me arresting Mrs. Whedon at church. I misunderstood the sheriff. I was supposed to wait until she came out, but I was just trying to be more proactive. Sheriff says we need to stay on top of things. And maybe interrupting Sunday service and using the handcuffs was a bit much. It was my first arrest."

Oh. My. The town would be talking about this for years to come.

"Is Greg available?"

My brother must have heard me because he stepped from behind the wall at the back of the reception area and waved me toward him.

I nodded to Kevin, and then followed Greg to his office.

After settling George in the corner on the bed my brother kept for him there—George Clooney is very popular—I sat down in front of his desk.

"I'm not discussing this case with you," he said. "You're too close to it."

I took a deep breath and just stared at him.

We sat like that for a few minutes. I should probably mention that when we were kids, I *always* won the staring game.

He rolled his eyes. "Fine. I know she seems an unlikely

suspect given her age, but we have evidence that is mounting against her. That and she had motive and opportunity. And that is all I'm saying."

I shook my head but still didn't say anything.

He grunted. "I bet you didn't know she used to be a pharmacist."

I shrugged. I didn't. And had no idea why that would matter.

"The tea was what killed her. She probably died within a few minutes of drinking it. And Kane was right. If he hadn't done that toxicology report right away, it would have been almost impossible to trace."

Poor woman. She might have been grouchy, and downright mean, but no one deserved to be murdered.

"Someone would have to have a thorough knowledge of drugs to be able to know how she'd react. That and Mrs. Whedon was alone in that store for at least ten minutes, while the rest of you were at the community center. All of the statements from the witnesses are the same."

I scrunched up my face, still keeping my mouth shut. At this rate, I'd come away with more information than I'd ever imagined he'd tell me.

Good to remember.

"Even after we brought her in, Mrs. Whedon said she was glad the Yarn Goddess was gone. Her exact words were: 'If I have to go up the river to rid the world of that horrible woman, I'm good with that.'"

I didn't chuckle but I had to bite my tongue to keep from doing it. That so sounded like her. But there was no way she murdered Yarn Goddess.

Mrs. Whedon is a grumpy coot but the two women had come to an understanding in my store.

"So that's it. That's all I have. It's a solid lead. She's already been released. She and Judge Garvner used to date, and he was kind of insistent about that. So we're done here, right?"

"Everything you have is circumstantial. And did you really have to arrest her at church?"

Greg rubbed his temple. "That was a—mistake. My guys were supposed to wait until she came out of the church and then escort her over. It wasn't supposed to be an arrest. She's just a person of interest. No formal charges have been filed."

"Can you trace the poison to her? How did Yarn Goddess get in my shop? She didn't have a key. And while Mrs. Whedon might have argued with her, that's a far cry from killing her."

"Sometimes things happen in the heat of the moment," Greg said. "I've been a cop for a long time, and arguments can escalate quickly."

"Um. I know you've got a lot going on—but poison takes some thinking through. It's a premeditated sort of weapon, right?" All of my knowledge of crime has come from the stories Greg has told me and reading just about every thriller and mystery out there.

"It would have taken seconds to put the poison in the tea. Mrs. Whedon admitted she wasn't happy the victim was in town. She'd been dreading it. Once you announced the book signing, she had plenty of time to prepare it. Or, she might have had a stash of it somewhere."

"A stash of what?"

He just stared at me. Whatever.

I sighed. "It's still a stretch. An old woman we all love just commits murder because she has a disagreement about yarn. It just doesn't add up." I held up my hands. "I'll stay out of it, if you promise you're looking at other suspects."

He frowned. "Of course we are. Ainsley, I've been doing this job for a while now. Just because you got a bit lucky—or unlucky there at the end, last time, doesn't mean we don't know what we're doing."

His ego was still bruised that the person who had committed the last murder had come after me. Greg had this idea that he was responsible for my safety. He wasn't. But I'd moved to this town because it was safer than Chicago—and even with the two murders, it still was.

"I never said you didn't." I tried to give him a reassuring smile. "I just know it isn't her."

"The evidence says otherwise. But like I told Judge Garvner, who was more than a little unhappy with the way we handled the situation this morning, the evidence is there."

So far. And rumor had it that the judge, who was known for being tough but fair in his courtroom, was still a bit sweet on Mrs. Whedon.

I stood up. "Thanks for the update."

He nodded. "This is between you and me, Ains. No murder boards, no snoopy townspeople doing your bidding. I don't need the waters muddied just because you guys all love her. I mean, she's a grouch, and I don't want to think of her as a murderer—but people never surprise me anymore. I imagine just about anyone is capable of killing."

That cynical attitude came with the job. I understood, or at least tried to.

"Promise you won't snoop."

"George and I are going home. Don't worry."

Right after I made a stop at Kane's office. I needed more information about that poison.

I should have probably felt some guilt, but I didn't. There was no way I'd let them accuse poor Mrs. Whedon.

I'd do whatever it took to prove her innocent.

Chapter Five

THE MEDICAL EXAMINER and coroner's office was in the same building as the police station, but I had to go outside to access it. George wasn't allowed in there. I couldn't ask Jake to watch him again, plus that meant going all the way home and then back to town. It wasn't a long drive, but I wanted to talk to Kane as fast as possible.

"Kevin, I need your help."

He eyed me warily. "I'm working."

I glanced at his computer—more like playing some first-person shooter game on the office computer. My brother would have his head if he knew.

"How about I don't tell Greg you're playing Call of Duty Modern Warfare, and you watch George for a few minutes for me."

He blanched. "Uh. Done."

There was a reason my brother usually only let Kevin work the front desk.

"George, you're staying with Kevin. Be a good boy and I'll dig up a treat for you." My beautiful dog cocked his head as if he understood every word. Then he went and lay down behind the reception desk. After today's debacle, Kevin would probably be stuck there for the rest of his career.

A minute later, I pushed the button outside Kane's office. There was a chance, since it was Sunday, he might not be there. He covered the whole county, as well, so he could have been in another town for all I knew. But I had to try.

He was a medical examiner, but also the elected coroner. It was an unusual situation but that was small-town living in Texas.

"Ainsley?" His voice came through the speaker. "Give me a minute and I'll buzz you in."

That was code for "let me cover up the body parts, so you don't throw up in my nice, sterile lab." I hadn't done so yet, but there was always a first time. I'll admit I'm not super fond of dead bodies, even though George keeps finding them.

The buzzer sounded, so I pushed in on the metal bar. Not sure what I might see, I focused on Kane's face. It wasn't hard since he's Idris Elba's doppelganger. He wore a white lab coat with an apron, which may or may not have had blood on it. I glanced back at his face.

We'd been on exactly four dates. He's fun and kind, but we didn't have *that* kind of chemistry. Right after the New Year, he started dating a doctor who works in a hospital a few towns over. She reminds me of Salma Hayek, and they are perfect together. I do consider him one of my best friends, and I'm pretty sure he feels the same way.

"I haven't seen you in forever," I said as I followed him into his office across the lab. Thankfully, this area was body free and he always had a candle or scented wax burning, so that the smells from the lab weren't quite as potent. Today's scent was vanilla, which happened to be one of my favorites. "Is that the one I gave you for Christmas?" I pointed to the candle on his desk.

"It is, and I ordered more from your friend at Bless Your Art. It's the only one I've found that keeps things smelling nice in here. Though I'm used to the lab, it's nice to walk in here."

I smiled. The first time I'd visited him, I'd brought lunch. I'd also stolen information off his computer. Um. Total accident. He left the screen up so I'm certain he wanted me to have the information. There was no way I could eat much with the disinfectant smell because I had a good idea of what it'd been covering up.

"How is Dr. Eva?"

He smiled broadly and then stared down at his desk. "She's great. I'm trying to finish up here so we can head up to Round Top. She wants some antiques for her new house."

In other words—spit it out, Ainsley, I have places to be. "I won't keep you long. I—um…" He'd been there when I'd promised Greg that I wouldn't meddle in his case. But that was before the sheriff had the crazy idea to bring poor Mrs. Whedon in for questioning.

He chuckled. "The poison that killed Yarn Goddess was digitalis, also known as foxglove. It would have taken someone extremely knowledgeable to know the exact strength and how much to put in the teacup."

I had not expected him to blurt it out like that. Something was up. "Did my brother call you?"

He laughed again. "Yes, right before you hit the buzzer. He said to tell you everything I know so far so that, in his words, 'she doesn't go off snooping.' He's doing his job and he really needs you to stay out of this one."

I snorted. "It's like you guys know me or something. And I did promise to keep out of it. But come on, Mrs. Whedon? You can't believe she did it."

He shrugged. "I've seen a lot of things that are hard to believe. Greg said she had means and opportunity. And she was upset with Yarn Goddess long before she arrived. So she had time to dose the tea when she was in the shop…"

"No." I sat down in the chair across from his desk.

"No?" He sat and then crossed his arms.

"I told Greg that she's old and she was only gone ten minutes. There was barely time to walk down the block, grab her things, and get back. I'd have trouble doing that in ten minutes and I'm fifty years younger, maybe sixty. No one is exactly sure how old she is, and she certainly isn't talking."

"I'm sure your brother told you about the argument."

I nodded. "I was there and they seemed to settle it. Arguing with someone isn't a reason to kill them. Mrs. Whedon can be a bit persnickety when she wants to, but I don't see her murdering someone because she's mad about the price of yarn."

He shifted in his chair and typed something on his computer. "I hear what you're saying," he said, "but she is old. Things may seem way worse to her than they really are. A couple of months ago, I had a case where the wife poisoned the husband because she thought he was keeping her prisoner.

"She had Alzheimer's and didn't realize who he was. At first the police thought he'd poisoned himself. But then she kept talking about how he was the prison guard and she had to break free."

I leaned back in the chair and crossed my arms. "Aww. That's just sad. Why did you have to tell me that?" Things like that had a way of sticking with me, even though I might not know who it was.

He lifted an eyebrow. "The truth is, we can never really know another person or what they may be thinking. I've seen it all, and I swear I won't be surprised. But then I come across a case that just blows my mind. I get that Mrs. Whedon is your friend. But do you know everything about her? Like why does she wear green every day? And do you have any idea what she did before moving to Sweet River?"

I'd wanted to ask more than once about her green color scheme, and I'd just found out she was a pharmacist.

"Do you know the answer to those questions?"

The side of his mouth quirked up. "Not the first one. But she was a pharmacist, a darn good one if your brother's report is correct—and we know it is. She was top in her field until she retired twenty-five years ago. There's a good chance she knows even more than I do about poisons, given how great she was at her job. Plus, she has that crazy garden in the back of her house with so many different types of plants, it will take weeks for the forensics team to identify them all. But she had a small bit of foxglove growing there. That's why your brother brought her in."

That was suspicious but foxglove was a pretty flower. I'd seen it in gardens all over Texas. Still, it was all circumstantial at best.

"I know you need to meet Eva and I don't want to delay your antiques shopping." And I had to get back to George.

"You don't have any other questions?" He seemed surprised.

I smiled. "Is there any chance Yarn Goddess was on a heart medication containing foxglove, and took too much?"

"This was a mega dose and it caused complete heart failure. She didn't look like she had any sort of heart condition before yesterday." He looked down at his keyboard.

There was something else, but he didn't want to tell me. I wouldn't push—at least not right now.

"If my brother meant what he said, do you mind if I call? You know, just out of curiosity about where the case is going."

He shook his head. "Riiiight. Curiosity."

We laughed. "I'll try to keep my word to Greg, but it won't be easy. I hope he's looking at other suspects. Like her business associates, and maybe one of her customers. Mrs. Whedon said some of the yarn from her company was faulty."

Kane stood. "He's thorough. And given the circumstances, he's going to do whatever he can to find the killer. Whether that's Mrs. Whedon, or not. You need to trust him on this. Besides, you learned the last time that his work can be dangerous."

I sighed. "You're right. But with the university back in session, he has his hands full helping out the college police. Every day it seems like they're having to deal with a different sort of protest. I love that kids these days are so active and fight for what they believe in. But occasionally, it would be great if they could go a day or two without causing some sort of riot. He has a great staff at the sheriff's department but there are never enough officers to cover everything."

Kane guided me through the door. I guess this was one time he was not going to let me look at his computer. "Ainsley, your brother has got this. He figured out the last murder you were involved in, and he will this one, as well. But you have to let him do it the procedural way."

That was true. He'd shown up seconds after the murderer had tried to kill me. So, technically, he'd figured it out before that murderous jerk hit Jake over the head and then busted into my house.

I held up my hands in surrender. "I'm just asking a few questions for a friend. Was there anything else about her death? Anything that might have seemed strange?"

"Why do you ask?"

I shrugged. "I just have one of those feelings."

He shook his head. "She had stage-four lung cancer, the kind there's no coming back from, and she probably only had months, if not weeks, to live."

"What?" That word came out like an exaggerated gasp. She'd been so put together and demanding. The last thing I'd have thought about her was that she might be ill. Was that why she'd wanted everything to be so perfect? That was one heck of a makeup job. I would have never imagined she was ill. And why didn't Hilary, her assistant, tell me?

"They found oxygen in her room, and a pharmacy in her luggage. My guess: this was her last big event. I'm surprised, from the size of the tumors, that she didn't have to use a wheelchair. Walking just a few steps had to have taken so much out of her. I'm not sure how—"

"What?"

He frowned. "I'd been about to say how she survived

that day. Your brother said she signed books and took pictures with fans for four or five hours. The sheer willpower she must have had—I know she gave you a hard time, but I'm not sure how her body made it through all of that. She was so weak. While her heart was okay, until the poison, the rest of her organs had begun shutting down."

No wonder everything had to be perfect. The poor woman had been dying and knew that it was her last chance to be with her fans.

Tears burned the rims of my eyes. I'd been nice to her, but I'd had so many evil thoughts that day. And why in the world would Hilary not have told me?

"I'll get out of your hair," I said as I pulled out a tissue. My nose had started running again. I'd been in such a rush I'd forgotten to take my cold meds.

"Is everything okay?"

I nodded.

He gave me a knowing look. "Do I get twenty bucks if I guess your next stop?"

"Nope," I said as I waved goodbye. "I'm pretty much a sure thing. Wait, that did not come out right."

We laughed.

Mrs. Whedon was my next stop—well, after I picked up something to take over. I'd learned early on that in the South you didn't show up at a friend's house without food or drinks. Ever.

But I hurried along, beyond curious what Mrs. Whedon had to say about all of this.

How did she feel about being tainted a murderer? And the thing that bugged me the most—was it possible, knowing she was dying, Yarn Goddess offed herself? Maybe she wanted to go out with a dramatic flair. It's not nice to think things like that, but she did seem to like that sort of thing.

Maybe Kane and my brother had it wrong.

Hmmm.

Chapter Six

WHEN I PULLED up to Mrs. Whedon's house on the edge of town, the driveway and the street were full of cars. I shouldn't have been surprised. This town pulled together for its residents—even ones accused of murder.

They'd done the same for Michael and Shannon, when Michael had been falsely accused a few months ago. Thankfully, he'd been cleared of all charges. The same would be true of Mrs. Whedon, once we figured out what was going on.

I had a feeling she'd be inundated with sweets, so I'd put together a fruit and vegetable basket. She'd commented more than once that her vegetarian diet was what kept her young and spry. That and a nip or three of bourbon every night.

Before I knocked, Maria opened the door. She wore her mom uniform, which was a sweater and jeans. That's what she called it. She had a lot of kids, so anything else just didn't seem practical to her. "What did you find out from your brother and Kane?"

I chuckled. Nothing in this town stayed a secret for long. "Let me say hello, and then I'll share. Where is she?"

"In the back den—just go through the kitchen. And feel free to grab a plate on the way. She's already complained that she has more food than she knows what to do with and she told us to save our money in case she needs to be bailed out."

Her home was a fairly good size, the moldings intricate, and the ceilings high. I'd looked at a few of these Georgian-style homes before I decided to keep the farmhouse I'd inherited from my grandmother.

It's how Greg and I ended up here. After years of being a police captain in big cities, he'd come back to the town where our grandmother had lived and became the sheriff.

Neither of us had been here much when we were kids, but what I'd remembered had been charming. My brother had been worried about me living so far out of town on the farm, but it wasn't that big of a deal—at least when people weren't trying to kill me or scare me to death.

Yep. That was a thing.

"Hi, Mrs. Whedon, how was your two hours in the big house?" I asked. She guffawed, and it was harder than I'd ever seen her laugh. She was in an avocado running suit. *I can't believe they make them in that color.* The leather recliner she sat in had doilies on the arms. And the room was a sun porch that had been converted to an interior room.

It was bright and filled with plants. A sofa and two other sleek recliners filled out the room, with a copper coffee table in the middle. It was like an old lady and Pottery Barn had a baby, but it worked with her personality. There were knitted afghans layered on all the leather furniture.

The woman did beautiful work.

"Hi, Ainsley, I'm hoping you have some news for me," Mrs. Whedon said as she knitted something pink. *Someone in town must be about to have a baby girl.*

"I brought you some fruit and veggies from Mr. Tully's

stand, and I may have heard a thing or two." I glanced around the room. People who had booths at Bless Your Art smiled up at me. "But you guys have to cross your heart that you won't tell anyone else. Greg will murder me, if he finds out I told you. I promised not to say a word."

True story—that was a big fat lie. Greg had to know I'd go straight to the source, which is probably why he'd told me what he did so easily. He'd see it as damage control. The rest of the town would soon know she hadn't been officially arrested but was most definitely a person of interest. I had a feeling none of them knew the truth about Yarn Goddess's health. That was something else entirely.

Don, who looked a lot like Santa and was equally joyful and kind, held up his hand as if to swear, and others followed suit.

"Let me put this down—" I lifted the basket "—and grab some iced tea. I'll be back." In the South, sweet tea is made from heaven. I only allow myself one glass every few weeks, because I'm fairly certain it has one million calories in every glass—and all of them from sugar.

That said, it's very refreshing.

I put the food on the center island and grabbed some tea. My friends Mike and Shannon walked into the kitchen.

"You haven't started yet, have you?" Shannon asked.

"I saw you going into the station, and then Mike saw you turn off Main Street and we knew you were coming here."

I laughed. "That would be super creepy if you guys weren't my besties. And no. I just got here."

Shannon did a little clap with her hands. "It's crazy. Right? No way she did this," she whispered. "What did Greg say?"

"Don't you dare say a word that we can't all hear," Mrs. Whedon grumbled from the other room.

We smiled. The woman didn't miss much.

There was no reason to hide anything. These people had helped me solve the last crime. We all made a good team.

After settling on the floor on a large pillow, because there were no more seats available, I told them what Greg had said. I thought maybe if Mrs. Whedon understood they were serious—she might speak up for herself.

"Hmmm," she said. "The judge followed me over from church and only allowed your brother to ask me a few questions. I had no idea they had so much evidence. And I guess you guys know my big secret—I'm a recovering pharmacist. That's a joke we made in the trade. But I've been retired for almost twenty-five years."

Then she closed her eyes and shook her head. "I'm guessing they know I have foxglove, since someone was in my garden today. They left muddy footprints all over my back porch." She sighed. "It was there when I bought the house, and the flowers are pretty."

"So, you didn't kill her?" Don asked.

He might look like Santa, but he was as curious as the rest of us.

"Of course she didn't," I said quickly.

Mrs. Whedon opened her eyes and stared straight at me. It was a cold gaze and sent a shiver down my spine.

Or, maybe she did.

"I thought about it."

There were gasps around the room.

She frowned. "But Ainsley's right, I didn't do it."

"Can you at least tell us why you were so upset with her? At the shop, you guys were arguing about her yarn."

She nodded.

"She was a fraud. Well, her products were. She claimed that the yarns were American made and all natural, but it wasn't true. They used cheap dyes and are trying to cover up the fact that it is causing rashes on a lot of knitters. It's all over the internet. I don't carry her stuff in my booth. More because I'm fairly certain she stole knitting patterns she claimed were passed down in her family. I've been around a long time and I've seen every pattern she said was hers before. She was all show and no substance."

"She had stage-four lung cancer," I blurted out and heard a couple of gasps in response.

"I'm not proud of myself, for confronting her like that. I'm even sorrier now that I know how ill she is—was. Still can't believe she's gone." A frown crossed her features.

"Do you think she knew about the problems with the yarn?" I asked. I'd done a bit of searching before bed last night and found a whole thread on a knitting chat room where people had been complaining.

Mrs. Whedon seemed to think on that for a few seconds. "Hard to tell. She wore sunglasses and her forehead looked like it was made out of plastic. But she frowned, and gasped a little when I showed her the pictures. Close up, she had at least a pound of makeup on. I keep wondering if maybe I'd walked a little farther into the store when I went back yesterday then I might have seen her or the killer. I was in a rush trying to get back to the community center to help you out. I grabbed what I needed and ran back out. I—" She went pale.

"What?" I asked on a whisper.

"I didn't lock the front door, Ainsley. I'm sorry. I'm old but I usually don't forget things like that. My hands were full, and I didn't take the keys out of my pocket until I handed them back to you. Darn it. If I hadn't left that door open, maybe it wouldn't have happened at your place."

I rubbed my head, trying to think about what happened when I went into the store last night. I'd put the key in, but I'd been distracted by Jake and George.

I hadn't actually turned it.

That meant anyone could have done it.

I needed to let my brother know.

Of course, that meant admitting I'd been talking to Mrs. Whedon, but he needed to cast a wider net for suspects.

Anyone could have killed Yarn Goddess.

Chapter Seven

On Monday, my head cold was much better, and I had a class to teach. We'd been studying several different genres from romance to thrillers over the last few months. This week their readings included *Murder on the Orient Express* and *The Murder at the Vicarage*. I'd picked those books because, in a way, every one of the suspects was guilty of something. And they keep you guessing to the very end. And, hello, Agatha Christie was the best.

The news about how fun the class was must have traveled because it had doubled in size from the previous semester. This was a slightly different look at genre studies, so some of my former students were also in this class.

And it made for lively discussions because these kids liked the idea of being able to read popular fiction and relate it to what's going on in the world.

We'd been moved to one of the larger lecture halls, and I sort of missed the small classroom where we just sat around a table. But if it meant more kids were interested in books, I'd put up with just about anything.

They were chattering when I walked in, and then there was a hushed silence. I sat my bags down on the long table at the front of the room, and then moved around to the front and sat on the table.

I was out of breath. I really had to start exercising—someday. George crawled under the table and yawned loudly.

Everyone laughed.

"Did everyone do the readings? Are you ready for your midterm?" I asked.

"Yes," they said in unison.

"There won't be any repercussions, but did any of you watch the movies, instead of reading the books? There are some key differences, so it's best if you tell me now."

No one raised a hand.

We'll see about that.

"Great." I reached into my bag and pulled out a stack of papers.

There was a general groan.

Even if they'd read the books, no one liked a test.

I chuckled, and then handed the papers to Lily, who had jumped up to help out. She and Jeff, who took the other half of the stack, had been in the previous class. They'd also helped me with some clues from the first mystery we solved and had become regulars at the book club we had every other Friday night at my store. I would never admit it out loud, but they were two of my favorite students of all time.

"You guys have a half hour."

More groans. My class wasn't hard, as long as you did the assignments. The tests were to keep them on their toes, so they didn't become complacent. The midterm was a requirement from the university. Once everyone had their test, I started the timer.

And then I opened my laptop to look up foxglove. More

than once, while I'd been at Mrs. Whedon's house, I'd stolen a glance out the back windows into her garden in search of the deadly plant. Then I'd learned before I left her house that it had been dug up as evidence.

After talking with Mrs. Whedon and learning about the yarn, I had a gut feeling that Yarn Goddess's death might be tied to that. What if someone in her company didn't want her to find out the yarn was making people itch? Or maybe someone was hurt by the yarn and wanted to get back at her.

I pulled up her obituary, which had run in *The Austin Statesman*, and then another one on CNN.

I wish I knew more about her family. But Greg had been tight-lipped in that respect.

I clicked through on the names of the survivors, her son and daughter. Brock and Emily were gorgeous and both looked like models. I clicked on Yarn Goddess's website. Emily was in charge of social media and her brother was vice president of production. There was also a Sam Winstone listed as a global consultant.

Well, look at that. If anyone would know about the yarn being tainted in some way, my money was on Mr. Winstone. But at the moment, I couldn't come up with a single reason that would make sense for me to reach out to him. I put that in my notes on my computer. I also made a note to research the kids a bit more, and her assistant, Hilary.

I typed in "Yarn Goddess" and "rash" and twenty thousand links came up. Many of them talking about the yarn creating rashes and even blisters on some people. After Mrs. Whedon had confronted her, had Yarn Goddess gone back to her room and called someone at the company? I tried to piece the fragments I had together in my head by typing out everything I knew so far into my notes.

Kane said she was dying. Maybe she'd stepped back and someone else was in charge of the empire. Had she gone to her room and called someone at her company or her family?

If someone had hid something about the changes in the yarn, and then Yarn Goddess found out, she wouldn't have been happy. That is, if she really didn't know.

I mean, there is no reason good enough for murder—but the motive would make more sense than some poor old woman worried about yarn. Especially if it happened to be some kind of cover-up.

The buzzer *dinged*, and the students passed the tests up. I stuck them in my bag and started our discussion on the various ways to commit murder, and the few reasons it actually happened. Sex. Love. Greed. Jealousy. Vengeance. Those were at the root of most crimes.

"And whether it's a classic or a modern book, the best villains have a reason for what they're doing. When the reader can sympathize a bit with the villain, or villains in the case of *Murder on the Orient Express*, then the author has done a great job with that character.

"That's what I want you guys to take away from what we've done so far. Creating rich characters leaves a big impression with readers." I glanced at my watch. "I'm going to end there. Your brains are tired from being tested, so go, guys. Go take a nap or study for your next exam."

"We were wondering if you found out anything about the case?" Jeff asked. When he'd helped me the last time I'd been "researching a case," we'd both nearly been run over.

After that, I decided no more investigating with anyone else.

I glanced up at the ceiling as if I were asking heaven for guidance.

When nothing came, I crossed my arms, and then sat back on the edge of my desk.

"I'm not on this case. The police are handling it."

"Yes, we know. But what did you find out?" Jeff asked again.

I laughed. "I don't know much more than what's been printed in the paper. Wouldn't you rather go do something fun with your free time?"

"No," they said unanimously.

"I'll give you a bit, as it relates to the thriller we talked about a few weeks ago: *Knives Out*. In that one, the family was shocked about who had inherited everything. The maid. All I'll say is that sometimes truth is stranger than fiction. Right now, the police are headed in the wrong direction—at least, that's what I believe to be true. That happened in the movie. There were several red herrings and many different suspects. It's possible the same is true here."

"But do you have an idea of who the killer might be?" Jeff asked.

"I really can't say. I don't know all of the players involved." I needed a plan to figure that out, which was something I would work on later that night.

"In mystery books and films, there are many twists and turns. Finding the perpetrator can sometimes be confusing when the clues shove investigators down the wrong path. And that…is all I'm going to say.

"You guys have a half hour to do whatever you want, but

you have to leave the class so I can lock the door. And be mindful of other students, who may not have the best teacher ever, and are still taking exams. Happy spring break, everyone!"

I wouldn't be taking any time off. With the spring festival, we were going to be more than busy at the shop.

Jeff was still on his computer. "Come on, big guy, time to go."

"I have something to show you," he said.

I rolled my eyes.

But I waited for him to come down the stairs from the top seats in the classroom.

"I took a deep dive into the son: Brock. He is a big-time player. There are lots of pictures of him partying, but also gambling. His sister's social media is one hundred percent fake. It's all selfies and products from her mom's line she's promoting. But every time she says, 'Yarn Goddess,' she gets a weird sneer on her face. Watch." He pushed the play button.

He was right. She was a beautiful girl but every time she mentioned the company, her eyes went to the left, and she smirked. It was just an instant but it was there.

So the son might have a gambling problem and the daughter wasn't crazy about working for her mom's business.

"Okay, thank you for this. But no actual investigating beyond your computer. Got it?"

"Yes, ma'am. Oh, there's one more thing. This is a photo of the daughter and the consultant guy from the website. Her brother said he took it."

As I squinted to take it in, he made it bigger.

Now that was unexpected.

"Can you text that to me?"

He nodded and then walked out.

"Come on, George." I whistled for him to follow me down to my office. Once there, I shut the door and sat down in my chair.

I picked up my phone and dialed my brother.

"Hey, Ains, I'm sort of in the middle of something."

"This is important, I promise."

It sounded like he put his hand over the mouthpiece, as his voice was garbled. "I want to know by this afternoon," he said. Then a door shut.

"So, what's up?"

"Are you by your computer?"

"Yep, just sat down at my desk."

"Pull up the social media page for Yarn Goddess's son, Brock—the page that's connected to the company website."

It took a minute. "Got it. What am I looking at other than some drunken frat boy who hasn't grown up?" I would leave out the drunken part, but I often thought about my brother that way. He never had a relationship that lasted more than a couple of weeks. And he still hung out with the guys and played poker at least once a week.

Still, who was I to judge on the dating scene?

"See the pics Brock took of his road trip? Just to the right of those. Look at who is in that picture."

"Right. Got it."

But he didn't, at least not yet.

"It's hard to see but Brock's the one taking the pic. You can see him reflected in Sam's sunglasses."

"Yep. I see that."

"Now look just over the car top. Does that look familiar?"

"Well, what do you know. Motive and opportunity."

YG's family was in big trouble.

Chapter Eight

ON TUESDAY, GREG let me open the store. Since it was midweek, I hadn't expected to be busy but as George and I drove down Main Street, there was a line around the door. Shannon was out there passing out coffee and cookies.

There were news crews parked on the other side.

"What is going on?" I asked George.

"RurrhRo," George said.

"Ruh Ro is right."

After parking in the back, George and I headed inside.

Don was in the break room, grabbing some coffee.

"What's with all the people?"

He grinned. "Isn't it great? I mean, the reason isn't. But think of all that business." A toymaker, he worked with wood and metal. His toys were meant to be played with, but they were also beautiful works of art.

I took George's leash off and hung it near the back door. "What's the reason?"

"They're coming to pay their respects. Some of them had flowers. Did you see that? I've been helping Maria set up a memorial booth where people can leave notes and flowers. And take a moment to reflect on their feelings for Yarn Goddess."

"Um."

"We talked to a lot of people in the line. That's why they're here. We put the booth where the signing was, so they'll be walking through the store. I—Oh. That makes us sound so greedy. Are you upset?"

I blew out a breath. "It's not that. I just don't understand why they'd come here. If anything, I thought we'd be known as the people who killed her. I'm more surprised that we didn't find the word 'killers' spray-painted on the window or something."

He shook his head. "Nah. This is the last place they saw her, and no one seems to blame you. I did call Mrs. Whedon and let her know she might want to steer clear. I can't believe the paper ran that story about her."

"They weren't the only ones. Yarn Goddess is national news. She's was beloved worldwide. I saw it on CNN this morning," I said. "They mentioned Mrs. Whedon, as a person of interest. The media just wants someone to blame. Greg put out a statement saying they don't comment on ongoing investigations, but they do have several persons of interest. I think maybe he got in trouble with the judge, so he's trying to make it look like they aren't just investigating Mrs. Whedon."

Don sipped his coffee. "That's a good thing, right? Since we know she didn't do it."

"Yep. I guess I better take a look at this memorial you guys have put together."

George followed me through the store. I loved this place. Being surrounded by arts and crafts just made me happy. Nothing, not even a murder, would take that away.

It was unfortunate she died here, but I had a business to

run. And Don was right: we needed to pay homage to Yarn Goddess. Even if we didn't sell a thing, it was a good thing we were doing. People needed a place to mourn. If the middle of my craft store was the place, then so be it.

The booth where she's been murdered had been modified a bit. They'd hung some flower garlands, put out a guest book and a couple of pictures from our event with Yarn Goddess on the back wall. It was tasteful.

"We checked with Greg before we touched anything," Maria said. "I'm not going to lie—after learning about the foxglove, I wore plastic gloves all morning."

I didn't blame her. "His forensics team went over the whole place with a fine-tooth comb. We're good. The only place they found the poison was in the teacup, which is locked up in evidence."

"Is there anything you want to add?" Don asked. Today he wore suspenders with green shamrocks, and a green button-down shirt and jeans. He always had some kind of holiday theme going on with his suspenders. His wife Peggy kept him well stocked.

"Great job, you guys," I said to Don and Maria.

I did a double take. "You look amazing," I said to Maria.

She waved a hand. "Oh, yep. I sort of dressed up for once. With all the news cameras around—I know it's vain, but I didn't want to look like one of those hicks from the sticks, even if I am one."

I laughed. "You're a lot of things, Maria, but a hick is not one of them."

She smiled brightly. "Thanks for that. Oh, I forgot to tell you the big news," Maria said. "So I heard from Ms. Erma, who will be here today, that they are looking closely at the family. Seems they aren't the perfect little picture all the magazines and news articles want us to think. There are gambling and drinking problems, and there were pictures that put them nearby."

Good. I hadn't heard what Greg had done about that information but I was happy his investigation was moving on. My guess was that Ms. Erma had wheedled it out of poor Kevin, her nephew.

Had Yarn Goddess called to complain to her family and had one of them killed her?

Since Greg promised to keep me apprised of what was happening with the case, I decided to write down all my questions in a notebook, and then I'd make him some food and grill him.

Ha. I made a food joke.

"It's fifteen minutes until we open," Don said. "Since there were so many people in line, I called in some of the gang to help out. I hope you don't mind. Or that we did all of this without telling you. I just—I made a quick run to get Peggy some espresso from Shannon's coffee shop this morning and there was already a line of thirty people. So I dropped it off, called Maria, who came right after she dropped the kids off at school, and I didn't even think about calling you. You've been so sick."

I must have been wearing my resting confused face. I put a hand on his shoulder. "Don, I'm grateful that you acted so quickly. I'm not even sure I'd have thought to do this." I waved a hand toward the booth. "Let me be clear: I never, ever mind help and ingenuity. You guys did a great job. And

I'm feeling a lot better."

I'd finished off the last of Mrs. Whedon's chicken soup after school yesterday. I did maybe pause for a second, when I remembered the older woman not being so sorry about Yarn Goddess's death. But since I'd already eaten some of it, I figured I'd be okay. That stuff was magic. I still had a bit of a cough, but overall, I was much better.

"Whew," Maria said. "I would have texted you at least, but we were so busy trying to figure out what might work that time ran away."

I laughed. "You guys are brilliant. Really. I may own the building, but this store is ours. Like I said, I'm super grateful to you both."

Noise from the back of the store meant the rest of the team had shown up.

"I guess I better get up front and open the registers."

Mike came around the corner. He had a booth where he sold goods from his winery. He and Shannon were experimenting with wine and cheese pairings, making both themselves. They had a new mild cheddar cheese that had Cabernet running through it. I may have eaten a brick or three of that one.

"Why don't I take George for his morning walk?" Mike said. "That way you can get the computers revved up."

"Awesome. Thanks."

The line lasted all day. Jake had one of his guys posted at the door, only letting in the minimum amount allowed by the fire marshal. At four o'clock when we normally closed, there was still a line. And there were news crews from all over the place out there interviewing those mourning.

Those mourners bought like crazy. It was as if they needed some kind of memorial piece from our store.

People are weird, but I was not complaining.

Poor George had been sleeping most of the day, while the rest of us worked hard. He groaned behind me and sat up.

"That's a very big dog," a woman in her fifties, who looked like she'd just stepped out of the sixties, said. She wore bell-bottoms, and a knitted vest over a flouncy shirt. A big floppy leather hat topped off her ensemble.

"He is."

"Is he the one who—found her?" That last part came out a whisper.

I didn't think anyone knew about George. Greg hadn't mentioned it and neither had I.

"Where did you hear that?" I asked.

George did his low whine.

"I can take him out," Samantha, Maria's daughter, said. She'd been helping me since she got out of high school around two. Customers loved her, and she added faster than the computers most of the time.

"Thanks," I said.

"People in line have been talking about it. I loved her knitting patterns," the woman said. "I made this vest as my first project of hers."

I smiled at her. "It's beautiful. Were you able to pick up her new book?" We'd had her sign several hundred copies to sell after the event. We'd almost sold out of those.

She put the book on the counter, along with several skeins of Mrs. Whedon's yarn. "Do you know who makes this yarn? It's amazing."

"Uh. Yes. She's been knitting for longer than I am old," I said. "She knows a lot about yarn."

Hoping she hadn't noticed I'd not answered her question, I rushed on. "We have more in booth twenty-seven." Probably, best to avoid revealing the news that the woman who sold the yarn happened to be a person of interest in the Yarn Goddess case.

"That's where I found this. I may be back for more, if I can find a hotel close by. Everything is booked up within fifty miles."

"Oh?" I wondered if maybe there was something going on at the college I didn't know about.

"A lot of us plan to meet up and do knitting circles in her honor this week. This seemed like as good a place as any. I don't do a lot online, but evidently, everyone who loved her is gathering here. I heard people discussing it while we waited outside. There's talk of doing some kind of memorial in town. I thought I might stick around for that. Do you know when it might be?"

No. Idea. I hadn't heard a word. Though Hilary had texted me earlier and said she'd call me later today. "I think the plans are still in the works, but I'll check with her assistant. If you want to put your name and email down in our guest book—" I pointed to the large book between the two registers "—I'll send out an email when I have news."

I wondered if Hilary had any idea all of this was going on. The family might want to do something closer to their homes either in Austin or Dallas.

"Oh, that would be great. I live in Marble Falls, which

isn't too far away. I may go on home and then come back."

"Are you guys talking about the memorial?" the young woman in the line behind her asked.

I stood on my toes so everyone in line could see me. "Just so you know, I'll reach out to Yarn Goddess's assistant about the memorial. If you want to put your name and email in our guest book, I'll contact everyone to let you know what I find out."

The line never seemed to stop. Everyone bought something from the medieval weapons Pete made, to most of the art hanging on the walls I'd picked up in Austin. My crafters and artists had to be happy with the results.

It felt wrong that we were benefiting from her death. I mean, it wasn't our fault people chose to gather here but it felt like we should do more than just have the booth inside the store.

At six, we closed. Shannon, who dropped off some snacks to keep my strength up earlier in the afternoon, had a great idea to give those still in line a business card with my initials on it, so they would be first in line the next day. That seemed to appease everyone. The line at six was still wrapped around the building.

And the news crews were still there.

Didn't they have something better to do? If filming a line outside my store made for an interesting story, it had to be a slow news day.

After we finally had the last customer out the door, I gathered everyone around.

"Hey, gang, I thought I might call Hilary, Yarn Goddess's assistant, and see if maybe we could set up a bigger memorial service here in town. Maybe at the community center. But I'd need your help, so I wanted to ask you first."

"We're happy to help," Don said, and everyone nodded.

"Okay. It will be our way of giving back. But first, I need to call Hilary." Samantha came back with George.

"Hey, Ainsley," she said. "There's some reporter out back. He wanted to talk to you. He tried to get in through the front, but Jake's men made him get back across the street."

Ugh. Nope.

"Don, could you please let him know that I will not be making any comments about anything to the press? None of us will." He might look like Santa Claus, but he was massive. No one messed with him.

"Done."

"Okay. Let's clean up and everyone get home to rest. Looks like it may be a very busy Wednesday for us if all those people in line come back."

My cell rang. It was Hilary.

"I was just about to call you," I said.

"Hi, Ainsley," she said breathlessly.

"Hello. Are you okay?" I put the phone on speaker, since everyone had walked away, and I worked on clearing out the register for the day.

"Yes. Trying to get away from some reporters who are staked out in front of the Austin house where I'm staying," she said. "I wanted to talk to you about something."

"What is it?"

"Well, we're having a private memorial service on Thursday in Austin for Yarn Goddess. I would love if you and Shannon would come. You guys were so great to us, and it would mean a lot to me and the family if you two would be there. You've been checking in through text, which I really appreciate, and you guys feel like a part of the family."

Um. What?

"We'd be honored, but are you sure it's okay with her family for us to come?"

There was a pause. "What do you mean?"

"Well, since she, uh—" Did I really have to spell it out? This was beyond embarrassing.

I chewed on my lip. Awkward, maybe. But it would give me a chance to talk to her children and if that consultant guy was there—I wanted to know when that picture had been taken.

"Died there?" Hilary's answer pulled me from my thoughts. "No. They…well, Yarn Goddess's family is unusual." She said the last part as a whisper, as if she were worried someone might hear. "They don't blame you at all. They don't think Mrs. Whedon did it either, even though the papers are trying to make her out to be some octogenarian serial killer.

"I honestly think she did it to herself. I'm not sure if it's come out yet, but it will when the autopsy is made public. She suffered from lung cancer and didn't have long." She sniffed. "It's terrible to say, but I wouldn't be surprised if she killed herself and maybe the crime scene guys were mixed up."

That wasn't true. Kane and his team were thorough. Also, there are easier ways to off oneself if she wanted to commit suicide.

"I mean, if it *was* murder, it had to be one of her crazy fans. She's been receiving some very strange letters the last few months."

"Oh? That's awful. The poor woman." Interesting, that Hilary had all these ideas. Maybe I should have added her to the suspect list. Except, she was with us the whole time.

"And then she had a stalker or two. The police in Dallas are still working on that one. It's one of the reasons she'd moved to the Austin house to work the last few months. No one knows about that place. Or they didn't, until now."

"I'm sure the police are following up every lead," I said. "But are you sure about us attending the memorial? We didn't know her very well—and since it's private, wouldn't that be awkward?" I thought for sure the family would hate us, especially me.

There was another long pause. "Not at all. You guys appreciated her art enough to have her at the store. I was grateful for that and I know she was, as well."

Riiiight.

Hilary's revisionist history was kind of weird.

"Like I said, we'd be honored. As long as you're certain, it's okay."

"Of course you're welcome."

I had a hard time believing that.

"So why were you going to call me?" Hilary asked.

I shut down the registers and then put the cash in a bank bag. I felt like I needed to call Greg to escort me to the night deposit at the bank.

"I don't know if you've seen the news coverage, but we've had a lot of her mourners here. We set up a small booth where people could sign their names and leave flowers or notes for the family. It's already packed with stuff."

"Oh, that's so sweet," Hilary said.

"Right. And the gang here and I wondered if it would be okay if we had a public memorial for her here. It seems to be a gathering place for those who loved her, and several people have asked. So, I thought maybe we could do something at the community center since it holds several hundred. And fans could share their stories. We heard a lot of them today."

"That just makes my day. I know she didn't show you her best side that day, but her fans do love her. I mean did. Oh—it's weird, ya know?"

I smiled, even though she couldn't see it. "I totally get it."

"I need to talk to the family, but if everyone is already gathering, I think it's a great idea to do the public memorial there."

"Okay, great. I'm going to go ahead and book the center for next Saturday and Sunday, just in case."

"Great. And thank you for doing that. I can't imagine any of this has been good for your business."

Um. "So the private memorial is Thursday. What time?"

"I'm still working out the details with the minister. I'll text you. Bye."

There was a bit of grumbling behind me.

"George, you ready to head home?"

He grunted. It was past his dinnertime. I handed him two of the treats I kept behind the counter for him. "Maybe these will tide you over." I shut off the lights in the front of the store.

I hit the middle where the book with all the flowers and notes were in the booth. More than thirty pages of the book Maria and Don had put out had been signed. Yarn Goddess was definitely loved.

Maybe we'd just seen her on one of her bad days. Well, it had turned into the worst day of *her* life.

A page had been wrinkled in the back. I opened it to that page.

You're next, was written in red letters. A nervous tingling surged down my spine.

What did that mean? Who was next? There'd been people signing the book all day.

Was it one of her stalkers? I had to check on that. How many did she have? What did they do? Did any of them take heart medication? So many questions.

Another shiver ran down my spine and my hands grew cold.

As if sensing my nerves, George grunted behind me.

I grabbed my phone out of my pocket.

"Busy," my brother said and then hung up on me.

Rude.

I took a picture and texted it to him.

My phone rang.

"Don't move. I'll be right there," he said and then hung up again.

"George, my brother needs to work on his communication skills."

I reached forward to flatten the page when a loud bang from the back of the store had me squeaking. George barked and ran for the back of the store.

And like those dumb heroines in horror films, I followed.

Chapter Nine

EVEN THOUGH I love my store, it's an old building that was abandoned for years. It makes strange noises all on its own. "Hello?" I yelled. George was a few feet in front of me, but he stopped and crooked his head as if listening. My stomach tightened with nerves and my hands shook as I picked up a giant hoop from Maria's cross-stitch table. "Is anyone back here? The police are on their way. For. Real."

No sound, except my chattering teeth and the *thumpity-thump* of my heart.

Something fell and George was off, barking like a mad dog. *What if whoever is back there hurts him?*

"George. Stop. Please." He paused, but still barked and snarled. The same sort of thing he did when someone had been watching me from my backyard. Oh, and when that same someone tried to kill me.

I grabbed his collar, and we moved more slowly toward the back of the store. Me holding up the giant cross-stitch hoop, like I'd be able to maim someone with the lightweight pine, and him snapping like a turtle gone mad.

"George, shush." But he didn't stop. We'd almost made it to the last aisle, when the back door slammed. And seconds later someone banged on the front door.

I may have screamed—loud. And while George took off

toward the back, I ran back to the front to turn on the lights, only to find my brother ready to break the glass in the door with his large flashlight.

"No, I'm here. I'm here." I rushed to fish the keys out of my pocket and dropped them. My nerves were shot. I finally managed to get them into the door.

"What's wrong? Why were you screaming? And what's going on with George?" He howled at the back door.

"Someone was here. I think they're gone now."

Two of his deputies rushed to the back and the door in the back slammed again. George quit barking, so at least there was that.

"Are you okay?" My brother looked me over from head to toe and stared at me like I'd gone mad.

That's when I glanced down and remembered I'd put the giant cross-stitch hoop around my neck while I opened the door.

"Weapon," I said as I took it off and sat it on the front corner. As if that made all the sense in the world.

His eyebrow went up.

No surprise there.

"I feel like I might hurl," I said, taking deep breaths to keep that from happening.

He ran around the corner, grabbed the wastebasket, and handed it to me over the counter.

I held it, just in case, but the nerves had died down considerably.

"What happened?"

"I texted you the pic that I took of the mean message," I said, desperate to sit down. As if he knew what I needed,

Greg brought around one of the stools from behind the register for me. "Right after that, there was a noise in the back of the store. George went nuts and took off, but by the time we were almost there, whoever it was slammed the back door. And then you were banging on the front one."

"Did you see them? Tall or short, man or woman? That sort of thing."

I scrunched up my face. "No. If the door hadn't slammed, I would have thought maybe one of the cats from the park had made it inside." During the winter, it wasn't unusual. The cats weren't feral, exactly. And the community, as a whole, decided to let them roam freely. They kept the vermin population down in the park and around the town buildings. We kept food out back for them, as did most of the stores on Main Street.

Someone squawked through the walkie-talkie on his shoulder, and he pushed the mic down. "Get Kevin and David to search the north side of the park. And I want video footage from the fire station."

"I don't suppose you got that back camera fixed yet?"

"No," I said softly. "No lectures."

"Ainsley, you promised me last weekend that you'd take care of it. If those back cameras had been working, we might have better leads on who killed Yarn Goddess."

"I've had a cold and my brain is not functioning at one hundred percent. Then you guys were in here for several days. By the time we opened the shop again, I forgot about it. I wasn't planning on having a murder or an intruder, ya know."

My brother has a thing about security, specifically when

it has to do with my well-being. Our mom and dad passed several years ago, and even though I'm way too old for one, he considers himself my legal guardian. It's because he cares. I get that. But sometimes he can be a bit overbearing.

He sighed. "Okay. Why don't you show me what you texted me?"

I really didn't want to get off my stool, but I did.

He followed me to the middle of the store. I pointed to the book that sat opened to the page.

He stared at it for a full two minutes and then did the weirdest thing. He leaned down and sniffed. When he stood back up, his frown had deepened.

"Where is forensics?" he said into his walkie-talkie.

"On the way, boss. ETA two minutes," someone said.

"What's wrong?"

"Did you touch the book, or was it open to this page?"

Crud. I'd touched evidence. "I'm sure lots of people touched that book today. Why?" Hundreds of people had come through the store today.

"Just answer the question, Ains."

"Yes. I opened it to the page. It was crinkled and I thought I'd straighten it out."

"Jake, I need you and the EMTs here. Ainsley may have been poisoned."

Bile rose in my throat and I very much needed my trash can.

"Whaaat?"

"The smell of almonds is distinctive. I think whatever ink this is, it's laced with cyanide. Did you inhale any of this powder?" I hadn't even seen it before. He brushed it to the side with a gloved hand.

Um. "Just the very edge of the page. Before I could flatten the wrinkles, there was a noise from the back room."

"Whoever it was probably saved your life."

"What?" The word came out on a squeak.

"You have to inhale or ingest it for cyanide to be effective. I still want them to check you out. Go sit down. Or better yet, go wash your hands."

"Can you come with me?" I blurted out. "Please. I don't want to sound dramatic but if there is a chance I might die, I don't want to do it alone." My body trembled. My brain understood that I was probably fine. But I was still scared as heck.

Greg frowned, but then followed me to the bathroom where I washed my hands and arms several times. Then I removed my shirt and put on a T-shirt from the shop that my brother handed me through the door.

My shirt went into an evidence bag. For good measure, I decided to rewash the top half of my body. And I'd take a blistering shower when I got home.

When I came out, George stood at attention, next to my brother.

"Better?" he asked.

I nodded. My dog was so intuitive that he sort of leaned into me so I could use him as support while I walked to a chair in the middle of the store where Jake stood by.

There wasn't a more handsome man on the planet. Nerves jangling for an entirely different reason, I sat down. George looked at me, and then Jake, and then sat down on my feet in front of me and put his head on my knees like some kind of guard dog contortionist.

Jake and I chuckled.

"You're going to be okay," he said. "But I need to check you out."

I bit my lip. More because I thought I might sound like some breathy teenager if I spoke. Jake had that effect on me.

"Your eyes are clear," he said, as he shone a light in them. "That's a good sign. I need to listen to your breath sounds." He stuck the cold end of the stethoscope down the overly large T-shirt and placed it against my chest. "Take a deep breath and let it out. And again."

I'm not going to lie—more than once I've dreamed of him touching me—just maybe not like this. Then his hands were gently touching my throat as he stared into my eyes.

Oh. My. Goodness. If I do die, I can do so happily now. That man's eyes were so blue—and I swore they changed color.

He let go of me, and I wanted to reach out and pull him back. "I need to draw some blood, so we can test to see if it's in your red blood cells."

I so hate needles.

I focused on my brother and his team, all of whom wore masks, gloves, and those little booties. My brother's booties were on top of his cowboy boots.

And as I am wont to do—when something is ludicrous—I started giggling. Like, shoulder-shaking, stomach-hurting laughing. And the more I tried to stop it, the weirder the noises that came out of my mouth.

Jake leaned down with concern on his beautiful face. "Is something wrong?"

I let out a huge snort and then covered my face with my hand.

I'm such a grown-up.

"I'm fine," I said through my fingers. I'd be better if the ground would swallow me whole. I pointed down to the boots.

Jake chuckled. "Yep, that's pretty funny."

Why does he have to be so nice?

My mind turned to the question of who had tainted the page. Was it the person who'd been in the shop? It had to be.

Jake distracted me by taking swabs under my fingernails, which he then put in an evidence bag.

"How did you get here so fast?" I asked softly.

"We'd been out on a burger run," Jake said, kneeling in front me. "We saw the deputies running through the park and then the call came in. Any dizziness or nausea?"

His sweet face made it difficult for me to concentrate and he was so concerned about me.

He's talking to you.

"Um. When Greg banged on the door, I felt a little sick. But I'm okay now. I think it was just nerves."

Jake had taken my hands in his. "I'd feel better, if you'd let us take you to the hospital so they can do a full workup."

I shook my head. I had a thing about hospitals. The last time I'd been in one, I'd been knocked unconscious for twenty-four hours in Chicago, where'd I'd been living before I moved to Sweet River.

The first time I woke up, they had me strapped to the bed. Later, we were told that I'd kept thrashing and they couldn't treat me—hence, the restraints. When I woke up,

Greg was there, and he convinced me to move to Texas.

It was so much safer.

Except when people tried to kill me.

"I'm fine now. I only touched the edge of the book."

Jake proceeded to check my ears, and throat, and took my temperature.

"It's cyanide," Kane said from behind my brother.

When did he come in?

Kane pressed his lips together. "It's not really that strong, according to the initial test I used. But it's definitely the real thing," Kane said.

"But why the hell would anyone do that?" Greg asked the very question I'd been thinking. "A killer would normally be after someone specific, unless they wanted to hurt all of Yarn Goddess's fans. It just doesn't add up."

"Ainsley, who had access to this book?" Greg squatted down next to George, effectively blocking Jake from examining me.

"Not done," Jake said. "Maybe you could give her a minute, just in case."

Greg stood and shrugged. "I heard you say she's fine."

"I believe she is but we won't know for sure until the blood samples are tested."

"About that guest book?"

I stared at Greg like he was nuts. I mean, I nearly died. Maybe that was a bit dramatic, but he could have given me a few minutes before the third degree. But he just stared right back.

"It's the book for the mourning memorial thingy," I said. "Pretty much everyone who was in here today signed it. It was constantly surrounded by people."

"Did you see anyone suspicious lingering?"

"No. There were a few oddballs in the bunch, but aren't we all? No one was scary or mean. Most of them were patient and polite. They bought a lot of stuff. I'll be honest, I was so busy with the register, I didn't pay much attention to what was going on in the store."

"Whose idea was the memorial?"

I shrugged, not really wanting to mention Don or Maria by name. They wouldn't have done anything like this, and I wasn't about to give him two more suspects. "There was a big line this morning before we even opened, so we thought it might be nice to put a book out where people could sign their name or leave notes and flowers. I was going to take it all to the memorial service on Thursday and give it to the family."

He blanched. "You were invited?"

No one was more surprised about that than me but the way he said it was kind of rude.

"Yes. Hilary called to make sure I'd be there."

"Huh." Greg turned to face Kane. "Anyway could we put a time on when that was put into the book?"

"The powder isn't matted down very much, so maybe a half hour," Kane said. "The book hadn't been closed for long, and it had to have been closed slowly, or we'd see residue on the table it's sitting on."

"Maybe the intruder wanted to scare me?" I asked. Though I couldn't imagine why. "Or maybe they meant it for Mrs. Whedon and didn't get to finish because George heard them?"

His walkie-talkie squawked again. "We found footprints, but it's raining. No way to know who made them. There were all kinds of people in the park today." At least, that's what it sounded like the person on the other end said. I had no idea how my brother understood everything that came over that thing.

Jake gently cleaned my hands and fingers with alcohol. "We don't want to take any chances," he said.

I smiled down at him, grateful for his kindness—and thoroughness. But the idea that someone did this… None of it made any sense.

"I talked to Hilary and she said the family thinks it might be one of Yarn Goddess's stalkers who killed her. She didn't think any of us here had a thing to do with it," I said. "And before you ask, she offered that info. I wasn't sure the family would be good with Shannon and me at the service. But Hilary promised it would be okay."

"Stalkers?" Jake asked.

"She's had more than her fair share," Greg said. "Dallas FBI has been looking into that. They'll be sending the files they have so far to me tomorrow. They had one more interview to do."

Being in the media like Yarn Goddess was, with the press watching every move she and her children made, she was probably more exposed to not-so-nice folks than most people. It just seemed weird that people would take yarn so seriously. Though I'm not much of a knitter, I know crafters who are very passionate about it, like Mrs. Whedon.

Had she been in here?

No. No. She wouldn't put anyone else in danger.

Or would she? Maybe if she wanted to throw law enforcement toward someone else?

Ainsley McGregor, you stop that.

That woman is innocent.

But why would someone dose that book, the one hundreds of fans might touch?

It made no sense.

"Sheriff." One of his deputies came in holding a plastic bag. "We found this."

It was a small blue vial.

"Where?" my brother asked.

"By Miss McGregor's car out back," the deputy said. "It looks like the perp might have tried to use it on the handle of the car."

My brother said some not so nice words. "Kane?"

"On it," the medical examiner said.

"We need to make sure nothing else was coated. Did it smell like almonds?"

"Yes, sir." The deputy's eyes became saucers. "It's like the book. Same sort of strong smell."

"I'm going out with Kane. Stay here," my brother barked, as if I would run after him.

I wasn't sure I could even stand. I don't consider myself a weak person, but a lot had happened in the last half hour.

"Do you think it's the cyanide?" I asked Jake, who'd been putting stuff back into his kit.

"I honestly don't know, Ains. I'd guess yes, but there's no sense in taking chances. Kane has the same test I do. It identifies poisons quickly, so we know what we're dealing with."

This time my eyes were saucers. I had nothing to do with any of this. Why would someone do this?

"It's the same poison," my brother said as he tromped back in. "It's nuts. Why would they pick on Ains?"

"I don't feel so good," I said, rubbing my head.

"Maybe you should go to the hospital," Greg said. The EMTs popped up the gurney.

I waved them all away. "No. No. I—It's just a lot. I don't understand why they'd do that to my car. And why drop the vial? It's like they wanted us to find it."

"If you'd touched more of that book and then your car—you could have died," Jake said. "Depending on how much is on the door of your car. It could have killed you within minutes, possibly seconds."

Ugh. Sometimes life was hard.

And as much as I needed to curl up in a fetal position and wish today away, I had to find out what was going on.

"You aren't helping with the me feeling nauseous thing. I don't understand why anyone would target me. I don't have any ties to Yarn Goddess except for the book signing. I thought maybe people would be upset, but no one seemed to care that she died here. Other than it was the last place she'd been, and they came to pay tribute."

My brother crossed his arms. "Well, obviously, someone isn't happy. And now they're after you. Or they want to make us think they are."

He rubbed his temple, which he did when he was nervous. "Are you sure you didn't see something the day of the murder?"

I tried to think back. My brain had been a bit fuzzy with

all the drama and having a cold.

"Maybe it was even before the signing," Greg urged. "Something Yarn Goddess said—or Hilary?"

I shook my head. "Yarn Goddess yelled about the booth and told me to get lost. I was busy at the register all day and then I went over to help set up the community center."

My stomach chose that moment to growl, and George whined at my feet. I tried to recall anything useful but all I wanted was some pizza—

Because that goes well with a sick stomach.

I didn't care; a giant cheese pizza was what I needed.

"I can't think of anything. I'm really tired and this guy is starving," I said as I rubbed his head.

"No arguments. You and George are staying with me tonight," Greg said.

Normally, I'd argue. But I didn't have the energy—also, the best pizza joint is around the corner from his house.

"I mean it," he said.

"Fine. But you have to feed us, and we want pizza." To be honest, I had no desire to be alone. And if I stayed with my brother, I could pick his brain about the case. Now that I was involved, I had to find the killer.

Hopefully before I was the next victim.

Chapter Ten

GREG'S HOME WAS two blocks from the center of town and looked like a miniature of Tara from *Gone with the Wind*. He'd inherited it from our grandmother, and it had big posts on the front and a wide porch on both levels. His friends and I sometimes called him Rhett just to annoy him.

I used my key to open the door and then flipped on the lights. His house could have been in *Architectural Digest*—thanks to one of his ex-girlfriends. She helped him update the house with timeless pieces—and then she decided small-town life was not for her. She left my brother with a broken heart, his first and only one, and a house that looked like it belonged in a magazine.

It was huge, with four bedrooms, each with its own sleeping porch and bathroom.

"I'll take George for a walk," Jake said from behind me and I jumped. My mind was so jumbled, I'd forgotten he was there. He put a hand on my shoulder. "Everything is fine. You're safe."

I tried to smile, but it was probably more of a grimace. I nodded. "Thanks. I'll call for pizza. Can you stay?"

He glanced at his watch. "Technically, I'm off duty, so sure. Lock the door after me." There was the reminder. The one that I might not be safe.

After calling Dino's for three large pizzas—the guys would eat one each, and I wanted breakfast the next morning—I ran upstairs to take a hot shower. Greg let me keep toiletries and a couple of changes of clothes here for nights when I had to work really late at the shop. I preferred my own home, but tonight I was fine with being protected by my big brother.

That and I needed a decent night's sleep. If I was by myself at my place, I'd be listening for every sound.

Once I'd nearly scalded my skin and scalp to make sure nothing was left on my body, I put on pajama pants with rainbows on them, and a hoodie that said, "I speak sarcasm." Then I pulled my wet hair into a knot on the top of my head.

Downstairs, I sat down in Greg's family room at the back of the house. I flicked on the television that took up most of the wall and flipped it to the news.

Yarn Goddess's name was on the crawl space at the bottom. It read: *Another attack in Sweet River, Texas. More at 10.*

Well, news did travel fast.

I switched over and started watching an episode of *Marple*, the one with Julia McKenzie. These old shows based on Agatha Christie novels gave me comfort. Murder shows should not be a go-to for settling the nerves, but I used to watch these with my mom when I was younger. I was twelve when Mom gave me my first Agatha Christie book. I'd already read every Nancy Drew.

Dad would make fun of us for watching the DVDs back then, but he'd settle down and view them with us.

"I miss you guys. And not just because someone tried to kill me tonight."

The doorbell rang, and I jumped—again. I wasn't sure my nerves would ever settle.

I peeked through the peephole to find Jake there. His hair was wet and there was some water on his shirt plastering it against his amazing abs.

Save yourself—don't look. But I couldn't stop.

"Ainsley?" Jake said through the door.

Oh. Right.

I unlocked the door and let him and George in.

"What happened?" I opened the door.

"I made a huge mistake," Jake said as he took the leash off of George. "I said p-i-z-z-a out loud. And he took off at a fast jog all the way back here from the park right through Ms. Helen's sprinklers down the street."

I smiled, this time for real. Glancing down at George, I wagged a finger at my dog. "You're not getting any. Last time you had cheese—well, let's just say Greg probably doesn't have enough gas masks to go around."

George cocked his head, as if he didn't believe me. He was probably right. Those sad puppy eyes, and groans like he might die if he didn't get a piece, would hurt my heart and he'd get anything he wanted.

Someone knocked at the door, and Jake opened it to the pizza guy. I'd already paid over the phone, but Jake gave him a tip.

"I would have done that," I said.

He just shrugged and carried the boxes to the kitchen island. "I'm going to borrow one of Greg's T-shirts he keeps in the guest room and dry off."

Before I could offer to help dry him off, he ran upstairs.

Ainsley McGregor, get a hold of yourself.

I sighed.

In the pantry, I found a container with George's kibble. Greg always kept a bag around, along with a food and water dish.

After getting my dog settled, I grabbed a couple of pieces on a paper plate. Jake came back down and I followed him into the family room.

"What are you watching?"

"A Miss Marple show from a long time ago. You can switch it to sports if you want to."

"Nah, I'm good."

We were about thirty minutes in, when George decided to come sleep on my feet again. I had a bit of a chill, so it wasn't such a bad thing.

"Hey," Greg said as he came in from the back garage. "Did you get some for me?" My poor brother looked beat down.

"On the island," Jake said as he pointed toward the kitchen.

We watched the show as Miss Marple went through one suspect after another.

It took everything I had not to ask my brother a million and three questions. But if I battered him with, what-ifs, he'd just close himself off.

"I think it was the pastor," Jake said.

"I think it's the artist dude. There's something fishy about him," Greg said.

I stayed out of it since I'd seen this episode about twelve times—maybe more.

Greg smiled when it was done. "I knew it."

"You can watch whatever you want," I said as I got up to get some more pizza. George was not happy that I'd moved. The two remaining slices were not going to cut it. I wished we'd order some of the cinnamon and sugar knots Dino's made.

"We can watch one more episode," Greg said. "It's kind of fun to guess."

Two grown men, the sheriff and fire chief, watching Miss Marple. Agatha Christie really did appeal to everyone.

They both followed me into the kitchen. I took the two pieces from my box. They took their boxes with them. Men. Neither of them had an inch of fat on them, and they ate like this all the time. It wasn't fair.

"Did you find out anything new?" Jake asked. I stood at the doorway, waiting for my brother to answer.

"We're checking more into the family now. Mrs. Whedon is still a person of interest, but she loves Ainsley. There's no way she'd ever hurt her. The son is in with a bad crowd in Dallas. Everything from gambling to drug runners. Bunch of rich kids who want to be gangsters. We're looking at him pretty hard. The daughter's ex has given us some pretty good leads. The family is definitely not what we thought at first.

"There are pics of the brother partying the night after he found out about his mom. And we have reason to believe the brother, sister, and Yarn Goddess's best friend were here in town near her time of death. Her phone records indicate she called each of them, about three hours before she died."

I stuffed pizza in my mouth to keep from asking any questions and kept standing there. I didn't want to stop my brother from revealing anything.

"That does sound suspicious," Jake offered. "Makes more sense than poor Mrs. Whedon offing someone. Though, she's a cantankerous one. She might think about it, but I can't see her actually doing it."

Neither did I. At least I had Jake on my side.

"She's definitely moved down the list. There's something deeper going on here. I just can't see it yet. I'm headed over for the service in a few days. In the meantime, I have several of my deputies going through bank records and we have a court order to investigate the company's holdings."

That was good because I'd bet a thousand donuts that her family had something to do with her death. They had the biggest motive of all—money.

"You can come in, Ainsley. I know you're listening."

I snorted and took my place back on the couch.

Greg flicked on the fireplace. "Before we watch the next episode, I need to ask you a few questions," he said as he pulled his notebook and pen out of his pocket. "This isn't official, I just need to know if you saw anything." He held up a hand. "I know you'd tell me. But I want you to close your eyes and just think. Why did you go to the booth?"

I closed my eyes and took a deep breath. "I have to walk past it to get to the back of the store."

"Right, but it was in the middle of the row. What did you see that made you walk by?"

"Smell. It was the flowers. So many of them and I'd been

busy all day. I was curious about how people were paying homage. There were knitted items and flowers. Stuffed animals. I was thinking we might need a much bigger space if it continued until her memorial."

"So you were standing there and what happened?"

"The guest book had a page turned under and I worried it'd get wrinkled. So I pulled the corner of it out. Then I saw what was written there. I called you and you hung up. So I texted you. I was about to flatten the page with my palm when there was a noise at the back of the store. Like someone ran into a shelf and things rattled. George took off and—"

"What?" Greg and Jake asked at the same time.

"I followed. I was thinking it was dumb since that's what the idiotic people do in horror films."

They chuckled.

"It's not funny. But I didn't want George to get hurt if someone was back there. I ran a few feet before the door slammed, and then you were knocking on the front door. That's all I can remember."

"Sorry I hung up on you. I was on the other line with the FBI in Dallas about the case. Kane has his hands full with a double homicide in Warrenton so we're actually sending the book and cyanide to the FBI's offices. They promised to move fast on it. They'll also be able to tell us what kind of ink was used in the pen the message was written with. It didn't match any that were on the table at the time. So we think someone took that red pen with them."

"But why target me? I don't understand." A chill ran through me again. I hoped my fever wasn't coming back.

"The note said: *You're next.* But honestly, Ains, it could have been for anyone. Or, it may have been a warning set to throw us off track. We can't be sure until we find the perp who did it. Until we do, you need to be cautious. Do not go anywhere alone."

I sat back against the couch and pulled my knees to my chest. "Wait, why is the FBI involved? It's a murder case."

"We haven't ruled out this wasn't a hit to show the brother what his new friends are capable of doing. Whoever did this was smart. Very little evidence, and like Kane said, if he hadn't examined the body right away—if you hadn't discovered it until Monday or Tuesday, no one would have suspected it was murder. Given her health troubles and the fact the poison would have been clear of her body, it might have been ruled a suicide."

Which made all of this feel personal. I disagreed with Greg. No way this was some professional hit. I didn't care how clean the scene was.

Someone in that family wanted her dead. The private memorial service might be just the place to find out who.

THE NEXT MORNING, I woke up way earlier than normal. After letting George out in the backyard, which was way smaller than what we had at the farm, I went in search of coffee.

My brother's laptop sat up on the island counter. He must have been doing a bit of work before he went to bed.

I might have accidentally bumped the mouse, and his

password screen came up. I might have accidentally typed in his password as well. For a lawman, he was insanely predictable when it came to his password. Favorite lines from movies we watched when we were kids.

Never Say Die worked.

I didn't want to do too much messing around, but I opened a few of the files he'd last looked at. One was on the son. This guy was most definitely mixing with the wrong people. All of the pictures were taken at parties, but people in the photos were tagged as those from drug cartels.

Holy moly.

I clicked on one of the pics in the file and nearly gagged. Someone had slit the victim's throat.

Yep. These were dangerous people but I couldn't see them killing someone with cyanide in a cup of tea. Maybe I'd seen too many movies, but the sort people in these photos used much more violent means.

The water upstairs started running. Crud. Greg was up. I clicked that file closed and opened the one on Sam Winstone. Interesting. He'd been a person of interest in a Ponzi scheme, but they didn't have enough evidence to charge him.

Yes. I'd most definitely start with Yarn Goddess's family.

Chapter Eleven

LATER ON WEDNESDAY, Kane still hadn't released the body. The family didn't seem to care about the formalities. They'd put together a private service for friends and family in Dallas today and were doing another one for her "Austin friends" tomorrow. That's what Hilary had said when she called to make sure Shannon and I were coming to Austin.

I promised we would.

My shop was still closed. A special team of investigators were testing everything at Bless Your Art to make sure the cyanide hadn't been anywhere else. And the vents would be cleaned and everything cleared before we could go back in to work. At least we'd had record sales in the days before so my friends would be okay financially. I felt bad for everyone with a booth, but there was nothing I could do.

Since the memorial here in town was set for next Sunday, the gang from the shop was busy at the community center getting it ready for visitors.

"It's weird," Shannon said, as she made me a dirty iced chai with two shots of espresso. Today, she wore a green sweater and jeans, with a big green bow tying back her long, blond hair. She always looked like the girl next door and seldom had a hair out of place.

Unlike me, who had piled my red hair in a messy bun on top my head, and maybe forgot to even look in a mirror. Hopefully, I didn't have toothpaste on my chin again.

"I mean, I've never seen invitations for something like this," she said, as she handed me my cup. "At the most, someone will post an announcement in the paper, right?"

The invitations had been FedExed to the coffee shop and my house. They were engraved white invitations, with black swirls. It was like a morbid wedding invitation.

When she turned toward the bakery case, I pointed at one of the chocolate croissants. "No matter how hard I beg, do not let my buy one of those." It wasn't that I was trying to lose weight—I rather like my curves—it's just that they were a gateway drug for me.

First a croissant, then someone would bring some kind of dessert to the shop, and then to keep that sugar high going I'd eat a piece of pie at dinner. If I didn't watch it now and then, I'd have to buy a new wardrobe. That, and Doc Marley had recommended at my last checkup that I cut back on my sugar intake or I'd end up with diabetes.

"I made power bars, which are packed with protein."

I scrunched up my face.

"They have honey in them, so they are sweet and healthy."

Ugh. "Healthy?"

She nodded and smiled. "Just try one." She handed me a piece in a napkin. It was like an oatmeal cookie.

"I'll take two."

"So are you going?" she asked, putting my goodies into a paper sack.

I'd forgotten what we were talking about. "Yes. There's a reception afterward, for some of the attendees. If you have a blue card, it gets you into the house for it. Who does that?"

"Rich people are strange," she said. "Who has color-coded cards for funeral events?"

It was weird. They didn't know us. Since she was killed in my shop, it made it even worse. The last people I'd want to see was anyone from Bless Your Art. The memorial was at a big church in Austin. Then the reception at their mansion.

"Hilary really wanted you to come. Will you go with me?"

At first, I didn't want to go. I had a feeling maybe they wanted to sue me and were checking me out. I can't help it. I have a suspicious mind. Then, I'd thought about asking Jake to come with me, since he was with me when we found her. But he didn't like me snooping any more than my brother, and I had so many questions.

"I guess I'll go," Shannon said, and then she asked, "Why did they use cyanide?"

"I don't know, but I've been opening every door with a tissue in my hand, just in case. Obviously, they wanted to scare me or someone at the store, but why?"

Was Greg, right? Did I maybe see something I didn't remember?

I'm a terrible person. Let's be clear about that. The main reason for going to the service was to get a look at this family. The rumors about them not being perfect had been true.

It made more sense that someone close to Yarn Goddess killed her, or maybe one of her crazed fans who loved her a little too much. They were an eclectic group for sure. We'd had a cast of oddball characters come through the store to pay their respects.

"The only person I know didn't kill her was Mrs. Whedon, even if she wasn't happy about the yarn. But then why did someone put cyanide on the door handle of my car? That feels personal, much like the teacup full of the stuff that Yarn Goddess drank."

I was only slightly bitter that my car had been taken as evidence in the case. I'd been provided with a rental, but still.

"Well, have you been snooping?"

I smirked.

"Of course you have." She laughed and shook her head.

"After I stayed with Greg, I tried to get a glance at some of the files he had on his laptop. That's how I found out that the gambling and drug problem of Yarn Goddess's son was the real deal. Word was, he owed some not very nice people in Dallas a lot of money. And that best friend guy, Sam, who was supposedly her right-hand man—has a sketchy past."

"Oh. Interesting," Shannon said as she wiped down the end of the counter where the drinks were delivered. "We should try to talk to all of them when we're at the memorial. Just friendly-like." She winked.

I loved her. She totally understood me and was just as curious about everything as I was.

More than anything, I needed to see how the family interacted with one another. I don't know why. I had this idea that if I saw them in person—I'd know which one killed her.

Dumb? Possibly. But I just had this feeling, and I'd

learned to trust my instincts the last time someone had been messing with me.

Maybe my brother wasn't willing to do what I liked to call research at the memorial service, but I did.

If he was nosy about why I'd chosen to go, I'd just say I was playing nice, so they didn't sue me, and because I wanted to pay my respects. I mean, I did. But I also wanted to find out who really killed her and who might be messing with me.

Then it hit me. What if the cyanide was just a distraction? Maybe to make the police think the killer was still in town?

"Hellooooo?" Fingers snapped in front of my face, and I shook the cobwebs away.

"Let me guess, you'll be on a fishing expedition at the memorial service and you don't want your brother to know."

I bit my lip trying not to smile. I cleared my throat. "Shannon, I'm just going to pay my respects. She may have not been the most pleasant of women, but she didn't deserve to die like that. And I feel somewhat responsible since it happened in my shop."

Shannon smiled. "Yep. Right. Doesn't matter. I'm in. Since you helped Mike a few months ago, I've wanted to get in on the super-spy action."

I laughed. "I'm not a spy. I'll just be—uh—observing. I'm curious about her family. I did a bit of research and the pics all show a happy family for the press, but there's a lot going on behind the scenes."

Shannon clapped. "I knew it. You're definitely sleuthing. I'm in. What time do you want to leave tomorrow?"

"I need to see if Jake can watch George Clooney. Probably around ten. The service is at noon and that gives us plenty of time to get there."

"I'll be ready."

George Clooney had waited patiently outside Shannon's coffee shop. I found Ms. Helen and her friend Erma petting him on the head and making baby-like noises, which he was totally into.

Nothing that dog loved more than being adored—well, maybe a large bone—but he was a needy toot in the love department.

"Morning, ladies, how are you?"

"Just fine," Ms. Helen said. She pushed a white curl behind her ear. "He really is an amazing dog. He just sat here quietly waiting on you."

"He can be a good guy." When he wasn't chasing squirrels. We had another go-around with that this morning.

"So?" Ms. Helen's eyebrow went up. Oh. No. She and her crew were some of the kindest souls in town, but they had their noses in everyone's business. "Are you going to the memorial service? We didn't get an invite, even though we were some of her biggest fans."

Since I was surprised to get one, I let it go. "I'll be going," I said.

"You should take a look at that son of hers. Erma's nephew says he's a shifty one. Had some gambling debts Mommy had to pay off for him." Erma's nephew was Kevin. If my brother found out he was blabbing to the whole town—again—he'd kill him. But Ms. Erma and Ms. Helen were formidable forces. They could get info about anyone, anywhere.

Poor Kevin never really had a chance.

"We're grabbing coffee to take over to Livira. The knitting circle decided to keep her company." It took a minute for me to connect the name—Livira was Mrs. Whedon. "You'll let us know what you find out, right?"

I shifted uncomfortably. The last thing I needed was them aware I might be snooping. The whole town would know by lunch—including my brother. Kevin letting things out of the bag went both ways. "I'm just going to pay my respects."

"Right. We'll see you at book club on Friday. You should be home for that. We'll expect a full report."

They took off, and I laughed.

"Well, George, let's go see if Jake can keep an eye on you tomorrow."

He grunted.

"Oh, let me check." Sure enough, Shannon had put an extra protein bar in the bag for George. Usually, it was an extra roll or peanut butter cookie.

He wolfed it down. "Well, if you love it that much, maybe I will."

My mind whirled with possibilities. I'd promised I wouldn't start looking into the case, but that was before they'd accused poor Mrs. Whedon.

And someone scared the heck out of me the other night.

I took a deep breath of fresh Sweet River air. It was early March, and we'd already hit the mid-seventies. It was nothing like Chicago weather, which would still be cold and miserable that time of year.

"I might do a bit more research into that family," I said to George. And into Yarn Goddess.

He barked and then burped really loud. People up the street turned to see what was going on.

At least it smelled like oatmeal.

THAT AFTERNOON, I sat down on the couch with George and turned the television to Animal Planet, which was his favorite channel. I thumbed through Yarn Goddess's autobiography: *My Favorite Yarn*. And it was a tall, tall tale. Except for starting her own business, which was true. The rest of it read like pure fabrication. Her sister had died of cancer. Her parents and her first husband had also died. But everything was whitewashed, used to make her look stronger in the face of adversity.

You're being mean.

Maybe so, but it just didn't jive with the woman I'd met that day. And why did everyone around her die? She didn't seem the type to sit at her sister's bedside talking about knitting patterns.

Or maybe I had her all wrong. Maybe it had just been a bad day. She'd been incredibly ill when I met her. I researched her online, and her family.

Her husband had died while hiking, when the children were very young. But the most interesting thing I found was that in just about every picture of the family gatherings or events, Sam, her best friend, was there. Most of the time he stared up at her adoringly and she smiled right back.

Maybe there was something to that. Could they have had a lovers' quarrel? Or, perhaps he'd steered her the wrong way with her business.

Love made people do awful things sometimes.

Chapter Twelve

THE NEXT DAY, we arrived at the service about thirty minutes before it began. There weren't many cars in the parking lot, and I checked the invitation Hilary had sent. She'd called the night before to make sure we were coming, since the invite arrived just a few days before the event.

She'd been stuffy-sounding, like she'd been crying. I felt sorry for her. Would she still have a job? She'd been a devoted assistant, who had done her best to make Yarn Goddess's life as easy as possible.

I thought we'd have a quick phone conversation, but it had ended up lasting an hour. She kept talking about the business and that she was worried that they wouldn't be able to go public. Then she'd been talking about flowers and party planning, and I realized just how awful I was. She'd been referring to the memorial reception. I'd totally missed the transition into that part of the conversation.

In my defense, I'd been watching George chase Mr. Squirrel, which was highly amusing. I had to stop myself from laughing so that she didn't get the wrong idea.

I told Shannon this as we pulled up to the huge church.

"Are we at the right place?" Shannon glanced around. "Maybe everyone in her social circle shows up at the last minute."

"Maybe." I parked the rental SUV. "Let's go in."

The church was a new Gothic-inspired structure that was made to look old. Like maybe something you'd find in Paris. There were polished marble floors and our heels clicked loudly as we walked.

Hilary stood near the door of the vestibule next to two somber-looking men, and a woman whose hat had a veil so thick it blocked her face. The son I recognized from the photos. The woman had to be the sister, but I didn't know the man in the middle. Yarn Goddess's husband had died years ago; that's when she'd decided to become a businesswoman. In the last twenty years, she'd built an empire.

"Oh, Ainsley, I'm so glad you came. She adored you," Hilary said as she hugged me.

Really? To my recollection, she'd told me to stay as far away as possible with my cold. But now wasn't the time to correct her.

"I'm so sorry for your loss," I said and tried to pull away, but she kept hugging me tight.

Okay, then.

Finally, she stepped back. "This is a dear family friend, Sam Winstone. He's been Yarn Goddess's confidant and advisor since she began the business." The man was handsome in a Hugh Jackman sort of way, with the most beautiful blue eyes.

He took my hand in his. "Thank you for coming. I loved her like a sister. It's so wonderful to have her friends gather during this sad time to celebrate her life." Then he smiled and it almost made me forget that I wasn't friends with the woman.

But I just smiled back, because even I know you just go with the flow at a memorial service. I'd seen the pics of the two of them together—no way that was just a brother and sister sort of relationship.

Behave.

I nodded, not really sure what he'd said.

"These are her children, Brock and Emily."

Brock looked a lot like Sam, which sent my mind all kinds of places it had no business going. They had the same eyes. Why hadn't I noticed that before?

"I'm sorry for your loss," I said to him.

"Thank you," he said stiffly and then shook my hand.

"We're so glad you could come," a soft voice said from behind the veil. "Mom would be so grateful."

"I'm fairly certain, with the exception of Hilary, the family have no idea who I am," I whispered to Shannon, as we moved toward the ladies' room at the end of the long hall.

When we opened the door, she ran and looked under all the stalls. I laughed.

"What are you doing?"

"That was weird," she said. "They treated us like we'd known her for years. That older man said that he knew how much she'd appreciate me being there. I don't know her."

"Right? This whole setup—where is everyone?" I asked.

She shrugged.

"We better get back in there."

Since no one else was inside the church, we sat in the middle. Usually, I'd pick a seat in the back, but it was too obvious with the enormous place so empty.

"I don't understand why no one else is here," I whispered, opening the program. There was to be a song, a moment of silence, a few words about Yarn Goddess. Most likely short and sweet. Except, a video montage was listed at the end. Even though I didn't know her, seeing photos plastered on a screen might make me weepy, especially with her kids watching.

It was like watching those Hallmark commercials that ripped your heart out.

I'd expected some three-hour event with choirs and tons of people talking about how much they loved her.

I was about to say something else when a few people trickled in, but it wasn't many. My brother showed up and sat by us.

"Promise me you're here out of the goodness of your heart," he whispered.

He was quite dapper in his dark blue suit, crisp white shirt. I seldom saw him in anything that wasn't his sheriff's uniform or a pair of jeans. Some people might call him handsome. Not me—ugh. But some people.

"Of course," I whispered. Was it bad to lie in a house of God? I glanced at the cross at the front of the church.

I'm going to hell.

"But isn't it strange that so few people showed up?" Shannon asked. "With all of her fans, I thought this place would be packed and people in line outside waiting to get in."

He kept his eyes forward and shrugged. "The daughter told me that they'd held the bigger service in Dallas. That this was just for her closest friends."

And yet, we were here.

"Oh." Shannon folded her hands in her lap.

I'd bet a dozen chocolate croissants that he was here to check out the family.

"So odd when we came in, they treated us like long-time friends," Shannon whispered, "and we barely knew her."

My brother's mouth tightened.

"You're here because they're suspects. I knew it." I might have said that last part a little too loud, and he and Shannon shushed me.

"Sorry."

"Can we please just pay our respects?" he said through gritted teeth. "The poor woman died in your shop. Have a heart."

I took a deep breath. Greg was right. I was being incredibly rude. No one believed in Karma more than me, and how would I feel if someone came to my funeral only to snoop on my family?

That evil part of me said: *You wouldn't care because you'd be dead.*

But I told it to hush.

A few more people came in, and then the family.

The daughter moved to the front of the church and lifted her veil. She nodded toward the pianist, and then she belted out Ariana Grande's "God is a Woman."

My eyes had to be as big as saucers.

What is going on?

Shannon coughed into her hand to keep from laughing and I stared down at the floor because if I saw her smile, I would lose it.

Never in my life have I been more uncomfortable sitting

next to my brother while the daughter sang about the way she liked it.

Don't get me wrong, I love the song. But not in a church—and definitely not at a memorial service for one's mother.

Stop it. You're being small-minded. Maybe Yarn Goddess really liked that song. Who are you to judge? You spent your formative years loving NSYNC.

I still listened to their Christmas album now and again.

I made the mistake of glancing at my brother, and the mirth in his eyes nearly did me in. I had to put my hands in front of my face like I was weeping. I was, with tears of hilarity.

The song ended and Emily brought a hand to her heart. "That's your favorite song and you know that I love you." Then she put the veil back over her face and took her seat.

To his credit the minister, who'd been sitting on the side, didn't miss a beat. He smiled tightly at the family, and then proceeded to extoll the virtues of Yarn Goddess. And yes, he called her that. Even in death that name wasn't changing.

"She was a kind and generous woman, who everyone loved," the minister said. Her kids nodded, as if agreeing.

Maybe she was a different person at home. Or maybe cancer had made her cranky. I mean, I would be. It was an awful, insidious disease. Kane had said he'd been surprised she could walk. She'd probably felt like hell that day.

My chest tightened and tears burned. I'd not been gracious or lovely today. My gran would be extremely disappointed in me.

"Let's take a moment of silence to remember our dear friend," the minister said as he held his hands in prayer.

Sorry, Yarn Goddess. I hope you are free from pain and suffering. Also, I'm going to find out who killed you. Promise.

A chill swept through the church and I shivered.

"I understand a few of her friends wish to say a few words. Ainsley McGregor?"

My eyes flashed wide and I gasped.

I'd only sort of been paying attention. Why in the world would they want me to say a few words? I didn't know anything about her other than she sold yarn and had knitting patterns people fought over.

My brother nudged me with his elbow, and the family turned to stare at me. Hilary waved toward the altar and the lectern to the right of it.

I stood on shaky legs begging my brain to kick into gear.

What am I going to say?

I glanced toward the back, as I had a feeling Greg and Shannon were trying not to laugh.

Never in my life had I felt more like a fraud.

Karma.

Ugh.

I tried to force a smile. "I—uh…" I coughed a bit. "Yarn Goddess was a talented and brilliant woman." Yes, that's good. "I know we're all feeling her loss, but none more so than her beautiful family, her friend Sam, and her assistant Hilary."

Hilary gave me an encouraging smile. She sat at the end of the pew with the family.

Oh. Lord. Please. Help. "What a wonderful life she created for herself. She knew exactly what she wanted." I swallowed hard. "And, uh, her fans adored her, and there will never be another Yarn Goddess."

And then nothing…no words entered my brain. I sniffed and quickly nodded, like I was about to cry. "Okay. Right. Amen."

Then I forced myself to slow down and not run back to my seat.

My brother and Shannon each had a hand over their mouths like they were trying not to laugh.

Traitors. "I hate you guys," I whispered. This time it was my brother who coughed.

They didn't mean to be disrespectful, and neither did I. But this whole thing—it was as if it'd been put on for show, but no one had any idea what was going on.

Maybe that makes me sound hard-hearted but this felt like her book. A bit whitewashed and unreal.

Thankfully, only a few others spoke. There weren't more than thirty people there and that included the family.

Hilary stood. "I'm so grateful for the opportunities she gave me," she said, and the words came from her heart. "As many of you mentioned, her fans adored her. Everything she did was for them. I've learned so much from you, Yarn Goddess," she said to the sky, as if she might be floating above her. "Thank you for everything."

Then she bowed her head.

When she lifted it again, she dabbed her nose with a tissue. "The family would like to invite you to the Austin residence. We hope you'll come and celebrate this wonderful woman's life."

Embarrassed by my awfully awkward speech, I was about to suggest we just head home.

"I'll meet you guys there," Greg said. "There's something I want to chat with you about." Then he moved to the side of the church and watched the family as they spoke to some of the other attendees. The son kept glancing to the back of the church where a shadowy figure was hidden by one of the columns.

"Who is he looking at?" Shannon whispered.

"Greg or her son?"

"The son."

She shivered. "I can't see who it is, but he's giving me the creeps."

"Do you think we should go to the house?" My head started to pound and wearing a dress with heels had an expiration date where I was concerned.

Okay, it wasn't the dress so much as the Spanx I had to wear to get into it.

"I have so many questions," she said.

I smiled. "Me, too."

We piled into the SUV. I opened my phone to sync it with the navigation system. I had no idea where we were going but according to Siri it wasn't far.

"So, is it just me or was that the weirdest memorial service you've ever been to?" Shannon asked.

I turned on the ignition. "I guess families grieve differently."

"Amen," she said and then busted out in giggles.

Of course she wasn't going to let that pass without comment.

"I had no idea what to say. And it's a church so—fine. It was dumb."

She waved a hand in front of her face. "Oh no. Ains, I thought you were great. I mean, what the heck were they thinking not even mentioning to you that they wanted you to do that?"

"It was…unexpected," I said. "Why would they ask me to speak? I'd only met her once. I spoke a lot with Hilary beforehand, but I had a cold last week and Yarn Goddess ordered me to stay away. I was maybe in her orbit for a minute at the most."

"That is weird," Shannon admitted.

"And where are all of her adoring friends and fans?" Shannon asked.

"Hilary mentioned they were keeping it small—just a few close friends," I said. "I just thought that meant, like, a hundred, not the usual thousands who show up for her events."

She pursed her lips. "I guess making it invitation-only limited the numbers."

"I'm sure you're right. I feel terrible for my thoughts while I was in there. Those poor people have a right to grieve however they want." I pulled out onto the highway. For once, the Austin traffic was light. That didn't happen often.

"Yep, I'm guessing she worked so hard, that maybe she didn't have too much time for friends," Shannon said. "That's just sad. But I'm with you, this was one of the stranger memorials I've been to. We can be awful about it together."

Siri told us to exit so we did. "When Mrs. Greenly died

last month, she wanted gardenia wreaths and for everyone to sing 'Old Rugged Cross' while standing in a circle. That was different, but you could feel the love. This was—"

"Cold," Shannon finished. "The woman wasn't easy to get along with—you know that better than the rest of us. Maybe she didn't really have any friends."

I couldn't believe it but I was sad for Yarn Goddess. At least she'd had a family who loved her. I think.

We pulled into a long drive and headed up a hill.

It took me a second to realize it was Greg's truck behind us. He loved that truck way more than he did me. Most of the time it stayed in the garage at his house and he drove the town's vehicles.

We pulled up to a gate where a line of cars waited to go in. "Oh, get the blue card out of my purse," I said.

The guard at the gate asked for our names, and then motioned us up the hill to where there was a valet stand in front of a large French Provencal-style home, which stretched out in front of us.

I handed off the keys to the valet, and we waited for Greg.

"And this is their second home?" I whistled.

"They actually have six homes," Greg said. "Two in Texas. One in Mexico, and the others are spread out over Europe. Her empire was international. From what I've learned, Yarn Goddess preferred to work here. Said it fed her creativity or something," Greg offered.

The family's limo pulled up while we stood outside, and we waited until they'd gone inside before following.

I was about to step forward when Greg put a gentle hand

on my shoulder. "Do not harass the family," he said softly. "How they choose to grieve is up to them."

I rolled my eyes. "Why do you always think the worst of me?"

"So you didn't come here today to snoop?"

I'm not so good at lying, but I shook my head. "Truth is, after my abysmal speech at the service, I was thinking of heading straight home. But then it was your idea to come here." I held up a hand. "I promise not to give anyone the third degree. All I ask is that you keep an eye out. There's something off with these people."

"Just behave," he huffed.

He's my brother, and I'd take a bullet for him. But there are days when I wish I could knock him out of a tree like I did when we were kids. Not that I could climb a tree these days. The very thought made me shudder. Too much like exercise.

"So, it's discreet snooping," Shannon said quietly beside me.

"Yep," I said as we made our way through the enormous double doors.

"What in the world is this?" Shannon whispered as she grabbed hold of my arm.

"I have no idea," I said softly.

Chapter Thirteen

IMMEDIATELY AFTER ENTERING the house, we were bombarded by a loud band playing a mix of techno and heavy metal. People laughed and chatted. There were definitely more here than had been at the service. The back of the house was all windows, which had been opened up so that the party had spilled outside.

And it was definitely a party.

"Uh…" Shannon said.

"Right there with you." The place was like something out of *Architectural Digest.* White wood, with washed-out fabrics on French country furniture. Pops of color came from the artwork, and the floors were stained a dark hickory.

Was that a Rembrandt over the fireplace?

It couldn't be.

Greg glanced back at me with one eyebrow up. Now maybe he believed me. These people were not grieving, only going through the motions. I know how that sounds. I've been to a few wakes, but they weren't like this.

This wasn't the somber reception most people had after a service or funeral. The kind of thing where you awkwardly told the grieving family you were so sorry for their loss, and then you ate bad chicken salad that made you throw up the next three days.

Or maybe that just happened to me.

A huge spread of food had been laid out on several tables lined up on the left side of the great room. Drinks were being served at the bar off the kitchen.

Hilary came to great us. Her face was flushed, and she held a plate full of shrimp. "Isn't it a great celebration? We didn't want to do anything too sad. Yarn Goddess would have been bored to death with that sort of thing. We're throwing the kind of party she would have had."

"Oh, that's nice," I said, feeling horrid inside for all the judging I'd been doing.

Perhaps, and I do mean perhaps, Greg was right. They were trying to celebrate her life and going about it in a different way. It wasn't like there was just one way to grieve.

Stop being so judgey.

I would—if just one of them seemed sad. Well, except for Hilary. Her eyes were puffy and her nose red.

"Are you feeling okay?"

She blew out a quick breath and then nodded, but tears brimmed.

"I'm sure she would have loved it," Shannon said beside me. She was so much better at these sorts of social things. "It's a beautiful setup. Did you do all of this?"

Hilary smiled. "Yes. I've done so many events for her, it's in my blood. The band's a bit loud. I'm going to ask them to tone it down a bit. She always said music should be a touch of atmosphere and nothing more. You go get some food. There are tables outside where you can sit. It's getting a bit crowded in here."

Greg was talking to Sam. My brother was good at his

job. He had a way of getting people to talk to him. I liked to give him a hard time, but he knew what he was doing.

As much as I wanted to know what they were discussing, Shannon pulled me toward the food.

"They have lobster *and* shrimp," she said, "and oh, those look like cheddar biscuits. This is nicer than what we're going to have at our wedding."

My stomach growled. Food didn't sound so bad. Plus, the daughter was at the end of the buffet, chatting with a friend. Since no one else seemed interesting in eating, Shannon and I made our way down fairly easily.

"I can't believe she's gone," the friend said to Emily.

The daughter scrunched up her face. "It's weird. I still feel like she's here."

"You guys were so close."

I happened to glance up as she frowned. But it wasn't a sad sort of look, more one of anger.

I stared down at my plate and moved on just to the side of the door outside, so I could listen a bit more.

"My heart hurts," Emily said. "We'd argued over my wanting to drag her into the next century with different types of videos and chats so we could bring in a younger generation. But she always treated me like I had no idea what I was talking about."

"Oh," the friend said, "that's just the worst. I'm sorry. Well—I mean—do you know if you and your brother are getting the company?"

I'd been wanting to know that very thing. "I guess. We'll know tomorrow when they read the will. I need a drink," Emily said and then her voice trailed off.

It was March in Texas, so there was a slight breeze, but it was a comfortable seventy-six degrees. We found a table on the other side of the pool where we could keep watch.

"Your brother was right," Shannon said as we sat down. "They just have a different way of doing things."

I shrugged. "It's more like a wake, I guess. I went to a few of them when I lived in Chicago. It's not so unusual, I guess."

"Yeah, my great-uncle Bernie had a wake. His mom was Irish, and he always liked the traditions. I don't remember much because I was nine. It was loud and everyone slept over at our house because they were all too drunk to drive home."

She stopped and then smiled. "I didn't mean to say that out loud."

I laughed with her. "Not quite as fancy as this one, I'll bet. This is like some Hollywood party or something."

"Only the best for our mom," Emily said, walking up. She'd changed into a short black skirt and a glittery top. How she walked in her eight-inch heels on the pool decking was a miracle.

"Thank you for speaking today," she said, sitting down and crossing her legs and arms. "It was great of Hilary to find people who were Mom's peers and really respected her work."

"It was—I'm honored I was asked."

Shannon kicked me under the table.

"Right," Emily said and then glanced back at the house. Her brother was arguing with some woman. "I'm sure Hilary spoke with you. We wanted to do a bigger…I guess you'd call it a send-off for fans. Since you guys had such a successful event for her last week, we were so happy you said you'd help out. Hilary said you guys could pull it off. I'm sure you can imagine how crazy it's been around here."

"It must be so hard for all of you," I said. "I can't believe anyone would want to hurt her. She was so beloved."

"That she was. It was probably weird for you guys today with so few people at the church. Most people went to the one in Dallas. But the one here in Austin was for those closest to her. We felt really bad that someone attacked your store." She rolled her eyes. "This was mine and Hilary's idea of apologizing that you got caught up in this."

Oh. Wow. "That's actually very kind of you. For the record, I don't blame anyone but your mother's killer."

"I know she's gone—" she pointed to her forehead "—here. But it still doesn't feel real. Like, why? She had stalkers and people like that, and business rivals, but she's always had those things."

I sipped my tea. "I promise I won't say anything, but I know she was very ill."

A tear slid down Emily's cheek.

It's official: I'm the worst person in the world.

"She didn't tell us." Her voice was rough and raw. She lifted the sunglasses she'd been wearing. "Why wouldn't she tell us? For months she's known she would die soon. And she let us go on living in Dallas like normal, while she was hiding out here. We'd figured she'd had some botched plastic surgery or something. She didn't want us coming here, and she'd stopped doing video calls with her execs at the company. Sam had to handle it all. If only she'd told us."

Shannon handed her a tissue. "You poor thing," she said.

"I'm betting she just wanted you guys to be happy and live your lives."

The young girl's shoulders shuddered. "Maybe. Hilary swears she would have been fired if she mentioned anything. She showed us the NDA Mom made her sign. So I can't be mad at her, but I wish she would have said something. We haven't seen Mom for six months. She was here the whole time."

She blew out a breath and then took another one in, deep. "You guys probably think I'm some kind of weirdo crying like this in front of strangers."

"Not at all." I put a hand on hers. "We respected your mother a great deal. And we hurt for your family. I'm honored that you guys want us to hold a memorial in our town. We all are."

She gave us a watery smile. "Thank you. It's so easy to talk to you guys."

The arguing escalated between her brother and the other woman. "He's in the worst mood," she said. "He's been taking this all really hard. The last conversation with Mom wasn't great. She was about to pounce some tough love on him."

"Really?"

Emily nodded. "He hasn't been a very good boy—that's what she'd say—the last couple of years. And she was sort of over it. I better go see what's going on before it gets out of hand."

I turned to face Shannon.

There was a coffee barista bar on the other side of the pool where the argument grew even louder. "If it weren't for the band, I could hear them," I said softly.

"I'm going to go get us a couple of coffees," Shannon said as she jumped up. I was about to follow when someone waved at me.

"I see you found a quiet place," a man said.

The sun was behind him, and only his outline was visible—until he sat down.

The super suave Sam sat next to me, which was odd since there was an entire table with about eight other chairs he could have chosen.

"Hi. Yes," I said. Knowing that sounded a bit rude, I added, "It's too beautiful to be inside."

"I don't disagree," he said, leaning toward me. Maybe he looked like an older Hugh Jackman, but I have a thing about personal space. And he was in mine.

As handsome as he was, in a movie star kind of way, the bourbon on his breath wasn't appealing. Bile rose in the back of my throat, and I pushed the lobster away.

Sitting back in my chair, I crossed my arms. "This is quite the party, Sam. You guys spared no expense. The food is amazing."

He smiled in an "isn't it wonderful" kind of way. "It is. My Ellie was great at throwing parties and I feel we did her justice here. This is exactly the sort of send-off she'd want."

I didn't think Ellie, a.k.a. Yarn Goddess, was the partier type. She'd seemed more the garden-party type.

Perhaps, Hilary had been truthful. The woman could have just been in the middle of a rotten day when I met her.

She was D-Y-I-N-G. That would put anyone in a bad mood.

The pain she must have been in. I had to keep reminding myself of Kane's words. I judged her by how she treated me, but it wasn't fair.

Guilt formed a tight knot in my chest.

"So, were you just friends—or did you work together?"

He chuckled and then put a hand on the arm of my chair, effectively trapping me there.

Yep. This guy was a predator. I ran into his kind all the time when I was in Chicago. Men who thought they were God's gift.

My brother had taught me many moves, but through the years, I'd also learned to use what I had.

So, I smiled sweetly. I batted my eyelashes and then remembered I'd put on my sunglasses.

I'm smooth like that.

"I thought you were going somewhere else with that question. We were the best kind of *friends*," he said, and then waggled his eyebrows for effect.

Yuck. Friends with benefits. Somehow, I couldn't imagine Yarn Goddess's hair mussed.

Ewwww. Bad visual. This guy and her having sex.

No. Bleach my brain. Bleach my brain.

"But I consulted with her business. That's how we met. I do conferences for up-and-coming businesses. You should check them out sometime." He handed me a slick business card, but I didn't bother looking at it.

I nodded. "Sounds interesting." That's what I always said when I had no interest at all in something. I'd definitely have to do some more research on this guy. Charming, but lethal, that's how I'd describe him. I had a Spidey sense. I'd developed it after dating a few of his type when I lived in Chicago.

"When you say consulting—in regard to Yarn Goddess—what did you help her with on the business side? I'm just curious so I can check out your seminars later."

Then he launched into how he helped take her global. That when he'd met her, she'd been thinking local only. So, he'd showed her a way to create an empire with fans all over the world. Keeping her profits high and her fandom huge.

Funny enough, none of the success had come from Yarn Goddess. At least, according to her consultant. It was all him.

Right.

"Oh. I'm curious. Since you were so involved on the business side, do you know anything about the dyes in the yarn being bad? A friend of mine saw something online about how it was making people break out in rashes. Maybe that's why someone wanted to hurt her?"

He sat back, his eyebrows coming together in a rather mean expression. It was as if I'd flipped a switch. "Your friend better be careful about spreading rumors and innuendo. That sort of thing might get them a slander suit. If there have been complaints, I'm not aware of them. And we're getting ready to take the company public. The media is always looking for lies to tell. But I'm going to make it happen. It was Ellie's dream."

Was it?

Somehow, I doubted it. I didn't believe a word he said. He was used to people just falling at his feet. And I'd bet all of Shannon's healthy oatmeal bars that this guy knew exactly what had happened with the yarn. Had he tried to keep it a secret from Yarn Goddess?

The argument in the corner escalated even more. "If you'll excuse me, I need to check on the kids. Brock hasn't been taking his mother's death well."

Hmmm. *That guy is hiding something.*

Chapter Fourteen

A FEW MINUTES later, Shannon came back with two cups of coffee and a couple of Bavarian cream kolaches balanced on top of the paper cups.

"What did Mr. Smooth have to say?" She sat the cups on the table and the plates of sweets beside them. "Something about him sends my creep-dar blaring."

"Mine, too," I admitted. "He wasn't happy when I brought up what Mrs. Whedon said about the yarn. In fact, he lied and said he didn't know anything about it. But he's very involved with the company and is taking it public, so he's aware."

She picked up her cup. "How do you know he was lying?"

"He grew angry quickly, and threatened lawsuits. My guess is he may have something to do with all of that." I wouldn't have put it past him to be the one responsible for the bad yarn, since he was so interested in keeping costs low.

Did Yarn Goddess, who'd obviously been very ill for months, lose track of what was going on with her company? Had she been surprised by the news from Mrs. Whedon? "So what did *you* find out?"

"That woman, Felicia, loaned Brock money and now she wants it back. Something about investments and gambling—

she's a bit hysterical, and I had trouble understanding her. But he was having none of it. He didn't even apologize for whatever he'd done. He told her that not all investments pan out and she knew that before she gave him the money."

"What about the gambling?"

"It was hard to understand, but from the gist, I'd say he didn't invest the money but gambled it away. Somehow, she found out. He's posturing, but my guess is he did exactly that. I'd say YG's son has a big gambling problem. The woman stormed off and then he was arguing with the sister. She begged him to get help before he destroyed *everything*."

"Wow. That's a lot of info. I'll have to send you on errands more often."

I took a bite of kolache. The pastry was filled with cream and so good. Greg came back with a plate and sat down with us.

"What have you found out so far?" he asked.

My eyes went wide. "I have no idea what you're talking about." I sipped my coffee.

"I saw you from the house. What did Sam say?"

I sat the cup down. "He mentioned his seminars to help business owners. And that he'd helped take YG's business global."

"YG?"

"That's what Shannon calls Yarn Goddess."

She nodded. "I think it's weird to call her that, especially now that she's dead."

"What else did he say?" Greg asked.

"I wasn't snooping." I frowned. "When I brought up the dyes in the yarn, he was defensive. He acted like he didn't know, but I'm sure he did. It made me wonder if some of the counseling he gave the victim wasn't the best. Maybe she wasn't aware of the problem with the yarn."

He stared across the pool toward the brother and sister who were now in a heated conversation with Sam. "Kane told you about her having cancer, didn't he?"

Shannon gasped. "What?"

Greg glanced back at me. "Look at you, actually keeping a secret!"

I rolled my eyes.

"She was dying of lung cancer and didn't have long," I explained. "But Emily swears she and her brother didn't know. The way she was crying, I believe her."

"I feel so bad for laughing earlier," Shannon said sweetly, and put a hand to her heart. She was one of the kindest souls I'd ever met. "If she hadn't been murdered, she would have died soon?"

Greg nodded.

"I think they're all trying to hide something," I added. I'd never seen a guiltier lot.

Greg smirked. "I'm not discussing the case with you. The foxglove used in the teacup, and the cyanide on your car and the book were the same."

Shannon and I exchanged glances.

I followed his gaze, which was still trained on YG's family.

"How could they even tell?"

"A lab in Dallas specializes in poisons. Kane drove it up there himself. We can still put Mrs. Whedon at the scene, but…"

"You really don't think she did it?"

He just turned back to the party and put his sunglasses back over his eyes.

Shannon leaned forward. "I wasn't snooping, either, but there was a big argument between Brock and some woman about gambling and investments. Might be something to check out." She stuffed some pastry in her mouth, as if worried she'd said too much.

He sighed. "You two need to understand that I'm investigating all possibilities. I came today, probably for the same reason you did."

"To pay your respects," I whispered.

This time he chuckled. "To see what was going on with the family. When I drove up to talk to them the first time, the daughter went into hysterics, but the brother almost seemed relieved. And that guy Sam pretended to be sad, but he was forcing himself. I haven't liked any of them from the beginning, but I had no evidence—or I didn't."

I waited for him to continue, but he didn't speak.

"Dude," Shannon said. "You can't just say something like that and not follow up."

"I have a feeling Sam would have done anything to make sure the business went public. We've traced payouts to certain individuals who had complained about the yarn. And there's some sort of cover-up with the financials. We're looking into the accounting, but the numbers aren't what they projected." He held up his hand. "But you two stay out of it. Let law enforcement do its job."

I sipped some more coffee. The afternoon sun was setting, and a cool breeze had picked up. "This whole charade today, and that's what it is, just doesn't make sense," I said as I sat my cup down. "I get the feeling they're hiding a lot of somethings. What if she disagreed with Sam about taking the company public? And did you see those guys in the shadows at the back of the church? Maybe one of them killed her to teach her son a lesson."

Greg shrugged. "Did either of you get a look at those guys? I was busy listening to the family, and when I followed them out, those guys were gone."

"No. They stepped behind some columns."

"I tried to glance back," Shannon admitted, "but then I was kind of weirded out and ran to catch up with Ainsley."

My money was on the son, or Sam, and I was definitely leaning toward Sam. *Maybe, I should check out one of his seminars.*

"Whoever killed YG—it had to be premeditated," I said. "I don't know much about the poison that was used but they had to have that ready and gloves, or they'd be dead, as well—did you guys look for gloves?"

He nodded.

"And the note was in YG's handwriting, right?" I asked. "So she'd been about to apologize to someone. I've been thinking about that, and whoever killed her, made her write that. Maybe she died before she could finish. The killer wanted everyone to think it was a suicide or natural causes. I'd hoped by now I'd have a better idea of who our key suspect might be. But the list is even longer."

While I didn't want to die and had personal motivations to find the killer—it was my brother's job. And other lives might depend on him. Sometimes, it was easy for me to forget the kind of pressure he was under.

I cleared my throat. "I think what we've seen today is cause enough to explore more. I know you want me to stay out of it, but I've become pretty good friends with Hilary. She might be the best way to learn about the family."

He shook his head.

I gave him my best grin and did jazz hands.

Even when we were in the worst trouble as kids, that always made him smile.

"Fine," he said grudgingly. "If it'll keep you off my back. But be careful. At this time, everyone is a suspect. Don't trust anyone. I don't want you getting into trouble *again*." He stared hard at me.

"I know. I know. Just friendly chats, no snooping. Got it."

He smirked. "I wish I believed you."

Chapter Fifteen

As we gathered up our trash from the table by the pool, a waiter swooped in and put it all on a tray. The food had helped my headache a bit, but thoughts swirled through my brain at F5-tornado speed. More than anything I wanted to go home and take a nap. Funerals and memorials did that to me.

Shannon and I walked around the huge estate in search of Hilary so we could say goodbye. It wasn't easy since we were in heels. We were about to traverse the private lake below the cliffs the house sat on, when we ran into Emily. She seemed a bit the worse for wear since the last time we'd seen her less than an hour ago. I asked her where Hilary was.

"I think she's in her room. Second door on the right upstairs," Emily said and then guzzled down her martini. She waved goodbye with the glass and then picked up her phone and shot a selfie.

"She might be sleeping," Shannon said. "I can't imagine she's had much rest since YG died. She had to plan two memorials and this party. And she's helping with the big event in our town next week."

"True. But I'd feel bad if we didn't at least try to tell her goodbye."

I knocked lightly, just in case. But no one answered.

There was one room with the door ajar at the end of the hall. "Maybe Emily was too drunk to remember," Shannon said.

I did my "I don't know" shrug and we ambled down the hallway.

I knocked gently, and when I did, the door opened a bit wider. The room was fit for a queen, except for the medical equipment all around. Amongst the Louis XV furniture, there were IV poles and heart machines. Two different types of oxygen machines.

"She must have been really sick," Shannon whispered.

"That's what Kane said." I closed the door behind us and locked it.

"What are you doing?"

"Snooping—what does it look like?" I rummaged through some papers in the nightstand. Nothing major. The books by the side of her bed were business ones on how to run an empire. "You stay by the door and listen for anyone coming down the hall."

"I really don't like this." Shannon's sweet voice was taut with nerves.

"If anyone comes in, we'll just run out there." I pointed to the big verandah beyond the French doors. There was a beautiful view of the lake.

"Just hurry."

I flipped through some of the books and found a photo inside. It was of Brock partying. There was what looked like cocaine all over his face, and he was asleep on a couch holding a bottle of champagne with women all over him.

Why didn't police take this as evidence? Clearly, her son

had a drug problem.

I stuck it in my purse.

"Someone's coming." Shannon's eyes went wide.

The door handle jiggled and Shannon stood there with her hands on her face and I was worried she might scream.

"Darn it. Who locked this door?" It was Hilary. "Probably them looking for the will again. Crud. My keys are downstairs."

"We have to get out of here," I said as I opened the door slowly. I locked it again as we stepped out.

We were halfway down the hallway when one of the doors opened and Brock stepped into our path.

"Ahhh." Shannon screamed and then put a hand on her chest. "You scared me. Sorry. I almost peed my pants." Then she slapped a hand over her mouth, realizing what she said.

I cleared my throat. "We were trying to find a bathroom—the two downstairs are occupied. And we're lost."

He sniffed and then looked from me to her. "It's right there," he growled and pointed across the hall. Then he pushed past us and stormed down the stairway.

My heart pounded and Shannon had gone pale. "We might as well go." I shoved her gently toward the door.

"Come in with me," she said. Her hands were shaking.

Poor thing. I shouldn't have made her snoop with me. It's just…the opportunity was there.

Thankfully, there was a separate room for the toilet, away from the shower and vanity. I reapplied my lipstick, which was almost gone. And took my heels off for a minute and sat down on the huge marble vanity. The walk-in shower was probably bigger than my whole master bathroom. But everything was just as tasteful as the rest of the house.

When Shannon came out, she had more color in her cheeks. "You okay?"

"Yes. Sorry about that. If I'm honest, that's the most scared I've been in while," she said as she washed her hands.

"I should have sent you back downstairs."

She waved a hand. "Goodness no. That was the most fun I've had in ages. It was like being in an episode of *Sherlock*."

"Ahhh. Benedict Cumberbatch," we said at the same time and then giggled.

"Let me take my turn, and we'll get out of here. I don't know about you, but I need a nap."

"Yes, all this cloak and dagger stuff has worn me out. Plus, if we leave now, we can hit the Junk Gypsy store in Round Top and maybe grab some food from Teague's Tavern."

"We just ate." I laughed.

"Yep, but that's like an hour away and we'll be hungry again."

She wasn't wrong.

"Then we can rewatch the first season of *Sherlock*."

"I very much like the way you think," I said and then bumped straight into Hilary, who stuck her arms out to keep from falling down.

We all laughed.

"I'm so sorry," I said. "We ran into Brock the same way when we were looking for the bathroom. I didn't realize this was the autobahn."

Hilary smiled sweetly. "No problem. I was looking for you guys. I have something I need to brainstorm, and I just don't know who else to talk to."

"We're happy to help however we can," Shannon said.

Hilary's shoulders seemed to sag with relief. "I know I haven't known either of you for very long, but I'm so glad you've come into my life. You're so solid and sane."

And I just broke into your boss's bedroom—but sure.

She led us to a room two doors down on the left, which explained why we couldn't find her the first time.

After kicking off her heels, she climbed into the middle of the bed. It was a huge four-poster, and the room was only slightly smaller than YG's had been. It was decorated in much the same way.

She motioned for us to sit on a plush sofa by the bay window.

"Thank you so much for coming. And sorry I threw you under the bus at the service. At the last minute, the family backed out of giving the eulogy." She sniffed. "I guess, from the turnout, you realize she didn't have a lot of people who genuinely cared about her. She'd stopped socializing the last several months."

"Because she was sick?"

She blinked rapidly. "You know? Does anyone else?"

I put a hand on her arm because she seemed so worried. "No. Just me and the police. And, Shannon." Oh, and everyone at Mrs. Whedon's but she didn't need to know that.

Shannon bit her lip. "I won't tell a soul."

"Her kids didn't know," she said. "For the last year, she's been limiting her exposure to the public on purpose. At first we thought she might kick it, but then six months ago—the news was awful."

Guilt hit hard in my chest. "Why wouldn't she tell her family?"

She shrugged. "She's their rock, and she was doing everything in her power to make sure they had great lives going forward. We were overseas seeking several different types of treatment. None of which worked. Even though she was going through all of that, she worked her butt off for the company. All in an effort to make sure their futures were secure.

"I'm mad. It doesn't make sense but I am. They don't really seem that upset by her death. She was the meanest boss I've ever had, but I still loved and cared about her. She'd softened this past year. She insisted I learn the ropes and taught me how to run an empire. I will be forever grateful to her for that."

Rap music boomed up the stairs. Somehow, I had a feeling that wasn't YG's favorite.

She glanced down at the floor. "It's a bunch of the kids' friends downstairs," she said. "None of them had anything to do with Yarn Goddess." She sniffed again. "If she hadn't been so—"

"Difficult," I suggested.

Shannon cleared her throat and gave me the evil eye over Hilary's head.

"Yes. She wasn't always like that, though. It's just…the pressure of the last six months…and not being able to trust her own family. Oh. I didn't mean to say that."

Curiosity piqued, there was no way I'd let that one go.

"It's okay." I patted her shoulder gently.

"Were they taking advantage of her?" Shannon asked.

"Yes. More and more. Even Sam was getting on her nerves. I don't know what was going on there. They'd always been so close, but the last few months—she'd just been crankier than usual. Nothing I or anyone else did made her happy."

I'd learned long ago that each of us were responsible for our happiness.

"That's what I've been doing up here. I know the police are going through her emails, but I am, too. And I snuck into her office and got a copy of the financials. Things just aren't adding up—and I'm fairly certain that's why she was upset with Sam. I handled her day-to-day, and her personal life. But most of the actual business she took care of—until this second go-around with cancer. Then she handed a lot of the bigger stuff off to Sam.

"He was hell-bent on taking the company public, but I'm not sure she believed it was what was best. She kept saying she wanted to keep it in the family." She rubbed her forehead. "Sorry, I…shouldn't lay all this on you, but there's literally no one I can talk to."

I'm not a hugger, but I jumped up and wrapped my arms around her and squeezed. I felt so sorry for her. She was trying to do the right thing and was all alone. I'd been there a few times myself. "Hey, I'm here for you."

"Me, too." Shannon hugged her as well.

"Anytime you just want to chat, hang out, or get away from all of this, you have an open invitation to come stay with me," I said. "You gather all this up." I motioned toward the papers. "And come with us now. We'll help however we can. Amazing what a couple of days on the farm can do for your soul."

"Be careful, I may take you up on it," she said and then gave us a sad smile. "Thank you, both. For coming today, and for being so friendly. I sometimes feel like I'm the only one who is sad she's gone."

I didn't disagree with her—at least, when it came to YG's family. "Just know, we're here for you. At the very least, we can figure out the profit and loss statements and tax stuff. I've learned a lot over the past several months with my shop."

"I'll be taking you up on that, as well as any job advice. The family has been good so far, but I don't know how much longer that will be the case. It's kind of strange staying here with her gone. I mean, most of the time we were here the last two months, and the rest of them were in Dallas. So it kind of feels like they are the invaders. That's terrible to say. It's just—this place, its solitude, had come to feel like home. And even though she wasn't feeling great, she was a lot more relaxed here. And I'm rambling."

"It's okay," I said. "And as for a job, I'm sure you'll find something within the company. You're one of the most competent people I know. You'll land on your feet."

She took a deep breath and let it out. "Thanks for everything today. Just this little chat has made me feel better about life. And I'll be calling you tomorrow about the event next week. I can't believe it's only a few days away and still so much to do."

Shannon hugged her. "Don't you worry. Sweet River pulls together for its friends. We've got your back. I heard from the gang at Ainsley's shop. The list you sent has already been taken care of."

This time when Hilary smiled it was the real deal. "Y'all really are wonders. I've never in my life known such kind human beings."

Poor thing. My heart really did hurt for her. She's been through so much helping YG with her illness, and then dealing with the murder and funeral.

"Most of the B&Bs and hotels are booked up with her fans, so why don't you come stay with me? That is, if you don't mind nosy Great Danes."

Hilary smiled. "Thank you. I keep saying that. You guys are the best. And I will stay with you. The reading of the will is in the morning and the lawyer said I need to be there for some kind of formality."

There was a loud crash from somewhere in the house.

She glanced up at the ceiling and then sighed. "I should probably get down there."

We took that as our cue to leave and waved goodbye.

ONCE WE WERE in the car, Shannon turned to me. "We should get out the whiteboard again and write all this down. It helped when we were trying to solve the last murder. And you know ten minds are better than one."

I laughed. "I don't disagree with you about the needing more minds, but that's the last thing I should do. Greg will have my head if he finds out. But here." I handed her a notebook and pen. "Write down everything we learned today before we forget."

She was right: this was turning into a real mystery. I might not know who killed YG, but I was certain it wasn't Mrs. Whedon. From what Greg said, the woman in green was off his list, as well.

Someone had put cyanide on my door. That attack was all about me. I don't care what my brother said. Putting it in the book was one thing—but my car was something else.

"Uh, Ainsley. Why are you going so fast?" We'd just pulled out onto the street and Greg followed us.

I pumped the brakes a second time. "Um, something is wrong." I tried again and the pedal went straight to the floor.

"You're scaring me," she said, her voice becoming high-pitched.

"Uh. I don't know what to do." Inside my head, *we're going to die, we're going to die*, played on an endless loop.

If this is the Karma for not being respectful of YG, I'm so sorry, God. Really. Super sorry. It will never happen again.

Please don't kill, Shannon. She's a much better person than I am. And Mike will never get over it.

"We're coming up to a curve," Shannon said. "You've got this. I believe in you, Ains."

I didn't, but I was too focused on not flipping us over to say so. We slid around the curve. A steep drop-off was on Shannon's side.

Please stay on the road. Please stay on the road. I begged the car. My hands shook hard, but I forced them tighter around the wheel. And I made myself breathe.

She grabbed her knees to her chest like that would help us from falling off the side.

It might have been funny, if I hadn't been so scared.

"Siri! Call Greg."

The phone dialed.

"Why are you driving so crazy?" he asked calmly.

"Brakes aren't working," I shouted. "Crud, we're going too fast for this curve." The car skidded to the right as we wound our way down the hill.

"Please, help us," Shannon said softly.

I wasn't sure if she was pleading to God or my brother. Maybe both.

"We're picking up speed," Shannon whispered.

"Hell," Greg said.

Thankfully, no one else was on the road out here—one of the benefits of having a house on a private hill, but we were heading toward some crossroads and I had no way of stopping.

"Try pumping them," Greg said, and then he put his lights on top of his truck and turned his siren on. He whizzed around me.

The high-pitched siren did not help my nerves.

"I am." I tried again. "The pedal is going straight to the floor. I promise you I'm trying. It's nothing but air."

My brother mumbled bad words under his breath. The speedometer hit ninety miles an hour.

"Try pulling up on the emergency brake—wait! Don't do that yet."

I had my hand on the brake, as he sped ahead.

"There's a culvert coming up on the right. It's filled with leaves and someone's thrown a mattress in it. Pull off into that and put on the emergency brake as hard and as fast as possible."

"I've got the brake," Shannon said and then she put both hands on it. "You keep your hands on the wheel."

"Thanks."

"There's the culvert." Everything happened so fast, and in slow motion at the same time.

"I love you," I said to Shannon.

"I love you, too," she said. There were tears in her voice, but I didn't dare glance at her.

I guided the car toward it, bile rising in my throat.

I didn't see the mattress but I trusted my brother.

"Ready?" she asked as we hit the culvert. We bounced hard and my head hit the headrest as my elbow cracked against the door. She pulled up the brake and we jerked to a skid. "Our Father who art in heaven…ohhhh." Shannon's prayer was interrupted by sheer fear. I was right there with her.

We skidded and fishtailed, but then the car slowed. Up ahead, Greg had pulled sideways into the culvert. "What are you doing?" I yelled.

Before he could answer, we hit the mattress and the car slowed even more, dragging the piece of foam along the bottom.

Screeeeeech. The noise was deafening.

He jumped out and ran to the other side of the road, and by the time we hit him, it was a slow, soft bump.

Tears burned my eyes. "Are you okay?" I turned to face Shannon, and she threw her arms around me. My stomach churned with nerves and we just stayed there for a minute.

"That was scary," she sobbed. I hadn't seen her cry like

that since her fiancé had been falsely accused.

I wanted to cry right along with her, but one of us had to be strong.

Of course, my whole body shook.

Greg was at the door trying to pull it open.

I had to unlock it.

"That rental company is going to get an earful from me," Greg shouted.

"I know you're worried, but yelling isn't helping me right now."

He put a hand on my shoulder. "Are you two okay?"

We nodded.

"Let's get you out of there," he said, tugging on my seat belt. "Shannon, I'm going to need you to crawl over to Ainsley's side. There's a barbed-wire fence right outside your door."

He helped us out of the car, and an ambulance and a fleet of police cars arrived seconds later.

"We're surrounded," I joked.

Shannon giggled and I did the same. That was way better than crying.

Greg grunted. Then he stooped under the car to take a look.

More bad words under his breath.

"What is it?"

"The brake line is hanging in two pieces. It either broke or…"

It was cut.

I stared back up the hill. Had someone in that house tried to kill Shannon and me?

Chapter Sixteen

THREE HOURS LATER, my brother dropped us off at my house. Well, not really dropped off. My brother wasn't leaving anytime soon. His truck had barely been scratched. He'd have to take it for repairs at some point, but it was drivable. The rental had been hauled in for evidence.

This was a theme for me, lately.

Mike waited on the porch. He'd been working in the vineyards and freaked out when Shannon's call finally went through. He'd been determined to drive to Austin, but we were already on our way back.

She ran to him and he hugged her, swinging her off the ground.

I want that. We could have died today, and I would have done so without having had a great love in my life. I'd had boyfriends. I'd dated a lot of jerks. But I'd never had that connection Shannon and Mike did.

"You're not staying out here by yourself," Greg said. "I just heard back from Captain Joe in Austin. He says the line was deliberately cut."

My stomach dropped to my toes, and the world tilted to the right. "Can a woman sit down before you hit her with more bad news, please?" On the way to my house, we'd all been eerily quiet. The troubles of the day, and what could have happened, weighing heavy on us.

He sighed. "Come on. I think we could all use a drink."

I didn't disagree.

"I thought you didn't drink when you were on duty," I said as I wrapped my arms around my stomach.

"I'm off today, and since I'm sleeping on your couch, I'm not really worried about it."

"Oh. I thought you'd make me, and George, stay with you."

He made a funny face. "George did nasty things in my backyard when you were there the other day. I'd rather he do that here where you have to clean it up."

I started laughing and I couldn't stop. In fact, I giggled so hard I had to sit down on the step.

Jake's truck pulled up. After he let the tailgate down, George jumped out and bounded toward me. As if he sensed something wasn't quite right, even though I was still laughing, he sat down in front of me and put his overly large head in my lap. I rubbed his ears and it calmed me.

My hands still trembled.

My brother went into the house, as did Shannon and Mike. "I'm getting the good bourbon out," she said.

"Yes, please," I said.

Jake cocked his head, staring at me with such intensity.

"What? Do I have something on my face?" I wiped my hand over my chin and cheek.

"No. You're perfect, Ainsley. I'm just glad to see you in one piece."

He sat down beside me and took my shaking hands in his. "That was scary," he said softly.

Tears rimmed my eyes. "Yes."

We stayed like that for a good five minutes. His strength calming me. "You two coming in?" Shannon said from the doorway. "Your brother ordered pizza. I hope you like meat."

We all chuckled. I do like meat, a lot, just not on my pizza. I'm more of a four kinds of cheese and just a hint of sauce kind of girl.

"Just kidding," she said. "He ordered a couple of cheese ones for us."

Jake stood and then pulled me up, which wasn't easy since George didn't seem to want to move. "He's tired," I said as we walked in.

"After hearing what you went through, we played not-Frisbee for about an hour."

"Not-Frisbee?"

"You know. He makes you throw it and he chases it. Then he sits and stares at it until you pick it up again."

"Oh, he was so messing with you. I just refuse to go get it. Eventually, he'll bring it back."

He chuckled. "Well, then I switched to the ball. And then his rope and then back to the Frisbee. After an hour, he sprawled out in the middle of my field and just lay there with his feet up in the air like he was dead."

George grunted. He'd be snoring minutes after he ate.

I smiled. "That sounds like him. Thank you for taking care of him. I'll be honest, I kind of wish we'd never gone to that memorial."

"Well, you're here. There's pizza and bourbon. Life is looking up, right?"

Except for the part where someone wanted to kill me.

He still held my hand and it hit me. He's always kind to me, but that was the first time we'd had a moment.

A different sort of nervousness shot through my body, but this one was warm and spread through my limbs.

I became twelve years old and wondered if it might be possible that he liked me—in that way.

Shannon handed me a glass with two fingers of whiskey. "Sorry that I interrupted your moment," she whispered. "Your brother asked where you were."

I grinned. It almost felt like someone hadn't tried to kill me a few hours ago.

"I'm going to freshen up and change clothes," I said. "You have some sweats in the guest room you left here last time," I told her. "They're clean, if you want to change. And I have a pair of bunny slippers that are too small for me."

"Oh. You are my favorite human in the world," she said, and then she hugged me. We stayed like that for a full two minutes, the men walking awkwardly around us like they weren't sure what to do.

"We're okay," I said.

"We are." She high-fived me.

We changed and I might have added some lipstick to make myself a bit more presentable in my yoga pants and Captain Marvel T-shirt. I sported unicorn slippers and there may have been a few snickers from the men in the room when I plopped myself down on the couch.

"Only you, Ains." My brother winked.

"I know. I'm special."

He snorted.

"I think they're cute," Jake said.

I may have blushed a loud red, as the heat in my cheeks was at an all-time high.

My brother glanced between us with a strange look on his face.

"So do you think Mrs. Whedon is still a suspect?" Shannon said and then cleared her throat. "I mean, it had to be someone at that party who cut the brake lines, right?"

My brother bristled. "I'm not going to discuss the case with you guys. It's an—uh—"

"Ongoing investigation," we all said, and then laughed.

His phone *dinged.* "Pizza's here."

"Saved by the bell," Mike said.

Oh, my brother wasn't getting off that easily. We'd learned so much today and that family was absolutely up to no good.

"I should grab plates and napkins, and water for everyone," I said.

Jake jumped up from his spot on the couch. "You rest. I'll get it."

Man, I could get used to this.

My brother came in with the pizzas about the same time Jake brought in a stack of paper plates and napkins. Normally, we'd use the real stuff, but I didn't want to do dishes later.

"Thanks," I said as Jake passed things around.

There was a college basketball game on television. Leave it to my brother to find some kind of sport to watch. That and the news—well, maybe a few action movies, were all he watched.

"I wrote everything Hilary and the rest of them told me down in the notebook you gave me, Ainsley," Shannon said. "While Greg was driving us home. I think—because it's obvious someone is trying to hurt you—that it should be all hands on deck. Like, Greg, you should tell us everything, so we know how to protect her and who to look for."

Go, Shannon.

I stuffed pizza in my mouth.

My brother stared up at the ceiling as if asking for strength.

"I just want to eat my pizza," he said. "And drink my beer." He raised a bottle. It must have been one from the six-pack I kept stashed in the back of my fridge for him. None of us drank much, but it had been an eventful day.

"Shannon is right. Mrs. Whedon, as far as we know, was nowhere in the vicinity of the memorial or the party afterward. And she had an alibi for the night someone tried to break into my store and poison my car."

That was still weird to say. Still, every time I opened a car door, I used a tissue. And though the entire shop had been cleared, I still planned to wear gloves while handling merchandise until the killer was caught.

"She is no longer a person of interest," he said.

I did an internal fist pump. No reason to gloat in front of my brother. He'd almost watched me die today.

He sat his beer back on the coffee table. "I have people following up in Dallas and Austin on the family. The brother has a history of gambling addiction. Turns out, he owes a lot of money to some not-so-nice folks. Some of whom were tagged by the FBI as persons of interest on another case. He's in pretty deep."

"Oh. We forgot to tell you," I said. "His sister told us YG was about to throw some tough love at him. Maybe she refused to bail him out this time? That could be a good motive for killing someone. Or, like I mentioned earlier, someone did it to teach him a lesson."

He pulled out the tiny notebook and pen he kept in his shirt pocket. Even wearing a suit today, he had that little book. He flipped it open. "The sister is trying to launch a cosmetics line and is also up to her eyeballs in debt. I overheard her talking to Sam, after the brother stormed upstairs."

I knew it. They were after Yarn Goddess's money. Any one of them could have killed her and then tried to pin it on Mrs. Whedon. Though, why? How would they even know who she was?

"Hilary thinks Sam is up to no good with the company," I blurted out. "I mean, she says YG wasn't as excited as he is about the company going public. She's trying to make sense of the financials, but things just aren't adding up."

George, who had plopped himself at the end of the *L* on my sectional, grunted. "That's his 'I need one last trip outside' grunt," Jake said and then jumped up to let him out.

What just happened?

I mean, George *had* been spending a lot of time with him.

"So right now they all have a motive, but not opportunity. They were in Dallas or so they say. The time stamp on the photo could be wrong. I don't know. There's a possibility they could all be lying and maybe drove down and killed her. But that next morning, they flew down in the company jet to meet me at the Austin house," Greg said.

"So none of them were in the vicinity?" Jake asked when he came back in.

George did his three turns on the couch and then settled down with his head on my leg.

"I don't know," Greg said.

This was almost better than the whiteboard.

I groaned. The book club was tomorrow night and then we had the big memorial on Sunday.

"Who backed up their alibi?" Mike asked.

Greg frowned. "They were each other's alibi."

"Did they really fly to meet you? Or were they already there?" I asked.

"A flight plan was filed. My guys checked. But someone could have messed up the dates. Hmmm. I'm going to double-check that."

"So they could all be guilty," I said. "Maybe they're all in it together. Sam seemed pretty close to those kids. But why go after me? It doesn't make any sense." I brought my knees up to my chest.

Jake sat his water on the table and wiped his hand with the napkin. "Maybe they think you know something. There's a chance you could have seen something you shouldn't have."

He'd obviously been giving this some thought.

"I agree," Greg said. "Or we have one of YG's stalkers going after you. The two things may not be related. The poison was part of several news reports. But we never specified what kind. They probably just assumed it was cyanide. Maybe they do see you as responsible for the murder. It did happen in your store."

"Her fans are passionate, but none of them were at the party," I added.

"That we know of. There were all kinds of people there. I was able to get photos of most everyone. And remember, you left the car with the valet, who was parking the cars. Anyone could have tampered with the car. There was a local announcement about the private memorial, even though the paper didn't put an address. If someone knew about the Austin house, and a stalker would, they could have been staked out there."

My appetite left, which is saying a lot where I'm concerned. "So they waited for me to show up? But I wasn't even in my car. It was a rental."

"Which means that person had to know what you were driving," Greg said, not really even looking at me. His eyes were on the game. "They've been watching you."

"Greg," Jake said.

My brother glanced over at him. "What?"

Jake tilted his head toward me.

"Oh. Ains. Sorry. I didn't mean to scare you. That's why you're going to have round-the-clock protection until we figure out who this is. I have patrols checking out your fence line and doing drive-bys, twenty-four seven. You're going to be fine."

I shivered and it wasn't cold in my house.

"I get that they might be upset about what happened at my store—but I'm not responsible for killing her. This all feels personal. Are you sure that this has to do with YG's murder?"

Greg sat up straighter. "What do you mean?"

"Well, I know that the killer used poison…"

A million thoughts whirled through my brain. "The killer wants us to believe that the murder has something to do with me."

"Your brake lines were cut," Mike said. "You and Shannon could have been killed."

I pursed my lips. "Yes. But we asked a lot of questions today. Maybe one of them thinks we might be on to them. It would make sense; we all walked out to the parking lot together. Anyone who had been at the private memorial would know the vehicle we were in."

"Right," Greg said. "But I can't see any of them crawling under a car to cut a brake line. Did you maybe overhear something at the party?"

Shannon and I stared at one another, our eyes growing wide.

We'd both heard more than we probably should have, and someone had figured it out. Now, her life was in just as much danger as mine.

Well, heck.

Chapter Seventeen

THE ONLY SOUND in my living room was the television. Was I right? Were Shannon and I both in danger?

Shannon, who sat between Mike's legs on the floor, squeaked. "No. I told you everything they said. It wasn't really anything you guys didn't already know about the brother."

Mike leaned over off the couch and wrapped his big arms around her. "Well, no one is going to hurt my Shann."

I chewed on my lip. "When Sam walked over, what exactly did he say to them?"

She took a deep breath and closed her eyes. We were all watching her like she was the most interesting thing in the world. "The girl kept saying over and over: I want my money. He made it seem like it was her fault that she gave it to him. Kind of classic narcissism stuff. I know because I used to date a lot of them."

She opened her eyes and kissed Mike's knee. "Until I met you, honey."

He touched her cheek.

This time, she opened the notebook she'd been writing in on the way home. "When the sister came over, she told the girl they'd figure it out. But to please let them grieve their mother, at least for today.

"After the girl left, she kept telling him to get it together. That he was making them all look bad. It was like she was more worried about what people might think or something. Not long after that, Sam came over. In a really mean voice, he told them to stop acting like toddlers. The son stormed off. Then she yelled at Sam and said he wasn't in charge. That she—oh. She said, 'We'll find out tomorrow if you're still around, old man.'"

"What's tomorrow?" I asked.

My brother rubbed his temples. "The reading of the will."

I slapped the sofa pillow I'd been holding. "Oh. No. I just remembered something.

When we were upstairs…trying to find the bathroom," I said slowly so that I didn't slip and tell him I'd been snooping, "we overheard Hilary say that they must be looking for the will. She seemed kind of perturbed about it." Then I told them about what she'd said about the books not adding up.

"I don't disagree with her. The judge approved the court order and we have a forensic accountant going over the files. I'll have a deputy pick up the records Hilary has as well."

Money. Power. Sex. Maybe all three. "I know we don't have much evidence," I said. "But that Sam—there's something smarmy about him. Like, he's too slick. And the way his face changed when I mentioned the problem with the yarn. It was like the devil showed his true face."

Shannon shivered. "His voice when he was talking to the son and daughter was scary," she said.

"It's hypothetical," I said, "but what if he's done something? I looked him up, and I know you are probably already aware, but he was accused of embezzling funds before. Maybe she found out. Or maybe she found out he'd done something like outsourced the making of the yarn without telling her. If she confronted him and threatened to go to the police—"

Greg nodded and glanced at Jake. "Any chance you can hang with Ainsley tonight? I need to check up on a few things."

"Not a problem," Jake said quickly.

"Hey. Hello? Sitting right here."

They all laughed.

"And I don't need a babysitter. I have George. I'm perfectly okay taking care of myself."

"Nope. Jake's staying or I'm bringing half the station to your house."

I rolled my eyes.

After everyone left, I tried to give Jake an out. "I really will be okay. You're just a mile away."

"Nope. Sorry. I'm not leaving. I wouldn't be able to sleep worrying that someone was trying to poison you or kill you. At least if I'm here, I can get a bit of shut-eye."

"At least sleep in the guest room, so you can rest better." He shook his head.

"Your couch is all I need. George and I will be great down here. Come on, George. Time to go to bed. You ate a lot of snakes today, so let's go out one more time." George cocked his head and I swear he smiled.

"Can I at least offer you some pie?" I said as I opened the fridge.

"I might grab some later," he said. "I'm still full of pizza."

I yawned.

"Go to bed, Ains. You're exhausted. You've had one heck of a day." He leaned back against the kitchen sink and crossed his arms.

I chuckled. "Truth. It feels like this one day has been a hundred years long, and that is not an exaggeration. My head has hurt all day. I don't know if it's from stress, or if I still have a bit of sinus congestion from my cold."

"Give me your right hand." He reached out and when our skin touched, I swear his burned into mine.

He turned my palm over and then pinched between my thumb and forefinger. It didn't hurt but it was uncomfortable.

"Jake?"

"Give it twenty more seconds." I had no idea what he was doing but he held my hand, so I just stood there and let him do it.

He let go, and I wanted to grab his hand again.

"Make a tight fist and hold it."

I did what he asked.

"Now let go and take a deep breath."

Was he making fun of me or something? Like some weird version of Simon Says?

"How is your head?" He crossed his arms again and leaned back on the counter.

I closed my eyes. All of the tension and tightness was gone.

My eyes flashed open. "What did you do? I've had that headache for a week."

"Acupressure. We get a lot of aches and pains doing what we do and I'm trying to lead the guys toward looking at alternate methods, rather than reaching for painkillers."

"Huh. I'd like to learn more about that. Any ideas on what to do for my elbow?" I shoved up my T-shirt sleeve to show him. It was already a mix of dark blue and purple bruises.

"What is this? Greg told me you guys weren't hurt." He cocked his head as he lifted my elbow up to the light. "Did they X-ray this? You may have some fractures."

I pulled away. "I'm not going to the hospital. It hurts, but I can move it." I swung my arm around like some maniac.

He smiled. "You really hate hospitals don't you?"

"Nothing good ever happens there."

"Okay, fine. No X-ray. But let me get something for you."

He moved around my kitchen so fast I couldn't keep up with what he was doing. "Keep this on for twenty minutes before you go to bed," he said. "I've got an ice chest out in my truck. I'll make you a couple more and set them in your room. If it hurts during the night, you can ice it again. You need to keep the swelling down and it will help with the bruising."

George barked at the back door. I started to reach for the door, but Jake held up a hand.

"I'll take care of George. You go on upstairs."

I turned to walk away but then stopped. "Thank you, Jake—for everything. You're a good man."

He chuckled. "I'd do anything for you, Ainsley."

I went upstairs with the biggest smile on my face. I climbed into bed and stared up at the ceiling, laying a towel on a pillow and propping up my arm. After ten minutes of that, I sat up and turned on the light.

How could I be so tired and unable to sleep?

The answer: my mind was running in circles about Jake and YG, and my brother and Shannon. I grabbed one of the books from my nightstand. This one was about the Renaissance era and the art produced by women during that time. Many of the paintings had been stolen by their husbands and presented as their own. That sort of stuff was still happening today.

It was fascinating but calming. I'd just drifted off when my cell rang.

I answered without looking at the number.

"Hello," I said sleepily.

"Oh. My. Gawd. Ainsley. You're never going to guess what happened," Hilary sounded terrified.

And then the phone went dead.

Chapter Eighteen

THE NEXT MORNING, George barked and then growled, just as the doorbell rang. "Be nice." I pointed at him. "We have a guest." I peeked through the eyehole not surprised to see who stood there. "And maybe she doesn't like giant dogs growling at her."

I swear, he rolled his eyes. He definitely huffed. But he sat down behind me.

I opened the door to Hilary. She'd been crying, if her blotchy face and red eyes were any indication. She held a pillow with one hand, the other was attached to a small roller bag.

"Are you okay?" I asked as I ushered her in. I left her suitcase and pillow by the table in my entranceway and guided her into the living room.

"Thank you so much for inviting me here," she said as she pulled a tissue out of her pocket.

"Don't be silly. I was expecting you today, just not so early."

Ainsley! "I mean, welcome."

Just be quiet.

She sat down on the opposite end of the couch from where George usually lay, so he took that as an invitation that it was okay to claim his spot. But rather than facing the television like he usually did, he turned as if he were keeping an eye on Hilary. George, my sensitive boy, was tuned in to the humans around him. Maybe he was as worried about her as I was.

She looked like I did after the car crash yesterday.

She, too, had been through the ringer the last few days.

"Would you like some tea? Or I have some hot chocolate a friend of mine in New York sent me."

She gave me a wary smile. "Chocolate sounds great. It's been a very long day."

It wasn't even nine a.m. yet.

When she shivered, I popped back up. "Here, take this." I handed her a blanket from the basket by the fireplace. "I just turned the heat up, so it should be warming up soon. Let me grab the hot chocolate, and I think I have some of Shannon's cookies. You can tell me what happened."

I hadn't heard much from Greg. I'd texted him when I woke up this morning. But he never answered back.

For about twenty minutes the night before, I discussed with Jake if I should call the police. I worried that someone had killed her.

Finally, she'd called me back and apologized about her phone dying. Then said she'd tell me everything the next day.

Like I could sleep after that. I had to know what happened.

I put everything together on a cute little tray I'd bought at Junk Gypsies in Round Top, and headed back to the living room.

"It doesn't look like you've had a great day, but Shannon's snickerdoodles, dipped in this hot chocolate, will help sort out anyone's troubles."

She smiled again, this one a bit more genuine. "Thank you, Ainsley. And I really am sorry for just showing up on your doorstep. With the memorial Sunday—even if they don't want me there, I wasn't going to leave you in the lurch."

"I told you that you'd always be welcome here and I meant it. What happened? When Shannon and I left, they'd said they couldn't live without you."

I hoped I wasn't being too pushy.

She put her face in her hands.

"Oh no," I said. "You don't have to tell me anything." I picked up the remote. "Let's watch a Hallmark movie or something. There was a scientific study done that proves those films lift spirits."

She took her hands away from her face and used her tissue to dab her nose. "No, it's okay. I need to talk about it, but it's all so overwhelming."

I turned the volume all the way down, but left the movie on, just in case.

Sipping my coffee, I waited for her.

"They all hate me," she said. "I don't blame them. This is so weird, and I can't wrap my head around it."

"I'm sure they don't." I reached over from the chair and patted her hand.

"Oh, they made it perfectly clear." She wrapped her arms around her waist.

What had they done to her?

"After everyone left yesterday afternoon, the family insisted the lawyer read the will immediately. It was like they couldn't wait to get their grubby hands on her money. He'd been at the reception but left to go get it and then we all sat down in the main living area."

I folded my hands in my lap. She needed to vent.

"There's no easy way to say this." Tears poured down her cheeks. "Ainsley, she left everything to me. The houses, the business, her money. All of it. She said in her letter to the family that I was the only one she trusted. For the last five years, she'd been training me to take over because I was the only one who seemed to understand her business. That all of them seemed determined to run her business into the ground and ruin the reputation for quality she'd created. They just took and took. I mean, it's true but you can imagine how that went over."

Those kids were something else. "Yep. Hostile to say the least. From what I saw yesterday, her children will have a hard time making it on their own." I sat my cup down on the table and moved to the chair beside the sofa. I didn't want to hover over her.

"You have no idea. I didn't handle her finances, but what she gave them for cars and clothing alone would probably feed a small nation for a year."

They were spoiled—that much had been evident. "Though, they'll have Sam to look after them. Turns out—big twist—he's their dad. It's one of the reasons he stuck around, even when he wasn't getting along with Yarn Goddess. That and he knew she'd been ill. My guess is he thought she'd leave the company to him because he would take care of the kids."

I sat back hard in my chair. "Wow. I mean, at the reception I sort of figured that Brock might be his. Even though they have different-colored hair, they have those intense blue eyes. So the kids had no idea who their real dad was?"

Hilary slipped off her boots and crossed her legs on the couch. "No. According to the letter, Yarn Goddess's late husband couldn't have children. He wanted them though, so they went through artificial insemination.

"What the husband didn't know, is she'd been having an affair with Sam for years. The man who was the husband's best friend. I don't know if you are aware, but he died in a weird accident. He fell off a mountain while walking a trail in Colorado. A trail that five-year-old's climb. Sam and Yarn Goddess were there. I don't like to think one of them pushed him but who knows?

"The police said it was a freak accident, that it looked like he tripped on some rocks and then couldn't get his footing. But I don't know. With all the weird stuff that's been happening to me, lately—Anyway..."

"Wait, weird stuff has been happening to you, too?"

She put down her cup. "What do you mean?"

"Someone cut my brake lines on the SUV and broke into the store. Oh, and they put cyanide on my car and in a guest book here at the shop. How strange is that?"

I shivered again and pushed the remote button that made the fireplace jump to life. George slipped off the couch to lie in front of the fire. We weren't the only ones who were cold.

That was the crazy thing about March in Texas. One day it could be a high of eighty, the next forty degrees or lower.

"I had no idea that happened to you guys. Are you

okay?" She pulled the blanket tighter around her.

I shrugged. "Yes. We're fine. What sort of stuff has been happening to you?"

"Someone standing just outside my doorway and trying to turn the knob. When I looked out in the hallway, no one was there. I thought it might be Brock since he's right across the hall. That was the night before the memorial. So I started putting a chair under my door. Last night, after everything that happened, I ran up to my room. Brock and Sam were banging on my door for hours. That's when I tried to call you. But by the time my phone charged, they'd gone away.

"I decided to leave early this morning, before they woke up. Then when I got in my car this morning—there was a dead rat in the passenger seat with a note that said: *You're next.*"

She trembled from her head to her toes, and then the waterworks really kicked in. I was gutted for her. That had to be so scary knowing how alone she was.

"Do you want to stop so you can rest?" Even though I was dying to hear about the rest of it.

She shook her head. "No, I have to tell someone. What if they do kill me? Someone needs to hear what happened."

I handed her some tissues and she gave me a weary smile. "Thanks."

"How did the kids react to the news about Sam? And who tells their children like that? It's crazy. I feel kind of sad for them—I mean, if they're not trying to kill you."

Hilary sniffed. "They just sat there. Sam seemed more shocked that they now knew the truth than they did. Maybe, since he's been around so long, they figured it out. But they just all sat there staring at one another. So. Awkward."

"I can imagine." This was all so weird and I needed to tell my brother as soon as possible. Poor Hilary was definitely in danger since she'd received the same note I had.

"Then there was this long list where assets were divvied up. Like cars and each of the kids also had a trust fund they can access when they're twenty-eight. Each kid was given one of the houses in Europe. They both seemed grateful, which surprised me. It was the only time I've seen any real emotion from the pair of them.

"Then the lawyer read a letter to Sam from Yarn Goddess. It stated that she no longer trusted him, but that he had been a good friend to her for many years. As the children's father, he was to receive an allowance of two hundred thousand a year for ten years."

Wow. That might not be the millions the family received, but it was still a lot to give a friend. If I had that kind of money—no, I'd still be living here in Sweet River running my shop. I really did love it.

Hilary blew her nose. "But then—she left me all the rest. Millions more than the rest of them—and the business. For a few minutes, I thought Brock might explode from anger. He screamed nasty words at the lawyer and me. Saying I was—well, it wasn't nice. But I swear to you no one was more surprised than me. She treated me like…the assistant. Always.

"I mean, I was probably closer to her than anyone else the last few months. On her good days, we talked about everything. And there were good days. She was peculiar and exacting, but she was also brilliant and so funny at times." A tear fell down her cheek. "She taught me to knit the last two months. She said her daughter never wanted to learn and she wanted to pass the love of knitting to me."

My heart ached for the young woman on my couch. But why in the heck would YG leave her everything? Something wasn't right here. "Sounds more like you were friends."

Tears streamed down her face. "In the letter last night—she said she was sorry. She apologized for the way she treated me. That it was all in an effort to make me strong so I could take over the business someday. That I would understand what it took to take the business to the next level."

She was really crying now, so I ran and grabbed another box of tissues from the bathroom downstairs.

"Here," I said, handing her the box.

"They're going to contest it all, but it's ironclad the lawyer said. And, um… Well, there's something more—I'd thought maybe the last few months…but I wasn't sure."

She stared off into space as if she were trying to gather her thoughts.

"You don't have to tell me."

"It's not that. I just feel so guilty."

"What do you mean?"

"I don't deserve all of this. Her family may not be the greatest, but, in her way, she loved them. I was the one person who put up with her but also didn't take crap from her. It probably seems like I did, but it wasn't like that. If I suggested something, she did it. Her demands—well, I kept her happy that way. But she kind of liked that I had attitude with her.

"I always looked out for what would be best for her and

she listened. I keep wondering if that's why she did this."

For the life of me, I couldn't imagine YG being fun in any way. But Hilary had been working with her for a long time. Still, if her family had learned about YG possibly changing her will, that would be motive for murder. And poor Hilary wasn't safe.

"She trusted you."

She nodded. "When the lawyer finished, I had to get out of there. Brock was throwing things and yelling at the top of his lungs. Emily and Sam were trying to calm him down. I honestly feared for my life. I ran upstairs and locked myself in, until this morning."

I smiled. "It's a lot to process but you realize that house belongs to you now. You could have called the police and had them escorted off the property."

She gave a short laugh. "I didn't even think of it that way. I just had to get out. It's all…too much. Ya know?"

I'd never inherited millions from a boss, so I didn't, but I nodded.

"Let me go make sure your room is ready. I have a feeling that after today, you could probably sleep for twenty-four hours."

"And then some. I can go stay at the B&B. I mean, I brought my suitcase in, but now I feel guilty for laying all of my crazy on you and asking to stay."

I waved a hand. "Nonsense. Friends look out for one another. It won't take me a few minutes to put some clean sheets on the bed. I'm going to grab you an extra blanket for tonight. Just in case you need more than the quilt that's on there."

"Thank you. I was wondering about one thing."

"What's that?" I asked, stopping at the bottom step.

"Does your brother still suspect Mrs. Whedon of killing YG?"

"Uh. No. New evidence turned up that cleared her. And then they found security cameras at the bank showing her coming in and out exactly as she said. And because of the position of the camera they could see images behind her. Someone was hiding. So she's in the clear."

"Images?"

"Yep. They tried to make the pictures clearer, but it was impossible to identify who it was. The whole thing was too distorted. For all they know, it could have been YG at that time.

"Anyhoo, she's in the clear. I'm not sure I should say this but he's looking closely at the family. Do you mind if I call him and tell him what happened today?"

"Not at all. I can't imagine one of them would try to kill her, but they may be guilty of something else. Brock—he's been rolling down a hill of angry for months, only made worse by his mother's death. And he's mixed up with some scary people."

I bit my lip. I had thoughts about that kid. He might not have murdered his mother, but he may know who did. If he owed as much money as Greg said—*Stop it, Ainsley.*

"My brother says everyone experiences grief differently. I'll be right back. Let me just make sure you're set."

I ran upstairs. After doing a quick dust, I changed the sheets. Wiped the bathroom down with the natural cleaner that Bernadette sold at my shop. And did a quick check to make sure the toiletries were all fresh. The only person who had stayed here with me in the guest room was Shannon, when we did our girls' night. On the rare occasion my brother was here, he liked staying on the couch, as did Jake last night.

By the time I was heading down, she was coming up with her pillow and her suitcase. "I'm exhausted. Do you mind if I take a quick nap?"

"Not at all. Get some rest and wake up whenever you want tomorrow. We'll handle everything to do with the memorial."

"No," she said sharply. "Sorry. Did I mention I'm tired? But I want to be there for the setup. I know how she would have wanted things. After what she's done for me, I want things to be perfect. I'll meet you at the community center, after my nap."

Poor woman had been through the ringer. She deserved a rest.

And I needed to call my brother.

Chapter Nineteen

I CHANGED CLOTHES, and then loaded George into my car. Greg had given it back since they no longer needed it for evidence. We'd also been allowed to open Bless Your Art, since they didn't find the cyanide anywhere else except my car and the book. I had no idea everyone from the shop had been cleaning since about five this morning, so they could open on time.

I sniffed. I really did have the best crew.

After calling Greg and telling him what I found out, I stopped by the shop, which was busy. I'd planned to donate a part of my proceeds from the shop's earnings this weekend to YG's favorite charity. I just had to remember to ask Hilary what that might be.

As I walked out of the break room, a flash of something caught my eye upstairs. We didn't have any classes scheduled for today.

"You go on up front with Maria," I told George, and then waited for him to find his way.

Upstairs, there were voices coming out of one of the larger classrooms we'd set up for everything from arts and crafts, to cooking classes.

"They all sound guilty to me," Mrs. Whedon said.

"I know, right?" Shannon's voice chimed in.

At the door, my jaw dropped. Mike, Shannon, Mrs. Whedon, Helen, Erma, Don, as well as Lily and Jeff, stood around the whiteboard we'd used when Mike had been accused of a murder he didn't commit.

"What. Are. You. Doing?"

Ms. Helen threw a hand over her heart.

Shannon jumped.

"It's too late to hide, isn't it?" Jeff asked.

I had to bite my lip to keep from laughing.

Shannon gasped. "Mike, I thought you locked that door."

"What does it look like?" Mrs. Whedon asked. "We're solving a murder."

Count to ten, Ainsley. Be polite to your elders, Ainsley.

"You all know that I promised Greg I wouldn't get involved. If he sees this, he'll murder me himself."

Shannon made a funny face. "I might have mentioned to Ms. Helen this morning at the coffee shop that the killer might be out to get you."

"Then I decided that we should get the book club together a little early," Ms. Helen said. "Maybe if we wrote it all down, it might help in some way."

"It's so much easier to read on the big whiteboard," Erma said quickly and then glanced away.

I stared at Jeff and Lily. "We just thought we'd come over early to help set up for, um, book club," Jeff said, and Lily nodded.

"It's not for six more hours." I put a hand on my hip.

They just smiled nervously.

Why fight it? *They're going to do it whether I'm here or*

not.

"Fine. What do you have so far?" I moved forward and sat down in one of the chairs opposite the whiteboard. They'd put the family, as well as Hilary, on top of the board.

"Why do you have Hilary up there?" I glanced at Shannon.

"She was the assistant. It's more to keep track of her actions than anything. And you never know, she did have access to YG. More so than most people."

I told them about the will. "No one was more surprised than she was. She can't even comprehend yet what it means. And I'm fairly certain she didn't know."

"Well, my money is on the son," Mike said. "From what Shannon saw and heard at the memorial."

"And my nephew just texted me." Erma held up her phone. "He says they've taken the son in for questioning. The FBI has taken over that part of the investigation."

Nothing I didn't know already, but I told them my suspicions. "This town has been full of visitors since YG's event. Anyone could have slipped in and hidden out for the right time to kill her. And a professional killer would know how to use poison and cut my brake lines. The poison is a big deal. As Mrs. Whedon will tell you, it's extremely effective. A novice wouldn't know how to use it."

"She's right," Mrs. Whedon said. "Though, it would have been safer if they used a syringe. The tea—she didn't ingest much of it from what I heard. The only reason she died was because she was ill." The older woman shrugged. "It's just not how I would have done it," she said.

Mike might have stifled a chuckle.

"Good to know," I said. Something niggled at my brain. "So why risk putting it in the book and on my car?"

Mrs. Whedon leaned forward, her green pom-pom hat shifting as she did. "I have a theory about that one. Maybe, since they were all supposed to be in Dallas then, which is five hours away, they wanted to make it look like it was someone here. Someone like me."

She had a point.

"Or maybe not you," Jeff said. "Mike told us that the person in your shop was running like crazy to get out of there. The bottle was found on the passenger side of your car, not the driver's side."

I didn't know that. I thought someone had said it was on the driver's side—or maybe they were mistaken. I'd been worried about dying just then, and Jake had distracted me. I could have misunderstood.

My friends were right—we needed all of this written down.

"What if the bottle was open as they were running away from you and George?" Jeff asked. "They could have tripped, dropped the bottle and it splashed on the car? It was dark and they were in a hurry, so they just left the vial there and took off?"

That kid was going to be a great mystery writer someday.

"Hmmm." Ms. Helen snapped her fingers as if something was on the tip of her tongue.

"So the perp doses the book with cyanide," Ms. Helen continued, "and writes a frightening message to who?" Perp. Ha. She's been watching her FBI shows again.

I pursed my lips. If they hadn't been after me, or someone in the shop, it had to be—

"The family," Jeff said.

"The killer didn't plan on me finding that page." I gazed at the board. "We would have handed that book off to her family so they could read the messages. Whoever it is may be trying to knock them all off."

I had to call Greg again. The family might be in danger. Or, at least one of them. The creepy brother might be trying to kill his sister and Sam. Or creepy Sam was trying to kill his children to get more of the inheritance.

"Oh, I forgot to tell you guys." I snapped my fingers, and everyone jumped. "Sorry, I'd been so surprised by you guys that I forgot about my call with Greg. And Jeff found photographic evidence of Sam, Emily, and Brock here in town, near YG's time of death. So their alibis are no longer valid."

"This is so confusing." Shannon sighed. "I thought for sure it was one of them. And if they're in town—maybe they're trying to make it look like someone else. And they're all in it together."

"You might be right," I said. "Sam's got motive. The brother could be trying to kill the sister to get her inheritance. People will do horrible things when they're desperate."

"Still wasn't me," Mrs. Whedon said. "I think we all know now that I would have been a much more efficient killer."

We all chuckled.

"No one says anything to anyone about this. Swear." I held up my hand. It was funny to see them all do the same.

"I mean it. If you all have so much free time, you can help us get ready at the community center."

Ms. Helen gave me the evil eye. "We'll stay mum, if you promise to let us know if there are any new developments."

"Done."

This case was more confusing than ever.

Chapter Twenty

FRIDAY NIGHT, I came home to find George and Hilary playing Frisbee in the backyard. After we set up the community center, she'd offered to take him home since I had to hang at the store a few more hours for the book club.

George didn't always catch it in the air, but he loved running after the blue disc. He did the same thing he did with Jake. He'd make her throw it, chase it, and then sit there and wait for her to pick it up for him.

I laughed when he made me a liar and jumped up with all four paws off the ground.

I hadn't seen him this happy in a long time.

"How long has he been at it?" I walked up to near where she stood.

George ran up and nudged my hand. He was sweaty, smelly, and super slobbery but I pet him anyway. Then he ran back out and waited patiently for her to throw it again.

"Just about ten minutes. I hope you don't mind. He was pacing in the house, and I thought maybe he needed a little outdoor time. To be honest, so did I. It feels good to get outside and just have fun. I don't think I realized what a bundle of nerves I've been."

I squeezed her shoulder. "I'm glad and grateful you took him home for me. So, he runs around like a crazy dog for about ten minutes. Then he eats an entire bowl of food and sleeps for the rest of the night."

She smiled. "He's a very smart dog. When I was letting him out, he went over to the pantry you have with all of his food and toys. When I opened the door, he grabbed the Frisbee and took off."

"Sounds like him."

He dropped the Frisbee and started sniffing the ground.

"We don't need to see this part, trust me." I motioned her back toward the house.

She laughed and followed me in. My house smelled amazing and the oven was on.

"Yum. What are you making?"

She leaned down to look in the oven window. "I hope you don't mind. I made us some chicken pot pies. I'm in serious need of comfort food. I also made a Bavarian chocolate cake."

"I'm not sure who you hang out with—but I'm never offended when people cook for me."

We both laughed.

"I had to keep busy. If I stop and think about everything that's happened the last few weeks—It may be that George was feeding off my nervous energy. I'm sorry. You've been so kind to me, and I just wanted to return the favor."

I washed my hands in the sink. "Give yourself some grace. It's something my friends say all the time. You're smart, Hilary. You'll figure it all out. And I've been thinking about it—she wouldn't have given you her life's passion, if she didn't think you could handle it."

She leaned back on the cabinets and crossed her arms.

"It's just…a lot." Dressed in leggings and a sweatshirt, she seemed so young, and a lot less like the prim-librarian type I'd first met.

"It is. I tell you what. Let me go change and then we'll have chocolate cake for the first course, and chicken pot pie for dessert. Shannon taught me that one."

She smiled. "You're the best, and that sounds like a great plan."

"Great. I'll be back in a bit."

After changing into some yoga pants and giant graphic tee that said: "You do you. And I'll do me," I headed back downstairs to find her talking on the phone.

"Yes, I'd be happy to discuss it if you've calmed down. But I think I'd like to have my attorney present."

She was silent while the other person spoke for a bit.

Then she pulled the phone away from her ear and stared at it before pushing the off button.

"Is everything okay?"

She put it down on the counter and went to pull the chicken pot pies out of the oven.

"That was Sam. He said he wanted to talk. He apologized for Brock's behavior the other day. He was in the middle of explaining that it was all a big surprise—then he stopped and said, 'The police are here. I have to go.'"

"Oh. Wait. I forgot to tell you."

The flat pizza pan she'd put the pies on clattered against the burners on the stove. It slipped enough that it hit her arm, just above where the mitt stopped. She'd made six of them; she must have been very hungry.

"Ouch," she cried out, just as someone knocked on the

door.

"Run cold water on that, and I'll find the Neosporin and some gauze."

The banging intensified. "Ainsley, are you okay? I heard someone scream," Jake said through the door.

"Come in," I said as I hunted through the basket where I kept all my meds downstairs.

"What happened?"

"It's just a small burn," she said.

Jake, being the conscientious fire dude that he is, took her hand and examined her arm.

"Let me grab my kit from my truck. I've got some stuff with aloe in it that should heal that up pretty quickly. I'll be right back."

She blinked as he ran back out the front door.

"That's Jake, by the way. My neighbor, friend, babysitter, and the chief of the fire department. Oh, and he owns the feed store where I get George's food."

She blinked again and I had to laugh.

"He is not Chris Hemsworth. Though, he looks so much like him I find myself doing double takes all the time. Most of the men in this town are—well, let's just say the medical examiner could be Idris Elba's doppelganger."

Her eyes went wide. "Did you watch *Luther*? That ex of his, what was she thinking divorcing him?"

I laughed. "Exactly."

"I was so busy the last time we were here I didn't notice how gorgeous the men are. But I may have to check out moving here if they look anything like him."

"Trust me, there are loads."

"Are you and Jake dating?"

I snorted. "No. He's just a friend."

She lifted an eyebrow and I smiled.

"He hangs out a lot here. Like a few times a week. We eat. We binge television or watch movies. But we're just friends." I did air quotes. I had no idea what was going on with Jake, and I didn't want to ruin it by asking.

"It might be closer to dating than you think, Ainsley. He's—uh..."

"Yes, he is."

"Your brother is cute. He looked so handsome in that suit the other day."

"Gross," I said, and we both laughed.

Jake came back through the door with a small kit. Then he doctored and wrapped her arm. "I promise, you'll only see a bit of red when you take this off in the morning."

"Thanks, Jake. I'm Hilary."

"Oh, I know," he said. "The whole town knows. When you asked for directions to Ainsley's house from the gas station yesterday, the town gossip chain was alerted."

She put the mitts back on and moved the tray with the individual pot pies back a little more on the stove. "I've never lived in a small town; it's quaint. But I'm guessing everyone is in your business?"

"You have no idea," Jake and I said at the same time, and then grinned.

"We were about to have chocolate cake for dinner and chicken pot pie for dessert. Would you like to join us?" she asked Jake.

"Let me guess, Ainsley came up with the order of the

menu items." Then he smiled at me so sweetly, a swarm of bees took off in my head and heart at the same time.

"She did. It's almost like you know her."

"I do. But I don't want to impose if you guys are having a girls' night."

I waved him off. "Don't be silly. We have enough to share." Maybe he'd smile like that again. "But I'm curious why you're here."

"Uh. Oh. I'm guessing Greg didn't call you." He glanced down at the floor, holding his hands behind his back.

"Let me guess, you're checking up on me."

He gave me a sheepish grin. "Greg asked me to make sure you're doing okay. He's in Austin—uh…" He glanced at Hilary and then back at me. "Following up on the lead you gave him. The FBI is involved."

It all came together. Greg was why Sam had hung up.

"Let me guess, you'll be sleeping on my couch tonight?"

This time he didn't bother trying to hide his grin. "After the last week, he's worried someone might try to hurt you or Hilary. And, you're perfectly capable of protecting yourself. It's just when you're not at the shop. Until he finds the killer, he wants someone to be with you. He says there are some pretty rough characters involved in all of this."

Same routine, different day. They did this the last time someone had tried to scare the heck out of me.

"Okay," I said.

"Well, that was way easier than I'd thought it'd be."

No way I'd fight hanging out with Jake, even if I did plan to give my overprotective brother what for later on.

AFTER WE ATE, I told them about the photo with Emily, Sam, and Brock in front of my store.

Jake had offered to do the dishes, and I helped him clear off the table.

"But they said they were in Dallas." Hilary sat down on the couch.

"Yes, and they were each other's alibis. But the photo proves they were here in front of my store, maybe a half hour before Mrs. Whedon walked in. Since the video from the bank showed her only grabbing her knitting things, we know she didn't do it. There are shadows in the store behind where she was.

"So the camera doesn't show any of the family going in, but that doesn't mean they didn't drive around the back," Jake offered. "There's a way to circumvent the security cameras back there, and they weren't working. Though, after everything that has happened, Greg's making Ainsley add a few more, and one to look onto the park."

"Oh, he is?" I smirked.

"I think that's a great idea," Jake said. "We live in a very safe town, but you do seem to attract trouble."

I started to argue with him but stopped myself. He wasn't wrong.

"Is your brother arresting them?"

"Yes. Right now, for obstruction of justice since he doesn't have any evidence to link them to the crime. But he and his team aren't just any old small-town force—they'll figure it out. I do feel sorry for Emily, unless she's involved."

Hilary nodded. "She was the only one who didn't freak out when the lawyer announced who was getting the company. It was almost as if she were relieved. While Brock was screaming and Sam was trying to calm him down, she just sat there staring down at her hands."

"Hmmm."

"I imagine they'll make bail fairly quickly. Sam has all kinds of lawyers working for him," Hilary said as she pulled a sofa pillow to her chest.

"I'm still staying on the couch," Jake said.

"I figured. Let me grab you some blankets and a pillow. And you know as well as I do that George snores like a freight train."

He chuckled. "We were just fine last night. He's no worse than the guys at the fire station and I sleep through that. Bunking with George isn't a big deal."

It's tough, when Jake is so perfect, to keep my expectations low. But I'd been disappointed enough by men to understand that taking it slow was the best thing for me.

That said, I'm human. While getting ready for bed, I may have imagined a wedding out at Falk's Creek where the trees have wound into a natural arch on a cliff there, and the sound of rushing water makes it one of the most peaceful places on the planet.

But I did not have a specific groom in mind.

At least, that's what I keep telling myself—to stay sane.

When I came back down, Jake wasn't there. Then George barked out back.

I followed the noise. They were playing catch. Well, more Jake would throw the ball and George waited until it hit the ground and started rolling before he ran after it.

"Trying to wear him out?"

"We needed a stretch," Jake said as he threw the ball again.

"You're welcome to sleep in my bed—I mean, I can take the couch."

Dear ground, swallow me whole right now.

I sat down in one of the rocking chairs on the back porch. Jake and Greg had built me a great deck when I moved in. At night, when the weather was mild, and the mosquitos weren't out, it was the perfect place to hang out and unwind. Sometimes with wine, other times with tea. It depended on my mood.

He chuckled. "I appreciate the offer but I'm good on the couch. I had kind of a rough day and playing with George helps."

"Do you want to talk about it?"

He shook his head. "Nah, but thank you. I found out a friend of mine is really sick and there's not much that can be done."

His normally smiling face was tight with tension.

"I'm so sorry. Is there anything I can do for you? Would you like a beer, wine, or some tea?"

He shrugged. "I'm fine."

George ran around chasing dragonflies, which had come out early this year. Everyone said it meant we were going to have a hot summer. I was not looking forward to that. I didn't miss the winters in Chicago at all, but Texas summers were hot and muggy.

He sat down in the rocker next to mine. "Your brother

and I both worry about you being out here all alone," he said softly.

"You live less than a mile away. And I'm not alone. I have George."

My crazy dog was racing as fast as he could from one side of the fence to the other.

"He definitely needs the space to run." Jake laughed. "You're perfectly great at taking care of yourself and George, though I can't help but worry. I like you, Ainsley."

He took my hand in his and we sat there in silence.

I should have said it back, but I didn't want to ruin the moment.

The warmth of his hand spread through my body like wildfire.

Simmer down, Ains. Simmer down.

George came up to the porch and plopped down in front of us in a full sprawl.

We laughed.

"This is nice." He squeezed my hand but didn't let go.

"It is." And it was almost an hour later before he let go and went inside.

I sat there trying to catch my breath.

That was a moment.

One I would never forget.

Chapter Twenty-One

THE NEXT DAY, I woke with a start. I'd dreamed all night of a wedding at Falk's Creek.

Get it together, Ainsley. He held your hand. It's just a friend sort of thing.

Didn't keep a woman from wishing.

I was about to get out of bed, when there was a knock on the door.

Worried it might be Jake, I pulled the covers up to my neck. He'd been staying every night on my couch. Greg had gone mum about the investigation, as they were working on several leads.

But according to Ms. Erma, who'd been talking to Kevin, or more like haranguing him, they were close to making an arrest. I had a plan to pop by my brother's office after the big event celebrating YG this afternoon.

"Come in."

"Hey, Ainsley," Hilary said as she opened the door a crack. "I brought you some coffee and I was about to leave a note. I'm headed out to check on the community center. I know everything is done but I just have a lot of nervous energy. I'll feel better if I get a chance to look at the venue one more time. And I've got this. You rest."

I shook my head. "No, give me five minutes and I can be

ready to go."

She walked in the rest of the way and set the coffee on the bedside table. "You've done so much for me. Your team has already done most of the hard work. I'm just going to make sure a few minor details are tied up in a bow. I probably won't be gone an hour and then I'll be back."

I frowned. "Are you sure? I mean about me not coming with you."

"Absolutely. I'll be back soon."

I sat back against the bed, and then grabbed the coffee. It wasn't often someone brought me my favorite beverage in bed.

I wrapped my robe around my pajamas and headed downstairs. After letting George out, I opened the warming drawer on my stove. There were scrambled eggs, bacon, and toast.

"Yum."

I ate, and maybe shared a little with George. Then I sent Jake a text thanking him.

He sent back a smiley face emoji and said he'd drop by in a bit.

It was warm in the house, so I made sure the heat was off and then went upstairs to open the windows. Today, we had a high of eighty awaiting us.

The guest room was spotless. You had to love someone who made their bed every day and kept their things put away—even if I didn't do those things myself.

I grabbed my cleaning bucket with all my products and some rags from the hall closet. At least, she could come back to a clean bathroom. I stuck my head out the window to check on George and found him chasing leaves.

I did a quick scrub of the walk-in shower. I wiped around the sink but when I picked up her toiletries bag to get underneath it slipped out of my hands and hit the floor.

A distinct crack as it hit the tile had me scrambling. I had my cleaning gloves on. Shannon had made them for me, and they had ruffles where they hit my elbows. I'd rolled my eyes when she gave them to me, but I use the heck out of them.

I opened the bag, careful to take out her toothpaste and brush and set them in the sink. The crack had come from a small blue vial. There was an almond smell, which may have scared me the most. I dropped the vial back in the bag and quickly washed my gloves.

Bile rose in my throat.

This had to be poison.

Everything flashed through my brain so fast, I stumbled back. Crap. Hilary was the killer. I ripped off the gloves and ran down the stairs, just as she was coming up. Stomach tight with fear, I forced a smile.

"You're back early," I said tightly.

"Yes, I forgot my phone." She smiled but gave me a strange look. Crud. As soon as she went up there, she would know.

"Good." I coughed in one hand, as I grabbed my phone from my back pocket. "I need to let George in."

She let me pass. "Are you feeling all right?"

No. My head swam with dizziness and I worried I'd pass out before I could call my brother.

"Yes, just need some air."

I ran toward the back door desperate to get away from

her.

But when I opened the door, George bounded in, ready for his breakfast.

"No," I whispered. "We have to go, now." But moving a two-hundred-pound Great Dane, who outweighs me by a good sixty pounds was impossible.

Double crap.

I texted Greg and Jake. *Help! Home! Hilary did it!* My breath caught in my chest and black dots formed in my eyes. I must have inhaled more than I thought of the poison.

After grabbing George's leash, I hooked it to his collar but he wasn't budging. There was no way I'd leave him behind with a killer, but I had to get out of there. "George, please."

I tugged again but he still ate. My vision blurred and my ears rang. I stumbled out to the porch, coughing. Nausea boiled in my belly.

I've gone and killed myself.

"Going somewhere?" Hilary was there with a rolling pin in her hand.

This is a terrible way to die.

"Don't," my brain was not functioning.

"I don't want to, but you saw what was in my bag. My guess is the poison is coursing through your veins. In five minutes you'll be passed out—and depending on how much you ingested—dead. You should have left my things alone."

"I didn't mean to. Accident." My words warbled. "Why?"

She sighed. "I was perfectly willing to be your friend, you know. You've been so kind, and I don't want to kill you."

"I won't tell."

She laughed but it wasn't pretty.

"Right." She lifted the rolling pin higher, as I stumbled off the deck.

"If you bludgeon me to death, they'll know. I've already texted them." I tried to hold up my phone to show her but my limbs were weak. I could barely stand.

She frowned. "Shame on you. Now I'll have to make it super painful, like I did for Aunt Ellie."

My brain was a whirling mass of crazy. "Aunt?"

"Yes," she said, moving closer.

"Why?"

"I had to make her pay," she said with a sneer. "That bitch destroyed my family."

"George," I yelled, but it sounded more like *Yorg*. Crud. I didn't have much time and I had to save him.

Finally, he bounded out. "Runzzz," I yelled. He jumped around like we were playing a game.

Hilary's arm rose and the rolling pin was headed toward my face.

I popped her in the nose with the heel of my hand, and then shoved her as hard as I could. She fell backward over George.

There was a shriek, and an angry growl.

And then darkness.

Chapter Twenty-Two

SOMETHING TIGHT AROUND my head made it impossible to open my eyes. Why did my head hurt so bad? I tried to focus on the words. Someone was trying to talk to me, but I couldn't focus.

"Please wake up."

Was that Jake?

I had to be dreaming. Why would Jake want me to wake up?

Wait. Did Jake and I—no. No I'm pretty sure I'd remember that.

"Open your eyes, Ainsley. Please."

Hey now, that was a full-on beg.

This was a really great dream. I tried to reach out, but someone held my hand.

Jake. I was safe. Or in heaven.

I tried to blink my eyes open, but it was like one of those dreams where you're paralyzed, and you can't wake up or open your eyes.

Or maybe it's just me who has those.

"What's going on?" my brother asked.

Ewww. What was he doing here?

Way to ruin a hot dream, *Greg*. Okay, so it wasn't exactly hot.

I blinked but the light was so bright, I turned my head.

"Turn the overhead light off and close the shades," Jake barked. "The brightness is too much. It's hurting her eyes."

"Isn't it too soon?" my brother asked. "Kane said it might take twenty-four hours before she actually wakes up."

I'm awake. Sort. Of.

"George," I croaked out.

"Well, look at that," my brother said. "Welcome to the land of the living, zombie sister. You've been out for a while."

Jake squeezed my hand tightly. "George is fine. Maria and her kids are looking out for him. You gave us quite a scare."

"Poison," I said scratchily. Had I swallowed some glass?

"Your brother figured that out pretty quickly. The EMTs and I were working on you. Luckily, you just inhaled a small amount. Otherwise…"

I'd be dead.

"Where is she?"

"In jail," Greg said, "and she's going to be there for a long time."

I tried to smile but I have no idea if it actually made it to my face.

"Tired," I said as the blackness closed in again.

THE NEXT TIME I woke up, Jake sat holding my hand, but his head was on the blanket and his eyes were closed. My brother snored lightly in the corner. They both appeared disheveled.

I was about to reach out and touch Jake's handsome face, when there was a knock.

A nurse came, and he rolled in a big machine with him. He reminded me of a tall Kevin Hart. "Well, hello there, Ms. Ainsley, you're looking better than when I saw you two days ago. I'm your charge nurse, William."

My brother and Jake stirred.

"Hi," I said hoarsely. "How long?"

He stuck a thermometer on my head and rolled it back and forth. "Just two days. The toxin had to work its way out of your lungs."

Two days?

"These two have been with you the whole time. Maybe now that you're awake, one of them will go take a shower. It's starting to smell ripe in here."

The men chuckled.

"Kane said you'd be fine. Jake was there fast," my brother said. I had to force myself to listen because Jake was still holding my hand. He'd been here two days with me.

My brain was too tired to comprehend what that might mean.

"You could have died," Greg added. "It was way too potent. We found the gloves and figured out what had happened."

The door opened and Kane walked in, his eyes on my brother. "How is she?"

"Better," I said.

His head swiveled so fast, I laughed.

Which set off a coughing spree and it was as though an

anvil had landed on my chest.

"Ouch." I put a hand on my heart. "What's happening?"

The nurse put a blood pressure cuff on my arm. "There was a lot of irritation, which can cause your lungs to be sensitive for a bit," Kane said. "That's what's causing your chest pain."

"You didn't inhale much, or we wouldn't be here," Kane said.

Why does everyone keep saying that?

"You went into respiratory failure but Jake and his EMTs were on the scene fast. They saved your life."

Jake hadn't let go of my hand. "Thank you," I said.

We just stared at one another.

"I think maybe the patient needs to rest," the nurse said. He glanced at Jake and then me. "One visitor can stay."

My brother and Kane said their goodbyes.

"I've been so worried," Jake said huskily. "There was a minute when I first found you—but you're here." He kissed my fingers, and warmth spread through my limbs.

This has to be a dream. I'm going to wake up and my stinky brother will be sitting here.

I blinked. Still Jake.

"My brain isn't quite where it needs to be," I said. "What do I say to someone who saved my life? How were you even there? I thought you were at work."

He shook his head. "I'd run to my house to take a shower and grab my truck. I rushed back because there was something about that woman that didn't sit right with me."

"What do you mean?"

"She grabbed some food at breakfast and was just making

small talk. We'd been chatting about the event. I don't think she knew I heard her, but under her breath she said, 'And when it's over I can live the life I've always dreamed about.'

"Right then, I didn't think much about it. But later, I was in the shower and it hit me. What if she was the killer and had masterminded this whole thing? And I knew you weren't safe."

I sighed. But breathing that deep hurt. "I had no idea. Truly. I mean at first, she was on the suspect list, but we'd all seen her at the community center."

"Your brother thinks she did it when she said she went back to the hotel. They've done one interview with her, but she just stared at him. He's making her sit it out in county. The judge refused bail. Greg's hoping that if she stays locked up a bit, she'll be more willing to talk."

I shivered. "I invited a killer to stay in my house. I feel…dumb."

Jake squeezed my hand again, and then pulled the blankets up to my neck. "You aren't. She had everyone fooled, including your brother. He's been beating himself up over all of this."

"Note to self. Do not invite killers to stay at your house."

We both laughed, even though it hurt.

"I passed out. But what happened when you got there?"

He smiled. "George had a rolling pin in his mouth, and she was face down on the ground with him sitting on top of her. Same thing he did with the last killer. He was whining so loud. She'd hit her head on the deck."

"I shoved her," I said.

"And either you or George broke her nose. She was unconscious when I arrived on the scene. Your brother showed up two minutes after I arrived. From what I hear, he'd been headed back to your house to talk to Hilary about the family. At that time, he still thought one of them had done it."

"I feel very lucky right now."

"So do I."

Oh. Wow.

"Can I ask you a favor?"

"Anything."

"Can you ask William the nurse to come back in? I want to go home and see George."

"You just woke up."

I shrugged. "I'm not a big fan of hospitals. And if Greg is going to talk to her again, I want to be there."

I'd thought we were friends. My heart hurt and not just from inhaling the cyanide. I'm not sure I could trust anyone ever again.

I wanted to know the truth, and I wanted to see her pay.

Chapter Twenty-Three

THE NEXT DAY, I sat in a side room at the station with Jake. My brother had special permission from the judge for me to listen in to his interview with Hilary, who was on the other side of the mirrored glass. Greg wanted all of this by the book.

"She's going down," he told me a few minutes ago in his office. "We have the evidence, but I want to seal the deal with a confession."

Hilary sat in the interview room, staring straight at the wall above my brother's head, answering his questions with a monotone "no comment." She was so unlike the woman I first met.

She wore prison white, and her hair was in a dirty ponytail. She still looked as young as she did the other day but there was a hardness in her eyes I hadn't noticed before.

"If you don't want to talk, that's fine," Greg said. "Did your attorney inform you of the terms of our agreement?"

She turned her head to glance at the attorney. He just nodded. She shrugged her shoulders.

"If you cooperate, the district attorney will take the death penalty out of the equation. But if you continue with no comment, the jury will decide your fate."

She nodded again, her lips a tight line.

"Why did you kill Yarn Goddess?" Greg asked, watching her carefully.

She glanced down at her hands and started picking her nails.

"We're done here," Greg said and then stood up.

Hilary leaned over and whispered in the lawyer's ear.

"My client will talk," he said. From what I understood, he was court-appointed. Hilary hadn't taken possession of her inheritance and had no money to speak of. There was a good chance the family fortune would be returned to the family.

Greg sat down again.

"Why did you kill Yarn Goddess?" he asked again.

"Because she killed my mother."

Wait. What?

I leaned forward.

"Your mother?"

She chewed on her lip. "My mom was her sister."

I wished I could see Greg's face. Did he know?

"She had cancer, and Ellie wouldn't give her any money to help take care of her. We didn't have any insurance. I was supporting her with my job as a pharm tech, but it was never enough, and the bills just kept piling up. I swear Mom died because she just gave up. The fight was too hard."

She stared down at her hands again. "At my mom's funeral, that witch had the nerve to offer me a job. Can you believe that?" She leaned forward and shook her head. The bitterness in her voice sounded nothing like Hilary. It was almost as if she was a different person.

"But she willed everything to you. She must have cared

about you."

"The only reason she gave me the business was because I didn't suck up to her or beg like the rest of the sycophants in her family. And I didn't take her crap. She thought I was tough like her—and I am. When she got sick, I played a role. I was the one person she could count on. The one person who genuinely cared for her. And she believed it. Changed her will the week before the big event. The docs weren't sure she was going to make it another month."

"You knew about the will?" Greg asked.

"Yes." She smirked.

"She told me I was the only one she trusted to take over the empire. She had a feeling Sam had been embezzling. Her son was a degenerate gambler. And her daughter didn't have the sense of a flea. Her words. Not mine."

"So why would you kill her?"

She rolled her eyes. "She had second thoughts. I heard her talking to her lawyer the day before the event. She thought I was out grabbing her favorite tea. She told him that she'd made a mistake, but she was going to fix it. I couldn't let that happen."

"How did you get the poison? That must have taken some planning and you only had a day."

"Well..." She scrunched up her face. "Thing is, I didn't want to wait for her to die. As soon as she signed that will, I'd come up with a plan. I needed something that would make it look like the lung cancer had killed her."

"Had you been dosing her tea before you came to town?"

"Yes. Just small amounts so she'd get used to the taste. I thought I could make it look like suicide. Like she couldn't take the pain anymore."

"But where did you get digitalis from?"

She rolled her eyes again. "Like everything else, I bought it off the internet."

"But why do it in such a public way? Why not wait until she was home? No one would have been the wiser."

She slammed a fist on the table. "My only mistake was being in a rush."

A chill slithered down my spine. There was no remorse for what she'd done. Sweet Hilary was a cold-blooded killer.

"When that old woman was so cranky, I finally had a way to do it where no one would suspect me. I could make it look like a crazy fan did it or one of her many enemies. If no one found her quickly, it might have looked like suicide or natural causes.

"Aunt Ellie was a truly vile person. She didn't want anyone knowing she had relatives who lived in the projects. It was as if we didn't exist. She'd created this make-believe world and I don't think she lived in reality a day of her life. Even her kids didn't know I was related to them. She said if they found out, she'd fire me. That me and my mom were from her old life, and she was never going back there."

Ainsley swallowed hard. It had to be tough not being loved by your own aunt.

"How long had you been planning on killing her?"

"Pretty much since I went to work for her five years ago, I've dreamed about it. Then when she signed that will, I didn't want to be around her one more second."

Greg leaned back in his chair and crossed his arms. I'd give anything to know what he might be thinking.

"And you got her into the shop how?"

She drummed her fingers on the table.

"I'd planned for it to happen in her hotel room, but she wouldn't let me in there that day. She was in one of her moods. Before we left the shop, I put a bit of tape on the lock on the back door, so I could get back in. When it was time for her to go to the community center, I made an excuse that I'd left her favorite needles inside. She walked right in and then sat down. She had to make sure I picked up the right ones. For an hour, she'd been on the phone with one of her vice presidents trying to figure out what was wrong with that yarn.

"I knew exactly what happened. While she told everyone her products were American made, they weren't. You'll see it in the accounting. Sam had outsourced it to other countries and was skimming the profits.

"That was something I planned to change. The only way to control the quality was to bring it all back to the States. I may not have liked her, but I loved that company. It had so much potential."

She sniffed. It was the only sign of any emotion I'd seen from her since she'd been arrested. "Now those stupid idiot kids of hers—they're going to take the whole empire down."

"And the teacup with the poison?" Greg brought her back to the question. He really was good at what he did.

"She was busy looking through several skeins of yarn in the booth, while she was on the phone. She asked me for a cup of tea and I just knew this was it. I quickly dosed the tea and gave it to her. It took about twenty minutes to work. She'd just passed out when that old woman came into the store, and I ducked us both under the table.

"Everyone thought she was missing. No one suspected she'd been in that shop. And it was closed the next day. After twenty-four hours, the poison would have been undetectable. But that stupid dog found her earlier."

George is far from stupid.

"So why the note?"

"I panicked. I worried that if she was found with the poison in her system, someone might think it was murder. So I tried to make it look like a suicide. I've been able to forge her signature since about six months after I started working for her. She's given me some well-deserved raises over the years. Of course, she didn't know that."

It was nearly the perfect murder, or would have been, if it hadn't been for George. Truthfully, if he hadn't been there, I probably wouldn't have noticed anything wrong or gone that deep into the store. I'd only planned to put the boxes on the counter and then go to dinner with Jake.

"Why did you frame Mrs. Whedon?" I liked that my brother never added anything, just followed one question with another.

"I didn't. The old biddy had been so mad that day. I'd been keeping them apart at the store. It just worked out that she had an argument with Ellie before we left the shop. I was as shocked as anyone when you arrested that old woman. Since you guys had her as a suspect, I decided to put the cyanide in the book, but Ainsley and that dumb dog almost caught me. When I ran out, I skidded into the car. It had been raining. The vial broke, so I just left it all there. I drove back to Dallas and slipped into the house there. No one knew I'd been gone."

This woman was a piece of work. I couldn't believe I hadn't noticed this dark side earlier. She was quite the actress. Though part of me felt sorry for her. Wanting a family's love—it had driven her mad.

That, and from her emotionless state, I had a feeling we might be dealing with a psychopath, but I was not a psychiatrist.

It was scary, though, how different she was.

"And what about the attempted murder of Ainsley?"

She twirled her messy hair around her finger.

"When she came out of my bathroom, she was acting weird. I knew she'd seen the bottle with the poison. You know what happened after that."

My brother's mouth was a straight thin line.

She was lucky he had witnesses. Not that my brother would ever do anything out of line—but he might think about it when it came to me. Normally his protective instincts drove me nuts, but this woman was something else.

My brother leaned back in his chair and crossed his arms. "Are you sorry for what you did?" That wasn't a question he normally asked but it wasn't often he dealt with such a cold-blooded killer.

"All she had to do was accept me. Make me one of the family and none of this would have happened. It's her fault she died."

Wow. She wasn't about to take blame, even though she'd confessed.

"If you liked Ainsley so much, why did you cut the brakes?"

"I didn't mean to cut hers. She was driving the same sort of SUV as Sam. That disaster was meant for him. He drinks a lot but he kept looking at me weird during the memorial that morning. Like he knew something. I figured when he left the house, they'd just think it was a drunk-driving accident. His blood alcohol level is usually at a lethal level."

This was just too much. She didn't care who she hurt along the way.

"I'll need you to put this down on paper and sign it."

She shrugged again. "I'm glad she's dead." She stared straight at me, and I shivered. No way she could know I was there.

On that note, my brother stood and then walked out, leaving Steve to get the written statement.

I LEFT, KNOWING Greg needed time to process. Even though he'd seen the very worst in the world between his tours in Afghanistan and in his police work stateside, it had to hit hard that this young woman had thrown her life away, and her aunt's.

Jake ushered me out of the small room, and we picked up George from where he was hanging out at reception.

"How are you feeling?" Jake asked. "That was—something else."

"It was. I can't believe I let that woman in my house."

He chuckled. "It's scary. Your brother is always saying you never really know people—it's true."

I slid in and sat back in the seat, more tired than I'd ever been in my life, even though I'd been sleeping for days.

"Did Greg mention anything about the photo with the family? Why were they in town?"

Jake smiled. "You really don't stop, do you?"

"Can't help it, I'm curious," I said as I pulled down the sun visor.

"Yarn Goddess had called and told them to meet at the B&B but when they couldn't find her there, they went to the shop. They never tried the door, just saw the lights were off. They went back to the B&B, but were told that time that Yarn Goddess had checked out. That must have been what Hilary said when she was there. She'd checked them out.

"Their phone records show that they all tried to call her but she never answered. So they went to the Austin house, thinking she might show up there. That's when they found all the medical equipment in her room and realized she'd been sick."

"But she was already dead. Hilary must have had her phone and known they were trying to find her. I wonder if she was on to Hilary, or maybe she thought one of them was responsible for the dyes in the yarn being bad."

"I'm not sure we'll ever know. Greg did say they were looking into that Sam character. He was definitely embezzling funds."

"I wonder what happens to the Yarn Goddess empire now."

"I have no idea. Probably will go to her kids."

I sighed. "Hilary was right. They might just destroy it."

"You never know about people. Sometimes they'll surprise you." He gave me one of those devastating smiles.

He ran around and opened the driver's side door. "I know you're a good guy," I said as he sat down. "And I know that I have a fantastic group of friends."

"We're lucky to live in this town with these people," he said and then turned on the ignition.

"Truer words were never spoken. You're a good man, and that's the second time you've saved my life," I said.

"Um. I wish I could take credit but that goes to George," he said. And then he scratched him under the chin. "I was coming around the corner and he had that rolling pin in his mouth. If I hadn't been scared to death that you were dead, I would have laughed. I left him sitting on top of her until my guys arrived about five minutes later. I was busy trying to keep you alive."

"My heroes," I said to both of them.

"There's something I need to talk to about, Ains." All of a sudden, he was so serious.

"Did I miss something?" *Am I in the* Twilight Zone*?* Maybe this was a dream. I kept having those ones where people were talking but when it came to the important parts, I couldn't understand what they were saying.

When he reached out and pushed my hair behind my ear, I forced myself to slow my breathing. That touch sent shivers, the good kind, down my back.

"I like you, Ainsley." His voice was a whisper.

"I like you, too, Jake." I tried to smile, but I'm not sure it worked. My head still hurt pretty bad.

"When I heard you screaming—I don't want anything to happen to you."

"That's sweet." I wasn't sure where he was going with

this, but his hand was still on my cheek. So it was all good.

"I think we should go on a date—a real one."

"Now?" *Hush, Ainsley, let the poor man speak.*

"Uh. No. You need to rest, but maybe tomorrow or the day after that. We could go to Teague's Tavern in Round Top and get you some of those jalapeño deviled eggs and a burger with the bacon jam. Or the rib eye."

I put a hand on his. "I get it, I like the whole menu."

"Right. I want to take you out. If I keep you busy, maybe you won't keep getting yourself in the middle of these situations. She could have killed you. And that just won't do."

More confused than ever, I just stared. I couldn't tell if he wanted to date me because he actually liked me in that way—or if he just wanted to keep me out of trouble.

"Uh. Is this some sort of pity date?"

He shook his head. "Goodness, no. I'm doing this all wrong. I like you in *that* way. I have since the day I met you. It's—well, your brother. Then I couldn't tell if you were dating Kane or not. I'm not the kind of guy who interferes that way. I have a code—crap. I'm doing it again."

Through the fog that was my brain, something hit me.

"Jake, are you nervous?"

He nodded.

I touched his cheek. "Me, too. And I like you *that* way, too. Even though every time one of us says it, I feel like we're in sixth grade and passing notes. I'd like to go on a date, but I can't promise I'll stay out of trouble. I won't ever let my friends down—I just hate injustice. So, if a bit of snooping might help a friend, I'm going to do it. Though, hopefully, that will never happen again."

"We can only hope. Okay, so we're going out. Right?"

I smiled, even though it hurt my face.

"Yes."

He turned toward the wheel. After backing the car out of the parking spot, he shifted to drive and then took my hand in his.

Well, look at that. Ainsley McGregor has a boyfriend. Sort of.

And she's talking about herself in third person.

I desperately needed a nap.

But as we drove off into the sunset, my heart may have done a little Southern two-step.

Now, just don't mess it up.

The End

Want more? Check out Ainsley and George Clooney's adventures in *A Case for the Winemaker*!

Join Tule Publishing's newsletter for more great reads and weekly deals!

If you enjoyed *A Case for the Winemaker,*
you'll love the next book in....

The Ainsley McGregor series

Book 1: *A Case for the Winemaker*

Book 2: *A Case for the Yarn Maker*

Book 3: *A Case for the Toymaker*
Coming October 2020!

About the Author

Bestselling and award-winning author Candace Havens has had more than thirty novels published. She is one of the nation's leading entertainment journalists and has interviewed countless celebrities from George Clooney to Chris Pratt. She does film reviews on Hawkeye in the Morning on 96.3 KSCS.

Visit her website at candacehavens.com

Thank you for reading

A Case for the Yarn Maker

If you enjoyed this book, you can find more from all our great authors at TulePublishing.com, or from your favorite online retailer.

TULE

PUBLISHING

Made in the USA
Coppell, TX
15 April 2026

75940642R00127

What Are You Waiting For?

by Stephen J. Kauffman

DORRANCE
PUBLISHING CO
EST. 1920
PITTSBURGH, PENNSYLVANIA 15238

Dorrance Publishing Co
585 Alpha Drive
Pittsburgh, PA 15238
Visit our website at *www.dorrancebookstore.com*

ISBN: 978-1-4809-8376-2
eISBN: 978-1-4809-8397-7

Contents

Forward

What are you waiting for?

Are you sick and tired of being sick and tired? Haven't you suffered enough yet? You know, suffering *is* optional. Of course, I didn't know this either. How could I? I hadn't yet learned every decision and choice I had ever made was actually not my choice at all. It was a programed reaction, a conditioned choice, not *my* choice. It was only when I became aware of this I was able to understand it.

Twenty years ago, I was diagnosed with cancer. The news was devastating to myself, as well as my family. I was still fairly young and probably in the best shape I had ever been in. I was a chief in the Naval Reserves then, and was required to be ready to deploy at a moment's notice. I kept myself in good shape by running and doing hundreds of push-ups, pull-ups, and crunches, as well as weight training. I was a poster boy for the ready reservists.

I loved being in uniform and I was *always* squared away. I have always respected the brave, unselfish men and woman who proudly wear the uniforms of the various branches of our military forces. My dad retired as a master chief with over thirty-two years of service. I also retired from the US Navy as a chief petty officer with nineteen years. I grew up with discipline and consequences and learned early on not to whine, complain, or question my parent's authority. Little did I know then my life was being programmed and I was being fed ideas, concepts, and conditioning that would decide how I reacted to the world. Little did I know my reactive mode was my only mode.

Why was I always making the same mistakes and suffering the consequences of those mistakes over and over? Why wasn't I learning from my errors and choosing differently? Was I slow, or was I just too stupid to get it? Why was I always punishing myself? Why did I hate myself? Why were my life's lessons so hard on me?

Change was needed for sure. Time after time, I would try to alter my ways, and when the time came to act, without thinking, I would overreact. Repeatedly, I would make the wrong choice and suffer the consequences. I had a 50/50 chance of getting it right. Not good odds at all.

> ***"You cannot change by effort of the will; you cannot change through ideals; you cannot change through building up new habits. Your behavior may change, but you don't. You can only change through awareness and understanding."***
> *Awareness- (Anthony de Mellow)*

It was only after I found this statement and I understood what it was telling me, that change occurred. I couldn't change on purpose, and change would only happen when I gained enough awareness and understanding to allow change to just happen.

I had always thought that *I* made things happen and *I* had the control necessary to get things done. The more I failed, the more I would punish myself for not choosing rightly. My punishments were severe. My usual choice was to not allow myself to have fun, be happy, or enjoy anything. This, of course, would make me miserable and impossible to be around. Instead of learning the many lessons being presented, I was too busy finding fault, condemning myself, and further hating myself. I was not a "happy camper". Tension was always in me. I was angry and moody and blamed people, places, and things for the way I felt. I didn't know then that: "*I was the source of my own joys and sorrows, and through my choices, my own wealth or poverty, and all that I experienced.*"

When I first read this, I immediately found fault and blamed myself for every wrong choice I had ever made. This was my normal reaction when wrong. Why wasn't I trying to understand instead? Why wasn't I learning? If I was truly responsible for my experiences, why did I constantly make the wrong decisions? It would take an intervention of some kind to wake me up. The answers to my questions were available somewhere and all I had to do was find them.

Only when I was ready to do the inside job, to "know myself", would I begin to find relief. I had to be serious and focused on my own well-being and health. I had to observe my interactions with others and the emotions being triggered. It would be rewarding, as well as perilous, and eventually through self-observation, change started to come about, little by little.

I want to personally thank those who helped me along the way. I want to also thank the authors of the books that influenced the changes that occurred and helped guide me. Many of the quotes, statements, and phrases found written are from these great works of literature. If I made a list of those who helped me, I would certainly fail to recognize everyone. Some of these folks are gone forever, although, their wisdom remains with us through their words and writings. People come in to our lives and often are there only for as long as it takes to impart something we may need at that time. Every relationship is an opportunity for personal growth and to help us to gain in "awareness".

I have my good days and bad days. Even my not-so-good days, pale in comparison to the misery I was in. The world is cyclic and the ups and downs go on and on. I once told a friend I might as well enjoy the bad times because I knew it was going to get worse, *way worse*.

Old habits are hard to break and can only be broken when we understand them and have the *awareness* to know they exist. Once we see them for what they truly are, we can then *accept* we have them. Once known and accepted we can then *act*. The final gain we make is the freedom and *autonomy* we get when our choices are truly ours. Imagine, if you can, a time when your decisions and choices are based on facts, not beliefs, truth not programming. In "awareness," you will do no harm, and every decision we make is the right one.

Healthy Routine

Many years ago, I would start every day by doing my morning routine. I would begin with a little stretch then a lengthy meditation, this would be followed by a three-mile walk downtown. After the walk, I would shower and eat a good healthy breakfast. Only a few months earlier, meditation wasn't even on my radar. I had participated in group meditations a few times and I tried meditating by myself, to no avail. It was difficult for me to sit for any length of time and not be doing something. My belief systems and programming told me to do, do, do. Thoughts told me it was a waste of time that could be used doing something, anything, except sitting there doing nothing.

I mentioned my dilemma to several friends and sought their advice. I saw the results in others who practiced meditation regularly and saw firsthand the positive effects meditation brought about. I noticed they seemed more at peace and relaxed, something I desperately needed in my life. Soon after sharing my dilemma with my friends, one of them introduced me to someone who would guide and teach me. His very presence and demeanor totally convinced me meditation was beneficial. I wanted what he had. I wanted to be relaxed instead of anxious, I wanted to be able to let myself be instead of doing. He laughed as he said, after all, I am a human being! Now, mediation as part of my routine was important to me and I would seldom alter it in any way. I made this routine important and vowed to do it no matter what! I needed something in my life to give me some direction and continuity. I needed discipline and to regain my strength and health.

My life was in turmoil, and I very much needed order. I needed discipline, and the routine gave that to me amid the chaos. Several years ago, I had undergone a major surgery. The after effects had a monumental impact on my life in every way. Four years prior, I was as healthy as a goat. I exercised, ate decent, and was fairly happy. My children were doing fine, and my son had a son of his own. My spouse was very content with her nursing career and enjoyed the company of her working companions and clients. I also had a great job with good benefits. I felt I had done well in my working career, and with only a few years to retirement I would start the next chapter of my life. Wrong! Every plan I had put into place over my lifetime was upended. Every dream was busted. I thought I had covered every base and felt secure. I took pride in knowing my future was set in stone and my family and I would be just fine. Sadly, this was not the case.

So, every morning, without fail, I'd walk through the neighborhoods on the outskirts of the downtown district and visit the park. This small seaside city was home to many retired folks as well as a healthy mixture of working people. There was also a large population of students who attended several colleges in the nearby area. The park I would visit had trails that wound through a large wooded area, where sometimes I'd scare a rabbit, and, occasionally, I would surprise a deer that would jump up off its bed and scurry away. I loved this part of the walk. Being in the forest and tuning into nature brought out my hunter instincts as I quietly walked and watched for wildlife. Nature has a way of helping me become aware, it makes me feel alive. Any noise or movement catches my attention, and as my senses are tuned into my surroundings and giving me feedback, I feel excited not anxious. Nature, in all its glory, is surely a remarkable sight. Nature is the perfect place to see reality. That is if you can manage to stop the past and future thoughts bombarding us at every moment, it seems. I sometimes call it the "committee" inside my head that is always chirping. I didn't know then our thoughts and memories all have an emotional attachment. I wasn't aware yet when I was present and focused, the committee would stop talking. I surely wasn't aware when I intentionally chose to look into my past or future, I would also see the good and bad. I would search my memory for a happy event and remember it and be happy, and suddenly a sad event would be exposed. I hadn't learned the concept of duality Yin/Yang, light/dark, and in order for anything to exist, it had to have the opposite. I hadn't been made aware or learned there was a balance of nature.

After working my way through the trails, I entered the fields and saw the playgrounds off in the distance. Sometimes I would sit on one of the benches and watch the people enjoying themselves. I would see parents playing with their children or having fun with their pets. I would see dogs chasing Frisbees or other dogs, and the children playing on the swing sets, monkey bars, and slides as parents laughed and cheered their kids on. I would watch and remember my own family and the times we shared with each other, like the folks I was watching. These memories would sometimes make me smile, and other times made me sad. The mood I was in would determine how long I would watch the events unfold in the park. More often than not, my mood would force me off the bench and onward.

During this time, I was experiencing a low point. It seemed all the plans I had made had all gone awry. Nothing was going my way and I was feeling a fear inside me that came about from the uncertainty of my future. This day, my visit to the park was cut short because of my mood as I got up from the bench and forced myself to walk on. I had only begun my walk and had a long way to go yet. Now it was time for coffee.

Little did I know, today would be a new starting point. I had no idea what would transpire; this very morning would set me on a course I didn't know even existed. Beyond my wildest imagination, I could never dream how my way of thinking would have a new fly in the ointment.

THE COMMON

From the very first day and on, as part of my walk I would go downtown and purchase a cup of coffee at the halfway mark. I remembered the first walk the very first day I started my routine was when I stumbled upon the common. The fact is, I was looking for a good cup of coffee, my first of the day, so finally, after asking directions, I was guided to the coffee shop. Before entering the coffee shop, I glanced over and saw an old man sitting by himself on a bench.

Across the street from the coffee shop was a small common area with benches and a trimmed lawn. Seasonal plants bordered the lawn and, depending on the time of year, would sometimes be in flower. The town kept the common area in great shape. The lawns were cut and the sidewalk up the middle was swept and kept in repair. At the far end of the walkway was a historic church and a small graveyard with headstones weathered and some impossible to read. This common area was very popular with the older crowd who would sit on benches in small groups or alone, enjoying their surroundings. There were plenty of trash receptacles and a few dispensers for bags pet owners could use for their dogs. It seemed a little odd to me then, as I looked around, there were no children or dogs anywhere to be seen. Maybe it was because there was no playground equipment for them, or was it because of the location and setting?

During the many years I frequented the common, very seldom did I see young people enjoying the tranquil common area. I did notice that day the common had a soothing energy I'd felt even some distance away. It was a welcoming, serene energy and for me to pick up on it seemed strange. That morning, the benches were empty except for one. That bench held an older gentleman sitting alone on the bench seemingly enjoying the sunshine. I looked at the old man sitting there and, although I didn't want to stare at him, I couldn't break my gaze. Looking, I saw his eyes were shut, he had his hands resting on his lap, and he had a slight smile on his face. The smile was really what caught my attention. It was a mischievous grin, the kind of smirk you'd see in children who just got away with something. It made me curious of what he was grinning about. Nothing in my life was putting a smile on my face in those days and I was a little envious of this old man because he seemed happy, and I wasn't. He looked carefree and relaxed, and it seemed he was genuinely enjoying himself as he sat there by himself on the park bench. I then realized I had seen this smile on other people many times before. It was a grin I'd seen before on those who seem to be at a level of awareness most of us didn't know existed. They knew something others didn't.

I'm not a religious man, but more of a free spirit. I believe every human being is born free and, in order to stay free, must protect their birthright. We must guard our autonomy and enjoy it as well. I believe the programming and preconceived notions we were all given may have been useful to a point. That is, until we realize they are no longer a help, but a hindrance. Early on, our survival may have depended on them, and later in our lives the same conditioning threatens our very existence. There will come a time in our lives when all of us must ask ourselves if we are genuinely happy or not. We have to decide if change is needed. The time will come sooner or later for everyone. Hopefully, we will stop blaming others and making excuses for our difficulties and realize we are responsible for our own happiness. No one and no-thing can make us happy. Happiness is a choice and we are ultimately responsible for the choice and the consequences of that choice. I thought my own happiness and the conditions I set were appropriate. Little did I know when I set certain conditions that had to be met in order to have it, I was making my happiness conditional.

"I will be happy *if* I had money, *if* I was in a relationship, *if* I had a new car, *if* I was tall, dark, and handsome. Conditional happiness isn't happiness at all.

I'm realizing happiness is in me all the time, just like its opposite, sadness. It's a conscious choice I make and isn't dependent on conditions. Sadly, belief systems installed in me as a child tell me I can't be happy unless... So, unless the conditions are met, happiness is unattainable.

I see through self-observation my happiness also depended on others being happy as well. I am also seeing I didn't allow myself to enjoy or have fun until those around me were happy. It took a long time before I realized I couldn't make anyone happy. I have failed repeatedly at making anyone happy, especially myself.

Ricky Nelson, a great singer and guitar player, wrote a song years ago called "Garden Party". He had been invited to attend the party and his band was lined up to perform. Everyone was there, Yoko Ono, The Beatles, The Rolling Stones, and many other popular bands and entertainers were in attendance. When Ricky Nelson went up, he had a new song with a new beat, and used an electric guitar instead of his usual acoustic. Within minutes after he started, he was booed off the stage. The crowd wanted Ricky's old songs, his old performance, they wanted him as he had been long ago. After the failure of his band, he wrote a song and the catch line was, "You can't please anyone, so you got to please yourself."

Today, I see people everywhere and most of them seem to be miserable. They, like myself, want someone to step up and fill us with happiness. Why were we conditioned and programmed this way? Why didn't someone tell me I was totally responsible for my own joys, and sorrows, and *all* I experienced?

The reason is simple. My programmers were programmed as well and all they did was pass this information on as it had been passed on to them. On and on it goes, and it seems to me to be an endless cycle. I would rather blame people, places, and things for my lack of happiness instead of knowing the truth.

"I AM RESPONSIBLE."

HIGHER CONSCIOUSNESS

Throughout my life, on many occasions, I'd run across certain, what I call, *special people.* Men and women all appearing to be in their seventies and eighties, although, I have also met young folks who were "*special*" as well. The older types all had a youthful look and a spring in their steps, despite their ages. These folks were all a little (or a lot) different from the average person. They all stood out in a crowd, although they weren't seeking to draw attention to themselves. They all had an air about them that was hard to explain. It was like they knew something no one else did. I always wondered what it was. All these people seemed relaxed. They had a confident look, and their eyes were bright and shiny with life. I was drawn to them, although I never made the approach. Something inside me feared making contact and, at the same time, a voice told me I should. What was I afraid of? I remember on several occasions I had intentionally stared their way to get their attention, and if I succeeded I would actually feel their gaze on me, looking through me, seeing who I really was. They knew the truth about me. I knew that was what I feared.

All these thoughts were a little mindboggling as I found myself going through the doors of the coffee shop. I wasn't familiar with the coffee shop this first time, and as I looked around I saw students from a nearby college busily working on assignments as businessmen and women were texting or talking on their phones. The place was alive in a very different way from where

I had just been. Outside there was a calmness, a feeling of serenity. Inside, everyone was busily connected, although not in a human way. No one in the shop was talking to each other, no one was making eye contact, and it seemed hectic. Once my eyes became accustomed to the light, I finally discovered the coffee line and took my spot. As I waited my turn in line I noted no one was making smalltalk as you usually hear where people are gathered. I also noticed the wait staff weren't smiling and seemed edgy; if they weren't taking an order they were connected to their phones or tapping away on the keyboard of computers behind the counter.

As I waited in line, my mind drifted back to the old man on the bench. Immediately, my attitude shifted to calmness, and a sense of peace took the place of the anxiety I felt just moments earlier. It was then I decided, if the old man was there on the bench when I went outside, I'd at least go and say hi. Today I would take the chance. After what seemed an eternity, I was finally served. With coffee in hand, I walked out the door and across the street to the common. The bench was empty, and, to my dismay, the old man was gone. I walked to the bench and sat where he had been seated. Strangely, I thought I could still feel his warmth on the bench. I sat back and started to relax as I sipped my hot coffee. I gazed out and took in the sights and sounds of nearby waterway and saw people window-shopping the small shops that lined the cobblestone streets. Occasionally, I would see runners pounding the pavement as they checked their times or quenched their thirst drinking from bottles stored in a pouch along their waistband. I felt peaceful sitting there, something I hadn't felt for many years, if ever. At that moment in time, it seemed everything was okay. I decided that day the coffee shop would be the halfway point on my morning walks, and if ever I saw the old man again I would muster up the courage to say hi. I had to do this because I knew I needed his help. At this point in my life, I had no one to turn to. My trust issues prevented me from taking a chance, or risk being vulnerable to any emotional pain.

As I sipped my coffee and took in the view of the area, I was reminded of my younger days and remembered when I worked on the docks unloading the huge wire baskets of fish from the boats. I loved the ocean. Back then, as a young man I would sometimes daydream while unloading fish at the dock and see myself as a fisherman gliding through the water on a small boat heading out to the fishing grounds. I had always known somehow my life would be connected to the sea. Anytime I had a problem or needed to re-group, I would always find comfort on shore looking out at the never-ending ocean with the gulls flying above always looking for something to eat. Somehow, I would feel the enormity of ocean, sky, and shore and sometimes I wondered where I fit in with it all. I felt an intimate connection like I had when hunting or anytime I took to the forest and fields. Later in my life, I found refuge at sea while serving in the Navy.

I never had a fear of the water, even though I couldn't swim well at all. I envied those who could swim and felt at ease as they glided through the water and able to stay afloat without trying. Many people told me I had negative buoyancy and for me to float at all I had to tread water and constantly move my legs and arms to stay afloat. A major issue was I couldn't relax. I was wound tight as a drum and always on guard. With all the work involved to not sink, I found no pleasure in swimming, and, often, I would just wade out to cool down on hot days.

Looking back, I remember the several times boating when I'd have to swim in from my mooring. I had many close calls and once or twice I thought I wouldn't make it in. I didn't panic or thrash about, instead accepted my fate and relaxed. Somehow, I would manage to reach the shore and live another day. Someone asked me one time if I feared dying, and I replied honestly. I told them I didn't fear my own death at all, and to this day I don't.

THE BIG MOVE

The first time I saw the ocean was when I was a young boy. My dad was a career Navy man, and his job was to be at sea doing what other sailors had done for hundreds or thousands of years. Our whole family had just completed a long drive, leaving behind the familiar home of our births. It was just days before, uncles and aunts, cousins and friends had united at our house to bid us farewell. The tears flowed as the adults reminisced about "old times". Meanwhile, the children filled up on the food and soda there to be had. We had driven for 12-14 hours with only few stops. The fuel tank would determine our stops. Bathroom breaks were called "pit stops", and when it was time, one of us would ask my dad if he needed gas soon. My mom had packed plenty of food and snacks to keep us fed and watered. No one whined or complained. Complaining wasn't an option for us, especially during this trip. My dad ran a tight ship and when he gave us direction (orders) we obeyed, *period.* Sitting in the car, zooming down the highway, we watched the scenery go by as my dad drove steadily on. Mom and I, my two younger brothers, and our baby sister sat quietly trying to contain our excitement building with every mile.

Almost every Sunday, as far back as I could remember, our family would take a ride. We seldom knew where we were going, and I don't think my dad knew until we were down the road a ways. We would play car games, sing songs, and watch the countryside change from forests to fields and back again. Farms were scattered around and the old barns advertised tobacco. Of course none of these rides compared at all to this ride. The distance alone was huge compared to the couple hours for a normal ride. Sleeping was impossible for me. My brothers, especially the youngest, were asleep before we left the driveway. My baby sister was with Mom in the front seat being entertained when needed.

Now, after what seemed an eternity, we were there. We had finally reached our destination. The truck holding our family's belongings parked behind our car. I bet the man driving behind us, seemingly forever, was glad to finally shut off his engine. As we unloaded from the old Buick, back on solid ground, we all ran to the ocean and took in the brand new sights, sounds, and smells. Water, as far as the eyes could see, birds working the shore, and people, adults and children, swimming and surfing the waves as they washed upon the shore. The beach was rock and sand, and as we approached the water I slipped on the kelp and other seaweed that had washed ashore. I reached down and scooped up a handful of sea water and had a taste. It was salty alright and had a smell that, from that day on, I would always associate with the ocean.

ABOUT MY PARENTS

My father was the middle son of three boys. My grandfather and grandmother were divorced before my dad reached his teenage years and he was left to fend for himself. During the few times I could get information from my dad, he mentioned he was basically on his own at a very young age. He said his first real job was working in a bowling alley setting up pins. That was well before it was automated and then setting the pins was done by hand. Back then the wages were low and the work was hard. He also mentioned he had worked with his uncle cutting hardwood for timber used for mine ties in the coalmines. He also worked the mines for a while and eventually landed a job at the steel mill in town. He had quit school in the tenth grade and went to work fulltime in order to support himself. He mentioned his younger brother of several years was with his mom, and although my dad still lived with his mom, she couldn't give him the support he needed. His older brother had left home and was also on his own from an early age. My dad was a bull of a man and his physical stature as well as his no BS approach to life was a force to be reckoned with. When Japan bombed Pearl Harbor, my dad was then too young to join. His older brother had enlisted before the war. The military was a way out of poverty, and although the pay was minimal, the service provided everything needed to survive. My uncles on my mother's side who were of age joined the war effort in the Navy, Marines, as well as the Army.

My mother was the only girl in the family. She had five brothers: four older and one younger. My mom's dad died when she was a small child and soon after his death my mom went to live with her aunt. Up until then, she and her brothers had enjoyed a good life. My grandfather had a great job, a fairly new car, and they lived in a nice home. Money wasn't a concern for the family, and my mom took dancing lessons as well as gymnastics. She and her brothers were well-fed, well clothed, and all was well. After his death, the house and car went by the wayside. My grandmother couldn't work even if employment was available. She had diabetes and other health issues that kept her back. Her small widow's pension couldn't support six children. So, as was the case with many families in hard times, Mom was shipped off to live with her aunt. This was a common practice and moving in with her wasn't out of place. My aunt lived in her own home and was financially set. My mom was in good hands. My uncles, those who were old enough to work, stepped up to the plate and took jobs to help make ends meet.

When my dad turned seventeen, he enlisted in the Naval Reserves and went to basic training, and then to "A" school to learn to be a boiler man. The war was raging and he wanted in. After his training, he was sent to the pacific onboard USS TOLLBERG (APD 100). After his hitch, he finished out his six-year contract as a reservist. When his obligated time was up, he decided to reenlist for six more years and remain in the reserve. It was a paycheck and a much-needed supplement for his and our growing family's survival.

Looking back, I can remember seeing him in uniform. He was all business, especially when it came to his Navy service. He was squared away and had successfully climbed through the ranks despite his education. During these years, supporting himself and the family was a struggle. Layoffs at the mill were putting many men out of work. With the war over, steel wasn't in demand and only those with years of seniority held onto their jobs. My mom worked selling Avon, and she eventually was employed by a large store downtown. Her Avon experience helped her land a job in the women's department selling and demonstrating the use of cosmetics. My dad was laid off and now took care of us kids while my mom worked. We lived in low-income housing and moved many times. Our family lived in housing we could afford, and we occupied an apartment in the projects most of the time. As a kid, I didn't really know or understand how dire our situation was. I figured everyone was in the same boat as us and it wasn't far from the truth.

In 1961 with few options, and after having many conversations between my parents, they decided to request a waiver for my father to go on active duty and into the Navy fulltime. Besides the money, or lack of, there were many other circumstances that forced their decision. The one major factor driving his decision above all was my baby sister's health and welfare concerns. My infant sister had severe health issues after her premature birth and, as a result of measles she caught while in the hospital, had developed meningitis. She was in the hospital and wasn't expected to survive. I remember going to see her with my younger brothers in tow. Seeing the tubes and needles in her arms, as well as the bags hanging, scared me. She was a fighter and did survive, although the meningitis had left her deaf. My sister would require special schooling, hearing aids, and continued medical attention. There was no way my dad could afford this extra care. We were hanging on by a thread. So, his option, and the only alternative, was to go on active duty.

I seldom heard my dad or mom complain. My mom would sometimes share a little now and then when pressured, things about my dad. They had known each other long before he had quit school. My dad's best friend happened to be my mom's brother. As I look back, I understand now why my dad was the way he was. I very seldom heard my dad laugh, and a smile was few and far between. I remember only a few occasions when there wasn't tension in the air. Life was hard and he and my mom tried to keep us kids out of the fray. Even before my dad went back to the Navy, he'd seldom be home. Well, he would be home, but he'd be asleep. Back then, third shift work was all he could find. We had to play quietly or not at all.

Most of the time, we were outside anyway. No matter the weather, we would run the fields and venture into the woods that bordered the projects. Some of my fondest memories where while in the woods swinging on wild grape vines, or playing like we were hunters. We would have spears or our slingshots and practice our skills. We would always, and I mean *always*, remember my dad's words. "Never kill anything you won't eat." My dad hunted often to supplement our food supply. We were brought up eating rabbit, pheasant, frog legs, and venison. I remember biting on the small lead pellets missed during cleaning. It was a game we played when eating wild game. Somehow, I'd always manage to find the most and we would all have a good laugh.

THE NOTE

Now, back on the bench and present once again, I went to sip my coffee and surprisingly realized I had already finished it. The coffee was steaming hot and now it was gone. I had been daydreaming for a while and it was now time to move on. Looking around for a trash can, I saw the nearest receptacle was at the entrance to the common. During my search was when I noticed a scrap of paper on the ground by my feet. Looking down, I saw the paper was folded neatly and when I looked closely I could barely see the words written inside. At first, I thought it was probably someone's grocery list or a note to remind them of something they had to do that day. As I bent forward to retrieve the note, I noticed the folded paper was stapled closed. I carefully removed the staple and opened the note when I noticed the excitement that had enveloped me. I saw my hands were shaking a little and an odd feeling came over me. I felt as if someone was watching me as I sat on the bench. I slowly looked around and concluded no one else there. I was alone as I had been when I first sat down.

I felt very weird sitting there with the note in hand. I thought for a moment the note might be something personal and maybe I shouldn't open it. I also thought I should place it back on the ground where I found it. The calmness I had felt earlier in the common was replaced by an excitement; I felt like a child ready to open their Christmas presents.

After what seemed to be a long while, I mustered the courage to read the note. The note only had a few words written on it. The note said: "*What are you waiting for?*"

I re-read the note as I looked around the common. I still had the feeling I was being watched. Was the note for me? Was it left there for me to find by the old man I had seen sitting on the bench? Or, was it just a scrap of paper that wasn't my concern? I carefully re-folded the note and placed it in my wallet for safekeeping as I stood to leave. I quickly looked around the common. Again, I had that feeling I was being watched. After a few more minutes and another look around, I finally started my walk back. I had about a mile and a half to cover before my walk was done. As I pushed myself forward, I thought of the note. I couldn't get those words out of my mind: "What are you waiting for?"

As I continued my walk back, I took in the scenes of the harbor with the lobster boats tied to the dock unloading its yummy cargo. I hadn't had a good lobster dinner in a long time. I then remembered a time when I had an old wooden skiff I had bought from a friend I worked with.

It was a small fourteen-foot wooden boat with a small twenty-five-horse Evinrude outboard on the back. The boat had spent its life in fresh water on the lakes in Maine. The boat leaked a little and had to be bailed every few days. It sat on the mooring that used to belong to my wife's dad. The mooring was an old engine block with a chain secured to it. In those days we maintained our moorings the best we could. Every year I would wait for a good low tide, so I could inspect the mooring and replace chains or ropes worn or rusted through. It wasn't a difficult job, and usually in the process I'd manage to gather a few quahogs I'd carefully open with the knife I always kept on my boat. The clams were delicious and fresh out of the bay. I remembered my first resident lobster license and how difficult the process was to get it. The license permitted me to have five pots and the law required them to be checked weekly. After many trials and lots of errors while learning to set lobster pots, I eventually managed to catch a few. Working on the water fishing for bait would always remind me of the first boat I had owned.

My brother and I were down at the water's edge one morning when we spotted a small wooden pram. It was floating twenty-five or thirty yards off the beach. Neither of us could swim, and I wanted that boat. I ran back to the house and retrieved my fishing rod; I had rigged it for catching flounder off the docks. Running back, fishing rod in hand, I finally reached the spot where we had spotted the pram. The first cast was short, and I wound in the line as fast as I could, hoping I wouldn't snag the bottom. The second cast went over the boat, and as I slowly reeled in I managed to snag the boat. The rod bent in half and made cracking sounds as I carefully reeled in the line until I could wade out to finally grab it. I didn't know there was a deep drop-off where the channel ran, and in I went. I was well over my head as I struggled to stay afloat. I swallowed a few mouthfuls of sea water and choked it up. As I struggled to touch bottom, my brother finally reached out and gave me a hand. He was laughing and seemed to enjoy the show. Back on solid ground, I dragged the small pram on to the beach. I was exhausted from the whole event and sat on the edge of the pram to catch my breath.

We both heard a vehicle approaching and saw the dark forest green truck pulling in just yards away. The truck belonged to the environmental police as I read the markings on the vehicle. The driver sat for a few minutes before the door opened. We waved to the man in uniform and he waved back as he approached. He asked us about the boat and we filled him in on what had happened. He had received a call regarding a boat drifting in the area. He looked over the boat for any clue as to whom it belonged. Finding no name or markings, he said it looked like we now had a boat to use. He would put word out, and if he didn't hear from anyone in a month or two the boat would be ours.

Our house was several hundred yards away. As my brother and I tried to carry the boat, we struggled. The policeman laughed at our attempt and offered to put it in the back of his truck and haul it up to the house. There wasn't room for us, so we ran up the road following the truck until he stopped at the edge of the yard. He dragged the boat out of the truck bed and flipped it upside down on the lawn for us. He promised to let us know if anyone claimed the boat; if anyone did he would come by and pick it up to return. We thanked him for his help as he drove away.

The boat sat upside down in the yard for a month and a half when the officer showed up to inform me no one had claimed the boat; it was mine to keep. He took my name and address and said he would file a report. He told me to keep the report when it arrived. I thanked him, and he said: "Enjoy the boat and be careful." He also mentioned to be sure to wear a lifejacket.

Once on the water, after buying secondhand oars and a quick paint job, I had new freedom. The boat brought me many years of use and transportation by water to fish and row. Not long after putting the boat in, I met another kid on the water. He had red hair, freckles, and would soon become my best friend. My new friend lived up the cove from me, and his parents owned a large, old house on the water. The house was from an age gone by and at one time was owned by a wealthy man who had several homes in the area. My friend came from a large family. His dad was an arborist and did tree removal and lawn care. He was always working and seldom home during the day. When my friend brought me to his house, I met his mom and brothers and sisters. His mom asked me if I was looking forward to Thanksgiving, which was only a week away. I filled her in on our family's dilemma. We weren't having turkey for the holiday and instead had whatever my mom could scrounge up. After hearing my sad tale, she filled a large cardboard box with all the fixings for a good, solid meal. We packed it in her car and drove to our rental apartment. I was scared to be scolded for letting the cat out of the bag regarding our family's desperate needs. She even included a couple quarts of beer after she asked if my mom drank.

After a quick introduction, my mother and my friend's mom sat for a long while talking. We kids left when the tears started. It was hard to see my mom in her emotional state and it reminded me of the many sad times we had experienced. From that day on, my mom knew if I wasn't home I would be with my friend, probably rowing in our wooden boats. Before my friend's mom left, she invited our whole family for Thanksgiving dinner at her house. My mom was proud and not to hand-outs, and politely said no. It took an hour before she was finally convinced to accept the invite. My dad was at sea and our first holiday was spent with another family. We all enjoyed the feast and the adults had a few drinks and smoked their cigarettes afterwards.

HARD TIMES

Only two months before, our family had arrived after our 12-14-hour car ride. The truck carrying everything we owned had left the parking lot. We piled into the car and drove off. All of us were overtired from the trip; the two smaller kids, my baby sister and youngest brother, were making a fuss. My mom did all she could to keep them quiet as my dad searched house numbers looking for the one we would occupy. The relator my parents hired was waiting in the small shell covered driveway. He got out of his vehicle and approached our car as we pulled in. Once stopped and after my dad finally shut off the engine, we kids unloaded. My parents talked to the realtor for several minutes as we waited. After talking with my parents, I noticed my dad shaking his head and my mother was really upset. The house my parents had rented wasn't available yet and we would have to wait another four to five weeks to move in. In the meantime, we would stay at the house where we were parked in front of.

The house was a small stucco summer home located not far from the state beach only ½ mile away. My dad opened the front door with the key he had been given only moments ago. As we all crammed our way through the front door, we were all taken aback. The cottage was a tiny, two-bedroom summer house that belonged to a family who had left for the season.

I remember how hectic it was during those first few days after arriving from our long drive. All our personal belongings were stuffed into the trunk of the old Buick. The first evening I woke up to find my mom and dad talking. My mom was crying, and my dad had a look I had never seen before. He was comforting my mom and looked like he needed comforting as well. They saw me standing there and forced smiles on their faces to change the mood. That was when I learned my dad would be leaving in a few more days. The ship to which he was assigned to was getting underway for a six-month North Atlantic/Mediterranean deployment. I was twelve years old at the time and my dad said I had to step up and help my mom; he expected me to keep my brothers and sister safe. I sat there as my mom wept again and I joined her with tears rolling down my face. I snuffed them away and tried to act more grown-up. My dad was counting on me and I didn't want to look like the child I really was. I felt a heavy load on my shoulders and didn't know whether I would be able to step up.

The next day our family drove around the area to take in the new sights. It was very different compared to home. I noticed there were few forested areas. The beaches that usually held scores of sunbathers and people wading in the water held only a few. School was in session now, the beaches were sparse with only a few people sunning and swimming. My brothers and I were enrolled in schools close to where we were supposed to be living. None of us knew it would be many, many, weeks before we'd actually start.

I was the only one of us kids who knew what was coming down the pike with my father. Only my mom and I knew my dad would be leaving very soon and wouldn't be around for a while. I was trying to act the part of the big brother and felt inadequate for the job. Instead of enjoying myself as a kid, I had taken on a serious demeanor. I was afraid. The little cottage was one of the few houses occupied at the end of the summer season. Everyone was back to their jobs or at school for another year. There was only one small store a short walk from the bungalow. They had beach type snacks including premade sandwiches and cold drinks. The grocery store sold milk, eggs, and bread, as well as packaged hot dogs, lunch meats, and cheese. The store was also pricey and, because of its proximity to the beach, was a goldmine for the owner. A large food chain supermarket over a mile away offered prices in-line with the markets down home. We stocked up on food supplies and odds and ends we would need and drove back to unload.

The days passed quickly, and it wasn't long before my dad gathered us kids for a family talk. I knew what was coming as he and my mom had filled me in on what was instore. My younger brother asked a lot of questions that couldn't be answered as my parents tried to make sense out of our predicament. My dad packed the car with his belongings and, with a wave and a few tears, drove off. My mom didn't drive, so the car was useless to her. My dad had made arrangements for the car to be taken to the new rental house and parked until his return. He also had made arrangements with the realtor to collect any mail for my mom once a week. We counted on my dad to send checks while he was gone. He emptied his wallet, except for the small amount he kept for himself. Although my dad would often be away for a few weeks now and then, this was the first time my dad wouldn't be around, period.

THUNDER AND LIGHTENING

A couple weeks went by and we adapted to life in our little bungalow. The furnishings were sparse, and we were using someone else's beds, furniture, and even the pots, pans, and dishes weren't familiar. We had no TV set and only had a small radio that used batteries. Stuck away in the two-bedroom summer home all of us were experiencing cabin fever. It was raining hard outside and the wind was blowing a gale. We didn't know what was really transpiring with the weather as we tried to entertain ourselves inside our cramped quarters.

Suddenly, without warning, thunder shook the cottage and lightening flashed everywhere. The front door was shut and we were all huddled in the living room scared out of our wits. BOOM, lightening struck the house. It came in through the keyhole of the locked front door. The ball of lightening bounced around the living room and vanished through the back-screen door. Everyone was screaming. As suddenly as it started, it was over. My mom got up after a few moments and went to each of us asking if we were alright. My sister took the brunt of the shock and, although not injured, was screaming out of control. Little did we know we were in the middle of a hurricane bearing down on us, and the worst was yet to come.

Not long after we had been hit, there came a knock at the door. We tried to open it but it wouldn't budge. The door had been struck badly enough by lightening as to make the knob inoperable. With his help from outside, we finally forced the door open and standing outside was a uniformed policeman. My mom let him in and filled him in about our situation. They talked for a few minutes and then my mom told us to pack our toothbrushes, toothpaste, and a couple changes of socks and underwear, and said we were being evacuated because of the hurricane. Moments later, we all piled in to the squad car and drove off to a nearby high school. We unloaded and went in the school to find dozens of families sitting on cots and laying on makeshift beds to wait out the storm. We stayed at the school for two days. While there, we were fed well and looked after by Red Cross personnel who had volunteered to take on this monumental task.

Returning to our temporary place, we returned to what a warzone might have looked like. The trees in the neighborhood were stripped of their leaves and other trees were uprooted and laying about. The ocean waves were huge, and seaweed from wind and tides had piled up on the beach. The kelp piles were eight-feet high and fish and shellfish had washed up everywhere. The gulls were the only ones who seemed to enjoy the hurricanes aftermath. There was water in the house; the carpet in the living room was soggy and it smelled like the low tide at the beach.

Not long after our return, a Red Cross van pulled in front of the stucco house. They had been tipped off by the policeman who evacuated us. A young man who had been driving came to the door and asked if we could use some help. The woman with him asked my mom if everything was okay. That was when my mother broke down in tears as she explained our dilemma.

She and my mom walked into the small kitchen and sat at the table. Meanwhile, the young man brought in boxes of food, new blankets wrapped in plastic, and other items they thought we might need. We would be all right now, I thought to myself as the Red Cross van slowly left us there to fend for ourselves. Although we now had food and warm blankets, we were not exactly okay. Money was our major problem and the checks we were sure my dad would send were our only salvation.

The only phone available was at the little grocery store half a mile away. Every day we would all walk to the phone booth and wait for my mom to finish her conversation. We were hoping for good news, and again we were disappointed. This was a daily occurrence: the walk to the store, the phone call, and the disappointment that followed.

The move as well as the hurricane and now our isolation with no transportation was having an impact on my mom. One day she told us she was going to walk down to a restaurant several miles away. She would be back as soon as possible and promised us burgers and fries. My baby sister was three years old and needed constant watching. My younger brothers were no help with taking care of her. I was the oldest and my dad had told me to be sure the kids were safe. I felt the weight of this huge responsibility as soon as my mom was out of sight and on her way to buy us food. Hours passed, and it seemed like every few minutes one of my brothers would ask when Mom would be back. I would say soon and try to change the subject. More time went by and I was getting a little worried.

I gathered everyone and decided we all would surprise my mom and meet her. She was probably walking the road back from the restaurant and I thought she would be glad to see us. We walked on the side of the road well off the pavement as we slowly made our way to the restaurant. We could see a fair distance as we walked, and we were also looking out for my mom. My sister was getting tired, and I eventually lifted her onto my shoulders and continued walking. With our goal in sight, we finally made it. I peaked in the window of the restaurant and saw Mom sitting at the bar drinking a beer. We all walked in and caught her by surprise. She was the only patron until then and she asked the server to give us all Shirley Temples. We sat at a table and I spotted a highchair in the corner and retrieved it for my sister. My mom ordered food for us, and we drank our sodas and waited for our meals to arrive.

When the burgers and fries were finally done, the server brought them over and we all ate. After our meal, we walked a few blocks further and my mom went into a package store and bought a couple six-packs of beer and several packs of cigarettes. My brothers took turns carrying the bag and I carried my sister on my shoulders the whole way back. My mom was very quiet as we walked along, and I could tell something was up. She held her gaze on the ground as we walked and when I looked back I could see her eyes were red and tears were flowing down her face. I stopped and asked her if she was okay and she said:

"No, I'm not okay," and didn't say another word until we finally made our way back.

My sister was getting cranky and my brothers were fighting over something. I felt responsible for everyone, including my mom. I suddenly felt alone, very alone. My mother sat by herself at the kitchen table. She didn't seem to notice the chaos from kids fighting and my crying sister. She had her back to us as she looked out through the screen door leading to the small backyard. From time to time, my mom would turn to us and smile. I noticed, although she was smiling, her eyes told a very different story. She sat drinking her beer and smoking while hell broke loose around her. I had no way of knowing what I needed to do to make things right. I was twelve years old and felt like the only grown-up. My mom was in another world. She had disconnected from us and coped in her own way.

As I tried to sleep later that evening, my mind was racing. I was trying to figure out what to do next. I managed to finally doze off; my night was filled with vivid dreams I wouldn't remember.

The next day was a repeat of the day before. My mom was at the table having coffee and looking out the door as she had done the day before. I didn't know what was going on with Mom. All I really knew was Dad was out to sea and it seemed my mom was too.

Over the course of the following weeks, I had managed to make sure we were fed, bathed, and taken care of. My childhood was over, and now I was responsible for everyone's wellbeing. My mom would be there with us although she wasn't *really* there at all.

I was angry. I felt hate. How could my mom and dad do this to us? How could they do this to me? I was just a kid, and although I had learned early in life to do what was needed, I didn't feel I could handle it all by myself. I felt like running away from it all. The responsibility my dad had so casually given me was more than I was prepared to handle. Contacting my father was not an option. He was at sea and the mail was the only line of communication we had. Only in an extreme emergency would a message be able to reach him.

Later that day, the realtor came by to drop off the mail and bring us up-to-date on when we would finally move. He and my mom talked as they were making arrangements to go to the bank and cash the checks she had received. My sister cried as my mom left, and it took a long time to settle her. It seemed like forever until they returned. We would stand in the living room, taking turns watching and waiting. There was excitement and, for me, relief when they finally drove in. My mom called us out to unload several full bags of groceries, a case of soda, and two cases of beer. After the realtor had left, I noticed my mom's mood was better. I guessed the money issues were resolved, at least, for a little while.

The days ticked by, and although all wasn't well, it was better. Mom left us alone only once or twice when she made the six-mile roundtrip to buy beer. We were all ready to get out of there and our patience was running thin, to say the least. It wouldn't be long now, we hoped.

Every day we would take a walk to the beach. My brothers and sister would run in the sand and let off steam that had built up while cooped inside the small cottage. My mom and I would sit and watch as they played. I felt very different now. I wasn't smiling or cracking jokes like I always had. I was in a very serious frame of mind. I was at the mercy of something I had no control over and didn't like the feeling at all. The fun was gone, and I wouldn't allow myself to have any until I knew we would be okay. From that time on, having fun was impossible for me to obtain. Guilt and fear kept even the idea of fun an unreachable distance away. It was okay for everyone to have fun, except me. I had no time for that anymore. I was too busy looking out for everyone, except myself. I had made myself responsible for making everyone happy and was failing. With every failure, I would ultimately, after blaming others, hold myself accountable and punish myself in some way. Usually, I would repeatedly keep myself from having fun, joy, or any kind of pleasurable experience. My misery would build, and I would find some poor soul to blame or punish, all the while knowing it was me at fault.

I started smoking during this time and would sneak a few cigarettes from Mom and go to the woods. It wasn't long until I was smoking regularly. My mom tried to convince me to not smoke, but I did anyway. I felt I was a man and could take care of my own business. I was no longer a child in my eyes, and would call the shots and take care of myself. I withdrew further into myself and constructed more barriers to guard my heart so I could endure. I was in survival mode and would be that way for most of my life.

Even with strong protection, I still felt the emotions and turmoil. I felt them, although no one would have ever guessed by my appearance that anything was wrong. I would put on my war face and fortify the wall I had painstakingly built to protect myself. Sadly, the wall worked both ways, and when I walled myself from heartache I also prevented any love I might have for others to ever be expressed. Nothing coming in and nothing went out.

Later, I would learn the risk of heartache was worth the reward. It would be many years until I would take the chance. I would suffer until then, and I was the cause.

HOME SWEET HOMES

Three weeks later, we were able to move to the original house my dad had rented while he was at sea. It was a three-story home in a sparsely settled neighborhood, located behind the strip. The strip was an amusement area that ran the length of the street. A huge circus looking building held an indoor merry-go-round and carnival type booths lined the circular walls. The strip also had a now closed indoor skating floor, as well as restaurants, bars, and food stands on both sides of the street. The strip was now closed for the season and the only business that stayed open were two bars and a restaurant that served local seafood.

The rental house itself was old and needed painting inside and out. We didn't even notice it because of the excitement that came with seeing our own furniture set up and waiting for us to enjoy once again.

A few days later, we started school and my mom packed a suitcase for my three-year-old sister. She would be picked up by a taxi driver from the School for the Deaf. My sister would leave the house on a Monday morning and return home Friday afternoon. These arrangements were known by my parents and news to us. Looking back now, I'm glad she was in safe hands and being cared for, even if it meant her being away. At least she wouldn't have to be disrupted like the rest of the family. Disrupted didn't even come close to what we would have to endure.

My mom continued with her drinking; she would slow down a bit and stay home only when my sister was home from school. Then, Mom would act like a mom and tend to her needs for the two days a week she was with us. She would cook meals, tidy up the house, and carefully wash, iron, fold, and pack my sister's little blue suitcase on Sunday evening.

As soon as my sister left for the week to attend school, all bets were off. We would go to school ourselves, and after school walked from the bus stop and find Mom wasn't there. The strip was a block away and she would be at one of the two bars, nursing a draft beer. At first, we would go in and try to talk her into coming home. She would buy us a soda and chips or maybe a Slim Jim and tell us she would be home soon. Repeatedly, we would find her sitting alone sipping her beer and staring off into the distance. I gave up after a while and didn't bother to try. I didn't care. I closed myself off from any feelings I might have. I was in pure survival mode. Little did I know then, it would be for a long time, for the rest of my life.

Over the course of the next nine months, our family had to move, lock, stock, and barrel, seven times. Imagine moving and not having a car or even local transportation to use. Ironically, my dad missed all of them except the final one. The reasons we moved so often were many, and it really didn't matter. Now, we were finally living in Navy housing and wouldn't be uprooted any time soon. Funny, we would actually move two more times while staying in the Navy housing community. The other two moves were a breeze. We were all professionals by then and had it down to a science. The next four years were tough all around.

MONEY

Money was the big problem, the real problem we had. This money situation drove me and was always on my mind. I became obsessed with money. I knew firsthand how being broke felt. The lack of it showed me how bad it could be. I made a promise to myself to never be without enough money to get by decently. I collected bottles and scrap metal and exchanged them for money. I did odd jobs for neighbors and one time threw bales of hay onto a farm truck and cut the field behind the elementary school. I started to accumulate coins and cash and kept it safely stored in my wallet. To this day, I always have Mad Money, tucked away behind my driver's license for "just in case".

My sister was in school and had only the weekends to endure. We, on the other hand, were below water. I would baby-sit the neighbor's children, and once word got out, I was busy from school's end into the night. At thirteen, I had gained a lot of experience with my youngest brother as well as my sister. My mom had taught all of us how to cook, clean house, and to wash, fold, and iron our clothes at a very young age. To this day, I'm a hell of a good cook and keep a clean house.

Although I was busy earning some money, it wasn't enough. I talked the neighborhood newspaper kid out of his route and had to pay him for it. I promised I would when I got my first check. I remember I had eighty-four newspapers to deliver every day after school and 135 Sunday papers to hand off and collect for throughout my route. I held on to that paper route for over a year. I continued babysitting and doing odd jobs after delivering the newspapers. I wasn't making a fortune after giving a large portion to my mom, and I was buying my own clothing as well as everything else I needed.

As time went on, things started to level out a bit. My dad was back at last, for who knew how long, and things were better when he was home. He was the family's protector and provider and when he wasn't home, I was. It wasn't long before I landed a dream job for a young person. I was now a stand-by grocery bagger at the commissary on the base. I'd catch a ride from school to the base and hope to bag groceries for a few hours after school to earn cash. Every day, I would run from the lot to the commissary. It was over half a mile jaunt. I was young and could go like a deer. If lucky, I'd be assigned an isle and take over for the day bagger waiting to go home. If not, I would gather grocery carts from outside and bring them in for use by the baggers. There were twelve aisles that needed carts and the baggers had to leave them unattended while food items piled up. In between customers, which was only moments, they'd run outside to get carts. The rule was if you went for carts you had to bring in a full load. I was paid by each aisle a dollar an hour to insure a cart would always be available. I'd sometimes make $25-$30 for the several hours I worked. Baggers did way better moneywise and the commissary was busy all the time. We were paid by tips only and bagged and offered to unload no matter tip or not. All the customers were military dependents, just like every bagger. We all were dependents, even the cashiers. Our moms or dads were mostly enlisted men and women stationed on base, on one of the two aircraft carriers docked there, or from the air wing command.

In the sixties, military pay was just above poverty level. We were all managing okay. All of us knew times were tough and some were worse off than others. I never heard any of the military dependents complain. With only one exception, we all wished our parents were home.

I worked at the commissary for a while before being offered another job. I joined the galley crew that served three meals a day at the two largest eating halls that provided meals to the Navy men and woman stationed there. It didn't take long before I was the shift boss of our crew. I was earning good money and able to help more. The work was hard and we stayed busy with very little time for breaks. My studies went by the wayside as I continued working. I had purchased a small Honda motor scooter I'd ride to school and then to work. My grades were just passing, and by then work and earning money was a higher priority. It wasn't long until I had enough of school. I decided to quit and go to work fulltime. My dad, back from sea, came home to find me sitting in the house and not at school. He gave me a choice, go back to school, go to work, or go into the military.

Later, I drove to the Marine recruiter and started the process of enlisting. When we finished, I brought the paperwork home for my parents to sign. I was seventeen years old and needed parental consent to join the military. That evening, my dad talked me out of joining the Marines. Vietnam was raging, and he thought I would be better off in the Navy. At that point, I really didn't care. I just wanted out. I was tired of the responsibilities I had been forced to take on. I had enough and it was time for me to be on my own. Everything was settled. I would be sworn in at the Boston Naval Shipyard, and then I'd be flown to basic training at the recruit training depot in Illinois in two months.

During those two months, I started dating my future wife. I borrowed a neighbor's car and drove down to where she lived, hoping to see her. I was a little shy (afraid), and after several tries, I finally mustered the nerve to knock on her door. We hit it off, and soon we were dating. We spent long hours talking about our dreams. I worked up until the week before I was due to leave. A few days before I was to depart, I got a buzz haircut and my father gave me a few tips on the ways of the Navy. He said I should keep a low profile and not volunteer for anything. Little did we know after completing basic training I would be assigned to a ship docked on the west coast in San Diego, California. Soon after reporting aboard for duty, the ship would be underway heading for Vietnam.

I was seventeen years old, just out of basic training, and I remember my walk down the pier. The USS Ogden LPD 5 was tied off docked and at the far end. After a few awful days in a holding company on base, I was finally reporting aboard. Although I had been given two weeks leave after boot camp, I decided in less than a week after returning home I wanted out of there. My dad was home, which was a good thing. I talked it over with him after dinner one evening. He said he understood my excitement for reporting early. My dad never knew what had transpired during the long months he was away. None of us kids would dare talk out of school. We were all affected by the happenings, and to this day only a few people know some of the details of what really went on.

NEW CAREER OPPORTUNITY

Sitting in my apartment, shortly after noon that day, as usual, I checked my mailbox and found a letter waiting. The envelope immediately got my attention. It was from my work and marked, "Official Business". My heart skipped a beat before it started pounding in my chest. I took the letter inside, sat down, and took a deep breath, probably my first breath since retrieving the letter. My hands were sweaty and trembling as I carefully opened the official letter in my hand. I was expecting news from my employer this week, and although I knew it was coming, it still caught me off guard. Wow! I was being informed I was officially retired. The letter went on to say I had paperwork that needed my attention and I was scheduled to go through the check-out process on Friday of that week.

The rest of the day I was in limbo. I thought I had a few years to look for a new career and train and be ready for the day I'd retire. Now, apparently, I was retired. Although I knew we could live off my retirement wages, I also knew it would be tight, moneywise.

Only a few months before, I found a very interesting possibility to the question of what I would do after retirement. This new opportunity was in the holistic field and an energy healing system that encompassed the various philosophies as well as Eastern and Western medicine. Sadly, I didn't know what holistic really meant and had to look up the word in the dictionary. My understanding, after reading the various definitions, was holistic medicine was all encompassing. It treated the whole person physically and mentally, not just the injury or disease. I thought, as I tried to wrap my head around the words, this new career would be taking me out of my comfort zone for sure.

This new opportunity would require me to attend training in a field I had never been exposed to. The training wasn't local, and I would have to travel from coast to coast, from the Great Lakes to Florida, and many places in between.

Luckily, I had started a savings account for this purpose. Although, I thought I had a couple of years to add to it, I had managed to accumulate enough to at least get me started. With the official letter in hand, it was obvious now my training would start sooner than later.

That night as I tried to go to sleep my mind was racing. I was excited about traveling to learn my new trade, and also scared of this unfamiliar territory I was about to enter. I was also a little afraid, as I anticipated tracking down the old man from the common. With the note, I now had a perfect excuse to approach the old man. I would ask him if the note was his or just a scrap of paper that meant nothing. After what seemed an eternity, I finally drifted off and my sleep was filled with disjointed dreams. I was in uniform and on the frontlines fighting any foe that came along. My alarm startled me as I woke up from a restless night. I felt anger in me and blamed it on my lack of sleep. Or, maybe I was angry at the letter informing me of my forced retirement, or maybe I was just pissed off about it all.

Suddenly, in a moment of clarity, I realized the anger was in me, and not me. I didn't **have** to be angry; I had a choice in this matter. I actually felt myself smile, something I seldom did. It was time to do my routine.

THE MEETING

With my stretching and meditation complete, it was now time for my walk. As I opened the door to leave, I noticed my wallet on the table. I picked it up and took the note out to be sure this wasn't just a dream. The note was real, okay. I felt an excitement come over me as I left the house for my walk. I felt like skipping the trails and playground and going straight to the common downtown to find the old man. Habit took over as I entered the forest to walk the trails. I was glad I took to the woods as I loved this part of my walk. Nature had a way of putting me in the moment. No crazy thoughts bombarding me, no tomorrow, no yesterday, just this very moment. I felt an alertness you see in the various animals found in nature, totally aware of everything around them; alert, yet relaxed, going about their business. Their senses gave them all they needed to stay safe.

I used to hunt in my younger days. I would usually hunt by myself. I never found anyone who would hunt like me. I was a stalker. I would move very slowly through the forest. I took a step or two and then stopped, looked, and listened. I learned this method while watching the very game I was hunting. I felt alive now as I walked the trail leading to the fields when I noticed someone walking the trail ahead of me wearing a red and black checkered coat. It reminded me of the hunting coat my grandfather wore in the field hunting small game and deer. I hadn't thought of him for a long while. I didn't have any fond memories of my father's dad. He was a heavy drinker and very rough. He was never gentle with me, and I was scared to death of him.

The only thing constantly on my mind lately was my predicament. All the plans I had put in place that were about to come into fruition, had fallen through. Suddenly, a deer jumped up feet away from the trail. It startled me for a moment, bringing me back to my senses and the walk. I looked for the other person I had seen moments ago, but they were gone. With the many trails winding throughout the forest, they could be anywhere. It was a little odd though. Very seldom, if ever, did I see anyone walking this trail. In fact, it wasn't part of the park and was on the boundary. The path was made by kids taking a short-cut to school. The trail was overgrown with bushes and green briar. Deadfalls obstructed the path in several places. There was also litter. This really bothered me. The one place you didn't expect to see trash is in the forest. I thought, *Tomorrow, I'll bring a bag and pick up and dispose of what others have left.*

It was hard for me to understand why people discarded their waste. From my earliest days, I remembered my parents always telling us to never throw litter on the ground. My dad would say, "If there are no trash cans, bring it out with you."

The end of the trail was near as I spotted the opening to the fields. I was leaving the forest and would soon be back in civilization. Oddly enough, I felt the energy change as I walked into the fields surrounding the playground. I immediately noticed traffic noise and the voices of children nearby.

As I walked farther out in the field, I noticed someone sitting on the park bench. They were wearing the red and black checkered coat I had seen on the trail earlier. I was still quite a distance away when I realized the man in the coat was the same man I had seen in the common yesterday. As I got closer, I could make out his features. Judging by his long, white hair and snow-white beard, he appeared to be in his mid-eighties. He was watching a golden retriever chase a tennis ball thrown by his human friend. He had a smile on his face, the same smile I had seen yesterday. After a few moments, he glanced in my direction and our eyes locked. He had bright blue eyes. He had a look you'd see in the eyes of someone who had survived the onslaught of a long and hard life. As we looked at each other from a distance, I noticed a softness about him. I could actually feel his acceptance of me; there was no judgement, desire, or worry. His eyes were an invitation of sorts to come over. The fear I had conjured over the meeting was gone and in its place was neutrality. At this moment, everything was okay, just like I had felt yesterday sitting in his spot on the bench at the common.

I slowly and deliberately walked his way and noticed his smile had broadened. It was as if he and I were long-lost friends and he was happily waiting to see me again. Everything seemed to be in slow motion. There was a strange silence in the park and playground then, and even though I knew the children were playing, and the dogs were barking, it seemed the noise had been tuned out. My total attention was on the old man, the note, and what it said. As I approached the old man, he stood and offered his hand and I offered mine. As we shook hands, the sounds of the playground returned as well at the church bell off in the distance. We looked each other in the eyes and both smiled. I had never met this man, yet it felt like I had known him all my life. His handshake was firm and warm, and I felt welcomed.

I said, "Hi, my name is Stephen."

He said, "Great to see you again, Stephen. You can call me Chief." He sat down then and I asked if I could join him on the bench. He said, "Of course you can, you are free to do anything you want," as he smiled.

At first, there was a long, awkward silence until I remembered the note in my wallet and the reason I was there at all. As I took the note out, I glanced over, and he was watching the golden retriever and his human friend playing fetch with a fluorescent tennis ball, again. I waited until he returned his attention to me. I asked, while handing him the note, if he had dropped it the day before down at the common. He said it wasn't dropped; he had put it there for me to find. I was silent and a little edgy as he continued saying he had seen me around for a while now and was wondering when we would finally meet. I mentioned the first time I saw him was yesterday and, for some reason, I was drawn to meet him. He laughed out loud, a great belly laugh that was contagious. As I laughed along with him, I wondered what I was laughing at.

After a few moments of laughter, I suddenly opened up to him. It was if a floodgate had opened and I was pouring out what had happened in my life over the last four or five years. He gave me his undivided attention. That in itself was refreshing. How many times had I had a conversation with someone who really listened?

That morning flew by as I unloaded what I usually kept to myself to a total stranger. Although I didn't know Chief, I trusted him and knew this conversation was just for us. I had a real connection with Chief and felt totally comfortable in his presence. I had a respect for him that could only come from another chief. Yes, I was a chief myself and knew what it took to become a chief petty officer in the US Navy.

A shiver went through me remembering my father had retired from the Navy as a master chief petty officer. I remember him saying when he been promoted to chief, it had been the highlight of his career and one his most memorable days. I knew *exactly* how he must have felt.

I remember every detail of the day I was informed I had made chief. I was on my two-week active duty required for reservists. I was at the barracks when the duty runner came to tell me to report to the commanding officer, immediately. He continued to say the C.O. wanted to see me right away. I was caught off guard for a moment or two, trying to come up with a reason for this summons. I had just returned from the weapons range after a full morning of shooting and requalifying the men and women for training. I had been delegated to be the weapons range officer and was responsible for the safe operation of the weapons range, as well as the safety of over seventy-five men and women qualifying on rifles and pistols that day. I remembered I had a heated discussion with a senior chief that morning. During range ops, the senior chief had forced me to use the authority I had as range officer to politely, but firmly, tell him to leave the range. He had disrupted our operations and was deliberately being an ass.

We had never had a great relationship. He was my boss and a thorn in my side. It seemed every time we had any interaction, he would try to degrade or embarrass me. He knew from day one I didn't care for him one bit. It was very difficult for me to show him any respect. I did respect his rank and had told him on several occasions, it was the only thing I really respected about him. It wasn't a secret to anyone, especially that day I didn't respect him personally. He was a bully and braggart, and it was apparent to me he didn't have much respect coming his way from anyone.

I arrived at the C.O.'s office and waited outside. Within a few minutes, I was called in by the commander and noticed him sitting behind the fancy wooden desk. Although I was nervous, I noticed he was smiling. That smile helped relieve the tension I was feeling, somewhat. He stood and walked from behind his desk to where I was standing at attention. As he approached, he extended his hand to me and said, "Congratulations, Chief."

I was floored for a moment or two. We talked for several minutes before I was dismissed.

After I left the C.O.'s office, I immediately called my wife and children. I also called my parents and spoke to my dad. I told him I had made Utilitiesman Chief Petty Officer and would be initiated the following month. I invited him to attend the initiation and ceremony that followed, and he said he would be honored. It felt a little weird for my dad to be honored to be at the ceremony. I could count on one hand the number of positive strokes my dad had ever given me. He would say, "Why expect compliments or 'atta-boys' for doing what you're supposed to do anyway?"

It made some sense, and no sense at all.

WORDS OF WISDOM

Back on the bench now, and after what seemed to be a long time, I finally wrapped up the (one way) conversation with Chief and had one final question to ask. "What do you mean by 'what are you waiting for?'"

The Chief let out a howl that was probably heard miles away and laughed as hard as I had ever seen anyone laugh. He actually choked a few times and had tears rolling down his face. Again, I laughed with him as if I knew what he was laughing about.

After what seemed to be at least ten minutes, he final calmed down. As he wiped his face dry with the sleeve of his coat, he said from what he gathered, I had to make up for lost time and get moving toward my new career. He said in order to manifest anything in our lives, we had to go through a deliberate process, step-by-step. This process required a plan be drawn up based on what we wanted to happen. He mentioned the "gunas", and explained this theory had been around for thousands of years in India. He went on to say the gunas were in all living and non-living things and were the quality of nature, according to Hindu philosophy.

I really didn't know what he was talking about and was a little confused by this new term, *gunas*. He continued to explain in layman's terms that the gunas were in everything we saw, and there were three gunas: Tamas, Rajas, and Sattva. Tamas equaled form or inactivity, Rajas was movement or activity, and Sattva was consciousness or mind. He went on to say the plan itself was Sattva. The plan was in my mind and had to go through the process of form, movement, and finally into fruition.

We discussed what needed to be done, and he guided me in a way that helped me understand. He said I needed to write my plan down and had to be specific in what I wanted to accomplish. He said, "Leave no stone unturned," and gave examples of how to proceed. I was to find the courses to attend and look for the dates and times the courses were offered. I had to book flights that would get me there and home, and I would also need lodging and food for my stay. He said I had to pack for the trip with the clothes I would need, a shaving kit, as well as any supplies needed for the course. I had to really take extra care when I made my plan, and instead of having it all in my head I was to write it all down. He listened as I added to the list and he mentioned a few I hadn't thought of. He asked about taxis, rental cars, and other transportation I might need.

I didn't realize how complex this plan actually was as I formulated it in my mind. I was impressed by Chief's knowledge and the way he explained these new ideas in a way that was understandable. I had traveled extensively with my civilian job, as well as when I was in the Navy, and knew what needed to be done. Putting it on paper and into a well-thought-out plan seemed logical.

Thinking of how Chief took the time to explain, in detail, reminded me of the way I learned best. Throughout my life, I would ask lots of questions when learning something new. I wanted it to be clear to me, and would always make sure I understood what I was learning. If not, I would continue with questions until I did. I had a lot to process from our first meeting. I mumbled under my breath I hoped things would change in my life for the better. There were a few moments of silence before the chief turned to face me, eyes tearing. He spoke in a voice and manner like that of a father when an important lesson was being presented.

> ***"Real change will come about only when it is brought about, not by your ego, but by reality itself. Awareness releases reality to change you."***
> *"Awareness"- (Anthony de Mello)*

He went on adding another statement that struck a chord. ***"You cannot transcend what you do not know. To go beyond yourself, you must know yourself."*** He then turned forward and looked to the skies and said, **"Know thyself."** He stood abruptly with a huge smile on his face and suggested I go to the library or access a computer and look into the gunas. He also said, "What are you waiting for?"

This time, I laughed out loud and said, "Well, I better get to it then."

I didn't go to the common that day for coffee. I went straight back to my apartment to check out gunas and start the process of manifestation. When I thought about Chief, I realized what he had given me were words of wisdom that could only be expressed and understood through his own life's struggles. Seeing his facial expressions as he imparted these profound, yet simple, statements convinced me he was sincere, non-judgmental, and totally neutral. He was simply stating facts others before him had discovered and passing them on as others had for him. My heart was suddenly filled with gratitude and love.

I was caught off guard by this unusual feeling. It was many years ago, at the age of six or seven, and then for the rest of my life, up until now that is, when I had purposefully made a conscious decision to never expose myself to heartache of any kind or let my feelings control me. I had experienced this pain and it was far too much to bear. Over time, I would build a wall around my heart to protect it. A childhood trauma had taught me to never, ever, trust anyone. I had learned firsthand what it was like to have no one cover your back, no one protecting you, no one in your corner. I realized then, as a child, I was **really** on my own, and if I wanted to survive, I would have to be fearless. It was then I decided I would not be bullied or tolerate anyone bullying others. Over time, I developed a reputation through my many trials and just as many errors. I became a loner and was fine looking after myself. I would not let myself down as others had. I carried this loner attitude everywhere I went. I wore it as a shield and it had served me well, I thought. Up until now, my heart protector had kept my feelings at bay. I had survived many challenges I might not have. Life's constant battles had bloodied me, but I had endured.

It then dawned on me in protecting myself from any heartache and emotions coming my way, I was also preventing any love from getting out. It was no wonder I had only acquaintances and not friends. I was keeping everyone out and sadly that meant everyone. I was afraid of being hurt; if I let anyone in, I would be vulnerable to the pain I had experienced early on.

Thinking of this, I felt a sadness come over me. Not moments ago, I was feeling gratitude and love, and now I was overwhelmed with sadness and depression. It suddenly dawned on me, my emotions were what caused my thoughts. If I was in a good mood, I would tune into happy times, and if my mood was bad I wouldn't feel happy. This understanding was profound as I realized it was all about my choice. Again, I was able to see I had a choice on how I felt, and I really was the source of my own joys and sorrows. I couldn't blame anyone or anything for how things were.

THE STRANGER

It was only a few months earlier, while my wife and I were on vacation, that I had met a man while we were out for breakfast. He came over to our table and introduced himself. He knew we were from out of town and came over to welcome us. I thought that odd and my warning signals put me on guard. He mentioned he was a DR in Chinese medicine and had studied there. He had recently studied and was certified in a new modality and offered to give us a healing session using his newly acquired skills. He was practicing his techniques and needed someone new to work on. He went on to explain the fundamentals of this new work. As he talked, I decided, what the heck, nothing ventured, and nothing gained. My wife, on the other hand, decided to not take him up on his offer. He and I set up a tentative appointment for later that day as he handed me a card with his phone number and directions to his clinic. Before opening the door to leave, he asked I call to confirm the appointment.

After he had gone, my wife and I had a little chat. She thought all this was weird, and I agreed. She was very nervous about what had just transpired. Here we were on vacation, far away from home, and of all people, I was trusting a total stranger to do some kind of voodoo on me. I laughed and didn't really have a cute comeback.

We talked some more and decided we needed to check him out. My wife and I walked the beach and several hours later we drove to the clinic, following the directions he had given us, and sure enough, there it was. We spotted his acupuncture clinic located in a neighborhood shopping center. The little shopping mall was home to an outdoor food stand offering fresh produce and fruit, as well as prepared food items and beverages.

As we pulled in to park, I noticed there was also a beauty parlor and nail salon nearby. The outdoor food stand was busy serving people buying goods or ordering meals. The place had a friendly atmosphere and we decided to have something to eat and plan our next move. The young woman serving us had a beautiful smile and welcomed us. She told us we could order when ready, as she pointed to the handwritten menu on the chalkboard over the small counter. We were seated at one of the few tables available and I had to get up to read the neatly printed menu. Our server gave us the time we needed, and after I sat down she returned to the table to take our order. Before I ordered, I asked about the clinic only yards away. She smiled that beautiful smile again as she told us of the many people she knew, including herself, who had been helped by the sessions in the clinic.

My mind was made up at once. I would follow through with the appointment scheduled for later that day. After eating an enjoyable, simple meal, we drove back to relax and enjoy our stay. The hours flew by and, before I knew it, it was time. I showered and changed cloths as I thought about what might be instore. I had to admit, even though everything seemed to be on the up and up, it was still very weird. I arrived a few minutes before the appointment and parked in front of the clinic. I had done what he had asked and called him to confirm the appointment. Nervous, I entered the clinic and noticed a small waiting area and took a seat. Only a few minutes had passed, and I heard people talking as a young lady came out of the room located off the waiting area. I stood as she walked only feet away, and she turned to me and smiled.

She said, "Enjoy the session," as she left the clinic.

Moments later, I was greeted and herded into the treatment room that moments ago the young lady had exited. The "stranger", now a new friend, and I talked for a few minutes and he explained the process used on me. Although a little anxious, I was okay with what was to come. As he treated me, he explained his findings. He found several things he brought to my attention and explained them in a way that made sense. Just before the end of the session, he taught me a simple technique I could use on myself. He had started the session with this technique and now he was showing it to me for future use.

As I got up from the table, I noticed a sense of wellbeing. All this was mindboggling and way beyond my present knowledge. My whole life was either in the Navy, or working for them as a civilian. My philosophy knowledge was nonexistent. I was conditioned to be a survivor, and my every thought and actions were always about not getting picked off.

As I left the healing session, I felt he had touched on things I didn't know or understand. I was a hearing words and holistic jargon for the first time, and it seemed foreign to me. This was all confusing and exciting at the same time. Above all, and although I felt a little scattered, I noticed I continued to feel the positive effects of the session. I felt serenity.

Since being somewhat forced to retire from the Navy Reserves earlier than planned and having an idea of my pending retirement as a civil servant, serenity wasn't in my vocabulary. I was really angry and there was no peace in me. Fortunately, I had nineteen years in the Navy and would receive a pension when I reached sixty. That was a long way off, and the income I earned as a drilling reservist would be gone. That money was put into a savings account for safekeeping. Not that I was making a bundle, but it did add up over the many years.

Funny, I would use those funds for my education learning something very new and a little out there. I didn't know this then and didn't have any idea the "stranger" and his "energy work" would start me on a path I never knew existed. I would be thrown into a world I had not ever envisioned and wasn't prepared for. I would be a student and exposed to "new age" philosophies and concepts that would rock my boat.

BY MYSELF

Now, seven month later, I was on my own. During those seven months, I had decided I needed time to sort out my life. My Navy service had ended, and my civilian career was all but over. All the plans I had put in place were unraveling and there was nothing I could do. Not having control over any of this was causing me emotional turmoil. Never in my life had my mental and emotional state caused me so much pain and anxiety. I needed space and time to myself, as well as a place to concentrate on me instead of the responsibility I had with family and careers. I had to be on my own with no family distractions. I needed to be able to focus on me and *my* stuff. After all, I reasoned, my children were grown with kids of their own. My wife had her work and friends, she was happy, and seemed to be content. I rationalized to myself the house was paid for, we owned our cars, and maybe I wasn't really needed anymore. It dawned on me then I had felt like a fifth wheel for a long time. I *always* felt that way! I never actually fit in and always felt contrary.

For many years, I had thought about moving away. As usual, I would talk myself out of it and stand my ground and never run away. This time was very different though; it felt absolutely necessary and I needed to do this for me. I made my decision, and much to the dismay of everyone involved, I left. I received the cold shoulder from my parents, as well as my wife and children. At the time I thought they were upset I wouldn't be available to help them as I had all along. I later learned everyone was worried about me. Things were changing with me since my surgery. The changes were contrary to my norm, and my wife told me her sister had asked why I was being so selfish. I thought to myself if being true to myself was selfish, so be it. So, I rented an apartment and moved in. Now, on my own and with only my stuff to worry about, I sat at the computer to start learning.

Suddenly, my cellphone rang, and I had to rush about to find it. I very seldom used it; most of the time it was off and sat on the table. It took a few more rings to locate the phone, and when I answered I was taken aback. It was the gentleman who had given me the session while on vacation. He was calling to ask if I wanted to set up a class for him. Little did I know, not only was he a practitioner, he was an instructor. He was offering to teach the first two courses of the nine-course training I was in the process of getting ready to find and attend. He said he needed at least six students to justify the travel and suggested I use the pamphlet and a copy of the book he had given me to help explain the training to possible students. He also suggested I contact the local chiropractors, massage therapists, physical therapist, and acupuncture doctors in the area. Finally, he mentioned if I filled the class with six or more students, I wouldn't have to pay for the training.

After I hung up, the words "What are you waiting for?" echoed in my head as I located the phonebook to make calls. If I could fill his class, it would save me time and money to use for other future training. I suddenly remembered the gunas and smiled. If I wanted to manifest this class and training successfully, it had to be done through the gunas. Then, I thought of the chief and how he helped me that day with only a few words. Funny, no one except him could have gotten away with asking that question. What are you waiting for? Anyone else would have felt my anger and heard my reasons and excuses for not doing it. The chief was holding me accountable. No one else would dare. The respect I had for chiefs went way back to my early days as a young boy with my dad.

Fortunately, my recruit training company commander was an engineman chief, as well. When he learned I was only seventeen years old, he made it a point to keep an eye on me. Looking back, I realized I must have looked like a little boy in uniform at Halloween. Soon, men would surround me on a Navy ship off the coast of Vietnam. Luckily, another chief took me under his wing until I was able to fly by myself.

I may have been the youngest man in Vietnam then. I was a "fireman apprentice", and my duty station was in the bowels of the ship. I was in the boiler room, and in my wildest dreams could never have dreamt of how bad it could be. I would stand watch and write readings down taken from dozens of dials throughout the boiler room. When not taking readings, I would be wire brushing steel deck plates over the bilge. I stood four-hour watches and had four hours in between. During working hours, someone would do the readings and I'd work. I chipped and painted and greased and oiled.

"If it moved, grease it. If it didn't move, paint it," was the motto I'd live by. Those of us who worked in "the hole" were all sleep deprived and in a stupor. Day after day, week after week, on it went.

Meanwhile, on deck, helicopters were flying equipment and supplies to the troops who had just embarked on Amtrak's from our LPD (landing platform dock). We carried hundreds of troops, all their equipment, as well as bullets and band-aides they would need to take the fight to the enemy. I was in another world and seldom went topside. Time didn't allow me to be a spectator. I was on watch, working, or trying to get as much sleep as I could. I'd often skip meals and showers to get the much-needed sleep. This was not what I signed up for.

GIFTS

The week flew by as I finalized the written plan. It included names and phone numbers of possible students who might attend the training. I also practiced a two-minute presentation to give over the phone or in person. I had read the book he had given me and was practicing techniques and learning the jargon associated with this new healthcare modality. The written plan was complete in every detail. The Tamas of the gunas was done. Now was the time to move into the action gunas of Rajas. Even though the weeks were flying by at a record pace, I stuck to my routine. I was a little lax on the eating well part and used the excuse I was just too busy to cook and take out was okay. I always started off with my routine with light stretches before a good meditation. Then, off for my walk. Over the course of the last few weeks, I managed to walk through the woods, down to the playground, to the coffee shop, and finally a little rest at the commons before the trip back.

Sometimes the chief would be there, and sometimes he'd surprise me in the woods. I never really knew where he'd appear next. Often we would sit on the bench at the common or playground. He would ask me about my progress regarding the upcoming classes. Other times, he would tutor me on philosophy and the many religions, as well as the numerous belief systems out there. I realized I had a lot to learn.

I remembered one day after he mentioned how he had changed over the course of many years. I had chirped in telling him of the changes I was trying to make in my life. His reply caught me off guard.

> ***He said, "You cannot change by effort of the will; you cannot change through ideals; you cannot change through building up new habits. Your behavior may change, but you don't. You can only change through awareness and understanding."***
> – *"Awareness" (Anthony de Mellow)*

Little did I know I had been given a real gift with the words of wisdom I had just heard. It seemed every time I met the Chief, he'd always have a gift for me. On several occasions, the chief handed me a book to read.

The books he passed on were always much worn and usually dog-eared with writing on the sometimes torn pages. All the books he gave me were stories that had philosophy intertwined within the story, many quotes, profound statements, and proverbs that would provoke thought. He said one day while handing me a book this one was his favorite. I chuckled and mentioned he had said that same thing about every book he had given me. He smiled and said they all were.

He then stated, "This one is really my favorite of all the books."

After receiving the book, I said, "Awareness," as I read the title out loud.

He said, "Yes, awareness, awareness, and awareness." He firmly, but gently, suggested I might want to read the *Awareness* book at some point. He stated how much it had helped him in his earlier days. After reading *Awareness* and putting the effort in, the book had given him a jump start.

I said, "That's what I need, a jump start."

He looked at me with a firm look that got my immediate attention. He explained:

> ***"It is better not to go to extremes in self-discipline until you have achieved at least some self-awareness or self-realization". If a brittle twig is forcibly bent, it will snap."***
> *(Dan Millman)*

Continuing, he listed the many books that had helped him along the way and expressed there were many more titles he had forgotten. There were also many people, wise people, who had given him good advice throughout his life. He mentioned, most, if not all the books he had given me, were, in fact, gifts. He was genuinely grateful for the gifts. He laughed as he shook his head. Chief then said, "The gifts we receive in our lives come in all shapes and sizes. But, the gift I cherish above all is the gift of hearing, reading, and knowing the truth. 'The truth will set you free.' The truth can be pleasant, as well as be painful to hear, through self-discovery." He went on to say the gift of having the rug pulled out from under him would shake him to his core. Being stubborn would keep us from learning the lesson being presented.

> ***"In seeking wisdom, the first stage is silence, the second stage is listening, the third is remembering, the fourth is practicing, and the fifth is teaching."***
> *(Unknown source)*

Instead of learning from his mistakes and using the consequences as a tool, he would instead punish himself for making the mistake. He used to be a 2X4 guy and said a 2X4 whack usually got his attention. He was a hard learner and at one time had been proud of the fact. Chief leaned back on the bench and sighed.

I looked over and knew our conversation had been very personal and had probably stirred memories for him. I knew it had for me. I identified with everything Chief had said. Even the pride I had for my own stubbornness.

He sat forward and smiled, saying, ***"True to self is loving yourself."*** Loving himself was one of his biggest challenges. He continued, ***"Our big villain is self-condemnation, self-hatred, and self-dissatisfaction."*** Again he smiled, and said, ***"If the heart is unobstructed, the result is love."*** *("Awareness" - Anthony de Mello)*

I certainly understood what he had said and felt a sudden sadness take over. I realized I had made my lessons hard on myself, and never learned the lessons easily. I knew I punished myself, didn't like myself, and certainly didn't love myself. Up until then, I had never seen Chief find fault, criticize, or have any negativity during our discussions. As I pondered this, I understood it wasn't negativity I was hearing; it was the truth about me.

From the very first meeting and future times, he would remind me to always be true to myself. That day, I asked him exactly what he meant by that. So, he explained we had four things we must do every day. We must *meditate*, we need to *exercise*, *eat good food*, and *be in good company*. Then he said something that really caught my attention. He said:

> ***"All of us are the source of our own joys and sorrows, through such choices, our own wealth or poverty, and all we experience."***
> *(Unknown source)*

With that said, the chief abruptly stood, shook my hand, smiled, and said, "See you around."

I walked with him for several yards until he suddenly stopped. Caught off-guard, I continued for a step or two and abruptly turned to him. He had a strange look on his face. His eyes were closed, and I saw a peaceful smile filled with serenity.

The chief then said in almost a whisper,

> ***"In an instant, a life may turn around; a heart may open in a moment of grace. But, preparing for that moment can take a lifetime... Learning can happen quickly. Unlearning takes longer."***
> *"Journey of Socrates" - (Dan Millman)*

He looked like he was in prayer. He seemed to be making a statement and asking for grace as well. A change came over Chief as I looked on. One minute he was serene, and now he seemed lost. It didn't last very long though. Within seconds, he stated, "I am the source of my own joy, so I choose joyous." It was as if a switch had been flipped on. His smile and peaceful look returned and the energy around us actually shifted. Gloom was replaced by serenity and peace.

I stood there for several minutes enjoying the warmth and security I was feeling. He looked over and shrugged his shoulders. He had shown me we do have a choice and that choice was only available when we knew the truth. ***"The truth shall set you free."***

Now, more than ever, I wanted to find the *real* truth, instead of the false truths I was living. I wanted the choice instead of my normal reactionary behavior, and the freedom that comes through *awareness.* I was starting to understand, even if only a little, that choice would only come when my conditioning, programming and belief systems were discovered through **self-observation.** I wanted to be free of them and wanted the full autonomy that came with ***"know thyself".***

More words of wisdom and gifts from Chief. I thanked him and told him how grateful I was for his tutoring and guidance. He said the only way to keep our wisdom was to give it away, and that, was all he was really doing. This was exactly as his teacher and guides had done for him, just as their mentors had done for them.

TO THY OWN SELF BE TRUE

Standing there, trying to absorb what the chief had just said, I watched as he walked away. I had thought my life was well-rounded considering my lengthy military service as well as the thirty-two plus years of government employment. It was evident to me I had missed a lot along the way. Philosophy and religion hadn't been high on my priority list. With all that had occurred over the last several years, my main objective was trying to survive. Not that I was broke or homeless. Compared to many, I was really doing well. I wasn't in debt, my savings for training was there if needed. Except for the permanent side effects of the surgery, my health was decent. I knew I must continue my routine and not skip any of the four things needed. I realized my main priority would be "being true to myself". Without good health mentally, physically, and spiritually, it would be impossible to go forward with my plan.

I suddenly understood what the chief was getting at. It was my responsibility to take care of myself. I was also responsible for how my life unfolded based on my own choices. I couldn't blame anyone for my situation. I couldn't use excuses for not doing what needed to be done by scapegoating others. The ball was in my court and it was up to me to put myself at the top of the list. This new idea was contrary to what I was taught long ago in church, school, and in general. Putting myself first seemed selfish. I remembered that profound statement Chief had made about being responsible for my own joys and sorrows and everything else, and I wondered why I hadn't been taught that.

As I walked the trail back to my apartment, my mind pondered all this. Then my next thought was, today, I would start making phone calls from the list I had compiled. My elevator speech was good. It was short and covered what was being taught, and I had it down. On to action. It was now time to move to Rajas of the gunas.

Shortly after returning to my apartment, I showered and ate a good meal. Afterwards, I sat on my comfortable chair and placed the student list, the pamphlet, and other information I had gathered while doing my research on the coffee table and started my phone calls. All but a few listened to my two-minute speech. Those who politely listened usually asked a few good questions, and I was glad I had done my homework. I didn't stumble or mumble and had good, solid answers to their questions. I then thought this guna stuff was working quite well.

As I continued, there were quite a few people who were somewhat interested and said they'd call me back. I mentioned the class cutoff date and I was looking forward to hearing from them soon. My stomach growled and I remembered I had been on the phone for quite a while and it was time to eat a good meal and maybe go out and stretch my legs. I was becoming aware of the fact I had to be true to myself. This wasn't just a good morning routine and it's done. This true to self-stuff was *all* the time.

Remembering Chief, I thought, *the choices I make will define the life I lead.* I decided to take a short walk downtown, have a decent meal, and then walk back. Maybe I would bump into Chief along the way, or maybe not. I was in a good spot mentally and felt carefree, even though I still had calls to make and speeches to give. I didn't have to worry about that. I was prepared, ready, and covered. Why worry about something until you're doing it?

It was only a short walk until I smelled the aroma of seafood cooking. My stomach growled again and decided now was the time to eat. I followed my nose a little further to a small seafood shack, a fish and chips shanty tucked between warehouses down an alleyway. Up until then, I never knew it even existed. I went through the door as the doorbell rang upon my entering. I looked up at the handwritten menu hanging on the wall behind the counter. My choice! "True to self" rang in my ears and I ordered grilled flounder, a salad, and an ice tea. The meal was delicious and healthy to boot.

I sat for a while before heading back and noticed the anger I usually felt was gone. It seemed I always had a chip on my shoulders. Long ago I figured out I was just an angry person. It seemed I used anger to accomplish just about everything. Whatever the task, I'd feel the anger arise. Sometimes I'd hurt myself working and then I would be angry at myself for the mistake. Other times, I might be angry for having to do whatever it was I was doing. Whatever the motive, the anger always powered me through to complete the task, bloodied or not. Although, not funny, I'd usually wake up angry and then look for a reason to be angry. The best place to justify my anger was driving. It wouldn't take long once I was behind the wheel. Soon, and only a short distance away, someone would not use their turn signals, or maybe they wouldn't let me merge onto the highway. I remember my father and the way he'd swear at other drivers who did just that. Just then it flashed through my mind, I was doing the same as he. Maybe I inherited this behavior from dear old dad. I never understood until recently I was choosing anger over no anger. It was *my choice* and, at this moment, I guess I was choosing not to be angry.

Once back at my place, I started working the phone. It was back to business as I continued calling. I connected to four people who were sold on the spot. I had their information, they had the instructor's email to register, and they had committed to a four-day training with less than a month away. That was five students including myself. I only needed one more student to ensure the class would be taught. Back on the phone, I continued the calls to fill the class. I finished the calls and had nothing concrete for my efforts. There were several who were very interested and promised to let me know. I was a little disappointed I hadn't signed up any more students that day. Funny, it was only hours ago I was celebrating. It was sad how fast I had forgotten my success. I never seemed satisfied even when things turned out well. I had a negative attitude and was pessimistic about everything, especially myself. I remembered my dad again and suddenly realized he had been the same.

CLASS FILLED

I was totally out of steam. I felt as if I had run a marathon and had nothing left in me. I halfheartedly continued making calls to fill the class. Listening to myself on the phone for the few calls, convinced me to stop for the day. I wasn't thinking clearly and or focused like I needed to be. I wasn't present at all. I was in the past and especially the future. I decided to wrap it up for the night and noticed the pile of books Chief had given me laying on the coffee table. I picked up the "Awareness" book I had placed on top. I noticed the cover then immediately felt a peaceful moment. It was a beautiful sunset scene with a tree that reminded me of the bonsai plants I had seen in the gift shop while on vacation. I had been intrigued when I had stumbled upon them months earlier and purchased a beautiful bonsai plant growing out of a rock. I remembered how I painstakingly packed the plant to avoid damage on the long flight back from vacation. I looked over and saw that very plant in the window of my home away from home. I thought it strange how a simple plant could bring me such peace and serenity amid the chaos I knew existed.

Looking at the book again, I noticed a subtitle I hadn't seen before. It said, "The Perils and Opportunities of Reality". Funny I hadn't noticed the subtitle earlier. "Awareness" was what stood out, and now I was being reminded with opportunities came perils as well.

I decided to check my emails and was pleasantly surprised to see several of the folks and possible students I had called had gotten back to me. I also noticed one from our instructor and decided to open his first. He informed me three more people had contacted him directly and were signed up. That was seven not counting myself. He confirmed the class was a go and the more students the merrier. He also surprised me with free tuition for the class. Although he had mentioned it earlier, as class coordinator I was able to attend free and receive a monetary bonus for every student who signed up. Another gift! He went on to say the training site was locked on and I would have to supply six massage tables for the training. He suggested I contact the local massage therapist who had signed up and ask them to bring their tables to the training. The training would start on a Thursday evening with a free presentation and all students must attend. The presentation was open to the public, and after the open presentation was over he would get a jump on the class.

A sudden panic set in as I read on. Fortunately, all the students who had enrolled were aware of the change and everything was okay. Relieved, I opened the other emails from four people who had promised to get back to me. Three of the four had signed up and were aware of the change, and furthermore, all three would bring massage tables for the class. I opened the remaining email from a person I hadn't recognized. I quickly looked at my student list and noticed she was not listed. She asked me to call and had given me her phone number. I sat for a while and felt content. I had managed to fill the class, the venue was close by, and booked.

The remaining three tables still had to be found and for some reason it wasn't concerning me. Enjoying the moment, I reached for the phone and called the remaining possibility. The phone rang several times and was finally picked up. She said hello, then her name. I responded with my name and told her I was calling as requested by her email. After thanking me for the call, she said she was very interested in the class. A massage therapist friend had told her about the upcoming class and she really wanted to attend. She was a reiki practitioner and foot reflexologist. She had heard about this fairly new modality and was impressed with the great results she had heard it was getting.

There was a pause in the conversation, and I thought we had become disconnected. She was facing some financial difficulties and wanted to know if it would be possible for her to pay for the class in installments. She was so sincere and so matter-of-fact. She was simply being honest, and I admired that. I told her it wasn't a decision I could make; she had to call the instructor. I provided her with the contact information and wished her luck. We chatted for a few more minutes. Before ending, she told me she would call him right away. It was all out of my hands and had to be worked out between them. It felt odd not being able to resolve this situation. It wasn't my style, and the chief in me was at odds with reality.

I sat and pondered the challenges in front of me and realized things were okay. I continued thinking to myself. I should take satisfaction in what had been accomplished in a short amount of time. I had filled the class, and any additional students I could pick up would be icing on the cake. I glanced at the book pile. Instead of taking the book on top, I took the one under it. It had a blue feather on the cover and titled "Illusions". It was a thin paperback book and beat up. I wondered, as I held it and looked at the simple feather on the cover, how many people had read it.

The phone startled me back to the present; it was the woman with the money problems I had talked to only an hour earlier. She informed me she had worked everything out. I was happy she was able to sort it all out. She also informed me she would bring her table and see me at the free presentation the evening before the class.

I only needed two more tables and knew where to find one. My sister-in-law had one she had recently bought. Yes, she was the same sister-in-law who thought I was selfish. She agreed to lend it to me and I could pick it up anytime. She never brought up the subject of selfishness during our conversation. I was glad she hadn't mentioned the conversation she had with her sister. I really didn't want to defend my decision to be on my own. It wasn't any of her business anyway, as I felt the anger inside me stir. "My choice," I said out loud, and the anger suddenly disappeared.

Chief had given me a great gift when he told me about my choices in life. I was noticing changes in myself I hadn't intentionally made and realized change happens because of *Awareness* itself. If change is forced, only my behavior would change, I wouldn't.

All these new ideas I had been exposed to lately were helping immensely. I had a positive attitude, a slight smile now, and knew everything would be alright. I remembered chief talking about loving yourself, and although I felt good about myself, I was nowhere near loving myself. I then wondered if I really knew what love was.

With the class filled and less than a dozen calls yet to make, I would take a little break to investigate love. I was going to do this like Chief had taught me. The first thing I would do was look up the actual definition. I'd used the computer and read the definitions, and then compared and came up with one I could identify with and remember. When I wrote things down, it would help me remember. Looking back, I realized I had done this with most of my major plans throughout life. I had manifested my goals using the gunas and hadn't been aware of it.

WHAT IS LOVE

I sat at the computer ready to find out the definition of love. While I waited for the response, I looked at the shelf above the computer screen and noticed a blue paper taped and thumbtacked to the shelf. I noticed the writing was mine and became curious as to what I had written. When I moved in, I had moved the computer stand in and thought I had put everything in the drawers for safekeeping. I wondered how I had missed the only papers that seemed to be left. I sat there for a moment trying to figure out when I wrote them. There were actually two large sticky notes taped together. I had done a good job at hiding the seams. My eyes weren't what they used to be and I had to partially stand to read them. The top note had two quotes written by me. I struggled to remember where I was when I wrote them. I must have thought them important enough to save.

The first quote read:

> ***"Life is what happens while you're busy making other plans."***
> (Unknown source)

The second quote was

> ***"The secret to life is to fall seven times and get up eight times."***
> (Unknown source)

Both quotes made sense to me and were positive affirmations. I was still puzzled with the notes. I used sticky notes all the time and had never bought any color except a pale yellow. As I glanced up to read the second note, I immediately stood. The title of the hand printed note was the word "LOVE" in bold, capital letters. I read the words under the title as I stood with gaping mouth. It said:

> ***"Love is not an emotion. Love describes neutrality, the absence of judgement, censorship, desire, and worry."***
> *(Unknown source)*

Was finding the sticky note just a coincidence when my plan was to define love? What about the blue notes taped and pinned to the side of the shelf? I remembered I had removed everything I had taped to the computer stand and placed it all in the drawer. I even remembered taping the drawer closed for the move. What was happening? Things were really changing for me. There were too many coincidences, one after another. Problems that would normally agitate me were being handled easily. Everything I took on would be resolved in simple ways compared to my usual complicated actions. There seemed to be more order in my life, and my meeting Chief was the only reason I could come up with. He had guided me with a few simple words and the books he had given me. Change was happening, and I wasn't doing it.
Then I heard the chief's words echo in my head.

> ***"You can only change through awareness and understanding."***
> *"Awareness"- (Anthony de Mello)*

I sat and relaxed in my chair as I tried to make sense of what was going on. Although a little confused, I noticed I was calm. I was not fighting everything. My old ways of being contrary about every matter had been replaced by acceptance. I found myself more focused on what is, instead of what was, or what might be. Now, instead of worrying where the love definition came from, I decided to try to understand what it was trying to tell me.

Love wasn't a topic discussed around the water fountain, especially with men. I decided to look at further definitions as I typed the word "love" on the computer.

Love = a strong affection for another arising out of kinship or personal ties; affection based on admiration. These definitions didn't stir me as much as the one I had hand printed. I decided to go with the one I liked. As I read it, I tried to imagine how it applied to loving myself.

I took a break from the computer and decided I needed some fresh air. I felt an urge, a strange urge. I felt a force was pulling me. I remembered this sensation would happen to me, but usually when I was hunting. I would be sitting still, patiently waiting for my quarry to approach and suddenly get an urge to move. The first few times, I put it out of my mind, at least temporarily, that is, until I was forced to move. I had to pay attention to this urge that had me under its control. Many times, I would go along with the whole idea and go where the urge led me. Many times, I would be led to my quarry, the elusive white-tailed deer. Now in my front yard, I knew I had to respond.

After locking up the apartment, I ambled up the street that would take me to the park. I always had a choice to either walk the road to the park or take the shortcut through the woods. Today, I had no choice and was once again being led to take the trail. I took the trail most of the time anyway, so on I went. Another tree had fallen on the trail since my last visit. It was a huge oak, and as I glanced at it I noticed the base of the tree had rotted over the years and finally gave way. It wasn't fun at all as I crawled over the tree. Finally, on the other side, and after dusting myself off a bit, I looked up and there was Chief. He was smiling from ear to ear and I could see he was containing himself from one of his great roars of laughter. He couldn't hold it and let out his famous roar. It took several minutes before he calmed down.

I said to him, "That must have been a pretty sight, me crawling over that tree," and I laughed myself.

The urge that had pulled me here was gone. Looking him straight in the eye, I asked him if he had summoned me.

He looked at me with a smirk and said, "No, you called me."

We walked together for a dozen steps or so until Chief sat on a large tree branch grounded by wind and weather. He had chosen a spot well off the trail and out of anyone's view. I looked around and found a stump calling my name as I sat and took in the view. We sat for a while, and I noticed the sounds of birds chirping. I thought I heard a small animal rustling the leaves behind where I was sitting. I was on alert like always in the forest. Alert not afraid.

Chief broke the silence and asked, "What's up?"

"What do you mean? I called you," I said as I sat there.

He simply stated we were all connected and in tune with each other, and all that was needed was the *awareness* of that connection. Acceptance of the awareness given to us had to be totally accepted before we could make the right choice or proper response.

Although I didn't understand, I knew what Chief said was true. I brought Chief up-to-date on the upcoming presentation and four-day class to follow, and that I wouldn't be seeing him for a few days. He said just because I had a class to attend didn't mean I shouldn't do my routine; being true to self means 24/7.

I must have had a puzzled look, as he said I would have to get up a little earlier that was all. I thought for a moment and agreed with him. I hadn't started the "*Awareness*" book yet and mentioned our last meeting had triggered me to investigate love. What he had said about it being his most difficult challenge had prompted me to look into love.

"Love is a funny topic," he said, "and a serious one as well." When he began observing himself, he noticed how bad he treated himself, and he had been this way all his life. He called himself names and punished himself to the extreme if he failed in any endeavor. Continuing, he said, "How can anyone truly love anyone or anything unless they loved themselves?" He said,

> ***"Our big villain is self-condemnation, self-hatred, and self-dissatisfaction."***
> *"Awareness"- (Anthony de Mello)*

I understood everything he said, and felt a sadness come over me. Chief said when we were true to ourselves, we treat ourselves with kindness instead of punishing ourselves for our mistakes, we learn from them, instead. We put more importance in holding ourselves accountable than in learning our lessons. In doing so, every lesson he was supposed to gain from, he had sabotaged with self-degradation and self-hatred instead. He mentioned it had taken him a long time to finally realize what he had been doing. When we were children, we had been programed; the rules, this programming and conditioning was, in fact, brainwashing, and the belief systems we were subjected to were all lies.

As he continued, I could see the subject was stirring his emotions. He explained, as children, we had been convinced having success or being successful, was the only road to happiness. We were told to help others before we help ourselves, put others in front of us, and that loving yourself was selfish and narcissistic. We were told our happiness was dependent on something outside ourselves.

I identified with his every word and told him so. I asked Chief, "Why? Why would our parents, teachers, clergy, and the other important adults in our lives do that to us?

He smiled and said it wasn't their fault. They thought they were helping us and passing on what had been passed on to them. People had been doing so since the beginning, and we had done the same to our own children, and so on. It would only stop when we became aware of it. The only way forward was to see our programming through self-observation. He paused for a moment before saying it was probably good I hadn't started the *"Awareness"* book; it would be better to put my focus on the upcoming class.

He ended the chat by saying it was funny, yet sad for most people:

> ***"The world as we see it, is but a description. From day one we, have been told, what we see. We label all, and try to label even what we don't see. It is therefore an illusion."***
> *"Illusions"- (Dan Millman)*

I thought for a moment, trying to wrap my head around what Chief had said. I asked him, "What is real then? What is the truth?"

He chucked and responded that I would have to find those answers myself through *self-observation*, and not to get whacky about it. Again, he reminded me

I had a new holistic modality to learn over the next four days. To get the most out of the training, I had to be present and open to what was being taught.

> ***"It's not what we do, it's what we learn along the way. If we are present and focused on our task, we will do it well and with joy."***
> *(Unknown source)*

That said, Chief stood and stretched. I followed suit and thanked him as he walked through the brush towards the trail. He turned and said, "Thanks for what? I didn't do anything."

I heard him laughing as he continued on his way. I didn't bump into or summon the Chief over the following days, although I walked the trails and went to the common. Apparently, he had decided to let me be. He knew from his own experience I had to sort out these questions by myself. I wasn't disappointed not seeing him and instead followed his advice and put all my effort into learning the subject matter and techniques day-by-day.

As I made my way back to my apartment, I thought about how I had been programmed and knew I had done the same to my children. I thought about the way they overreacted to different situations and saw both my kids had inherited beliefs and programming from my wife and I. My son had a lot of exposure with his mom and grandmother early on. I was on active duty in the Navy and would be gone three months and back three months. I was a submariner and once submerged, there would be no contact for two full months while on patrol. My daughter wasn't afforded an opportunity to know her grandmother like my son. There was a fourteen-year age difference, and my wife's mom had dementia and wasn't mentally available. As I observed their behaviors, I saw a huge difference between the two. My daughter had most of my belief systems, where my son had a healthy (or not) mix of his mom's/grand-mom's and mine.

I felt a sadness take over when I realized how my conditioning, programming, and belief systems had impacted my children. I also knew my parents had imparted their preconceived notions onto me, as well as my brothers and sister. I was understanding the cycle went on and on forever, unless something changed. I also knew the only way to end the crazy cycle was through awareness and understanding of the beliefs and conditioning that took our choices away.

SHOWTIME

The presentation and first part of the class were starting that night. Over the course of a few weeks, I had managed to fill the class with nine students, not counting myself. I had talked to the instructor who would arrive late that morning. He had a rental car and drove from the airport to his lodging. I met with him when he called to say he had arrived. The classroom was set up and we had all the massage tables needed. I purchased refreshments for the presentation and was instructed to be sure to have plenty to go around. We didn't know offhand exactly how many would come to the free presentation, so I would be sure to have enough. We could use any leftovers for the classes and nothing would go to waste. Everything was locked and loaded.

I stuck with my daily routine and would think of Chief almost every day. What a kind man he was. I seldom, if ever, saw him angry or even anxious. He was a very humble man as well, and never took any credit for the help or gifts he had given me. Anytime I attempted to offer praise or even thank him, he would stop me and smile.

At every meeting, he would continue to impart his words of wisdom. I was like a sponge absorbing it all with enthusiasm. I kept Chief up-to-date with my life's happenings and what had to be accomplished in the near future.

One time, as I was talking about what I had instore, he stopped me mid-sentence with a raised hand. Chief had only on a few occasions interrupted me and usually let me go on and on. The few times he had stopped me were when something important had to be said. This time, he said, in the gentle voice I had come to admire:

> ***"Just handle what is in front of you now, and the future will take care of itself. Otherwise, you'll spend most of your life wondering which foot you'll use to step off the curb when you're still only halfway there."***
> *(Unknown source)*

He laughed out loud. As usual, I laughed along, even though I knew the joke was on me. He said having any expectation usually led to disappointment, and we usually set ourselves up for it to fail.

I complained and asked how we could ever accomplish anything unless we had a good plan? To make a plan, it would require me to think in the future.

He said plans were necessary and working the gunas from the beginning to the end was required. He said, "Just don't have any expectations on the way it'll turn out." When we did it correctly, it usually turned out much better than we could have planned anyway.

I thought about the class I had just filled and all I had accomplished recently, and I understood exactly what he meant.

The morning flew by, and after meeting the instructor at the bed and breakfast he had rented he offered to do a quick session on me. I felt great and didn't have any health concerns I was aware of and was going to ask for a rain check for a session later. Instead, I said a session would be great. He worked on me for about half hour. He used many different techniques during our session and mentioned soon I would be able to use these same techniques on others. He told me to just relax for a bit and enjoy the after-effects of his work for a while.

I closed my eyes and moments later woke myself up snoring. I apologized and quickly got up. I was a little embarrassed and told him, "That was a first for me."

He smiled and said it happened quite often to his clients after doing deep work, and it would likely happen to me.

Finally, I was heading over to the training site. I had showered and had on decent attire. Lately, it seemed jeans and a T-shirt was what I wore most of the time. Since retiring (early), I didn't need to wear the starched and pressed slack and shirts I had for many years. I had accumulated quite a wardrobe over my lifetime, and because my weight never changed, I kept clothing from year to year. Everything was on hangers and in good shape. Some of the higher quality clothing I had inherited seven years ago. My younger brother, forty-three years old, had died suddenly, and his wife gave the clothing to me shortly after his death. I thought about this because I was wearing a sport coat that had belonged to him.

Present once again, I noticed I was parked in front of the training site; the engine was off, and my hand was opening the door. I got out and walked through the doors, following the signs the staff had placed to guide us to our presentation. I was early as usual. I had a habit of being at least a half hour early for everything. I had developed that behavior during my years in the Navy, and, most of the time, it paid off to be a little early.

As I went into the classroom, I noticed I wasn't alone. There were twenty-five chairs set up with a massage table in the center of the half circle, and at least ten of them were filled with people or their belongings saving their seats. Only one would be attending the class. Everyone else was there for the free presentation. I introduced myself to everyone and sat in a chair I found in the back of the room. I was feeling exceptionally well, and, although I should have been a little excited, I remained calm and found myself at ease. I remembered I had a session earlier and somehow knew it was the reason for my great mood. The folks slowly filled the chairs and I rose to set up a few more just in case.

The instructor entered, went to the front of the room and sat on the massage table smiling all the while. He checked the time and right on the hour he started his presentation. As he explained this new modality, he looked around as he tuned into the audience. He got up from the table and escorted those who had volunteered to be treated up to the table and sit facing the audience. He worked with confidence, and it was obvious, at least to me, he knew his stuff.

The presentation was over now, and everyone was helping themselves to the refreshments we had made available. I saw three attendees talking to the instructor who worked busily on his laptop. I soon discovered those three folks who had come for the presentation had signed up for the class and would be staying on with the rest of us for the start of the class.

The first evening class went well and most attendees had a grasp about the concepts being taught. It was all foreign to me. I was a layman, and not only was the information new, it was difficult for me to comprehend. As was always the case with me, I asked a lot of questions until I fully understood. I made sure what I was learning I could use.

We ended for the night and bid each other farewell. We had twelve students in our class now, not counting myself. I was thinking during the short drive back I was the only one without a holistic background. Everyone else had credentials, practiced their trade on clients, and were comfortable working on vulnerable people, even if they were lying on a table being treated. I decided to watch and learn as much as I could on how to interact with others in this new setting.

The next day I was up bright and early. I had a restless night with thoughts bouncing around in my head. I was tired and a little irritable as I prepared myself for meditation. During my meditation, I noticed I was blaming myself for not getting enough rest. Then, I realized, I didn't have any control over those thoughts that had kept me from sleeping well, and therefore it wasn't my fault and I hadn't done anything wrong. The rest of my meditation went well, and soon I was on my walk. I cut the walk off after a couple miles and decided to head back to eat and shower and get ready for our class.

The first day of our training went by in a flash. We were given our manuals, and we were all biting at the bit. As I sat and gave my full attention to right now, I felt afraid. I was hearing terms new to me and noticed the other students seemed to be taking it all in as familiar. I was afraid to ask questions for fear I'd sound stupid. I saw this going on and pushed myself to at least get a little of my confusion resolved. As the day went on, I became more and more comfortable and understood that, yes, this was new information, and, yes, it was unfamiliar and a little "out there" and just tried to not fight it.

The following three days were filled with concepts and techniques that were odd, to say the least, and, above all, although I didn't fully understand much of it, I was starting to go with the flow and accept it at face value.

After wrapping up the training, our instructor presented us with our certificates. He told us we had to monitor these modules again before certifying, and the cost would be minimal. To certify as a practitioner, there were many practice sessions to do, as well as knowing the techniques by heart. He encouraged us to study what we had learned and to practice the techniques he had taught us. He wanted to return and do another class in four months and was looking forward to certifying anyone who stepped up to the plate. I knew I would be the first to certify from our class and would be ready for anything he threw at me.

Several of my fellow students lived close-by and we would get together to practice our newly learned skills. I took the lead, of course, and always knew I taught what I needed to learn. I put loads of pressure on myself, fine-tuning and memorizing the exploring protocol and procedures used to help bring about balance. I made many calls to our instructor when I got stumped, and he would always clear my confusion.

I started to feel comfortable with myself when working with clients on the table and developed a bedside manner to insure they felt secure. I picked up several clients through word of mouth and used my living room as an office and treatment room. I bought a massage table, sheets, and heating pad for the table. It was okay for now, and I knew eventually I would need a dedicated space out of the house to continue my practice.

DRIVEN

Three weeks later, I was sitting in another classroom filled with eager students. This was another four-day class and I was in New York attending the next two classes. They were being taught by the founder of this relatively new health care system. I had driven down to western New York to a holistic training compound located out in the country. Driving along the winding farm roads through the countryside brought me back to my childhood days and reminded me of home. I had opted to stay in the camping grounds to save a few bucks and be a little distant from everyone else. I liked being alone and most of the time I didn't feel lonely at all.

I had no clue what I was about to learn over the following four days. I was a little relieved and glad to see several men attending the class this time. Besides the instructor, I had been the only other male in our all-female class weeks before. For some reason, that made me feel able to relax. I would soon learn that man would be in the minority, and I might as well accept that fact. The class was illuminating, to say the least. Over the next few days, I would be exposed to philosophy and concepts I'd never heard before.

The first class was an eye opener as we dived into consciousness, beliefs, and the physiology of the five senses. We continued with the "Body, Mind, and Consciousness" and learned balancing techniques to work on the endocrine system, organs, and all the body parts.

Over the next days, we were taught about the Major and Minor Chakra's and were educated on the effect the planets and our solar system had on us. I learned about the Chinese clock and how every organ had a specific time for maximum energy and minimum at the opposite time. We dove into the twelve houses and life cycles. We also learned more techniques for balancing and to help make the techniques from the first two classes more effective. I was impressed with the way our instructor handled the advanced topics.

During one of the classes, the whole idea of control was discussed. Our instructor asked us if we had control of our thoughts. Every action we took was based on a thought, and if we didn't have control over our thoughts, we had no control. I thought for a moment and realized my thoughts came and went and I had no choice what thoughts I had. He then said control was important in feeling safe and secure, and we were brainwashed into thinking we had any control. The control issue and beliefs we had were a driving factor in our own well-being. Most people knew they didn't have control and, as a result, had a negative opinion of themselves. This negativity could lead to health issues and we would come up with this control issue time and time again with our clients. He finished the topic with an interesting statement. He said, only in awareness did we have a choice, and in unawareness our choice was not a choice at all.

During our class, a fellow student mentioned he would be attending the next class in Chicago the following weekend and told me he was a chiropractor. According to the description of the upcoming class, it would be right up his alley. Musculo-Skeletal work as a chiropractor paid the bills. I hadn't been handed my certificates for this class and was already thinking of my next trip. This new information had me in its grips. I wanted more and wanted it now.

I borrowed another student's computer and signed up for the class. I booked flights and was looking for lodging when my new friend the chiropractor offered to share his room since it had two beds and the restaurant offered a free breakfast from its menu. I was sold and now everything was lined up for my next adventure.

I packed my tent and cleaned the camping area. It was in much better condition than when I arrived. As I pulled away, my Bronco made strange noises and wasn't running well. I took a chance and drove off. I was over 200 miles from home and wanted to try to nurse my vehicle onward. No dice! I saw smoke out of my rearview mirror and knew I was in trouble. I limped off the highway at the next exit and coasted down the ramp. Luckily, there was a service station at the bottom and I managed to get the truck off the road and parked.

The transmission was shot. I would either have to wait until the next day for repairs or get a tow. I had coverage and chose the tow. For some reason, I wasn't upset like I would usually be under the circumstances. Instead, I was calm and collected. The tow-truck driver asked how I could remain so calm. I told him, normally, I would have been really angry; maybe the breakdown had prevented an accident up the road. I couldn't believe my own rationale and the words coming out of my mouth. Something in me had shifted for the better, it seemed. I knew I didn't have control over my truck breaking down. I also knew getting upset over the breakdown wouldn't help the matter. With all that was happening, I remained calm. This was not my normal reaction and totally foreign to me.

I talked to the driver all the way home. He was probably happier than I was to finally be there. In talking, I observed I was explaining my recent course and new learning as we drove along. He was interested and asked questions about energy medicine. I fielded his questions as best I could. I wrote down the website and told him he would find good information there. After unloading my Bronco, I slipped him a fifty-dollar bill and thanked him for a great ride. He took the money and smiled, got in his tow-truck and drove away.

I was glad to be back. After resting for a little while, I looked in the phonebook for local transmission repairs and found one I had used before. It was Sunday, and nothing could be started until the following day.

I unloaded the Bronco and loaded the washing machine with laundry from my trip. Usually, I would have done the washing and folding before leaving for home. I had always insisted only clean cloths should go into the suitcase. I had picked up this habit during my extensive travel working for the government. I understood why now as I waited for the machine to finish. I noticed my having patience hadn't been touched yet, and I chuckled to myself while I waited.

OBSESSED WITH LEARNING

With less than a week before my next adventure, I had just finished a great meditation. I was in a very up mood today. I knew by now there would be a 99% chance I'd see Chief if I wanted. He would probably be at the common sitting alone or with one of the few people I would sometimes see him with. He always sat on the same bench in the common and the park as well. He was a creature of habit, I guess, and I was the same. Even though Chief sometimes surprised me by showing up somewhere along the way, I had developed a knowing. I would feel his presence long before I would see him.

There he was at the common, sitting on his bench. Today, he had company. I looked over and saw him talking to a beautiful older woman, someone I didn't recognize, and wondered who she was as I went in for my coffee. There was no line and I was surprised when the coffee tender handed me my coffee just the way I liked it. I paid for my coffee and gave him the change. I usually kept any pocket change for my bank at home. After many months, I would count and fill coin rolls. Funny how change could add up over time. I'd put the rolls of coins in a Hefty bag, and when the bag was full I would drive to the bank on base and get cash in exchange. I always kept that cash for "just in case" money.

As I left the coffee shop and looked over toward the common, I noticed Chief was alone again. I was relieved as I walked over to say hi. He greeted me with a big hug. Over time we had become buddies of a sort. The usual handshake was replaced by a bear hug. At first, I was a little reluctant to be seen hugging another man, and now, for some reason, I actually looked forward to Chief's bear hugs. Slapping each other on the back was like a reunion between long-lost friends. We sat, and I filled him in on what I had learned, where I would be going next, and how long I would be away. He listened as I brought him up-to-date. I told him about some of my problems understanding this new information. He took the time to bring me up to speed. He always went the extra mile until I understood. For some reason, I trusted what he said and took it as the truth. I never doubted him, and this was contrary to my normal ways. He coached me along, explaining the philosophy I had been exposed to, and helped make it understandable. He seemed to know when I was stumped and found ways to help me understand. He would sometimes use funny examples and often make up a story that shone a light on my ignorance. As time went on, Chief eventually learned my deepest, and sometimes darkest, secrets. I knew he could be trusted, so I took the risk.

I informed Chief of my future plans, and that I was excited and seemed to be obsessed with learning. He said he was reminded of how he was when he was first exposed to the holistic world. I was a little fearful and wondered what I was afraid of.

He said,

> ***"Fear is born of the thought of failure when one is attached to success - Anger is born of frustrated desire."***

He continued,

> ***"Fear leads to disappointment, which leads to anger."***
> *(Unknown source)*

Another gift, I thought as I listened. I was impressed with Chief's wisdom and told him so.

He let out a roar that caught me off-guard and said in an unusually loud voice,

"He is a fool who cannot conceal his wisdom."

(Unknown source)

He chuckled and shrugged his shoulders.

I attended the training in Chicago. The first evening was a get-together to meet each other. After a while, the founder started his demonstration of techniques we were going to learn.

Afterwards, I had a session with the founder. He would invite people from the audience to come forward for a session with him. I had caught his attention while he was working on another student and he nodded to my being next. When the time came, I went up and took my place on the massage table. I was shaking like a leaf and almost frantic lying there as he worked on me. It took him quite a while to calm me; he used various Reiki techniques I was unfamiliar with. Finally, when I had calmed down, he stated to the class he was doing newly developed techniques and protocol he hadn't quite finalized. This new work would supercharge the basic courses and techniques we had learned and take it to a new level.

I was one of the very first to have these supercharged techniques done on them, and little did I know what was instore. As he worked, he explained what he was doing. That day, he would find I had, at an early age due to a traumatic experience, blocked my heart to prevent any emotional pain. He said I had spun a cocoon around my heart to prevent myself from feeling heartache. The technique he had developed was being used to open my heart.

He used Kundalini energy to break open the heart protector. It was out of my character and control as I lay shaking on the table. I couldn't stop myself from jerking around. It wasn't an act as I saw myself having some kind of fit. During the treatment, although I had no control of my body, my mind was clear and focused as I listened to him explain what was happening. He remained calm and collected, as if he had done this a million times.

When he said I was done, I lay still for a minute or two before I sat up. I looked around at the people who had been witnesses to the events and noticed some were unsure of what they had seen; some applauded the session.

After I returned to my seat from having this awesome work done, I felt a huge difference. I looked around and felt a connection with everyone there. I felt part of, instead of the indifference I usually felt. I also felt emotional, something I would never dare to feel. Something had definitely occurred while on the table. I would forever be grateful for the founder's help that day.

The next day our training started. Over the course of the next four days, I would learn more techniques and acquire important tools to use on my existing clients. I was practicing what I'd already learned and looked forward to bringing this new information back home to help those who needed them. Again, I was given privy to class information about the final training course I needed to complete. The course would be held in New York, although it would be in the city itself. I remembered the last time I had been in New York City was on my return from Vietnam.

While making arrangements for the final class, I decided I would take a train down to the city and stay at the YMCA. I had gotten a tip from a fellow student that it was very close to the training site, and the lodging was more than adequate.

The flight home was good, and the drive from the airport was uneventful. I was glad to be home. As I walked into my apartment, I noticed I had messages waiting for me. It was three new clients wanting sessions.

The following week went by rather quickly. The final class was on the weekend and two days of training. I saw Chief and filled him in on what I had been taught and what was instore. I told him about the session I had received and the positive results. I was considering going to massage therapy training in Massachusetts. I explained several well-meaning, fellow students and instructors had advised me I would need to have credentials. There were very few layman attending the classes I had completed. Almost everyone had prior training, credentials, and licenses to practice. I had none and wanted to be on the up and up. It was also important for future clients to know I was officially licensed and sanctioned by the state. I also became aware I was weak in anatomy and physiology and knew I had to get up to speed.

Chief said he understood and agreed with my idea. We continued our chat and had a few laughs as we wrapped up our visit. I always came away from our meetings feeling better. This time was no different. As I walked back to my apartment, I felt I was on track.

I had looked in to the various schools in my area that offered massage and found one that stood out. It was located in Salem, Massachusetts. Funny, not that long ago, anyone who spoke of energy work or was a little weird, was burnt at the stake in the very town of Salem. Now, I would go there every day and learn the very thing those people were condemned for.

I took a trial run to Salem later that day to get a feel for the drive. It was an hour and a half drive and all on interstate highways. I had to go through Boston, which always had heavy traffic, accidents, and construction. I found the school and saw it had plenty of parking and a handy restaurant close by. The building was brick and three-stories, and looked like it may have been a mill. New England was famous for the textile industry and there were many old mills remaining. I was glad to see it being used, instead of torn down and another one built.

I decided to give the little eatery a try and was happy I did. They served "Home Cooked" meals and there was always a "Special of the Day" offered. I drove back using a different route to see if it saved me any time. It would save me fifteen minutes, although it was twenty miles longer. This route skirted Boston and the traffic always present. I decided I would drive up using my new route and come home using the old one. At night, Boston traffic was a little lighter, so I would take the chance.

RESPONSIBILITY, AUTHORITY, POWER, & CONTROL

At an early age, I was given huge responsibilities by my dad and mom. Not just making my bed or taking the garbage out, but for the welfare of my younger brothers and baby sister. I didn't choose this responsibility, I was charged with it. At twelve years old, how could I possibly, or successfully, carry this out? How could I accomplish this duty unless I had the authority to do so? How could I manage this situation without the power to carry it out? How could I be successful unless I had control?

I tried my best, and through sheer luck, was able to, at least, keep them out of harm's way. I realized at that age having responsibility without authority or power was useless. There was no reward for taking on the responsibility. The prize of control was the reward I wanted and needed. The proof of this was right in front of me. I would give direction to my younger brothers and they would laugh and do whatever they wanted. I then thought to myself, *I didn't take on this responsibility, it was dumped on me.*

From then on, my focus and major concern would be my little sister. I knew she was unable to take care of herself and I would have to give her my constant attention. She was unable to communicate well because of her deafness; her words were almost impossible to understand. We kids understood her gestures and noises, although no one else would. I never stopped making sure my brothers were fed and somewhat safe. I would do this without being told. I was the oldest and it came with the territory.

Early on, the only thing I achieved by taking on responsibilities was some control. I was bigger than my brothers and could sometimes intimidate them with threats or by rewarding them and buying them off. I always got more than I gave and knew I had a little control of the situation. I was unknowingly building up the belief I was in control, that I had control, and control was a need. Little did I know I was feeding the beast in me. I was cementing in my mind the need to have control and the importance of having control overall.

Everyone wants to be in control over their own lives. In fact, everyone thinks they have control and are in charge.

I thought this way from an early age. I heard adults say, "Get yourself under control or I will," or "You have to control your emotions and behavior. What's wrong with you?"

I would see and hear teachers telling children, "You have to maintain self-control."

Control was something I thought I needed, and if I didn't have it, I was bad or weak. I also heard of how great certain people were with control over this or that and how they were respected for being able to control themselves. On and on it went. Even the church told their members to control their thoughts and actions and how they needed it, and to pray for control.

The need to have control, we were told, was necessary. We were also shown what happened if you didn't, and the price you would pay for losing control. Control was a necessity and expected. We were also taught having control was a priority; we had to have control of ourselves to be safe. Safety and security were only available to us if we were in control. These beliefs and programming, which were handed down from generation to generation, were actually causing us to feel inadequate and promoted guilt, fear, and anxiety for everyone. The idea of controlling others was born and became our goal in life.

As a father, husband, and son, I was told I had control over these important responsibilities and had to live up to them. Anytime I didn't, I would be asked if I had control, and if I did, why wasn't I in control? The answer would be any handy excuse I could come up with. Of course, backpedaling excuses hardly made the grade. Admitting defeat was not the way I operated.

I loved to control what I could and proved to myself repeatedly how well I could. All my life I knew to be in control was the most important job I had. To be successful, control had to be mastered. So, I controlled everything I could and took control away from others to be in charge. I knew and believed I would save the day. Of course, I failed over and over again. With every failure, I punished myself in some way, and then I would look for more ways to control and conquer.

Deep down, I wondered if I really had any control. I felt worthless when I thought this way and would punish myself for even thinking like that. I also needed to control my thoughts. What was wrong with me? Why didn't I have what it took to keep control? Why was I losing control when I wanted and needed it so much?

When I watched men in power, I would see the control they had over others. In the Navy, I witnessed control being exerted everywhere. Officers had control over the enlisted, and high-ranking officers controlled their juniors. In the enlisted community, the chiefs were in control of the men and women under them, and would train officers on leadership and discipline. I wanted that control and knew making rank and climbing the ladder was my way to control.

It's little wonder why I was so obsessed with control. I was taught and groomed and finally achieved a measure of control with each promotion. I was being fed a drug and slowly becoming dependent on it. The drug was control and I wanted more. I *needed* it! Any opportunity to take on more responsibility, I would take on. I wanted power and knew I would not gain power through wealth. I had to work for and earn power as if it was being doled out like money. I didn't have the education necessary for great jobs that paid high wages. I took what I could get and worked my ass off for years before I got the power I wanted through promotions. I attended college and received an associate's degree, and though it took a while to earn, I was paving the way for future opportunities that may present themselves.

I applied for new jobs being offered and worked on my resume and applications. I was eventually selected and was a maintenance foreman with sixty tradesmen working under my direction. I loved being a foreman and was good at my job. I had been in the trades myself and knew what had to be done and how to move forward. I enjoyed visiting the men working under me and spent time everyday seeing the different jobs being started and followed them to the finish. I received promotions, and with each one came power and more control.

As a maintenance foreman, I would plan and schedule jobs needed to be done. All the work orders had been estimated by someone from upstairs and sent to me to complete. I always questioned the amount of time they gave to complete the work. They always seemed to fall short of what was needed. I'd complain, and eventually they agreed to send me to school to learn the ins and outs of estimating work. I really enjoyed the schooling, and from then on knew for sure if the hours on the work order were correct. If not, I'd raise hell and send them to be redone.

I was a real pain in the ass for upper management. The good thing I had going were the facts were on my side. I eventually was promoted to planner and estimator, and then an engineering technician.

My two-year associate degree had finally paid off. It was down to me and another man with almost an identical background. After I was promoted, my new boss told me by going the extra mile to get my associate's, it had been the deciding factor. I never thought I would benefit from a two-year degree. I was wrong and glad my time and efforts were recognized.

More responsibility, more authority, more power, and more control came with each promotion. I also took on extra responsibilities I knew I could handle easily and was rewarded with more power and control. I received monetary rewards and many letters of commendation and appreciation for the results I had gotten in my work. All of these rewards convinced me further of the importance of having control and on it went. I wanted *more*. I was addicted to control and loved how it made me feel. I was important and needed, ask anyone. Sadly, I needed people to tell me I was good. I didn't feel it myself. I always had a nagging issue with self-worth, and now I was getting it from others. I needed their praise.

As my responsibilities grew, so did my importance to my employer. I knew I was needed and felt great being important. I needed them, and they needed me. It sounded good and the game went on. I had no idea of the monster forming in me. I had no idea I would have to feed this monster and tend to its needs, *all* the time.

SELF-IMPORTANCE

Little did I know then those hard realizations about control would set in motion the lifelong task of making myself important, in any way I could. I would have to maintain the self-importance by acting important and being needed by others. I took on responsibilities to show my importance and lived up to them. I only had people in my life as long as I was getting what I wanted. If they stood up to me or showed me any disrespect, *poof*, they were gone. I was very cunning in my ability to convince others to let me help them, and, as a result, I gained power over them. I made myself important to them and demanded the courtesy and respect I thought my importance deserved.

When I was an employee, I always stood out from others, and made sure I did. I stepped up and took on more responsibility, then proved I could handle it and carry them through to completion. I gained a reputation as someone you could count on. Although I had to follow through, I knew it would be worth it overall. I looked for ways to get ahead, and slowly climbed the ladder to gain leadership roles in the Navy and was promoted throughout my civilian career. More money, more power, more control was my goal.

This was all happening, and yet I still felt I needed to be more important. I was totally unaware what was happening. I didn't know I was holding people in my life hostage. I needed them to tell me I was good because I didn't feel I was. I needed to keep certain folks in my life for compliments and respect. I always received more than I gave. It was all about me.

This constant need for positive feedback was tiring. It was a fulltime job to maintain my self-importance and required me to always be on my toes and look like a man with a mission. Over time, and as a result of my constant anxiety, I started to drink to get relief. Before long, booze had me in its grip, and my drinking was no longer under my control, it never was. How could I let this happen to me? I thought I was in control. I thought I had everything handled. Alcohol was running the show; the more I drank the more I lost control. Now I knew, deep down, I was wrong, even when I was right. This self-importance and control I so needed was a thorn in my side as I took on more responsibilities and made myself more important.

> ***"I was so damned important in my own mind, I felt justified to be annoyed with everything. I was so important I could afford to leave if things didn't go my way."***
> *(Carlos Castaneda)*

I would get upset having to wait in line at the bank, shopping, or even during a doctor's visit. Why did I have to wait? Didn't they know who I am, and how important a person I am? If it wasn't all about me, all the time, I would get angry and lash out at anyone who didn't recognize my important role. I demanded respect, and if I didn't get it, there would be hell to pay. I dismissed anyone who questioned my abilities and look for someone new to need me.

RECOVERY?

My life was falling apart. Those who knew me well, saw I was spiraling downwards. The buzzards were circling overhead and I was going down the drain. I was drinking around the clock. I started every day with a couple beers to get my heart started and carried a full cooler. When the need arose, I quenched it. Very few of the people I worked with knew how badly off I was. I had to be better than average to pull it off while hiding what was really going on.

I was damn good as an air-conditioning mechanic and solved problems others couldn't. I *had* to be great to take the heat off my boozing.

The years went by slowly back then. Every single day I had to put on my show, and every day I saw how much of a fake I'd become. This made the drinking worse and more needed. One day, in a moment of clarity, I suddenly realized I needed help. I knew I was an alcoholic and I couldn't quit on my own. Admitting defeat was not easy for me and probably the reason I drank for as long as I did.

I came home and was well lit. The night before I had been out after work and blacked out early in the evening. I was in no condition to drive, but drove anyway. I remembered hitting something and drove on. The next day I woke up hungover and needing a drink badly. After showering and getting ready for work, I remembered hitting something the night before. I went out and looked at the dent on the front fender and couldn't remember what I had hit. Driving to work, I heard on the radio there had been a hit and run and they were looking for the driver. A panic set over me and, when I arrived at work, I carefully inspected my van. I was a wreck thinking I had been the driver they were looking for.

Shortly after noon, the news on the radio said the driver had been apprehended. *Whew*, I was off the hook. But not really. My drinking was taking me down the same road as it had with my mom. I drove home and my mind was racing. Once home, I sat in my recliner with my cooler only inches away. I watched TV and drank. I was consumed with the fact I couldn't remember what I had hit the previous evening.

A commercial came on advertising a brand-new alcohol rehabilitation facility. It had only been open for about six months, and they were offering help. One of my buddies had gone and he had quit drinking and seemed happy. He was a whisky drinker and could put them away. I thought he was much worse off than me and thought if he could do it, maybe I could too. I called out to my wife and asked her to call the rehab and see if they could take me. I had no sick leave and didn't have much vacation time. I knew I would have to miss work for thirty days and was worried about taking that much time without a paycheck. My wife came out after making the call and said they had a bed available and to come right over.

With my wife driving, I was on my way to a rehab. At one point while we were trying to find it I said, "Let's wait until tomorrow."

My wife knew if she didn't get me in that night chances were I wouldn't ever sober up. With directions from a homeowner, we were guided to the rehab. The intake nurse asked me how much I drank daily, and my wife chirped in saying, "He drinks a couple six-packs."

The nurse asked the question again, and I told her I was drinking one and a half cases of beer every day, and more on weekends. My wife was floored when she heard the truth about my daily consumption. I guess I had fooled everyone, everyone but me. I spent thirty days in the rehab, and after I was detoxed from the booze for five days, I joined other men and woman learning how to live without alcohol calling the shots. Fortunately, my employer had advanced me the sick leave I needed and said, once back at work, I could repay it over time.

After my time in the rehab, I joined a fellowship of folks who had the common goal of recovery. During my stay and education on addiction and alcoholism, I was somehow convinced alcohol was my problem, and if I didn't drink, I would be alright. To this day, I believe in every cell of my body that this fact was absolutely true, and I haven't touched a drop. I thought my problems were over, and everything would be fine.

Although I had quit drinking, I hadn't changed. I tried to be different from how I was when I drank. The more I tried, the more I failed. Of course, I punished myself for my failures. I could no longer blame the booze for my wrong actions. I had no credible excuse anymore. I might have been worse now than when I drank. The guilt I felt along with the constant fear I had was looking for relief.

I managed to not drink during those first few years, despite doing everything else wrong. Not drinking was my goal. It was a miracle I didn't drink. White knuckle sobriety allowed me to continue with my pursuit for self-importance and control. Up the ladder I went, and on went my game of self-importance, responsibility, authority, power, and control.

Even after accumulating many years of sobriety, I continued to have this drive pushing me to be important. I had gotten into the habit of attending certain meetings where I was respected. It had become routine for me. I thought developing good habits might help me change. I was meditating once a week in a group setting and exercising regularly.

One day, while reading, I stumbled across a couple sentences that triggered me. I read:

> ***"Habits are negative even though sometimes good. We must be inspired in what we do, this is the positive way."***
> *"Awareness" - (Anthony de Mello)*

That's exactly what I wanted. I wanted inspiration to guide me, instead of habits. I thought to myself and realized very few of my life's actions were inspired; they were all reactionary. I also understood habits may be good, although negative. The idea of being inspired in some way would make the task at hand something I wanted to do instead of forcing myself through habit. This whole concept of being inspired was very appealing to me. Instead of forcing myself to drudgingly complete my routine, I would want to do it. Instead of pushing myself, I would be enthusiastic instead.

Only when I faced my biggest challenge, my own health problems, would I be open to what would come next. I eventually met people along the way who offered me a way out. I started taking the advice of those few I somewhat trusted. I began by reading enlightening types of books on "The Power of Now", "The Secret", "Beyond Concepts", "Who am I", and "The New Earth". I looked deeply in to *Vedanta* and discovered the different yoga used for enlightenment. I listened to speakers talking about happiness and started practicing meditation. I now had a little understanding of philosophy with much to learn. I was still whacky as a bed bug. Only after learning to meditate did I make any headway toward stillness. It took many books and then reading them again, and again before I started to understand what they were all saying. ***"Know thyself."***

Funny, I already know myself, I thought. I am Stephen; I am a man and husband, a father, a son, a brother, an uncle, an engineering technician, a chief. What else is there to know?

I realized I was being sarcastic, even to myself. All the literature and philosophy I had read was making *knowing myself* something very different from what I thought. I thought it may be time to find the truth behind this *know thyself*. It was time to find Chief and pick his brain. We had talked about the subject off and on and I knew he was speaking the truth when he said, ***"Knowing self is imperative if you want to be free."*** He said, until we dug in to find what made us tick, we were not free. All our actions were kneejerk reactions based on faulty programming. Some of this conditioning we received may have helped us along the way, but it was time to "act" instead of "react". When we did the inside job, we would be convinced through self-observation we were really puppets on a string and not free at all.

His example was, someone says something to you, immediately it triggers an emotion, which triggers our reaction. No thinking at all. You're not making a choice, not thinking it through, just reacting.

Chief was really fired up as he continued,

> ***"Nothing is more terrible than seeing ignorance in action."***
> - *"Goethe"*

He laughed before singing "Amazing Grace". I loved that song when I understood it was written for me. I was indeed a wretch and totally lost.

I remembered a Johnny Depp movie where Keith Richards of The Rolling Stones was a pirate and said, ***"It's not about living, it's about living with yourself."***

I realized living with myself was the problem. The guilt and fear I had was eating me alive, and I had to look at and understand it. Only then would change occur.

I was sober and still had no clue of what was needed. This idea of *knowing myself* was rattling around in my head and needed resolution. I listened to Chief talk about the way he had uncovered the deep, dark secrets he had buried within himself and saw he had made huge gains according to his conversation. I wanted to have a little of the peace he seemed to always have. He was very calm, even when it was hitting the fan all around us. He seemed to have a way of not letting the fray touch him. Chief was non-judgmental, always. He was living in acceptance when I was fighting every battle being presented. I wanted to have the freedom I saw in Chief. He allowed others to be free and kept himself free as well. I wanted that and decided to do whatever it took to obtain real autonomy and be free at last. It was now time to do the inside job and be thorough when I did. I knew my only way to the freedom I saw in Chief was to dive in, head first, and take the risk involved in introspection.

SELF-OBSERVATION

I was starting to feel I was depending on Chief to guide me a little too much. I wasn't used to having any help at all. I always kept my personal problems or questions to myself. Sometimes not knowing how to proceed actually prevented me from getting started. I looked back and saw I had not taken on certain tasks because I didn't feel smart or educated enough. I was starting to realize in refusing help and guidance along the way, I became stuck and unable to go forward. All these thoughts were overwhelming me. As much as I knew I needed some guidance, and all of us could use some help from time to time, my pride was getting in the way. I wanted to stand out and impress others. I wanted everyone to know I was "the man". Self-importance was at it again.

I walked the trail leading to the park and saw Chief's bench empty. I felt a panic arise. I continued to the common and empty bench where Chief usually sat. My gut was rolling, and I felt sick to the stomach. I took a few deep breaths and became aware I wasn't breathing fully. I was a mess and didn't know what to do. I decided to get a coffee and went into the shop.

The coffee shop was packed that day, so I took a spot in line to wait my turn. The atmosphere was a little chaotic and after waiting for what seemed a long time, I was finally served. I paid the cashier and left the shop hoping to see Chief sitting on his bench. He wasn't there. I felt devastated and disappointed. I needed Chief's guidance and his calming energy.

I didn't bother to sit and wait that day. I was feeling lost and helpless anyway. I slowly walked on, almost in a stupor towards my apartment. I entered the park and the bench was still empty. I took to the trail and had given up on seeing Chief. I unconsciously continued walking and felt a sadness that forced me to stop. I looked around and made sure I was alone before I let the tears flow. I felt guilty about crying because, "*Boys don't cry.*" As soon as this thought entered my head, another thought suddenly appeared. *It's okay to cry,* and cry I did.

It took a long while before I was able to finish my emotional release, and I remembered how long it had been since I last cried. I was just a little boy then and remember sobbing like now. After a few more minutes, I was done. I felt embarrassed even with no one around. I also felt some relief as well. I slowly stood and continued up the trail to the pavement of the street leading to my apartment. I definitely felt a lot better. I said out loud, "Wow, that's a crazy belief about not being allowed to cry." I now understood how the crazy belief of "*boys don't cry*" had hurt me more than it had helped. I also realized how it had prevented me from letting go.

I slowly walked on and took a left on to the drive that led to my apartment. I looked down towards the house and saw Chief sitting on my front steps. On one hand, I was relieved to see him sitting there, and on the other wondered how he knew where I lived. He remained sitting there, comfortable by his appearance. I approached him, hand extended, and he grabbed it and stood asking for a little pull to help him up. Once up, he put both arms around me for his usual bear hug. I hugged him back almost as hard and felt the need to prolong the contact than quick hugs of the past. Chief and I both must have needed the extra time.

I explained I had been looking for him and asked how he knew where I lived. He said he had seen me move in months ago, and he had noticed the chief's sticker on the windshield of my truck. He had met my nephew who helped me move in. He had found a blue note, actually two notes, taped together on the ground. He gave them to my nephew who then pinned them on the edge of the shelf on my computer stand.

Finally, at last, the mystery was solved. I had racked my brain trying to figure out the blue sticky note mystery. He chuckled a little before he laughed.

I invited him in my apartment and offered him coffee, tea, or water, and he took the latter. I joined him and we both finished our glasses. I refilled both and told him why I was looking for his guidance. I asked him where to begin in *knowing myself.* I also mentioned the uncontrollable bout with crying I had just before seeing him.

He had seen my eyes were red and knew I had been crying. He used to have a heck of a time letting himself cry as well, and his conditioning had prevented him from crying until he realized it was just a belief system. He said, "'Boys don't cry; men don't cry' is one of many lies we have been programmed to believe. Everyone has this belief, especially males."

I was stunned. Only moments ago, I had come to the same realization. I told him I just had this understanding, myself. Chief commented on the book pile on the coffee table. He laughed and said his own coffee table was free of books. He noticed a brochure I used as a bookmarker and asked if he could take a look. I said of course, and he read the front page out loud:

> ***"Break Through...From Becoming to Being."***
> *– "Breakthrough" – (Esther Veltheim)*

He looked over and smiled as he read the brochure thoroughly as I looked on. He re-read the entire brochure again, held his gaze on the photograph, and said, "This might be the class that may help clear up some of your questions." He handed me the brochure and I read it over. The developer of this system had summed up the training goals of the class well.

I looked over to Chief and said, "I'm sold!" It seemed to be exactly what I needed to help me understand.

Chief then took the "*Awareness*" book off the pile and waved it in front of me, saying this class would help make it easier to understand this book. He knew I had a lot on my plate and had been just like me. He had also felt obsessed when he first discovered there were new possibilities he hadn't known existed.

MORE TRAINING...DAMN!

I sat in the classroom in New York City. I had checked into the YMCA and was okay with the sparse furnishings in the room I was given. It reminded me of the single rooms on the Navy bases time and time again. The training site was within walking distance and I took notice of the many eating establishments along the route. I looked around the classroom in time to see the founder walk in. He was accompanied by his wife, and after a few moments he introduced her to our class. I recognized her from her photograph on the *BreakThrough* pamphlet I had read when Chief was at the apartment.

She sat in the back of the classroom as the training began. Again, this training was new to me. New terms and jargon, and the feeling I was out of my league. It took a while to settle and soon I was taking in this new information and starting to obtain at least a basic understanding.

Our lunchbreak was announced and we all headed outside to one of the many restaurants close by. I followed the crowd and noticed the founder and his wife had gone in to a deli and decided to follow. I got in line and ordered a meal from the handwritten menu on a white board. After the server handed me my food, I continued to the cashier to pay. I looked around and saw there were few, if any, tables unoccupied. I usually sat by myself if possible. I also always had my back to a wall and a clear view of my surroundings. Old habits would keep me on guard.

The founder's wife spotted me and waved for me to come over to their table. I smiled and nodded as I walked over and took a seat. I introduced myself, and we talked about small stuff as we ate. I mentioned I was very interested in the *BreakThrough* class she had developed, and she described the teachings in more detail. I decided then and there I would attend her next class. Most of her classes were being taught in Florida. She also traveled to wherever needed if the class was large enough to make it worthwhile. I enjoyed our conversation very much. I told her I was planning to attend her class very soon, as it had been highly recommended by my friend, Chief.

Back in class, we continued on and I was like a sponge soaking up this new information. We discussed matrixes and how our life experiences and active memories were stored in matrixes for access. At least for now, that was my understanding. We finished the class practicing new techniques and procedures. The founder informed us he was finalizing his new supercharged training and soon the class manuals would be ready.

He informed us the class would be taught in New York and at the holistic site where he had taught before. It was a must class for all the instructors and would be open to everyone else by the next day. The prerequisite to attend was to have completed all the classes, which I had just done. Another requirement was the founder would make the final decision on who attended. He based his decision on more than course completion. He handpicked class attendees on his own intuition and from seeing them in classes.

Just when I thought I was trained up, four more days of training were added. I was a little upset and wondered if this adding of more and more training would be a fact of life. The courses were expensive, and with every class came travel as well as lodging, meals, and transportation. I knew by now holistic healthcare didn't pay much, at least in my area. It would take a long time, if ever, to recoup the money I had spent.

Suddenly, I remembered the session I had received not long ago from the founder. There was no doubt in my mind I would attend that training. I felt like a juggler trying to keep twenty balls in the air without dropping any. I realized massage school was not that far off from starting. I wanted to attend *BreakThrough*, and the new course as well. After the class wrapped and we were given our certificates, I managed to pull our instructor aside to ask questions about the upcoming course. I wanted to know if he thought I was ready for the training, or pushing it by attending this soon. Surprisingly, his wife joined in the conversation and she thought I was definitely ready. I was a little shocked and jokingly said she had more confidence in me than I did. We laughed and her husband agreed with his wife. I casually asked if she had considered teaching a *BreakThrough* class either before or after the New York class. Ironically, she had and it would be taught before the founder's "new class".

Two birds with one stone, I thought. I also felt a little panic. I had a lot on my plate for sure. I made my way home on the train and had time to think things through. I knew what I had to do. Once home, I would start the process of planning. I relaxed a little and heard music playing. It was on the speakers and had been on the whole time. I was now aware of it and listened to Bob Marley singing,

"Don't worry, about a thing, cause every little thing's, gonna be alright."

I joined in singing softly and smiling.

I went online and signed up for both classes. I checked my bank account and was glad to see I was still decent, moneywise. I would start massage training and be able to attend the other training as well. I might miss one or two days of massage training, which I could make up at night classes. I was attending fulltime days and would drive up and back every day.

Things seemed to be going my way lately. I took some credit for how my attitude was changing by giving credit for new awareness. I knew I was in the equation, and through awareness and understanding, I was able to make better choices and wasn't over-reacting nearly as much.

BREAKTHROUGH

"EVERYTHING THAT MAKES US WHO WE ARE IS PRIMITIVE AND AN OBSTACLE TO OVERCOME."

(Unknown source)

The *BreakThrough* class started in the morning. I had just finished a great breakfast and sat with other students attending the class. The setting for the training was excellent. We were in New York, although in the country instead of the city. The community who lived there grew their own fruit and produce and the menu was vegetarian. The food was awesome and I didn't realize this healthy way was so tasty. I hadn't ever been exposed to a diet like this and was very pleased at the taste and variety they offered.

As time drew near to start the training, we casually walked from the dining hall down the paths leading to our classroom. As we approached, I spotted our instructor talking to several other attendees. Everyone seemed to be excited about starting the class, and as I entered I noticed several people sitting quietly meditating. I didn't want to disturb their serenity, so I quietly tiptoed to a seat. It wasn't exactly the seat I would have chosen. The chairs were set up in the center of the room in a semicircle. There was no seating available where I could have my back to the wall, and that made be a little nervous. I thought about this and realized my way of thinking was purely self-protection and survival.

Here I was, in a tranquil setting, and I still had a drive dictating my every move. Even without thinking, my choices were not a choice at all. The choice was made before I had a chance to think it through. I knew I was in the right place to figure this out, and taking a class to learn how my programming was affecting my life. As I looked around, I saw everyone had been seated and discussions between students went on in small groups. I was the only male attending, again.

The energy in the room was a little weird, and I felt like the odd man out. I thought I had become used to this situation by now. Almost every class I had attended was mostly woman and it disrupted me a little being the only guy. I felt fear and couldn't understand what was actually going on. Maybe my role as a man was coming into play. I looked around again and noticed a table was set up with coffee, tea, water, and fruit and decided I needed a coffee to get my mind off my thoughts. I took a sip and enjoyed the flavor and the aromas it produced when our instructor entered the room.

You could have heard a pin drop as the anticipation we all had to start the class. After a few moments, our instructor welcomed us to her training. She told us a little about herself and asked we all do the same. One by one, we all took our turns saying our names and where we were from, as well as a little background information about ourselves. Everyone so far had seemed relaxed and a little giddy. My turn came, and I filled them in on my background and training so far. All eyes were on me and I really felt alone. Even with twenty-three fellow students sitting all around me, I didn't feel part of the group, and my defenses were up and scanning. I couldn't understand why I was so worked up. Something inside me took over and I felt the need to be on guard.

The morning class went by quickly, and eventually I started to relax. Our instructor was awesome. She was very comfortable with the subject matter, and it was obvious to me she was well learned. We were being taught how our programming, conditioning, and beliefs were running the show. As long as that was happening, we were being controlled and not free to choose for ourselves. When we were children, our heads had been filled with false notions and living this way was reactive, not responsive. Almost every decision was a knee jerk move, and most of the time a wrong choice. Children were like little sponges, sucking up information and believing everything to be true. After all, to us, grown-ups were gods. We believed them without question and followed the rules and laws they put forth.

We broke for lunch and I was a little off. I was sad and angry when I realized almost every choice I had ever made wasn't mine at all. They were my dad's choices, my mom's choices, uncles', aunts', teachers', and clergy's, everyone's except mine. Every action and choice was tainted. Why didn't I know this was going on? I felt stupid and ignorant as well as depressed. Even in feeling this way, I managed to pick up a lot of new information.

The morning flew by and it was now time for lunch. I chose a seat with my back to the wall as I ate by myself. I looked around and the mood seemed different for everyone else. They were chatting away with each other and laughing and enjoying themselves while I was distant and on my own. This caused me to see myself as I usually was, a loner, and okay with it. At least that was what I wanted everyone to see. What I actually felt was not independence as my choice, but fear and my reaction to it. What the hell was I afraid of? I was in an all-woman class, so what was my fear?

Back in class, we continued learning the techniques that would enable us to help uncover the belief systems and programming we had in us. I watched as our instructor worked on a student; she was so tuned into the process. By the end of the day, she had completed working on half the class with *Break-Through* sessions. She made it look so easy and carefree and at ease doing her important work. I was impressed and started to understand her teachings.

We finished for the day. As I walked out, I saw and heard several women at a table having an animated conversation. They were laughing and enjoying themselves immensely. Not trying to listen, but managed to overhear the words, "inner child." Immediately, something in me snapped. I thought they were talking about me. I felt "on alert" and I noticed my defenses go up. For some reason, those words had triggered the thought, *There's no child in me; I'm all man. Period!* I quickly walked out and headed to my dorm room.

Wow, it hit me then. I had witnessed my over-reactionary behavior first-hand. I, without a doubt, understood a major belief system in me had been triggered by those simple words. I had been taught about this very thing only hours ago and saw it unfold before my eyes. It blew me away for several minutes and shook me to the core.

I remembered Chief and a conversation we had not long ago. He and I were talking about truth. He said, "The truth will set you free," and explained truth didn't need defending. The truth was the truth. We knew the truth and it would be silly to want to defend it. If we were defending anything, it was our belief systems. We were standing up and defending a lie we had been programmed to believe to be true.

I thought I had understood what he meant, but obviously needed the rug yanked out from under me to finally get it. My past flashed before me, and I was seeing how that simple statement, "Boys don't cry," had impacted me; it had starting before I could actually remember.

I was stunned and felt a little shaken as I slowly walked toward the little wooden bridge that covered a small stream that wound through the holistic village. Many folks lived and worked there, and their community was close-knit. As I approached, I saw my instructor "Lady BreakThrough" talking to her husband "The Founder". *I could go around and take another route*, I thought as I slowly proceeded. Lady Breakthrough turned toward me and gestured to join them.

I walked up and smiled and knew I was forcing it. We chatted for a few minutes before Lady BreakThrough said to her husband she would join him later and told him "we", meaning her and I, needed to talk. I was caught off-guard and looked his way. I simply shrugged my shoulders and gave him a questioned look. He mirrored my gestures and walked away laughing. Lady BreakThrough took my arm and asked me to join her for a walk.

After walking in silence for a ways, she pointed to a bench and asked if we could sit down and talk. I agreed and we sat there together for a moment or two taking in the view. There was a small pond with a few swimmers out on a raft. I could see the water was too shallow around the pond to swim and probably had a muddy bottom loaded with weeds. *A good place for fish*, I thought. Lady BreakThrough asked if I was understanding her class and wondered if I had any questions she could help me with.

I saw the opportunity clearly and noticed I was relaxed. I told her of the experience and reaction I had been made aware of and how it had rocked me. Then I told her a little about myself. I didn't go into the gory details I had with Chief though. I felt I didn't have to. I knew I was telling her everything she needed to understand, where I was coming from. I knew our conversation was for us only and she could be trusted with my little secrets. I did most of the talking, as usual. I noticed in class, as well as now, when she listened to anyone she really gave her total attention. It felt good, and I remembered I had felt the same way when I was with Chief.

She did a *BreakThrough* session on me that afternoon. It wasn't her typical technique, as she asked me questions and I responded. I noticed my gut was settling a bit. I was calm when I answered her questions and felt I was honest.

Lady BreakThrough stopped suddenly and said I was a very difficult case. Over the course of my life, I had found many ways of protecting myself from, not just physical harm, but had succeeded in keeping my emotions at bay. She wrapped up by saying I had become a *master coper* and it would be almost impossible for anyone to do a full *BreakThrough* session, like the other students had received.

I was surprised at her comment and worried. I knew I was loaded with belief systems and programming causing me difficulties and I wanted to be able to discover and address them. Master Coper was now a new title I had been given.

We sat together for a while longer, and I eventually I made the first move and stood. Lady BreakThrough stood as well and arm and arm we walked back to the bridge. I was a little confused and wondered if my master coper could ever be penetrated. She told me not to worry, as she had been a master coper herself. Even though it may be a drawback, she knew, from her own experience, I, and only I, could make the breakthrough I needed. It would be difficult, although not impossible for me to find relief.

As I listened and saw her in action, I knew she was a power of example for me to remember. She was or had been in the same boat as me. Her kind words and the patience she had given me rang true. Although my inside job would be tough, I had to go forward. I knew the inside work would free me.

I slept like a log that evening. As I woke, I felt refreshed and invigorated. I did my meditation, took a walk, and after a good hot shower walked my way to the mess hall for breakfast. The place was noisy that morning, and after I filled my plate with great smelling food, I found a vacant table and sat by myself as usual. It wasn't long before Lady BreakThrough and her husband the founder asked to join me. I said sure and we made small talk as we ate. Not a word was mentioned in regard to the afternoon meeting or what had happened. I was happy it didn't come up as I was avoiding it like the plague.

Back in class, we continued learning and refining our *BreakThrough* techniques. Our instructor finished doing sessions on our class. I was the only one who didn't receive a session during class. One of the students noted this and asked why I hadn't been given the opportunity like the others. Lady BreakThrough explained she and I had done *BreakThrough* on me in private the day before and dropped the conversation before it started. I felt a little odd and at the same time a little special. The class would be finished soon and most of the students would soon be leaving. There were only a couple of us who'd attend the founder's new class, and Lady BreakThrough would be staying on with her husband.

I had made many discoveries about myself during my training and wanted to put it aside for a while before starting the new class the following day. I didn't want my mind loaded, but to make a fresh start. I knew I needed to be up and running if I wanted to understand and learn from the founder. Although I knew I was a little off because of my *BreakThrough* discoveries, I knew I was on track.

The founder's class was a real eye-opener. It took everything I had learned to the quantum level, literally. More new words and philosophy were finding their way into my orbit. Techniques using energies and "Mandalas" were all Neptunian to me.

I was wound tighter than a drum and thought, instead of worrying, I would let myself go, listen, and hopefully, learn. I had finally surrendered. The overwhelming talking and questions rattling around in my head just stopped. I was totally present and had an awareness filled with neutrality. Immediately, I thought of the *BreakThrough* and my Chicago sessions. Maybe my heart protector, the cocoon, was unraveling a little. I wasn't on-guard and felt serenity as I listened to the founder as he talked about Kundalini Energy. I didn't question it and listened intently.

The class wrapped up with a few sessions on the students attending. The majority of the attendees were instructors who taught the many classes being held worldwide. I was a little intimidated until I realized we were all in the same boat. This was new and all of us were hearing it for the first time.

The next day we continued learning new charts, procedures, and protocols for exploring deeper. I knew I would have to work hard once I got back and was glad I had a small clientele as well as family and a few fiends to practice my new work on. We finished the class shortly before lunch, and as we sat in the dining hall eating a great meal, I felt okay. As I finished my meal, I remembered something Lady BreakThrough said as we were walking. She said, ***"It's risky business when a man shows his gentle side and only a few see it."*** *(Unknown source)* I had found a gentler side of myself I had never knew existed.

Now, I had an option: either take a chance and risk heartache or continue to shut my heart and suffer the consequences. I was feeling a new strength inside and wanted to make the decision to take the risk. On the other hand, if my gentle side wasn't noticed, maybe my beliefs on what gentle really meant was gentle to me and to no one else.

Did I even have a gentle side? All my life I believed I had a very gentle, and nice side of me. I saw myself being kind, caring, and nurturing. I looked back and remembered the many times I helped someone unload their groceries or gather carts from around the parking lot. I opened doors for seniors and gave drivers breaks. I pondered on my memories of being a gentleman and suddenly the underlying truth was revealed. From my earliest memory, I was only caring for one reason. *It was all about me.* The only reason I was kind was when I needed something from someone else, and this was often. Even a thank-you, a smile, or an appreciative look would be my reward. I received the approval from others I wasn't giving to myself. I needed approval from others and understood I wasn't giving any to myself.

I thought of the belief systems and saw the programming and conditioning that had swayed me from my earliest memories as a child. Even as an innocent being, my programming was being displayed and I was acting the part given to me unknowingly.

I had learned more than I thought I would and gotten much more than I bargained for with my training. I had gained a little awareness and some understanding of what happened behind the scenes throughout my life. I had willingly followed the thread wherever it would take me. I also had a feeling there was much to be revealed and discoveries to make. This inside job was going to take me to where it had to go, if I was willing to chance it.

KNOW THYSELF

The massage training was exhausting. The drive was awful with tons of traffic as people drove to work. The time it took to drive up and back each day caused me much anxiety; I would be a basket case until I had a chance to recover. I hoped this huge inconvenience would be worthwhile. It definitely would be and was, as I continued to learn new skills with the hands-on techniques used in the various massage styles. The anatomy class was excellent. I was learning how complex our bodies were as I went deeper into the anatomy and physiology teachings.

I learned sports massage, Swedish massage, as well as basic Shiatsu. There were exams to take and the homework was time consuming. I finished my training in less than a year. I certified with the state within weeks of completing school, and it was now official. I had credentials, great training, and decent skills to practice. Along the way, I had rented an office/treatment/massage room. It was located in a small building by itself. My wife volunteered, and she and I worked many nights cleaning and painting. The remodeling needed was beyond my scope, and my son showed off his carpentry skills and made quick work of it. He and I were both pleased when the dust finally settled.

With certification approved and license in-hand, I continued adding clients as my business grew. I rented another office space on the eastside of the bay and was in a prime location. Now I was covered and clients were adding up. I offered reflexology, massage therapy, Reiki, as well as the new work I had spent a small fortune to learn. My business was booming, and I was practicing my new-found trade.

I saw Chief every time I went for my walks to the park, the woods, or downtown. I was starting to have a confidence in myself that wasn't an act anymore, and Chief mentioned I had just touched the tip of the iceberg with *BreakThrough*. It was now time to dig in and do the inside job of self- discovery. I remembered how I had felt in New York and was a little fearful of what I might find.

Chief said, "Now it is time to start reading the *Awareness* book." He reminded me to stay neutral when observing myself. What we discover would make us want to punish ourselves and loving ourselves was the key to prevent self-punishing. When we observed ourselves, we should try to imagine watching ourselves as if watching a movie. I would be the main character and witness and feel the emotional triggers when a belief system had been activated.

Before we parted company, Chief looked me square in the eyes and said, "Knowing self is a lifetime of hard work. Your findings about yourself will shake you to the bone. You have to stay neutral and not judge yourself." He reminded me to focus on my reactions when a negative emotion was triggered, and to be good to myself. Chief said one more thing before we parted. He said, "Emotions override logic and reason. We have very little control, which is contrary to what we really feel, and controlling the emotions is like trying to hold back the tides from rising and falling. All we can do is to be aware the emotions are in play and observe how they override our thinking."

I walked back to my apartment psyched to begin the book and to let it guide me. Funny, I really had no clue where this journey would lead me. I was glad I had gotten some great guidance from Chief and again was impressed with his wisdom and knowledge. I thought of the other folks who had helped me. Most of them didn't even know me, although, their written words in the dozens of books I had read had helped me immensely. I also spent many hours listening to wise men and women during lectures and heard facts and truths from all. I knew I wasn't alone on my journey. Lots of people were fed up with their lives as was I. I was feeling gratitude and knew my heart was starting to open. It was great knowing there was a way out. Although hard work was in-store, and many discoveries were yet to be made, I felt on track. I was seeing the light at the end of the tunnel, and knew it wasn't the light of a train coming my way. Instead it was the light of awareness and understanding beckoning me to go toward it without fear. I had to risk it all and take the plunge I heard others before me had to take. I wasn't exempt and had to step up.

"AWARENESS"

The Perils and Opportunities of Reality

With book in hand, I noticed the other words written under the title, the subtitle: "*The perils and opportunities of reality.*" Funny, at first, I had only noticed the title, and now I was seeing the subtitle, which seemed to stand out more for me now. I thought only of the opportunities I would get through seeking awareness and now I realized it would be a perilous journey as well. I understood *the perils*, as I thought back to my recent *BreakThrough* experience. I decided to read the book from beginning to end one time to get the gist. Then, I read a chapter and pondered what I had read. This wasn't a race to the finish to be done with it. This was an opportunity to actually reveal the belief systems, programming, and conditioning running my life. I had to muster all the patience I could and knew this wasn't going to be a quick fix.

Before starting the book, I read the back cover and saw Anthony de Mello, S.J., had been a Jesuit priest in India. He died suddenly in 1987 and the book was edited by J. Francis Stroud S.J. after his death. "*Awareness*" was written from transcripts and recordings taken during his many retreats, workshops, seminars on prayer, and his therapy courses. This all sounded good and I was excited and biting at the bit to start. I read the forward at the beginning of the book and had to laugh at the egg story. It gave me hope once my programming was revealed to me, I could hopefully reach my full potential, whatever that was.

I had always felt something was holding me back from being happy and content. Hopefully, I would soon find out what it was. I noticed while leafing through the pages they were in sections short enough to read and finish. I didn't like stopping in the middle of a chapter. So far, so good. I read the book rather quickly and then re-read. This time, I read a section, and then stopped to ponder. Sometimes I would re-read the section repeatedly to understand, as clearly as possible, what was being said.

Sadly, I reverted to my old ways and wasn't taking the advice of the book or Chief. I would immediately see my errors and judged myself wrongly. Every time I tried to see what happened when my emotions flared, I would be triggered to punish myself by name-calling or, again, anger at myself and the punishment of no happiness. I wasn't separating and observing myself in neutrality, but instead only finding fault and holding myself accountable. This went on for a long while as I read and re-read "*Awareness*". What was I missing here?

I stopped reading and sat on the couch wondering if maybe I was overlooking something. Even though I might be doing it all wrong, I noticed my awareness was growing despite me. Every time I picked it up to start over, it was like reading a new book for the first time. Over time, I did notice I wasn't as angry at myself as usual. Instead, I noticed I was beginning to laugh at my findings and smiling more. Above all, I was being kinder to myself. Changes were occurring despite me.

A few of my clients who wanted to pursue self-observation kept me on my toes during these troubling times. Some would call or come by for a visit and, as a result, cheer me up and inspire me to tough it out. I tried to explain what I was up to, and in explaining the way of self-observation I was convincing myself instead. I was thankful for those few folks who had recognized the benefit of doing the inside job. It gave me the push I needed to continue and not give up. Time was slowly creeping by and there were many days when I would be so frustrated I would have to take time away to sort out and search for gains I might be making. I saw an improvement in my mood swings and over time my anger wasn't running the show as it had been. I saw how learning about what made me tick was exposing the falsehoods I thought were true. I thought everyone should doing the inside job, and I focused on that and nothing else.

I bought dozens of books online, new and used, to give to my clientele. I would gift it to new clients and found many of them really liked it. Surprisingly, to me, there were many who didn't like the book. Some were really offended after a few chapters and stopped reading it altogether. Quite a few clients decided they would stop seeing me. I couldn't for the life of me understand this weirdness. The changes happening in me were allowing more freedom than I ever had. Why wouldn't anyone want this instead of the misery?

As a man, I was fairly free do what I wanted. I came and went as I pleased, and that was the reward I took for my hard work providing for family. This wasn't that kind of freedom at all. I was becoming free from some of my programming. I was experiencing wanting less attention or praise from others. The need for others was becoming, less and less. I was starting to feel good about myself, maybe starting to love myself. I was letting myself off the hook for decisions made in ignorance. ***"Forgive them, Father, they know not what they do."*** I thought, *Wow!*

Not that my conditioning was gone just yet. I would feel the emotions being stirred and watch my reaction start. Now and then, I would have a slight pause and choose differently. Sometimes I saw an alternative instead of having my normal, knee jerk reaction. This didn't happen all the time, and I knew I had to go deeper. I had to be convinced of the truth and see it play out again. All progress would soon be tested in ways I couldn't even start to fathom. The failing economy and the big bank bailouts started the ball rolling in a downward trend. The financial crisis was followed by the ongoing health issues with my mom, dad, and youngest brother and sister.

The economy was heading downhill and extra money for my services was drying up. It wasn't long before I ended up having to close one of my offices and treatment spaces, and as a result, I lost 60% of my clients. Money was tight for everyone and I understood why many clients had to drop sessions. I lowered prices and offered discounts to no avail. When it rains it pours, and pour it did. It poured for years as everything, and I mean everything, went from bad to worse. My business took a big hit and I was down to only a dozen or so clients.

Although I was getting great results with all I had learned and practiced, hard times were on everyone, and not just me. I took it somewhat personal sometimes, and the fear of failure constantly haunted me. It seemed the gains I thought I made were dissolving as more was piled on my plate. My parents were elderly and their years of poor eating habits, inactivity, and the lack of exercise, as well as their health issues were causing them serious difficulties. Both my mother and father were overweight, and my sister unable to drive either. She was depending on friends and me to help her in almost every way. My mom had several major health conditions that were life-threatening if left unattended. My dad had dementia, but my sister's health was the worst of all. I was so busy looking after Mom and Dad, I had lost track of her. When I went to see her, I was taken aback when I saw her condition. I had a feeling she was on her way out and it was only a matter of time before she would die from her many health problems.

I received a call from my mom one day that my brother was at the hospital. At first, I thought she might be calling about my sister. He was disoriented and having severe memory issues to the point his employer had called her. They had been concerned for a long while with his behavior at work. My brother lived by himself and had been divorced for many years. He was a grown man and their last resort was to call my mom. My brother was sent to a hospital that dealt strictly with the various mental disorders folks may have. I would travel a long distance almost every day to visit him and talk to the doctors in his care. One day, I agreed to become his power of attorney for all his medical, as well as financial, needs and everything in between.

My brother was diagnosed with Wernicke Korsakoff Syndrome, and would need 24/7 care for the rest of his life. Arrangements were made for his transfer to be a resident in a nearby nursing and rehabilitation facility. Everyone took this news hard, especially my dad. His dementia progressed rapidly and he would forget where he was going when he drove. I stepped in and took his license. I was concerned he may crash his car into a family or not know where he was when he went out. I made up a story and told him the cops knew about his condition and they had told me to take his driving license away and to bring it to the police department. Luckily, he believed me and stopped asking for his license. Now I was the transportation man and driving everywhere they had to go.

Shopping wasn't fun at all. My mom was using a walker, and my dad couldn't walk any distance without having to take a break to sit down. Here I was trying to manage Mom and Dad as well as fill the cart with food they needed.

Visiting my brother every day went on for months, and eventually I had to cut back to once a week. My business was circling the drain, and so was I. I had filled in Chief on my crisis and he understood. I think he sensed I wasn't open to any advice or philosophical jargon. He knew I was in a tough spot, and surely, he was aware I wasn't handling it well either. I was a great actor and should have won an Academy Award for my performance.

The daily routine which held me together ended. Meditation went first, and was followed by the walk. My eating went by the wayside, as usual, and I was not being true to myself in any way. My weight loss was brought to my attention by my wife. I hadn't noticed or, better yet, I didn't care. All the gains I had made over many years were lost or on hold. I forgot about loving myself and did the opposite instead. I had no control and I needed to have control. Why wasn't I able to see what I was doing to myself? The cost of my brother's care was phenomenal. He had done without during his working career to build his retirement savings, and now I had to spend it all on his nursing care. This caused me additional worries as I watched every penny spent and kept meticulous records of every expense.

My brother was transferred from one nursing home to another due to behavioral problems, and eventually I located a place very close to home for him. I loaded Mom and Dad, along with two walkers and took them to visit their youngest son once a week. I went a few times a week since it was closer. Every time I'd visit him, it took me down and hurt me to see his condition worsen. I called my few remaining clients and told them I was taking time off to attend to family matters; I promised them a call when I was open for clients again.

In the meantime, my sister's health issues were needing more of my attention. Ever since she was a baby, her health challenges were many. Because she was deaf, communication was very difficult. No one could understand her, and I had to be there to decipher. She had been drinking heavily for many years and smoked two packs of cigarettes a day. Even today, I feel a sadness when I think about how she had suffered for most of her life.

I put everyone in front of me when it came to living up to the responsibilities that had been dumped on me. I was responsible for everyone and this responsibility drove me to putting myself last, if at all. My own health started to suffer more as a result, and my wife and children were noticing my weight loss as well as my ability to focus. I couldn't continue this running around and being responsible for everyone and everything any longer; I felt like I was going to crack. Every now and then, I would get a little relief when someone else stepped up and took care of shopping or taking my parents to visit my brother. They had their own stuff going on, and although I knew this, I was angry at everyone for not doing more.

This craziness went on for many years and there was no end in sight. Little did I know there was an end, but I didn't know how it would finish. My dad was rapidly failing mentally, and my mom received horrible news after complaining to her doctor about swallowing issues. I was startled when the phone rang, and answered on the first ring. My mother called and informed me my sister had been rushed to the hospital. She was in bad shape and they had to put her on a ventilator. After several days in the critical care ward, she died from a massive infection making her toxic. I took my parents up to the hospital, not knowing it would be their last visit. My wife and sister-in-law were there for support as the medical staff took her off the ventilator. I couldn't stay and watch the outcome, and I took my dad back to the house to wait for the news. Although my father was mentally challenged, he knew what was going on with my sister. As I looked at him, I could see he was distraught and ready to cry. *Boys don't cry,* rang in my ears as I watched him sob. I had to leave the room and couldn't watch as my dad wept like a child. I didn't cry then, and was like the rock of Gibraltar instead. At least that was what I wanted everyone to see. In reality, I was crying inside and a real mess.

I made all the final arrangements for my sister at the funeral home, and my mom wrote my sister's obituary. My mom took it badly and would never be the same again, whatever that was. She had lost her only daughter and the loss took a huge toll on her already bad health. She had recently been diagnosed with tongue cancer and was required to have radiation treatments every week. I took her down and waited for her to finish, with my dad in tow. I would sit with her waiting, then go out with my dad for a while, and then back to Mom. Back and forth until Mom was finished with her radiation treatment.

The effects of the treatment were taking a toll on Mom and my concern for her deepened. She wasn't eating, and swallowing was difficult. She was also in severe pain, and I could see she was suffering and there was nothing I could do. *If I had control, things would be different.* I had a full plate with Mom, Dad, and my brother, and none of the responsibilities were of my choosing.

Crazy as it sounded, I decided to get a dog. For a long time, I was aware I needed a responsibility I had chosen, not one dumped on me. I needed to make my new responsibility important for *me*. I needed company as well. I felt lonely and knew a dog would fill that void.

No one, and I mean no one, bought into my taking on a new responsibility rationale. My wife and children thought I had gone off the deep end, and my parents didn't think it would be a good idea to add to my plate any more than I already had. I listened to their complaints and reasoning and it really fell on deaf ears as far as I was concerned. I had made up my mind and that was that.

PORTIA

The Standard Schnauzer

After looking at most of the dog breeds and figuring out the best choice for me, I decided to get a Standard Schnauzer. Looking back, I remember how much I liked the breed and had always wanted to have one. I started the search and found it more difficult than I thought it would be. Eventually, and just before I was ready to give up, it happened. I called a Standard Schnauzer breeder in Connecticut and talked to her about obtaining a dog. She bred show dogs and had won international competitions on many occasions. I was impressed at her show record and was hoping she would help me find a good dog. She told me she had a ten-month old female and was in the process of selling her. Another breeder was interested in her for breeding stock and he would have first bid on the dog. The breeder asked if I could come down for an interview in a couple weeks. The dog was being boarded in upstate New York and was being kenneled by her business partner. She would make arrangements for the dog to be brought to Connecticut, so the first guy and I could look her over and decide. I agreed and set up an appointment to be interviewed. I waited for the time to pass and kept busy with Mom, Dad, and my brother until the day arrived.

I drove down Route 95 heading toward Connecticut around mid-morning and got lost once on the back-roads. After stopping for directions a few times,

I managed to find the house. I rang the doorbell and heard several dogs barking inside. I was excited and happy to see three dogs looking at me through the front bay window of the house. A moment later, I was greeted by the breeder and invited in.

We went downstairs to the finished basement where she groomed and kenneled her show dogs for competition. She introduced me to her husband and then to the dogs that were as excited as I was. The schnauzer I had come to see was all over me. As I was petting her, I knew then I wanted *this* dog.

The interview lasted for a few hours and I felt I had a good chance of getting Portia. I had the money in my pocket, a dog kennel in my car, and had bought a few doggy toys as well. The breeder told me she had another interview with the other guy the next day and she would decide in three weeks who would get Portia the Standard Schnauzer. I thought I would be leaving with a new friend that day and was disappointed at the delay. I understood her concerns and knew she was looking out for Portia's best interest. That impressed me, and I knew I would have to let everything pan out as it would.

I wanted to call every day to see how everything was going, but decided not to. I waited impatiently until I received the call I had been waiting for. The breeder chose me instead of the other gentleman, and it was now confirmed. I went back down to Connecticut the following day and brought her home. The breeder told me how lucky I was to get a Standard Schnauzer. This was a very odd predicament and Portia had a home with a family in New York. They had picked her up but one of the family members experienced an allergic reaction to her. They brought her back and she stayed with the breeder for a few months before she was shipped to upstate New York.

I knew luck had nothing to do with me getting Portia. I had manifested her on my own. I remember while waiting for the call, I would walk the path and visualize her running just ahead of me. I called her and she responded, and then we played in the fields with the other dogs that would usually be there. I saw it as clearly as if it were real.

Hmm, the "*Illusions*" book came to my mind. The Messiah had taught Richard how to manifest anything he wanted. It was the "*Law of Attraction*" at work.

That afternoon, I took her for our first walk to the woods and the park. Portia played out my prior visualizations to a tee, and then some, as we found Chief sitting on his bench. We stopped and Chief and I had a long chat while Portia sat between us getting nurtured from both of us. She really took to Chief. I could see he was glad for me and my new friend. As we sat and talked, Portia took turns resting her head on either my or Chief's legs. When I looked at her, she seemed to be smiling with her eyes.

Now, I had to walk her several times a day, and be healthy to give her the care she needed. Portia was doing for me what I hadn't been doing for myself. I started meditating again and I was re-starting my healthy routine once more. Within several weeks, I gained a little weight and regained some hope again. My dad now had company when I was with Mom for her appointments, and Portia seemed to enjoy his company. It was odd to see my dad smile. Most of my life, all I ever saw was a serious look on him; now he seemed happy and content. The dementia had progressed and he was now free of all responsibilities and could finally relax. Funny, everyone loved Portia, and Portia loved everyone. She was always at my side, and I was starting to feel better, health wise.

I decided one day, after she slipped off her collar, she needed obedience training. I went to the park and talked to other pet owners and after some recommendations I signed her up for the course. I dropped her off in the morning and picked her up late afternoon every day for two weeks. This worked out well. I would see my brother or take my parents to their appointments in between.

Mom got worse; we were told there was nothing that could be done for her cancer. They gave her a year to live and she seemed to handle the news fairly well. My mom and I filled my father in on the prognoses and he shook his head and said no. He would not accept the facts and refused to talk about it. Both my parents were housebound, and my brother was in the nursing home. He had taken a turn for the worse and was also diagnosed with cancer as well. Mom and my youngest brother had the exact same cancer, although my brother's was too far along for any kind of remedy or treatment.

Months before, I had promised my mom if things got worse I would move in with them. The time was now, so I decided I would move from my apartment and live with my parents. I was getting calls day and night from my mom and the nursing home and living where I was wasn't working.

I'm glad I started; it took me six months to clean out their basement and have it remodeled. I hired a contractor to build a deck and handicapped ramp so my parents could go in and out without falling. The basement was dark and dank, and I decided to have windows cut into the cement walls for much needed light. Meanwhile, I was still living away and spent the night at my apartment when I could get away with it. My mom finally got to the point where she needed care day and night.

It wasn't easy for me to move in with my parents. I had left the house at seventeen and for good reasons. Now, here I was, with a grown family of my own and living with my parents after being on my own for most of my life. Just the thought of it made me feel queasy. I still had painting to do and truck loads of stuff to give away or take to the dump.

Over the course of many years, the basement and attic, as well as the garage and two sheds, were used to hold my sister's, my brother's and my parents' personal belongings. My dad never threw anything away. An old, worn T-shirt became a rag, and there were dozens of bags of rags. My sister had lived in the basement and everything she owned was in boxes and bags. She had clothes she hadn't worn in twenty years on hangers. All my brother's belongings were thrown on top, and it took me days to build the courage to sort and box everything.

Every day I would make dozens of trips to the Salvation Army and give those boxes, and boxes of clothing, household items, books, and furniture away. Anything they wouldn't take I hauled to the dump. Portia was with me always and helped keep me smiling through this arduous task. It took a long time before I actually moved in. I had been using the spare bedroom upstairs for myself and slept on a futon bed. I wasn't getting enough sleep. When I got up in the morning, I had low-back pain that would sometimes last all day. The mattress was old and worn from many years of use it had endured and was the cause of my back condition. The back and forth to the apartment, as well as doctor visits and seeing my brother, were wearing me thin.

I felt like I was in limbo and was happy and as well as sad when I finally moved all my belongings to the newly renovated and painted basement. The basement had been used by both of my brothers, as well as my sister over the many years. The furnishings were beyond use, and I had to purchase new furniture and carpets. It had a bathroom with a shower, a nice open kitchen, which had a gas stove and refrigerator. The refrigerator had to go and was replaced with one I had bought for my old apartment. I added to the counter space as well as making new cabinets for storage. When I renovated, I redid everything. I replaced the sink in the bathroom and covered the floors with laminate that looked like a hardwood floor in place of linoleum. I had as much space down there as my parents had upstairs. My mom was very pleased with the outcome, and Dad complimented me on the paintwork as well as the new floor. His first compliment as far as I could remember.

Portia loved her new digs. We had a huge back and front yard and a great wooded area for her to run. She loved chasing rabbits and squirrels, although she would never catch one. She would be within striking distance when suddenly she would stop her pursuit. She just wanted to play, not kill. I had everything I needed downstairs and it had a great energy to boot. I noticed the difference when I went down at day's end. I left the hectic upstairs in the evening after getting Mom and Dad fed, cleaned, and to bed, and went downstairs for the night. My mood actually changed as I walked down the eleven stairs to the basement, **my sanctuary.** I loved it and would relax for a few hours before going to bed myself. Portia slept with me for a little while before jumping down and up on my recliner for the rest of the night. It wasn't uncommon for me to have to help my mom or dad during the night. Although I slept well, it was rare I had the night off.

If I hadn't gotten Portia, I didn't think I would have made it. She sensed any emotional turmoil I was having and cheered me up as dogs can. She would entertain my parents during the day, and then me later. Every day I took her on a two-mile walk around the middle school only a few miles away. We would get in the car and go to the school at least once a day. On weekends, I took her there more often. Portia knew where we were going and talked to me, making funny sounds as her excitement built.

I loved the forest located behind the school. The track team had a trail that wound through the woods for their cross-country runners. Almost every time we visited the school, Portia and I saw wild game. Often, we would scare deer or turkeys would fly off. Every weekday afternoon, while school was in session, there were always kids playing soccer, baseball, or running track. They all knew Portia and called her name. Every day the walk through the ball fields and forest reminded me of my walks to visit Chief. With all I had going on with Mom, Dad and my brother, I couldn't find time to see Chief.

Chief came by the old apartment just before I moved out. We had a great talk and he was happy to see me making a rebound, health wise. He told me getting Portia had probably been the best thing I could have done, even if it was contrary to popular beliefs. He enjoyed Portia's company a lot, and when he was with us, she enjoyed his touch as he petted her. I told him I probably wouldn't be over for a while and felt my voice crack a little from my deep sadness. He said he understood and knew I was on track; he would be around if needed, and I knew where to find him. I knew he didn't have a phone and I never asked him where he lived, so contacting him would be unlikely unless we met in the park, the woods, or the common. I was sad and understood it was a proper response, although it was still my choice to be sad or not.

As we were sitting there, Chief pointed to the *"Illusions"* book by Richard Bach and said anytime he was having a rough time or felt out of whack he would read *"Illusions"*. Reading cheered him up and shifted his perspective to one of hope and freedom. I picked up the book and opened it where I had it bookmarked. I read the words, ***"Argue for your limitations, and sure enough they're yours."*** *"Illusions"- (Richard Bach)*

I needed some hope coming my way and decided to continue reading *"Illusions"* that day. I mentioned this to Chief, and he said, "It'll be good for you." He said it was a great story and I would definitely enjoy it. There were plenty of facts written and even if I thought some were farfetched, not to judge anything based on what I knew now. We really didn't know much when it came to what was real and what wasn't. It would take time and effort to sort it all out. He was very surprised to discover what he thought was true, was in fact a falsehood, and the programming we had been given early on in our lives.

Our visit ended sooner than I wanted. He gave me his bear hug and wished me the best. I noticed he was a little sad.

As he said goodbye, he said,

> ***"Your friends will know you better in the first ten minutes than your acquaintances will know you in a thousand years. The bond that links your true family is not one of blood, but of respect and joy in each other's life," and, "rarely, do members of one's family grow up under the same roof."***
> *"Illusions"- (Richard Bach)*

Chief gave me a mischievous smile and whispered those were not his words and he had memorized them from *"Illusions"*. I told him I'd re-start the book today; I really never had many friends and had mostly acquaintances. I also mentioned I didn't really have much of a connection to my own family. I was full of guilt for not being a better son and brother. He said not to worry, it had been the same with him and it was all about trust and respect. Early on, he had lost faith with everyone else, and his disappointments were many when it came to anyone except himself. He laughed and said as he gained more awareness, he realized he had been more disappointed with himself and had blamed others for his own shortcomings. He said, "It's too much for us to bear knowing we are the cause of our joys and sorrows, especially our sorrows." He smiled and continued, "We love taking credit when everything is going well, but, when it hits the fan, we find fault, and immediately find someone or something to blame. It's our human nature, but we think we are above that, with our misconception of having control."

As Chief walked up the driveway toward the street, a thought came to me. I may never see Chief again and he was probably my only friend. Portia sensed my turmoil and came over and nudged me. She needed to go out by the nudge, although I knew she was helping me to take my mind outside where I could possibly see a different reality. I was on my own, and if I needed help I would have to handle it myself. Chief was available, I guess, although he would be hard to track down quickly. I had the books Chief had given me and knew the answers would be found in the readings. The ball was in my court as it had always been throughout my life, and it was now time to get serious and look inside. I decided to finish the "*Illusions*" book and maybe, just maybe, I would find out what was real and what wasn't.

Portia lived up to my every dream and seldom let me down. Everyone who came to know her loved her, and it seemed everyone wanted to pet her. She loved it all and let them pet and play until it was time to move on. She especially loved the very young and very old and sought them out. She especially liked old people and made it her mission to say hi and to cheer them up.

Everywhere I went, Portia would ride along. She had her back legs on the rear seat and her front paws on the center console as she watched the road like me. The people at the banks I used, as well as folks working at the tractor supply store and Home Depot were used to seeing us together. Most of these places provided doggy treats, and she would sit at the check-out and wait patiently for her reward for being herself. Now and then, they would forget or run out of treats and I would provide her with one when we got to the car. I always had fresh water and a small variety of dog biscuits for her there.

The Standard Schnauzer was a people dog, as well as a herding breed. It had been said the Schnauzer had a human brain and could learn quickly the ins and outs of their owners. She could definitely play the games we played, and it was funny to see.

All dogs were all about food and Portia was no exception. I had to be sure she ate her food instead of relying on goodies. I bought her the best food I could afford and was sure she was groomed daily. I took her for a professional grooming every three months. When she was done, she looked like a champion show dog. The love Portia gave me daily was awesome. She didn't judge me and accepted me totally the way I was. I should take cues on love from her because she was a perfect example of love in all its glory.

GETTING SERIOUS

I re-read the *"Illusions"* book, and not only was it great entertainment, it was also educational. I had to agree with Chief that it gave him hope and a shift in perspective. I was feeling good despite the huge responsibilities I had taken on. My mom was getting worse and so was my brother. Dad was usually smiling and cooperative these days. The more I saw him smile, the more I looked back to see the very serious man who never smiled. I understood; I had become very much like him.

When I was a small boy, I wanted to be just like him. As a teenager and young adult, I had followed in his footsteps, almost exactly. As I aged and was able to see the family dynamics, I distanced myself first by quitting drinking, and afterwards, went with my new training, or seeing clients. I had also gotten serious with self-observation. My few clients were perfect mirrors to reflect my own stuff.

In my interactions with others, I observed myself as if I were watching someone else. I tried staying neutral which took a hell of a long time before I stopped beating myself up. I was making some progress though, and was starting to see how my belief systems were really running me. I realized it was all about me, and had **always** been about me. Some of my discoveries rocked my boat as I searched for more understanding. When I pointed my finger at anyone to judge or blame, there were three fingers pointing back at me. I was the problem, not them. When I judged others, I was trying to knock them down so I would be up. These discoveries were hard to bear at first, I mean, for a long while. I still hadn't learned to forgive myself for my ignorance. Suddenly, I thought, ***"Forgive them, Father, for they know not what they do."***

If Jesus Christ could forgive those who crucified him on the cross, maybe, just maybe, I could cut myself a little slack as well. I had to do this inside job if I wanted relief from my ongoing emotional turmoil. I thought I had done things for others out of the goodness of my heart. Through self-observation, I discovered I didn't do anything for anyone unless there was something in it for me. It was all about me; I hadn't known my selfishness was driving me. I wanted others to respect me. I mean *everyone*. I was so important in my own mind I expected others to admire and compliment me for all I had done for them.

One of my first gifts from this process was what I discovered when I was behind the wheel. I would always be on the look-out for other drivers not playing by the rules of the road. I thought everyone should be courteous on the highway. I thought everyone should use turn signals, yield the right of way, and drive the speed limit. Every time I drove, I became very angry when I saw other drivers not doing what I thought to be right. My dad used to be the same way. I remember hearing my first swear words in the car as a child.

Anytime I drove, I was more focused on others' mistakes than in my own driving. I thought I was the best driver on the road and found fault continuously. The drive set me up for the rest of the day, and I told others of my bad experiences and the reason I wasn't happy. I always had an excuse to cover my moods. It was always someone or something that caused me to be angry or fearful. Always someone's fault, not mine; I was a perfect driver.

When I discovered I had expectations with my highway experiences, I realized I was only looking for mistakes and recklessness instead of concentrating on my driving. I wanted people to respect and honor me and give me the road. It was all about me and no one else. I was important, and when others didn't live up to my demands, I would retaliate by swearing, shouting, waving my finger, and getting really angry. I was blaming everyone for how I felt, even when I drove.

I still have a little of this behavior left in me, although I have come a long way since I recognized my expectations. Today, when I drive, I focus on driving well, not judging others, and tuning into the joy of driving. Ah, yes, the joy of driving.

When I first learned to drive, it wasn't a joy at all. My dad took me out in his Oldsmobile to teach me to drive and park. He was a stickler for turn signals and moving quickly forward after the light turned green. He hated drivers who lollygagged at the intersection after the light had changed. He also hated anyone who didn't use their turn signals.

Just then, I remembered the song: *"I'm going to be like you, dad, you know, I'm going to be like you." "Cats and the cradle"- (Harry Chapin)*

After I passed the written exam and road test and the pressure was off, I **loved** driving. I would find any excuse, some made up of course, to drive the car. Behind the wheel, I would tune into the power at my disposal and the comfort of the seat and the sounds of the car itself. After lots of driving and practice, sometimes I felt I was being driven. Once we learned something well, it became a reflexive happening. We could feel good knowing our abilities were honed and we were good drivers. Then we could relax and enjoy the ride and not have to concentrate as intensely.

I don't know when I lost the joy of driving or when my belief systems kicked in with drivers being courteous. It might have been a good reason to just be angry. Through self-observation, I noticed I had anger constantly brewing. It was underlying and tainting everything as well. I would try not to show my anger by smiling a phony "all is well" smile, knowing I didn't mean it. Others would know too, and that really cemented the anger further. I saw myself people pleasing to get the gift of attention or compliments. Again, I saw *it's all about me* rearing its ugly head. Wow, I always knew I put myself first, and then others if I could get something out of them. I didn't realize how far I went to get what I wanted.

I thought I was a loner, but now was learning how much I **needed** people. I needed people to please **me**, make **me** happy, and feed **me** the positive feedback I desperately wanted. I didn't like myself very much, I learned, and might even say I hated myself. All I seemed to think about were my failures, and the many times I would disappoint others. It was impossible to meet expectations of myself. I set myself up to fail with no way of succeeding. I wasn't even aware I had been doing this until I started observing myself seriously. I was starting to realize the inside job couldn't be done half-assed. I had to make this work important and convince myself, beyond doubt, I had to push on no matter what.

Chief was right on when he said we must love ourselves. I saw it clearly now and wanted to be free. Freedom was the ultimate goal, and awareness of my belief systems, programming and conditioning, was the only way to achieve it.

BAD TO WORSE

I continued with self-observation and was finding more about what made me tick. I had discovered "self-importance" and "all about me" were major factors I had to accept. People pleasing and needing people to stroke my ego were also on my plate. I was also watching my remaining family members' health fail before my eyes.

My mother was in tremendous pain and her doctor was balking at prescribing medication that was needed. The "old" me came alive when I was fighting for my mom. Take no prisoners and charge on. I fired my mom's doctor and read him the riot act. As far as I was concerned, he was a hack. He should have caught her condition long ago and didn't. I was pissed off and suddenly saw I had used him as an excuse for my anger. I was mad at myself for not be able to save the day. I hated myself through him for failing everyone. The doctor was a decent man and had been my parents' doctor for over forty years. He was doing his duty when it came to pain medication and obeying the law. He had looked after their health and welfare and probably contributed immensely to them reaching past their mid-eighties.

I also observed I wasn't eating well. Meditation time had shortened, and my eating wasn't adequate. I checked the scales and saw I had lost ten pounds. I looked back and knew it had started when I had cleaned and renovated my parents' house. I ran myself ragged then and eating hadn't been a high priority.

I had been punishing myself then and hadn't learned the art of self-observation yet. I wasn't perfect at it, although, I did see changes occurring. I noticed another thing going on in me that was impossible to ignore. I was starting to grieve my brother and parents. I guess I was preparing myself for the inevitable.

Over a year had gone by very quickly. Hospice was involved with my mom, and she was getting the medical care I couldn't provide. The doctors at hospice were specialists when it came to their patients' needs. My wife and sister-in-law were both RN's and pitched in when they could. They were especially helpful when it came to bathing my mom. I was glad they stepped forward, although I was prepared to handle it myself if necessary. Looking back, I was seeing how my pride had prevented me from ever asking for help. I had to be in charge and prove myself to everyone. Rather than simply ask for help, I'd use my anger to do what needed to be done.

Anger again reared its ugly head and it was anger at myself that fueled it. More lessons on control, or lack of it, were coming my way through awareness. Seeing myself in action and staying neutral was still sometimes very difficult. By now, I would watch the show and feel the emotional charge ignite my programmed reaction. More often than not, I took action instead of the usual reactionary way. I noticed subtle changes occurring without trying to change. I then remembered the words Chief had quoted from "Awareness".

> ***"You cannot change by effort of the will; you cannot change through ideals; you cannot change through building up new habits. Your behavior may change, but you don't. You can only change through awareness and understanding."***
> *"Awareness"- (Anthony de Mello)*

Change was occurring because I had taken self-observation seriously. I was discovering the truth about myself. I was learning the lies and falsehoods fed to me like candy to a child. I also understood the people behind the programming were unaware they were doing me any harm. In understanding this, I seemed to be letting go of any ill feelings I had about all my family members. I saw them act out their beliefs as truths, regardless of the harm it might do to them or others. They didn't have a choice in their behavior either. They had no control and were overreacting just like I was. They were all programmed themselves, and their programmers didn't know either. The only way to stop the continuation of passing down these crazy beliefs would be to expose this phenomenon, so others would know.

My father was scheduled to be admitted to the veterans' home the following week. My mom had been worried about my ability to care for him. She had witnessed our outbursts on several occasions. I had also witnessed it and was ashamed of myself for not respecting my father. Then I saw my guilt and fear for not being able to control myself. I immediately wanted revenge on myself and saw that too. I assured my mom I would be kinder with my dad in the future and was sure I would. He would soon be at the VA home and in better care than I could muster.

After a horrible night trying to manage my mother's pain to no avail. I asked her if she wanted to go to hospice. She said, "Yes, it's time to go." My dad was oblivious to the matter, and he wasn't. My mom had a talk with him on several occasions to prepare him for what was to come. He would fight any talk of death and tell us to not talk about it again. I called the hotline for our case worker and she sent an ambulance for my mom. She had lost a lot of weight due to her not being able to eat. Her cancer made it impossible for her to use her tongue, so swallowing became very impaired. I knew she would be fed someway at the hospital. I thought she would stay at the hospital for a while and be fed and in a place where she would be cared for by professionals.

I contacted my wife who was working and left a message for my sister-in-law to inform her Mom would be taken to the hospice hospital. The ambulance arrived within an hour and took my mom away. I got my dad ready and we went about an hour later. I helped my dad with his walker and we went in. My mother was sleeping soundly and had an IV going. We looked at Mom and only stayed for a while longer. My dad tried to wake her, but she was fast asleep, so he kissed her good-bye and we headed home.

My wife and sister-in-law arrived only minutes after we had gone and stayed with her until the end. Her stay was brief; once she knew my dad would be taken care of, she was free to die. My mom was finally free from the pain and suffering she had as a constant companion for months. I received the call from the hospital, and from my wife as well, that Mom had died and the arrangements I had put into place were being carried out. I didn't tell my dad his wife of sixty-eight years had passed away.

The next day, I tried to broach the subject and he refused to talk or listen to what I was telling him.

Several days later, I picked up my mother's ashes in an urn and brought them back to store safely. My mom wanted to be interned with my dad at the veterans' cemetery and I had to keep her ashes until my dad died. It was hard to see my sister's ashes as well, as my mom's, sitting on a shelf in my mother's hobby room. My mom wanted my sister buried with her, and at the time I thought it plausible. I later found out it wasn't. I waited a while before I finally made arrangements for my little sister's ashes to be interned next to my younger brother at a cemetery up the road.

The next week I took my dad to the VA home. After getting him settled and staying for as long as I could, I left him there and went home. Portia was with me all the way, and my wife made the trip up and back. Her support made it a little easier. I managed to observe myself during those hard times and all I was able to think about during the last few days and today was *boys don't cry.* Suddenly, "*A time for every purpose under heaven; a time to be born, a time to die, a time to laugh, a time to cry,*" rang in my head.

I chose not to cry and sat in my dad's chair and tuned into the feeling of loneliness. Portia chirped in with a friendly yelp that brought me back to the present moment. She came over and rested her head on my leg and looked up at me with her loving eyes. That's all it took and I began to weep. My past flashed before my eyes and I began to sob.

The first night in the house without my parents was difficult. I was still listening for any sound, like I had trained myself to do. No sounds and no having to attend to my parents' needs. It was now just myself and Portia. She was an unbelievable dog in the way she nurtured me over the following days and weeks. We did a lot of walking and spent hours in the woods. I visited my dad a few times a week and took Portia along every time. The VA home had gotten used to seeing us both and the residents loved her visits. My dad was always happy to see us and I think he enjoyed her company more than mine. He was not able to remember me or my name as his Alzheimer's progressed, although he did seem to recognize Portia.

Four weeks later, I received a call from the nursing home my brother resided. They called to let me know he was quickly failing. I had informed him of my mom's passing the day after she had died, and his beliefs, *boys don't cry*, kept him from responding as mine had done to me. I went to see him and noticed he was in severe pain. He was in hospice care as well, so we called to up his medication. The nurse gave him his meds and he seemed to settle down a little. I had called my wife to let her know what was happening and she came over within fifteen minutes. We stayed with him for a couple hours and left when he fell asleep. Late that night, I received a phone call from the nursing home that he had passed peacefully and without pain. I asked them to call the funeral home and they said they had it all handled. I thanked them and hung up.

I lay in bed for a while before finally dozing off. My sleep didn't provide any rest and I woke up tired and irritable. Now I was really alone. My sister had died two years before and then my mom and youngest brother this year. It was just me and Dad, and I seemed to be mourning him as well as the rest of my family.

My father died a year later at eighty-nine years old. I made the arrangements for him and my mom to be interned at the veterans' cemetery together and had my brother placed beside them. He was an Army veteran and had earned that right. My sister was with my younger brother who had died at the age of forty-three from a massive heart-attack. When I had gone to buy a plot for her, they told me one was available very close to him.

In a matter of four years, I had lost my entire family and was now the sole survivor. During those tough times, I had managed to self-observe and witness the emotional triggers that normally caused me to overreact. Instead, I saw another choice and, often, I acted appropriately instead of reacting. I didn't know how I was able to continue my inside job, but I did. I noticed a feeling of serenity in place of sadness and sorrow. Even though I had been through a lot, I felt fine. My wife had been living at our house a few miles away and I invited her to move in with me. My daughter and her children needed more room, so they moved to our old house and kept it occupied. It would be nice to see children playing in the yard or fishing the beach once again. The house was in a great location and the neighborhood was safe. With forests behind the house and the ocean only a few hundred yards away, I thought it a perfect place for kids to explore and have fun. My son and daughter enjoyed and took advantage of the fun that could be had when wooded forests and oceans were in the backyard.

STARTING ANEW

It took several months before I started to replace furnishing in the house. I bought new carpets and bedding. The old couch and recliner were worn and too much of a reminder to live with every day. I cleaned out the old shed and put my stuff in its place. I was slowly making the house a home. One morning I woke up and thought of Chief and decided to pay him a visit. That is, if I could find him. We hadn't been in contact for many months and I wanted to touch base with him and bring him up-to-date. I showered and dressed while Portia visited the woods.

We drove over the bridges and headed downtown to the common. It was early and I knew I could find parking close to the common. Traffic was heavy, and I was glad my reaction to the many drivers was a smile instead of swearing. I still felt emotional triggers while driving, although I would only watch and understand what was behind it all. I wasn't rid of my crazy belief systems around driving, and sometimes took a drive to judge my progress with awareness.

I slowly made my way downtown and found a spot to park close to the coffee shop I had visited many times over the years. I connected Portia's leash and we walked toward the common.

Rounding the corner, I saw Chief sitting on his bench. There were a few folks enjoying the morning sun while reading the newspaper or just taking in the view. He was in all his glory sitting on his bench, eyes closed, and seemingly meditating. I felt the energy of the area and noticed Portia was acting a little odd. I then remembered I had very seldom, if ever, had seen other dogs around the common. She was reluctant, as I had to pull her along. Portia spotted Chief and all was well. She was now pulling me along toward where Chief was sitting. He looked our way with a smile that welcomed both Portia and I. He stood as we approached the bench, and it was obvious Portia was excited to see him. He held out his hand and gave her a small dog treat she gently took and sat down to eat. We hugged each other for longer than usual this time. I felt my emotional triggers pulling on me and remembered how odd I felt the first time I had hugged him in public. I had to laugh at the old me and was glad I wasn't overreacting like before.

We sat on the bench for a long time talking and laughing. Portia sat between us, taking turns resting her head on our legs and looking up at us with her loving eyes.

Our conversation was a little different this time. Chief hadn't changed and looked relaxed. I updated him with the news about my parents and brother and sister. He listened and said comforting words when appropriate. He saw a huge change in my demeanor and it looked like I was doing decent, despite the challenging times I had endured. We talked about "*Awareness*" and the many perils that came with learning the truth about ourselves. He also made sure we talked about the opportunities that came as a result of understanding what made us tick, as well.

He brought up a subject he hadn't before. He said over the years he had erased his personal history, and in doing so had freed himself of the need for people. Most of us tell others everything about ourselves and then created an expectation. I didn't quite understand his message, so he explained further. Most of the time we made ourselves important by giving people way too much information about ourselves. We set ourselves up and then had to live up to what we had told them. Over the years, he had learned not to give anything away and be himself instead of the pumped-up version he always portrayed. In deleting his past, he kept himself a mystery to everyone instead of an expectation to live up to. By not sharing details about himself, it had given him a real freedom from people pleasing. He said we were taught and programmed to need people to tell us we were okay, and once we learned on our own, over time, **we were okay**, we wouldn't need others to compliment, praise, or even respect us anymore. The people in his life had accepted him for who he was today, right now, instead of who he had been or who they wanted him to be.

It was a huge relief not have to play the game anymore, and now he enjoyed the company of others much more. He chuckled and turned to me and said he had lost a few "friends" along the way. Those he had lost were disappointed with him. He said, "We only have disappointment as a result of an unmet expectations."

I understood what he meant, and decided to ponder on it later that day. This self-importance and having to maintain it would stop when the need for people was looked into and accepted as fact. I agreed with Chief's assessment and understood how I had needed people even when I thought I didn't. I had, for most of my life, maintained a posture and acted out the part of an independent man who was above the fray. I was starting to understand only until I truly liked and loved myself would I be able to free others of the expectations they had of me. Only then would I be able to truly enjoy the company of others without the need of their approval.

Chief looked at me with his kind, understanding eyes and said sometimes our losses were really gifts for us to enjoy; often we took on responsibilities only to use as excuses for not doing what we knew we needed to do.

I thought of all the responsibilities I had been given and realized I could have said no to all of them. I said yes instead and took them on for the reward of power and control. I didn't do it out of the goodness of my own heart! I did it for me and my need to have control over someone or something. My life was out of my control, so, I would control others to prove I was in charge.

Suddenly, my jaw dropped when I realized I was observing my past experiences and seeing what was really going on. I felt a little embarrassed thinking I might have not been paying attention to Chief. I apologized and said I was distracted for a moment. Chief let out a roar of a laugh that could be heard for miles. After he settled, I told him what I had been thinking and he agreed with my findings. He noted I was beginning to understand a new awareness through self-observation. He complimented me as he chuckled saying I was doing well and to continue with persistence. Chief also said to be grateful for my discoveries, good and not good.

Portia was anxious to move, so we walked around the common enjoying the morning. The street noises were picking up and I noticed more people had arrived and were walking the streets shopping. It was time to head home and process all we had talked about. I enjoyed Chief's bear hug, and Portia enjoyed another treat he had slipped her. I told Chief I would be over more often. He said my excuses were all dead now and that, was the final gifts I had been given. The freedom of the responsibilities I had with my family were all gone. I had no excuse to delay or stop my search for more awareness.

I was driving back and remembered something Chief had said. He had noticed a tension in me even though I was more relaxed than ever. I was in a kind of survival mode, and he had tons of experience with this condition throughout his life. I immediately identified with the fight/flight part when I remembered reading one of my course books. It told of a category I hadn't heard of before. I knew about tend/befriend and fight/flight, and was informed we also had a freeze mode. It was well-known in theory, but never got the attention the other categories received. I was stuck in the freeze mode waiting for the arrival of a que to take action.

Chief explained it with an example. He said to imagine myself as a mouse in a field and seeing the shadow of a hawk circling above. The mouse would be frozen with fear and unable to take flight for the fear of any movement would give away its position. Many people were in the same boat as the mouse and stuck waiting to take action. This could go on for years, or even a lifetime, and during the waiting we were on fight/flight and pumping adrenaline. While in this mode of survival, all our energy and circulatory systems focused on fight/flight. This included the immune system, digestion, and the majority of our body's regeneration capabilities. When we were young, it wasn't even noticed by us, and when we became older the damage was already done and our health went awry.

I asked him how he had overcome this malady. He said he had to tune into the emotion of fear in the background all the time, and look deeply into that fear and be aware of it to understand it. We had to see it and to be aware it existed to figure out what the actual fear was, then we had to accept it as the truth. Awareness and acceptance of our new findings would lead us to act on our new truth and finally be free.

Chief had let out a loud sigh when he finished. He told me he hadn't realized he had been in fear, just being prepared and thought everyone was doing the same. I agreed and understood what he had revealed. I thought the emotion of fear I had been made aware of was buried deep within me and I had to "go down the rabbit hole" to find it.

I suddenly realized I was pulling in the driveway. I had no idea where half of the drive went. I didn't even remember going over two bridges that ran across the channel and bay. I didn't remember any of it. I looked at Portia and she was happy and ready to get out. I had a lot on my mind with the fear issue as well as my personal history deletion. Chief mentioned I might find some guidance from one of the many Carlos Castaneda books he had given me. He said Don Juan had explained self-importance and personal history to one of his apprentices. Sadly, he couldn't remember which book.

Once in the house, I looked at the books and saw there were seven by Carlos Castaneda stacked up. I guessed it was time to take a break and to start reading. I knew I'd uncover the self-importance and personal history subjects and I'd learn other new things along the way.

Portia was curled up at my feet with her head lying on my foot as I tuned into the tension in me. I thought of the mouse in the field seeing the shadow of the hawk and saw myself in the mouse's place. I dared not move else I'd give away my position. I shook from the adrenaline pumping through my body and saw myself figuring out what to do next. I was on hold and stuck on freeze with no options available. Imagine, living this way for a lifetime and never knowing who I was. I realized then how this all impacted my overall health. Of course, the emotional turmoil affected my thinking and took a physical toll. The fear was impacting my immune system as well as my digestive system and my body's ability to heal itself. Fight/flight/freeze was imperative to our survival and took number one priority over everything else. Danger and our response were the only matters at hand when it came to life/death.

I could almost feel the adrenalin coursing through my veins and supplying my muscles with the energy needed to react. My thoughts, driven by the emotions, were overriding any thinking except *danger, danger*. Rationality was absent and programmed overreactions triggered by emotions geared up. At the same time healing stopped and would not start again until the crises was over. My problem was I was always in a crisis and ready to react. I was stuck waiting on something that would never come about. I was prepared to protect myself to the death, if necessary. I was now aware of this new concept and now had to accept it entirely. Acceptance didn't mean I liked or condone it. Acceptance was necessary before action could happen.

Not only was I stuck in the freeze mode, I was stuck on acceptance, really stuck. How many times had I said, "This is not acceptable"? I had said and heard those exact words over and over by others. I realized we're all probably living in non-acceptance of the truth. Our programing, belief systems, and conditioning told us one thing, and reality told us something else.

How many times had I starred truth in the eyes and convinced myself otherwise. I would always revert to my conditioning, especially when emotional. Emotions overrode logic and truth, and I was starting to see how long I had defended the lie. Acceptance was being stirred and I was understanding how my non-acceptance of the truth had caused my many difficulties throughout my entire life.

THE MIRROR

I remember early in my adult life hearing the phrase, ***"The world is our mirror" (Unknown Source),*** and thought it sounded cute and took it as a nice saying. I didn't understand what the phrase was really telling me though. I went through my life never knowing that mirroring was going on all around me and lessons and facts were being given to me and everyone.

When I was forced to retire and had to retrain, I was drawn to the holistic community and trained for many years. I first came across the mirroring idea while learning Reiki, reflexology, and massage therapy. The mirroring concept wasn't explored much at all and brushed over as a thing going on and nice to see. When I started studying a newly developed holistic healthcare system, the concept of mirroring was brought to the forefront. As I became more aware of the reflections and had a better understanding, the more I used it for my advantage. My clients showed me the mirroring, and I could see how connected we were to each other. When I drove or went grocery shopping, the mirror was always there for me to see. As much as I didn't want to admit it, I was slowly starting to understand the ***"We are one,"*** philosophy.

I saw a side of me only visible when I closely observed every action and didn't judge myself for my reaction or overreaction. At first, it was impossible to see the ugly side of myself. I knew he was there, but I managed to turn a blind eye. I would get glimpses now and then of who and what I could become if pushed and realized that side of me was indeed my dark side. Not wanting to accept I had a nasty side prevented me from trying to understand and be aware it was there. I had to see other people lying, cheating, and breaking the rules before I saw them in myself. I didn't even have to leave the house to see the truth.

I watched the news and saw people of power and great authority stand in front of the camera and lie. I would also see the people conned by the best there was, believe him rather than the truth. The only reason I could see this happening was to observe the negative emotion within being triggered while watching TV. If it wasn't the news, coincidently, there would be a program, commercial, or movie with the exact character I needed to see, play their part perfectly for me to see clearly, myself. If I decided not to watch TV and read instead, I would get the mirroring concept through the characters of the book, article, or ad. If I was understanding self-observation and noticed I was being triggered, I would see again a program, a conditioning, or a belief system rearing its ugly head wanting me to overreact.

The world was my reflection and my inside was reflected outward and the outside was reflected within me. I understood the mirroring constantly happening all around me. At first, I compared myself with those who acted as my mirror and couldn't identify with them. They were very different from me, I was unique. Often, I'd notice the mirroring would be an exaggerated version and sometimes so exaggerated I couldn't see myself. I would discard the reflection and think it wasn't my mirror and only their behavior was being seen.

Over time, a long time, I was finally able to tune in and observe. What I saw may have been exaggerated for me to see the deep and subtle reflection being shown. I was being shown, in an exaggerated way, an image big enough to be seen clearly enough to know it was going on in me. By observing my actions with persistence and determination, I was gaining awareness little by little. I understood one fear I always had in the background. Fear of failure. I became aware I was afraid of being exposed as a fake. I was afraid of others knowing I was acting and had conned everyone with an award-winning show all my life. The high confidence and the bravado I portrayed constantly was really an act. I was living a lie and saw my behavior and reactionary ways were subject to what I had been taught. I was seeing the results of my conditioning, programming, and brainwashing. My hardwired belief systems were impacting my life in a bad way.

By now, I had been practicing self-observation for a while and positive changes were occurring little by little. I was excited and observing myself at every opportunity. Suddenly, I realized I had always observed myself throughout my life. I was waiting to catch myself making a mistake or failing. I would observe myself in any highly emotionally charged actions, then criticized, chastised, and harshly judged myself. I would find fault on the simplest of matters and never give myself any credit. It would never be perfect; the only thing visible were the imperfections. I wasn't observing at all. I was critically watching myself, judging myself, and waiting to find any fault.

Where the hell did this behavior come from? Why was I sabotaging opportunities meant to gain and learn from? Why did I hate myself so much and punish myself so badly?

I guessed, deep-down I wanted to be perfect, and nothing less would do. If I was perfect, I would have **complete control and the power and authority** to make everything be **perfect**.

Wow, in seeing my own imperfections, I started to realize, **my** definition of perfection was just another belief given to me along the way. Perfection wasn't having complete control. Perfection was the opposite entirely. I remembered my blue sticky note with the definition of love and smiled. By now, I had it committed to memory and often heard myself saying it when in self-observation: ***"Love is not an emotion. Love describes neutrality, the absence of judgement, censorship, desire, and worry."****(Unknown source)*

I thought love, and being loved, was what perfection was. I saw I was not enlightened, aware, woke, or God, (*yet*). I saw I was a human being and connected to everyone. I was starting to understand *"The world is my mirror."* I was gradually seeing and understanding my condition was the human condition. We were all, with few exceptions, loaded with crazy belief systems, and programming. Most of us were hardwired to behave and treat ourselves the way we do. In punishing ourselves for our imperfections, some of us went to the extreme. When I saw this in myself, and how my own thinking was impacting my health in every way, I was stunned.

ACCOUNTABLE

There was a price to pay for what we did in life, whether knowingly or not. Actions resulted in reactions, and every cause had an effect. The problem was sometimes the consequences of our actions took a while to manifest. This led to thinking we got away with our behavior and were free from consequences. Another problem we faced was being held accountable for our actions and overreactions. When we took on a responsibility, we were usually given the power to carry out the responsibility. We were also accountable for the outcome. Many times in our lives, we took an action to accomplish our goal and accomplished our task and were never held accountable for whether it turned out good or bad. All that mattered was we finished the job. This lack of being held accountable didn't seem to be a priority.

Often, we see people in power not living up to their responsibilities or being held to account. Repeatedly, we make wrong choices and are let off the hook as well, and the mirror is in full view. Of course, we have built-in excuses for failing and blame people, places, and things for our failures. But, deep-down we know it's really our fault. We punish ourselves and the lesson goes unlearned again.

I had observed over time my favorite (sic) ways to beat myself up were to not allow myself the simple act of having fun. By doing this, I could rob others of their fun and think, "If I can't have fun, you can't either."

I think, most if not, all of us, are very aware, of every mistake we have made in our past, and are aware of the consequences.

When we think we're off the hook, we are in for a rude awakening. We think we're exempt from the law of *causality* or *cause and effect*, and convince ourselves our wrong reaction or behavior was okay.

I also observed no consequences and accountability would guarantee I would not learn or gain from the experience at hand. The lesson went unlearned and would have to be eventually presented again, and usually at a higher cost. I had noticed, while observing my emotions and actions, I held myself accountable for every mistake I made. I also understood, through awareness, if I did this now, I must have been doing this all along. I became aware I punish myself in some way, usually at my health's expense. Usually, I would think badly of myself, call myself names, or, worst of all, not allow myself to have fun or be happy. I would choose to hold myself accountable for failing and see what a failure I was, instead. I'd also noticed the consequences of punishing myself, over the course of my lifetime. My emotional turmoil, I thought I was controlling, went unexpressed. This could be a big problem if left unchecked.

When I was a young man in my prime, I never noticed the effect of my falseness. I didn't know I was holding myself responsible and doing myself harm. I didn't know I was programmed and conditioned and had no choice most of the time. Being ignorant of facts would impact my success or failure, my winning or losing, and my joy or sadness. Important lessons in living were being presented all the time and going unnoticed or unlearned.

As the years pass, and I age, I now feel the impact and consequences I placed on myself for a lifetime of my failures. I continue to try and understand most of my failures came about because I just didn't know any better. I also know and am becoming more aware, there's a me in there who wants what he wants when he wants it. That side of me doesn't care anything about rules or laws when it comes to me or about what others think or care about him.

As I gain understanding and see what drives me, I find I am realizing my preconceived notions are being exposed. Once seen, I am becoming more receptive and less judgmental. In accepting my discoveries, I am allowing myself to move forward. Acceptance of what is, isn't easy. I know and have been convinced only until I accept my new truths will I be able to move forward. Non-acceptance has stopped me in my tracks throughout my life and I see it going on all around me. My mirror is showing me if I disagree or don't like something, I won't accept it. Acceptance is just complying with whatever it is. We may not like what is, it may not give us a fuzzy feeling, but we *must* accept it, period. Without acceptance, we stall and never move on; we are stuck and sometimes forever in the "freeze mode".

If I refuse to see my mirror, if I fail to accept the truth, it shows me my suffering continues. I see suffering and injustice and leaders slowly taking away freedoms we have let them have with little resistance. By luck or chance, I then understand and see the duality in everything, and know until I become aware, the battle in my mind is still happening. Good/evil, dark/light, yin/yang, duality in all of it glory. In awareness, in the now, and totally present, allows me to see the beautiful balance that exists. I'm still distracted and often choose to see the imbalance instead of the duality. I continue to have my mood swings and tough lessons in life, although I immediately recognize what's going on and usually find myself smiling. Every day, I tune into the show and see through others the programming and belief systems tugging at me. I am starting to understand if I look through soft eyes, I see more balance.

I AM RESPONSIBLE

"ULTIMATELY, ALL OF US IS THE SOURCE OF OUR OWN JOYS AND SORROWS, THROUGH SUCH CHOISES, OUR OWN WEALTH AND POVERTY, AND ALL WE EXPERIENCE."

(Unknown Source)

I wrote this quote or phrase down well over fifteen years ago. This quote struck a chord within me and shifted my then current perspective dramatically. It was an *Ah, ha* moment and I remembered how the shift in my understanding affected me at the time. I had heard the truth and it rang like a bell inside me.

The course lasted three days. Learning this new truth had shaken the old lie I thought was true. The first day after class ended, I decided to meditate and ponder what I had just discovered. I grabbed a decent meal and, after eating, took a walk. After showering and dressing, I relaxed for a while and started the process in *the art of drawing a conclusion.* In order for us to draw any conclusion, we must *analyze, synthesize, ponder, and consider.* I could understand this idea from (***PaRama College)*** charts I had purchased during my supercharged training with the *"Founder"*. This particular chart showed how the Thalamus of the brain was so heavily involved in the thinking process physiology.

After noting my breathing for a time, I began to achieve a neutrality and a feeling of detachment, and I further investigated. I thought about the phrase and how it made total sense. It indeed rang true to me; there was no doubt. I then saw I had always blamed someone or something for a reason for not being happy, wealthy, or successful. Ultimately, I would blame myself even if I managed to find a scapegoat. I always held myself accountable for any failure. I was starting to understand I was responsible for all my choices. At first, I thought what an idiot I had been. Immediately, another thought came to mind: "*Forgive him, he knows not what he has done.*" So, instead of beating myself up in some way, I was understanding my choices had been tainted by outside programming. I was responsible for the outcome regardless of whether the choice was good or not, or based in fact or not.

I had found a jewel in this quote and it could possibly change my life forever. I changed without trying to change. I started to have a kindness toward myself I had prevented, for a whole lifetime. I attended the rest of the class and noticed my behavior had changed as well. I had become quiet and seemed to be in deep thought. I was in attendance, but a part of me still pondered and analyzed. I was looking for any chink in my new trueness. I was trying to find any fault, any opening I could to revert to my old reasoning. I saw my conditioning and programming fighting truth. A battle was going on inside of me.

Many years ago, under enormous stress, I became interested and started Kriya Yoga. After reading "Autobiography of a Yogi", I decided to attend workshops and learn Kriya Yoga. I knew meditation was one of the keys to being true to self.

The book jumpstarted me. I went through the slow process of learning and practicing breathing exercises, energizing exercises, and the art of Kriya meditation. I also read the "Bhagavad Gita: The scripture of mankind". This great piece of literature spoke of a great battle coming and in the works. The battle in the Gita was on the battlefield with armies and drawn lines. It spoke of battle plans, strategies, and actions for both sides. In reality, the battle described was the war going on within all of us. We'd all heard the major opposites: Good/Evil, God/Devil, Yin/Yang, and Truth vs Lies. Don't forget, Angles/Demons, Right/Wrong, Sinner/Saint, and Dark/Light.

For thousands of years, philosophers, scholars, authors, and enlightened people have been helping us to see the truth. Through their writings, public speaking, and their actions, they have been showing us the many paths and ways to autonomy, and finally freedom. All these people and tools we have at our disposal can take us only so far. The buck stops with me and only I can go forward, or not. I must dig deep, stir the pot, and continue to learn, to understand, and become aware of *what makes me tick?*

The help I received along the way and the guidance I got from well-intentioned people is not a substitute to take them at their word. What they say or write is their truth, their own discoveries. I can't skip the inside work I must do on my own. I have to observe myself in action and find out my truths. I can't take any shortcuts or find excuses for not doing the job. To ***"know thyself"***, for me, is a work in progress. Sometimes, I think I have myself all figured out and, voilà, I observe myself finding a new character in the mix or uncovering another preconceived notion coming into the light. I am slowly discovering my beliefs, my outside programming, and my human conditioning have roots that go very deep. I am also becoming aware of the side shoots with deep seeded ties, and all the new programming I have added along the way. Everything must be looked at and concluded before we accept it as the truth. No stone unturned, dig, dig, dig, until I have exposed everything.

My wife and grown children have witnessed me before and after I started this process. I am more detached from their emotionally driven turmoil and look in the mirror. I've noticed more I'm not giving direction or advice and letting them figure it out for themselves. I see the damage done, and instead of hating myself, I find I am kinder to myself and understanding the *why* of what I've done. I am understanding by doing the inside work, I am changing and slowly finding the joy of living. There was no joy before, and now I see it little by little every day.

I have read and re-read "*Awareness*" well over 100 times, not counting the many times I just open it to wherever it happens to fall. I am still amazed at what I discover every time I read it.

One day, I opened to a page and was blown away at what I had missed. How could I miss the important message and how had I not remembered it at all? Every time I have read *"Awareness"* I am surprised by the new words that appear as I progress. The quote that struck me was one I heard ringing in my head when clients ask for help, or when family members ask for guidance.

"Until you are aware of yourself, you have no right to interfere with anyone else or with the world." *"Awareness"- (Anthony de Mello)*

This statement put me on my heels as I pondered what it was telling me. My understanding was blatantly obvious and without doubt. I had no right to interfere with anyone or anything. Holy crap! Did this mean I couldn't help folks who were seeking help or advice? Did this mean I had no impute in matters that concerned me? What did he mean 'to interfere'?

Back to Google for a search on the definition of interfere: ***Interfere; to impede, obstruct, hinder, inhibit, restrict, constrain, or hamper.***

I pondered this definition only a short while before I concluded, "To **in terfere** = to **control**". Wow! I'd been all about having control and controlling people, places, and things all my life. I thought it was a necessity to have control and to exert it as well.

Looking back made me realize I had, by my controlling, taken away the very freedoms from others I had so diligently fought for. I was controlling others so I had freedom while taking theirs away. I also became aware of something even more subtle and disturbing. I took on being responsible for many things I wasn't given responsibility for. No one asked me to be responsible for them and I took it on anyway, without permission or request. Ah, back to self-importance, authority, and power again, and *all about me.*

I didn't look to beat myself up or find fault with my discovery this time. Instead, I saw how my belief systems had given me no choice in most matters. A little sadness caught my attention just then, and self-pity came into my observation. It seemed I wasn't trying to blame anyone or even myself. I was accepting a truth as truth, even though I didn't like what I had discovered. Normally, if I didn't agree with or like something, I would not accept it in any way; I would fight and resist the truth I saw or heard, and my programming challenged the facts. I was becoming more aware.

DISTRACTED

"TO SEE AT LAST WITH A VISION THAT IS CLEAR AND UNOBSTRUCTED BY FEAR OR DESIRE."
(Unknown source)

In today's world, there are many, many distractions that can pull us away from what we are doing. Cell phones, computers, emails, and texts are some of the hundreds of things disrupting thought and goals. This is a common occurrence and didn't exist that long ago. I was slow on the draw when it came to technology and fought it until I finally had to surrender. Yes, I have a cell phone and a computer. I also have a TV and landline. Over the course of the last several years, I have been very in-tune with these distractions and become fully aware how a simple beep on a cell phone can stop me in my tracks.

Everywhere I go I see people, young and old and anywhere in between, looking at the texts, Googling, or talking on cell phones. I see it when I drive, (the highway is a battlefield for me) or when standing in any line. People, including myself, are being bombarded by information distracting them from reality. My grandkids, as well as my wife and adult children, can get quite preoccupied with their devices, and it's making me realize distraction is always trying to take me away from awareness.

I was trying to have a conversation with a contractor doing landscaping for me at the house. During our "conversation", he was called several times. First, I would hear the phone chirp and see the sudden change he displayed when he heard the phone and felt it vibrate. I saw a slight fear rear up in him, followed by obvious annoyance, and then anticipation of a response. I also saw the total disconnect that took place between me and him.

My immediate reaction was feeling offended, disrespected, and disregarded. Here I was, trying to make my point, and my words were not being heard and my presence wasn't even noticed. I felt invisible. I was just about to give him a piece of my mind when I realized the mirroring taking place. Although I wasn't truly aware I was self-observing this scene, observation was taking place. I was feeling the emotional tug and seeing the beliefs being brought to the surface. I had to really stop myself from overreacting like I'd normally would have done. I understood that wouldn't resolve anything. I might get a little satisfaction from expressing my anger, but my outburst wouldn't help me understand what was really going on.

It was very easy for me to revert time and time again. I observed when I overreacted, the programming and conditioning being triggered by the negative emotions or high emotional conditions triggered anger. The anger I wanted to release was *in* me and not me. It was my anger I was feeling and not anger at the contractor.

There are several outdoor programs I enjoy watching. I like them for the beautiful nature scenery, and I see a time of long ago being played out. I watch folks of all ages living off the land and homesteading or living on land they had purchased. I notice the more remote and out of touch they are from civilization the more they rely on tuning into their surroundings.

I know how it feels to be alert and aware of my surroundings; I can sense obstacles before I see them. I hear the almost silent sounds of game scratching for seeds and nuts, to smelling a buck starting their rut. It only takes a short time for me to feel nature around me and to be able to see the animals, birds, and insects living out their lives. Before it was brought to my attention, all I would see was tranquility and peacefulness all around. Then, suddenly I would be witness to the chaos going on all around as well. I would see an owl pluck a rodent from the ground in a flash, or see a coyote tearing apart its prey. I would see fish jumping out of the water for insects flying above the water. I was seeing a balance of both sides of the equation. I was seeing reality. If I take the time needed to look and to see, I will be present and in acceptance.

The distractions we have in the civilized world are only that. I can go to a park or playground and hear man-made noises from fire trucks using their blaring sirens, or the sounds of children yelling at each other and having fun. I can tune in to whatever I want and also tune out as well. I was meditating one morning, and as I sat and became still all I could hear was a lone bird chirping with its *squawk, squawk*. I was distracted by the sound; all I could hear was its unnerving squawk. I was about to give up, when I suddenly remembered something I had read long ago.

A Yogi had written: "That when hearing a sound that might be distracting, remember, in order for sound to exist, silence must exist as well. Tune into the silence that is there along with the sound and your distractions will disappear."

I sat for a moment or two and concentrated on the silence that existed in between the chirps and soon the chirps were covered by the silence. I was amazed and completely caught off-guard. No noise at all as I thought maybe the bird had flown away. As I smiled to myself, I picked up the sound of the chirping again. I went through the process again and tuned into the silence once again and the bird noise disappeared, like before.

Our world is full of distractions that can hinder our attempt at being present and in the moment. Some folks are lucky and have only a few, and some of us are distracted most of the time. I now know I am making a conscious choice at letting anything distract and take me away. I know if I really want this moment only and want the silence, I can choose that, or I can opt for the sound that always exists with noise. I have realized over time I might choose to be distracted and make that choice as an excuse for not wanting to be present or in the now. I know what needs to be done, and yet, I look for any reason that gives me a good excuse for not doing what I know is right. My mirror always shows me what is really going on if I really want to look and to see.

"I am the source of my joys and sorrows, and through such choices my wealth or poverty, and all that I experience."

"SEEKING"

"In Awareness there is truth; In Awareness is salvation; in Awareness is spirituality; in Awareness is growth; in Awareness is love; in Awareness is awakening" "Awareness"
- (Anthony de Mello)

Since day one, once I became part of the holistic community, I have been exposed to, and made aware of, the theory of enlightenment, self-awareness, awakening, and "higher consciousness."

I first heard the term "seeker" when attending courses in the energy medicine field as a practitioner. It seemed there were many people not satisfied with how their lives were playing out and looking for a way out. I received lots of advice along the way and saw there were many paths that supposedly would set me free or shift my consciousness for the better. Along the way, there were many times I would take on a new way and buckle down and force myself to master what I had heard from others. Usually the new way required huge discipline and complete dedication to the cause.

At first, I was enthusiastic and gung-ho to follow every detail, but in a short while I would get bored or quit. I was trying to force change and it wouldn't take long until I would give up. Of course, I had to hold myself accountable for failing and decided once again to be miserable. I blamed others for their whacky ideas, although I knew I had made the choice, not them. This would happen repeatedly and always play out the same. I would be exposed to a new idea or concept about the final goal of "oneness", and then take a course, go on a retreat, read a new book, or learn a meditation style that flipped my enlightenment switch on. I didn't stick to any one way long enough to see the desired effects of techniques come into fruition. When I looked around during my exposure to new ideas, I would see a lot of "miserable seekers" like myself. We were all trying to fulfill our true purpose of being true to ourselves and evolving.

I remember one experience that brought this to my attention in an awesome way. I was attending a retreat many years ago and looking forward to the offerings. I would be there a full week and didn't have to worry about lodging, food, transportation, or my safety. Everything was being provided for all that attended the retreat. After settling in and unpacking the few items I had packed, I decided to walk around my new home and get a feel for my new digs. I checked out the dining hall and helped myself to hot ginger tea always available. I then shopped at the bookstore and purchased a few items that caught my eye. I noticed several attendees, like myself, had gathered and were talking and smiling while they discussed the schedule of events planned for that day. The retreat would officially kick-off in a couple of hours with speakers and staff making their presentations. I noted the excitement and anticipation most of the group felt. Finally, the time came for our presentation to begin.

The speakers seemed genuine and sounded like the clergy with soft words and much smiling. I looked around briefly to not cause a distraction and noticed how most, if not all, the attendees seemed to be sad and wanting. I guessed they wanted what the speakers had shown them, happiness and serenity. Every person who spoke was smiling from ear to ear. They seemed to be filled with love and acceptance.

Shortly after the presentation, we were invited to the dining hall for our noon meal. I was caught, finding myself in the middle of the heard, and decided to step away from the proximity I was in. Instead of following the crowd, I decided to wait a while and sit on one of the benches scattered about.

As I sat and tried to wrap my head around what I had witnessed with the attendees, I overheard loud voices and an argument going on behind me. I sat facing forward, and although I was nosey and wanted to take a look, I forced myself to not. Instead, I tried to focus on what I was there for and tune out anything else. It wasn't working at all. I was hearing two people calling names at each other and sometimes swearing. I couldn't take it any longer and had to turn around. What I saw made my jaw drop. The two folks carrying on were two of the speakers we had just heard. One minute they were at the foot of the cross, and now they were far from that. I felt a little embarrassed for giving in to my curiosity, although I was glad I had.

I was witnessing myself in the behavior being displayed and seeing how I had done exactly as they had done. I was seeing "talk the talk" not "walk the walk". I would often criticize when others broke a rule. I would get on my high horse with my children, my spouse, and other family members. I would hold others accountable and chastise them for their wrongdoings when, in fact, I was the one in the wrong. Seeing my hypocrisy, I would eventually get around to punishing myself to hold myself accountable. The problem was I wasn't learning anything; I wasn't seeing the lessons being presented. Instead, I focused on how to punish myself for mistakes. I was talking the talk instead of accepting what was apparent. I was refusing to see the mirror and to see my own reflection. Until I became aware of myself and ready to take the time to introspect, and take the plunge to go deep, I'd continue to suffer and keep myself from joy.

"Walking the walk" could only happen when I was in acceptance of what is. In order to accept what is, I had to be present and aware of what is.

When I first started seeking "awareness", I had to force myself to see objects being presented. An example that comes to mind was when I was on a walk in the forest. I started off only thinking about the objective of going from point A to B. I thought of the route I'd take and the time it took to complete "the walk". The first time I really saw this, I was really upset at myself. Here I was, on a walk with my best friend, Portia, and the only thing I was seeing was the finish line. I wasn't enjoying her company or taking in the sights, sounds, and the smells going on all around me. I would keep an eye on Portia and not really be seeing her and her antics. Portia did funny, sometimes hilarious, things and looking at me for some kind of acknowledgement, at least.

With all these thoughts coming in, another one took over as I remembered Chief saying one day, "Don't look at the world like it's a dragon to slay. Look at the world through soft eyes, accepting everything you see as is."

From that day on, I would force myself to look around through soft eyes. I would look at a certain tree and gaze at it until I began to really see it, and then tuned into the glory it was showing me. I would look up at cloud formations and soon be mesmerized with their beauty and shapes. I would watch and be a witness, seeing Portia being the dog she is. I was being entertained by nature and her creatures. I was getting a taste for "awareness" and becoming present enough to enjoy its gifts.

I guess I am a seeker after all. What I am seeking is *awareness.*

GOOD/BAD COMPANY?

I learned early on when I started looking into the holistic world and taught being true to myself was a high priority, as well as a must if I wanted any kind of serenity. One of the four ways of being true to myself was "keeping good company". I contemplated this and saw a fly in the ointment, so to speak. On one side, I was to observe my mirror in others, and on the other side trying to handpick my company and those mirrors that would be good for me to see. This was a real conundrum for me and is still unresolved. *The world is our mirror*; was calling my attention and keeping good company was ringing in my head as well. I considered the dilemma and didn't know if my bad company was in fact good for me or not. I tried meditating on this puzzle and a conclusion was to no avail. I was stumped and stopped in my tracks. It was time to seek answers and advice from Chief.

The next morning, I loaded Portia into my car and drove over the bridges to track down Chief and ask for his guidance. As I drove, as usual, other drivers in their own world, and probably distracted themselves, were forgetting to use turn signals, lollygagging at intersections, or not playing by the rules. I laughed out loud as it dawned on me the rules I had thought were for all to obey, were *my* rules. In fact, they were hardwired rules and conditioning or someone's preconceived notions, which had been introduced to me long ago. I knew exactly where these beliefs and conditioning came from, and realized I had passed these same concepts and falsehoods onto my children as my dad had done for us kids.

Looking back, I remembered the many times I had been a passenger while my brother or sister drove. I would witness their overreaction to other drivers and egged them on to overreact even more. Then, at that point in my life, I had yet to uncover any of the emotionally charged conditioning in me. The highway, roads, and streets were a constant battlefield. Then, an opportunity arose when I was a passenger with my daughter driving one day. My grandson was playing soccer for a local team and instead of taking two vehicles to the game, we decided to use one car instead. I wanted to drive, and she did too. I decided to go with her, and a while later, she picked me up. She backed out of the driveway and before we even got to the street, my daughter was wound up. She was complaining about another driver not giving her a break to leave the driveway. We had a five-mile drive to the soccer fields and had to drive a four-lane highway until using a two-lane rural road. The highway was a nightmare with heavy traffic in our lanes. Vehicles were crawling along and stop and go traffic kept everyone on edge. My daughter was really triggered, overreacting and getting angrier by the foot. I saw other drivers doing the same. I smiled and kept my laugh to myself.

I was amazed to see her behavior and noticed the huge amount of anger she was venting that day. I immediately saw I was observing myself driving and seeing the way I overreact. I was also seeing the anger triggered both of us. I realized on this one occasion, she had, as I did, an anger that had to be justified. I remembered how I would wake up pissed off and knew deep inside I had a choice to be angry or not. I was seeing I always made the same choice and knew the choice was mine. I would have to find a good reason or excuse for choosing anger. If it wasn't the highway, I would search and be on the lookout for anything I could blame. This went on for many years until I finally became aware of what was really going on and finally understood. It was all my choice and the anger was **in** me, not me.

Being in good company was sometimes not a choice at times. *Choosing* to be in good company was. Do I avoid the hustle and bustle of the city where chaos seems the norm, or do I choose only good company and quiet surroundings? Do I subject myself to rowdy people or do I choose only the serene and wise people? I was having a difficult time trying to figure it all out as I drove onward to seek good, sound advice from Chief. I was also unnerved at the fact I couldn't figure it out on my own. Milliseconds after that thought, I saw myself criticizing myself and had to once again laugh. I smiled and realized I was a real piece of work.

I parked in the driveway where I had once lived. I took a chance and drove there in hopes of seeing my neighbor and friend. She lived diagonally from my old apartment. I was friends with her husband and son as well. As I entered the dead-end street, I saw our old driveway. I noticed her car parked and her working in the garden she kept every season. After a funny handshake and then a real hug, we chatted for a while as Portia ran around. Moments later, Portia's best dog friend, a giant male Akita came bounding up to greet her. Portia's a mid-sized dog at thirty-one pounds, the Akita quadrupled her weight and then some. He was very gentle with her, although sometimes would whack her with one of his man-size paws, knocking her about. It was funny to watch him afterwards nuzzle her to make up for his inadvertent actions. The Akita owner came up within minutes of his dog escaping his yard and we talked and laughed as the two dogs ran and played. He had an appointment to attend, so he took Portia's playmate and left us. Soon it was time for my friend to return to her work and I wanted to go on a walk like old times to connect with Chief.

Portia walked with me on the lead until we reached the shortcut and familiar territory. She was trained to heel, although I liked her beside me instead of at my heel. It took a long time until she understood what I wanted. It then donned on me old habits were hard to break, even for dogs. I also saw how habits, any habit, wasn't good and wouldn't led to change. Hmmm. I unsnapped Portia's lead and off she went after a rabbit I hadn't seen. Again, she would stop short of catching the bunny and would let it think it had escaped the jaws of death. I had to laugh at her antics and reminisced to when I had first brought her home. I felt a wave of gratitude come over me and realized how much Portia had done for me over the few years we had been united so far. I received unconditional love from her all the time; she showed me continuously what love was. Maybe, just maybe, that was her role in my life. She was definitely living up to the reputation dogs had as "man's **best** friend". Portia was *my* best friend.

We entered the park and Portia took off at full speed. She was low to the ground, and when she ran she could corner and stop on a dime. She had seen a few of her other best friends in the field with their human buddies. I called out to her and she stopped and waited for me to catch up. We visited for a little while, me with my human companions, and Portia with her doggy pals. I looked around and noticed the bench Chief normally sat on held someone else instead. As I continued looking over, I suddenly remembered the elderly woman I was staring at. She was one of Chief's friends. I had seen them together talking on several occasions when looking for Chief.

My stare must have been picked up by her as she turned my way and waved me to come over and join her on the bench. I called Portia over and said goodbye as I walked her way. I was trying to look casual and walk slowly to cover the overwhelming excitement building within me. I had apprehension and had conjured up a reason for her being there instead of Chief. Maybe he was sick or not around anymore. I thought something bad had happened as my mind raced. I noticed a fear and grief building inside as I fed it with my worry. I was tapped in to my lack of control over anything. I then started observing I was thinking future possibilities and being in the future or the past wasn't a good place for me to be. I said in my mind, *Now, Now, Now*, and was immediately present and focused on this very moment, and nothing else.

Years ago, when I was a civilian working for the US Navy, my job was to test equipment onboard Navy ships and submarines. Our team would help groom the computers, navigational systems, and sensors the ships used for their mission. We would spend several days making adjustments and fine tuning the equipment before testing them underway. During the testing phase, I would sometimes be on the bridge and combat center where the buttons were pushed, and weapons were fired from. It was a busy place and seemed hectic with sailors talking on microphones and looking at their computer screens. That was until the special words came loudly through the speakers. *Now, now, now* would be heard and everything would come to this moment in time and nothing else. On the first *now*, the bridge would become totally quiet, as the folks behind their instrument panels, sitting on station would be waiting in anticipation for the next *now*. When the third *now* came, there was immediate action that happened simultaneously without exception. The third *now* was *right now*, that very moment. Buttons were pushed, switches were flipped, and commands were given; the test was underway. From that day on, if I was mind boggled or overthinking, I would use those words to yank me into being present.

I approached the bench and the woman I had never met stood to greet me. I put out my hand and she took it, pulling me gently towards her for a hug. Portia looked up at us and I could see her eyes were smiling like we were. After a moment or two, we broke the embrace and sat on the bench. I introduced myself and she said, "Yes, I know. Chief has mentioned you many times in our conversations." I asked how he was, and she said, "He's great."

I felt relief hearing he was okay and relaxed a bit. She said he was attending a get-together, a reunion of sorts, out west in California. She said he would be gone for at least a month and to him it was a big event he had wanted to attend for a long time. I was genuinely happy for him, even though I wanted him for myself, I guess. I finally got around to asking what her name was, and she looked me in the eyes, smiling and said, "Oh, sorry, my name is Freebird."

I immediately thought of the Lynyrd Skynyrd's song with the same name. I remember it had been very popular in the late seventies. I wondered how she'd got her name and mentioned the song. She said it had nothing to do with the song. She had been presented with her name by a Native American Shaman as a young baby and shortly after birth. She was Native American. Her mom's father was full blooded Native American, and her mother came from Swedish heritage. Her father was 100%, full blooded Cherokee. I looked at her features and could see she was indeed of Native American blood. She was a tall woman and had a beauty you often saw in the Swedish people. Her hair was a mixture of blond and powdery white. She was very beautiful and had a command of herself that demanded respect, and that I did. I was feeling an admiration for her and didn't know anything about her at all.

We talked for a short while before she abruptly stopped in mid-sentence of our conversation. She caught me off-guard when she asked why I had come over to see Chief. On one hand, my being caught off-guard had surprised me, and now my guard was up like a wall. I was seeing this happen as I observed my emotional turmoil. A moment went by, and as I settled I saw Freebird' s eyes shining just like Chief's lit up when I presented him with one of my dilemmas. I told her I had come to seek advice and maybe for her to help shed a light on the "good company" concept in being true, as well as "The world is my mirror" phenomenon.

Freebird sat quietly for several minutes. She had her eyes closed and was deep in thought and seemed focused on providing me an answer. After another moment or two, she opened her eyes and looked over my way. She smiled and I noticed how her eyes were smiling also. It reminded me of the way Portia would look at me during special times. The special times were when we would sit on my couch down in the basement after a long day of doing, doing, doing. Those were the very hectic and troubling times we spent a full day running to appointments, shopping, or visiting the nursing home. I would be frazzled and probably hungry and overtired. The time had finally arrived to walk down the eleven stairs to my sanctuary. To this very day, I have always counted my steps when I go to the basement. I do this for one reason and one reason only: I want to be sure I'm present and focused on descending the stairs, without tripping or falling. I had a few close calls with the stairs while renovating and moving. As an older person, I have become very aware of how my reactions have slowed a little, and the fear of falling has crept into my consciousness. I'm sure these thoughts and fears arise in most of us as we gracefully (ha) age. It doesn't stop me or hinder me in any way and has protected me by keeping me focused.

After my careful decent, Portia would follow. She would run down the stairs or jump down several stairs at a time until she reached the bottom. She would then glance my way and give me a look I conjured up as her showing off her agility. Smiling, we sat on the couch and I would remove her collar. This was our "little routine" and done at the end of the day. After taking the collar off, I scratched her roughly where the collar had been and she would look at me. She seemed to be smiling lovingly at me; her eyes would be filled with pure affection. Every time I saw this display of affection, my heart flew open and I'd feel like crying with total joy. Joy didn't seem to fit the feeling I experienced. I might say I felt total bliss and acceptance.

As I looked at Freebird, I observed I was feeling the same with her. She started by saying mirroring was taking place always, and it was up to us whether to see the reflection it offered. Our conditioning, programming, and all our belief systems were like a film or coating we had placed on the mirror, and we could look at the reflection and did not see it for what it really was. She said, once we started the process of "knowing self", we started to clean the film and coating from the mirror, and more was revealed to us. Sometimes when we saw the true reflection, it was revealing to us there were images and things, we would have rather not be shown. We were seeing the truth and sometimes think it was too much to bear. This was when another belief system kicked in and we dismissed our findings and find a handy excuse like "bad company" or "not my mirror".

She laughed as she said we were all very cunning, and knew all the angles, and we had to observe this new cleaner mirror, even if we didn't like what we saw.

Acceptance is a must, and acceptance has nothing to do with liking or disliking it. Acceptance is only acknowledging what we are seeing is fact. We don't have to like it or even agree with it, but, we do have to accept it, period.

Freebird then said to me, "Be sure to always protect yourself. "Women are more vulnerable to being harmed than men are usually, and just the fear of man's wrath alone is keeping most women on their toes."

I wasn't understanding the protecting myself and asked her to help me understand.

She said, "As we start to become aware of our own programming, we also realize everyone else is as well. When we are in the process of becoming more aware, sometimes we start to become more passive, mellow, and forgiving. Sometimes we let others off the hook, and let them actually, do us harm. We let them yell at us, we let them blame and chastise us while thinking we are doing just great. We think we have arrived, and we think we are just letting them blow off a little steam. We must not let anyone harm us with their tantrums, and must tell them so. Just because we are changing, doesn't mean we should tolerate bad behavior or bad actions by anyone." Finally, Freebird said,

"Whether physical, mental, or verbal, abuse is abuse, and we must always be true to ourselves and protect ourselves at all times."

Freebird was very blunt, and I noticed she was in a very serious frame of mind. She was very different than Chief. I knew she didn't care whether I liked or disliked what she said, and she wasn't at all worried about hurting my feelings. I was grateful for her honesty and wasn't offended in the least. All she had given me were facts, and sometimes the truth could hurt a little; if I chose to be hurt, that is.

I was understanding her point and, for a moment or two, I thought about what she had said. I had conjured up my dilemma myself, to stall or stop myself from observing something I didn't like or want to see. I understood everything she had told me and realized even more, how cunning I could be and how I could turn the tables, **even on my own self.** A part of me wanted to hold myself accountable and call myself names and condemn my actions, and another part accepted what had transpired in total neutrality. I was seeing the battle going on inside and seeing love vs hate, acceptance vs non-acceptance, and how both sides were always there.

I then remembered what I had read in "*Awareness*" about caring. My interpretation was when I, or we, cared for someone or something, the only reason we cared at all, was there was something in it for us. I thought on this and again realized I never really did anything for anyone without there being something in it for me. It's all about me and the only reason I cared was the same exact reason. Even if I only got a good feeling for my caring, or a thank-you, or positive compliment, I was getting something and not doing, out the goodness of my own heart. I was always in the equation and always front and center to get my rewards.

Freebird and I had a great visit and I was enjoying our time together as I watched Portia sniffing a nearby tree stump. Suddenly, my stomach made a loud rumble that surprised us both. I apologized for the disturbance, and she said I didn't have any control and not to worry. Yes, the control idea again and my certainty I had some, was shining through. I turned to Freebird and asked if she would join me for lunch. I mentioned the seafood place I had discovered long ago on my ventures and earlier walks. She said yes, and we stood and slowly walked in the direction of the restaurant.

Along the way, Freebird would point out a specific tree or spot a bird and bring it to my attention. Anytime she would talk to me or when I would make a comment, she would stop walking and give me her full attention.

We eventually arrived at our destination and sat at a table outside. We had chosen our meals by now and the wait staff came and took our order. Portia was behaving well as usual and laying under the table at both of our feet. When we were served, we ate in silence. At first, I made small talk. When I did, she stopped eating and gave me her undivided attention. This happened several times, and I asked her about it, as well as when she stopped walking while we were conversing.

She laughed and said, "When you walk, you walk. When you eat, you eat, and when you talk, you talk. Multi-tasking makes us take our eye off the ball, and when we don't totally focus on the task at hand, we are apt to miss something that might be important." She continued by saying earlier in her life, especially as a woman, she was expected to multi-task. When she did more than one thing at a time, whatever she was doing would be done half-assed.

I laughed at that. She said it was sad society demanded multi-tasking, and if you didn't have twenty things going on at the same time, you would be called inefficient or lazy. Most people were like jugglers with six balls in the air, and would eventually drop one or two when they lost concentration by another distraction.

I pictured a juggler and clearly saw the similarity in my life. We took a long while to finish our meals, stopping eating many times so we could chat. I felt satisfied in every way. I had a full belly and a head full of ideas I would investigate further in time.

We finished our meal and walked our way back to the common and said our good-byes. I told Freebird how helpful she had been and thanked her for taking the time needed to help me along. She said our time is valuable and she was happy to spend a little of it with me and Portia.

Before she left, I asked her if she was available for counsel, and she said she was. Freebird also gave me her cell phone number and said if she didn't pick up to leave a message. I offered to give her my number, but said she would see it if, or when, I called.

Driving back home gave me an opportunity to evaluate our meeting. Suddenly, I said, "When you drive, you drive." That's exactly what I did. I tuned into driving and took in the view I would have otherwise missed. I saw the road in front of me and smiled as I tuned into my surroundings. No thoughts were blaring, no distractions pulling me around, and no multi-tasking. The only ball I had in the air was driving and being focused on what is.

On the way home, I had decided to take Portia to the beach at my old house. That thought came to me when I looked at the shoreline from the top of the bridge road. The exit was coming up and I pulled off and continued down the road to my home of over forty years. The house itself was much older and some of the wood used in its construction had come from ammunition crates from World War II. The house was in good shape considering its age. I remembered how much time I had spent keeping it up to par. My wife had moved in with me at my parents' old house, now mine. My daughter and four grand-children were now living there and enjoying it as I had.

I parked in the empty lot we owned and walked down toward the beach. Both Portia and I drank from the fresh water spring that had a hose connected. The Seabees, a Navy unit developed after Pearl Harbor, had dug the spring out and had made accessing the spring easier than it had been before. Back in the old days, the Seabees would do community project around town free of charge and used their construction skills to train and perfect their skills.

We walked the beach heading north and to the inaccessible, remote, and rocky beach. Portia was afraid of the waves as they splashed ashore and would go to the water's edge and run from the waves as the came rolling in. I laughed at her antics and enjoyed the show she provided. We stayed for a while, and finally, after another drink of spring water, we departed and drove back to my house.

I was in a great mood and decided to read one of the many dozens of books Chief had gifted me. Portia was happy to be home as well. She was sleeping at my feet with her head on my foot. She often did that and I enjoyed the contact. I was very grateful and tuned in to the things I should. I was also very grateful for the many things I didn't have either. My health was making a rebound, and my mind seemed less cluttered. I was feeling a serenity that could only come with being present and aware. I remembered the many times I complained about not having something I wanted, and some smartass would say I should be grateful for what I already have; I should be thankful I wasn't sick, disabled, or ill. I would look over and think to myself, *easy for you to say*, as I compared myself to them. Instead of hearing what they were telling me, I would shoot the messenger bearing the gifts. I was always on the defense with anyone who offered suggestions or find any fault with me.

At last, I was understanding what their messages were telling me and found truth in what I was hearing. Instead of closing myself off and going on the defensive, I took the information received and thought it through. Gratitude was now something I was aware of and saw how appreciative I should be instead of my selfish, all about me, attitude.

TIME

I chose one of Carlos Castaneda's many books and opened to a page where Don Juan, the sorcerer, was talking to one of his students he had taken under his wing. I'll paraphrase and say he was making his pupil aware of the time we waste during our lives.

He said we waste time as if we had an unlimited amount of it to use, and, in reality, we didn't have that much time to begin with. He reminisced about how he had used his valuable time recklessly throughout his lifetime by doing superfluous things that had no real importance in the scheme of things. Death was patiently waiting to tap us on the shoulder when the time came, and we had no control on when it would happen. Death was our constant companion and wasn't our enemy, but instead a friend. When we finally understood our death was inevitable, then, and only then, could we use death as a constant reminder of our immortality.

Another book I read had their student dig a grave and then spend the night in it as if he were dead. It may sound a little overboard to some until those some understand the point being made. Death *is* a constant companion for the living, and until we are aware of that possibility, we will continue to waste our very precious time to no avail.

Death, and the fact we all will die, isn't a topic you hear discussed often. As a matter of fact, death is a subject we try to avoid. As I read on, I was starting to understand the importance in seeing we were infallible and are all subjected to a beginning and an end. I put the book down and remembered what Freebird had said about time and knew exactly where she was coming from. I understood I had wasted a hell of a lot of my own time and had probably robbed tons of time from others along the way. I became aware of the importance of my time and I should try to not squander it away. When I thought of the concept of death being my constant companion, I understood, for life to exist, death had to exist as well. I was also very aware of my age and didn't have much time, statistically speaking.

Another idea flashed and revealed time was not on my side. I stopped reading for the time being and decided to take a nap. I went down the eleven stairs and counted each one I took. At the bottom, I continued to my bedroom and shut the window curtains and laid down. Within minutes, I fell fast asleep and rested for several hours in a blissful sleep.

I awoke to Portia staring up at me. She was wagging her stubby tail, happy I was awake. I sat on the edge of the bed, slowly stood, and walked toward the stairs going up to the kitchen. Eleven stairs as I again counted to prevent distractions. I opened the door to the deck and Portia ran out and down to the woods. Ever since she was a ten-month old puppy, I trained her to do her business in the woods. Not on the lawn or on paths or trails. I've carried plastic baggies just in case, but have never had to use one.

While she was gone, I thought of time and death and forming a plan to employ using my time more wisely. I must have digested all the newly introduced ideas about time and death while I napped. I did this a lot, and after a nap I felt refreshed and ready to jump in with both feet.

I watched a little TV when Portia came in and found myself enjoying the distractions. Observing myself all the time, and then digging deep when I would find triggers, then seeing reactions and overreactions was taking most of my time these days. I seemed inspired to continue on the search for self and was becoming more aware of the reality that had always been there, behind the coatings of paint we had covered reality. A thought came to me about how devious I had been with everyone, including myself. I was becoming aware of the ways I had lied, cheated, and, as Freebird had said, how cunning I had been along the way. I was a sneaky SOB and knew I could probably talk a dog away from a bone if I wanted it. I would go to any length to get what I wanted: control. I was living the very lies I had created and had justified it all in my mind as okay.

I observed a sadness envelope me as I thought about how I hadn't known any better. At the time, I was only reacting to my preconceived notions and hardwired convictions that were really someone else's ideas. I then felt the anger always in the background. I wanted to chastise myself and condemn my behavior, and blame myself, or those who had filled my head with such craziness. Instead of thinking badly about myself, or hating my programmers, I was just observing it all. I noticed a neutrality instead of resistance. I saw the absence of judgement, instead of the usual critical way I found fault. I then observed the missing desire and worry that tainted everything.

A chill ran through my body and I felt a little odd as I sat for quite a while taking stock of myself in an attempt to understand what I was really being shown. I felt detached and, at the same time, felt more connected than ever. I then looked to find a feeling of being alone and truthfully knew I wasn't.

I then remembered another quote Chief had said about loneliness. He said, "Loneliness is not cured by human company. Loneliness is cured by contact with reality."

I felt a little more carefree, instead of the worry I normally had over just about everything, I felt relieved. The definition I had written down on a blue sticky-note came to my mind, and I realized I was feeling **love**. I had stumbled upon the love inside me, and the neutrality at the center of loving. I thought maybe, just maybe, my heart was finally in play instead of being closed off by anger, fear, worry, and guilt.

> ***"When the heart is unobstructed, the result is LOVE."***
>
> *(Unknown source)*

HUMAN-BEING vs HUMAN-DOING

It seemed like ages ago, I remembered learning how to meditate. I was having huge problems letting myself sit for any length of time without getting up to do something. It didn't seem to matter what needed to be done, I just wanted to do something, anything. My meditation teacher laughed when I told him about my dilemma. I remembered him stating I was a human being, not a "human-doing". He laughed and I did as well. I agreed with his statement, found it to be true, and then dismissed it.

I hadn't yet started to observe myself when feeling a negative or powerful, emotionally charged belief being called out. At the time, I had felt some triggering going on and because I hadn't begun the "inside job" it had gone unobserved. I recalled feeling stupid when asked if I was a human being or a "human-doing". I had laughed along at the joke, but, at the same time, felt really dumb I didn't know what he was saying. It took many years of beating my head against the wall before I understood how profound the statement really was.

As a child, I would be told to keep busy and do what needed to be done. Not knowing any different, I soon developed into a human-doing. In school, in church, and in life, I would always try to be doing something so I couldn't be called out for being lazy or lax. For some reason, the word "lazy" triggered me. Even at a very young age, the word had bad connotations and triggered a defensive response like the word "stupid" sparked my anger as well. Those two those words, as well as many more, triggered a belief in me I was defending.

If at school, I would be drawing Navy ships with flags flying, weapons visible, and bombs dropping instead of the note-taking. To the teacher, I was doing what she wanted, doing was happening and that was all that mattered. At church, I would have hands in prayer while thinking about the girl who smelled so nice somewhere in the church. To the pastor, I was doing what was expected, praying faithfully. In life, I would walk fast, eyes focused on what lay ahead and presented myself as a man on a mission doing something that needed to be done.

Long ago, I remembered hearing the footsteps of my parents, and I would jump up and look like I was busy doing homework. I spent my early life always trying to look, to everyone watching, as a real go-getter. I continued this behavior when I started working, and it played out in the Navy, as well as my civilian job. I knew I wasn't the only one pretending, as I watched others doing, just like I was doing.

I was also aware of how I expected others to be busy and doing something. My dad once said to a worker fixing his car, "DO SOMETHING, PLEASE, EVEN IF IT'S WRONG, DO SOMETHING!"

Later in life, I would say the same phrase and have the same expectation everyone should be busy and doing something constructive instead of doing nothing. I don't think I'm alone; there are many of us who have been taught and programmed to behave this way. The only way to become "aware of what we are doing" is to observe ourselves while it's taking place. I've seen this constant doing most of my life and though we are all, or most of us, in the same boat, we need to see, or I need to see, the error of my ways. I must become privy to the other side of the equation and see the being side of my humanness.

It took many, many years before I allowed myself the time to be. Every time I tried to relax and enjoy the scenery as I sat at the beach, or on a fallen log in the forest, within minutes I'd be looking around for something to do. I saw others able to enjoy their stillness and noticed how at ease they looked. With me, there was an anxiety anytime I tried to be still for any length of time.

I saw myself standing in line waiting and thinking to myself, *if, they knew how much I had to do, they would check me out, so I could get going on my doing*. The same would happen at doctors' visits, and any time I had to stop my doing and wait. I would get impatient and feel the conflict going on. Sometimes I would finally be so triggered, I would overreact in some way. That is, if I felt I could get away with a tantrum. If I couldn't act out my frustration, I internalized it and heard the committee inside my head egging me on to an outburst. I would stand up, after a few minutes of impatient waiting, and pace the room or look through the magazine pile. I was looking for something to do while I waited. Maybe I felt my time was being wasted and that was why I was so angry, or maybe I was wasting my own time and angry with myself. I could use my waiting time for meditating or to read a good book. Not *my* fault, the committee says, and then to find someone to blame. The battle inside me was raging.

After many, and I mean *many*, years of observing my behavior and seeing what was really happening, relief finally found its way to me. I noticed a calmness instead of the anxiety I usually had. I tried out my new outlook and tested it on the highway. I knew there, driving my car, and knowing my triggers and buttons, I would clearly see if I was making progress. I was in the "smooth seas do not make a sailor" mode and putting myself out there in the heat of the battle. It wasn't long before my wishes were granted and I noticed instead of being only aware of bad drivers, I was also seeing courteous drivers. I was seeing a balance of sorts as long as I kept a non-judging, open mind. In seeing both sides, I noticed when I saw actions by drivers that upset me, often it would be offset by a kind driver giving another driver a break. I was seeing the balance that existed throughout our universe instead of the lopsided view I had before. I then had a realization: "If I was seeing more of a **balance** outside of me, maybe, just maybe, I had to have more balance within me as well."

Again, the mirror is at the reflection game it always is playing and showing us a true reflection. Another thing I noticed was less disappointment in me. I know expectations will lead to disappointment. Although I was aware of this, it didn't stop me from expecting certain things. I, like many others, would have an expectation, if we take our vehicles to be serviced it would be done right. How many of us have been disappointed after driving away and, within hours, or sooner than we wanted, the service light comes on, or our vehicle suffers some other kind of breakdown. My immediate overreaction would be to raise Cain with the dealership and demand my car be repaired right this time. Then, they discovered it wasn't something they didn't do, or wasn't poor service, and told us we needed further work done that wasn't part of their original service agreement.

This happen with cars, refrigerators, and even a dinner date. Not having any expectations is the only way to go, and it still isn't easy for me. My wants have lessened to a degree and my disappointments have as well. I still make a plan, and when I do, I know it may fall apart. I'm not counting on things to go as planned as much as I used to, and therefore, I'm not setting myself up for plans to turn out my way. I also know, by now, it may turn out better than I had predicted.

It took a long time, and a lot of investigating was done as I went further down the rabbit hole. Over time, change was coming about, and the change was only a result of having more awareness and understanding. I still had a long way to go.

> ***"In an instant, a life may turn around; a heart may open in a moment of grace. But, preparing for that moment may take a lifetime... Learning can happen quickly. Unlearning takes longer."***
>
> *"Journey of Socrates" - (Dan Millman)*

I'm not going to wait for the possibility of grace to solve my problems.

When Chief wrote my note and asked, "What are you waiting for?" I knew it would be up to me to do the dirty work and not rely on others to do it for me. They couldn't anyway. I have to dig deep and not take someone's word. I have to observe myself and cannot rely on what others have done. I have to learn my lessons and not take what someone else says as the truth. I must ponder, analyze, consider, and contemplate my findings and see my own truths.

I have read hundreds of books and taken classes, completed courses, and learned new techniques to aid me in my discoveries. I have to use all I have learned to unlearn most of it. My only focus nowadays is to observe myself. I do this by observing others and seeing the *me* in *them*. In "seeking" awareness, I have been able to hone in on how my crazy belief systems have affected me, as well as my family and everyone I know. Very few are free of the conditioning, programming, and preconceived notions most of us have. Those who are free, very seldom make it obvious to others. Well, they make it obvious for those who have **some** awareness. Sadly, most people are happy in their dream world and don't want to be disturbed or woken up. They are coping and have convinced or maybe conned themselves, that all is well.

I thought the same way. Long ago, I knew I was playing a game and decided to get good at the game rather than be free of it. I now know change isn't liked or wanted by most of us. Actually, we hate change. We're comfortable in our rut and think we can go on pretending. The longer we play the game, the better we get at it.

Unfortunately, or fortunately, a major for me, health crises hit me like the 2X4 whack I needed. My pride and stubbornness had kept me from seeing anything clearly. I had, through my belief systems and prejudices, placed coats of paint on the mirror the universe was showing me. Because of this, I missed seeing the true reflection I so desperately needed. Every belief system, all my conditioning and programming, and all the hardwired lies were keeping me from clearly seeing what was being offered to me. I understood there was a huge risk as I chipped away at the film and paint. It all depends on me and to what extent I will go to see the truth that has always been there all along.

Years ago, when I was reading the many books available on acquiring freedom, enlightenment, or awareness, and became privy to secrets others had discovered, I started writing down any statement, phrase, or words of wisdom being offered. Almost every day, I would hear a line from a movie that caught my attention, or hear a profound statement from a neighbor that sparked my interest or struck a chord in me. I would always have a notepad beside my chair to use to capture anything I thought needed further investigation. Over time, I managed to fill several notepads and had accumulated quite a lot of great information. Most of my notes were taken from reading, although it didn't matter where they were obtained from. I would write down whatever caught my attention, and it didn't matter where it came from. The truth rung like a bell when finally heard, read, or was seen. I'd heard the expression the truth can sometimes hurt. When I pondered this, I realized the truth is just the truth. I could choose to be hurt or I could choose to see the freedom the truth has at its core. I could argue and defend my lies or I could accept the facts. "Argue for your limitations, and sure enough, they're yours."

I understand now, I seek the truth no matter where it is found. Once a truth grabs my attention, I have to think it through. I have to dig and uncover what lies at the root. I have to shine a light into my darkness and see what needs to be seen. Freedom doesn't come without a cost. I find my own cost is the constant vigilance I need to give, to stand-up for, and to protect the very freedoms I am seeking. I am seeing in myself, the extreme difficulty to see the balance that exists in everything. Logic has convinced me there is always two sides to the coin. I must continually resist when I am being tugged away from this very moment, this now moment, by past or future thoughts. I see this occur when I'm distracted by thought and not present in the now. I must be fully convinced of the truths I uncover as I slowly remove the paint, clean and shine the mirror to see my true reflection. I have to be on guard to see when I am being distracted. The ego, the *me* who I think I am, wants attention and will distract me from being in this very moment. The me, *(ego)*, cannot live in the now. It can live only in the past or future, and that is not where I want to be.

Although, most of the programming and conditioning remains within me, I now know many of these preconceived notions have been exposed, even if just a little. Constant vigilance is the price I pay for my freedom. In the beginning, I would have to force myself to self-observe. Now, more often than not, I am inspired to find truth, wherever it takes me. I know, I am not there yet, although, I don't know how far or close I really am.

I've heard "others" talking of how much they wanted enlightenment", "full awareness", or the other many names we call "freedom". I have discovered there is a side of me that wants it, and another side that is scared of it. That side is seeking the truth, and fearful of the truth as well. In uncovering some of my own truths along the way through self-observation", I have found I am a little fearful of what will become of me, Stephen, when the actual time comes.

Upon deep reflection and consideration, I have finally begun to understand, "***It's NOT the final destination for me, and it's the journey along the way, instead.***"

I still have that part of me, which wants what I want, when I want it, now. I am surprised and taken aback when I observe how many *ME's* there are. I notice the programming and belief systems battling each other, all looking to be heard.

Over my lifetime, I have developed characters for any situation. My many characters all have to be fed and remembered, as well as be maintained. All the labels I have accumulated are the many *ME's* society has labeled. Of course, there are many more I took on for, self-importance, power, and control. Father, son, brother, cousin, and the many more we all have taken on or were given is unfathomable. Sadly, they all come with belief systems or programming you and I have to live up to, or be failures. We fail because we can't live up to the high bar we set for ourselves, or the expectations others have of us.

On and on it goes, forever for some. The more I faithfully look, the more that is exposed to me through self-discovery. I know I must continue to self-observe to gain the "awareness" I so much need. **Awareness** (of reality/truth), **acceptance** (of truth/reality), and **action** (if necessary) are necessary for me in order to reach my goal of **autonomy** (Freedom). There are no short-cuts, for me at least. I am slowly able to see distractions that are trying to keep me off balance. It's always past and future memories, events, and thought, which sabotage my present and now moments. They are trying to rob me of the "awareness" I achieve when in the moment. The battle continues until "the me" is gone.

The phone startled me and brought me to the now. It was Freebird calling to tell me Chief was back. We chatted for a little while and had a great conversation. I filled her in on some of my discoveries, and she had a lot of laughs at my expense. I wasn't angry or insulted and laughed along at myself. Not long ago, I would have overreacted to my emotional memories.

I still feel a slight trigger, although I seem to be able to choose otherwise more often than before. I am beginning to like myself more and consciously working on loving myself. I also find myself laughing at funny things I see and not caring if anyone sees it. My constant worry of living up to some expectation had of me is slowly fading. The need I used to always have for respect and recognition for my self-importance is less now.

Portia, my best friend, keeps me on my toes. She makes sure I get my walk in every day and keeps me off the couch or recliner. Portia even lets me know when it's time for me to eat. Whether she is concerned about me or is looking for a handout is for you to guess. Either way, none of this goes unnoticed, and I'm once again reminded to be grateful for what I don't have.

Having a choice based on the truth in all my matters, is my *motes of operando* now, as I continue observing myself in action and inaction as well. I am still amazed how I must follow the threads until the end. **"Half measures availed us nothing."**

I still look for and take any truth that comes my way. I seek the truth which will ultimately set me free. I thought of Chief and was glad he was home from his two-month retreat. Freebird mentioned he had been in a monastery he had found long ago. She had laughed when telling me it was for his five-year tune-up. I wanted more information about Chief and pressed Freebird to fill me in. She immediately clammed up and made me promise to never mention our conversations. I assured her I would be silent. I knew Chief's idea on "personal history", especially his own and understood how important it was. I decided maybe it was something I should focus on as well. The less anyone knew of me, the less expectations, and the more I'd be accepted, or not, by others. If I no longer needed approval from people and approved of and loved myself, it no longer became a need.

I was supposed to meet Chief the following day and was already feeling my excitement building. I decided to ponder on the things I tell people when I meet them for the first time. I know when I find someone who will really listen to me; I let them in on a lot. Way more than they need to know. Self-importance at it again. I saw this all play out and was amused at myself seeing my self-importance on display. I was walking Portia one day and bumped into another man walking his dog as well. I put the led on Portia and the other guy snapped a rope to his dog friend too. We approached each other as the dogs pulled both of us closer.

He said, "Mine's friendly. How about yours?"

I laughed and said she was fine as we unhooked both dogs. They got familiar with each other, as dogs do, and I had to laugh at their antics. While the dogs played and ran around chasing each other, we made small talk.

I was wearing a military, camouflaged blouse, which I had worn during my Navy Seabee days, and the man asked about my service. The next thing I knew, I was filling him in, with much detail, all about my military days and accomplishments. I saw it all going on and had to laugh at my bragging to make myself important.

The man said, "Welcome home," and I felt embarrassed. I was looking to him to give me accolades and respect I thought I deserved. If I liked and respected myself, I wouldn't need it from others. This was a great lesson for me, and one I hope stuck.

"CHIEF" & "FREEBIRD"

I sat for a while pondering and seeing the past events for my entire life unfolding, and now was starting to understand what really made me tick, (kind of). In the past, most of my life lessons had been hard, and I was entirely responsible for that. Lately, I'd noticed my lessons became a little easier to learn.

As I gain more awareness and understanding, I tend to act more rightly, and the consequences are gentler. "In awareness, you can do no harm."

Portia chirped in and brought me back to the moment at hand. It was not coincidental for her to know when I needed a break. This time, she needed a bathroom break and I needed to take her outside. Once she was done, she bolted in for her last treat of the day. I read a little and pondered off and on until I realized it was bedtime.

I slept well, although I had a few dreams of fighting battles of long ago. I was a warrior and fought for freedom and independence. As I saw myself fighting, whether it be for a king or some religion, or an empire, I knew I was fighting for myself first. Sitting there, I remembered the many battles I had in this lifetime, and knew in my heart there were more, yet to come.

After my meditation and a short walk, Portia and I drove over to see Chief. We would meet at the park and I was glad he chose the park. Sometimes parking could be hard to find and there were lots of spaces at the park. As I drove, I noticed a calmness in me and a neutrality hard for me to come by without effort. Something else dawned on me then. I was not being triggered while I was driving. There was decent traffic, a little construction, and many opportunities presented to push my buttons about driving and my rules I held others accountable to. I didn't question or try to analyze my feeling of neutrality and instead savored it.

After quickly finding a spot to park, I was happy to see Chief sitting there in all his glory. Today he was enjoying the sun on his face and the serenity he had worked so hard to earn. Portia let out a bark, which was not a common event. She had recognized Chief by sight or smell and was honed in on him as I held her back until she settled. Finally, she heeled and walked next to me as we approached the bench. Chief had his back to us and his head was slightly tilted up toward the sun. I was trying to be quiet and was quite a ways away when he turned toward us. He stood and walked our way with a beaming smile that lit up his whole being. I had to blink my eyes to be sure what I was seeing. I swore I had seen him glow. When I looked again, he was the same ole Chief I had grown to love over our many years as teacher and student.

After a long bear hug and a few back slaps, we made our way over to Chief's bench. It was vacant, as usual, anytime Chief was in the neighborhood. We sat for a moment or two while Chief nurtured Portia. The look in her eyes was pure joy, maybe even bliss. Chief started our meeting asking how things were with me. He never made anything about himself. He might have used himself as an example and laugh at his wackiness. Never selfishness or self-importance for him, ever. He always maintained his "true to self" and nonjudgmental stance. I truly appreciated his neutrality and his total independent way. I realized then Chief was showing me, through his actions, how to "walk the walk".

I pressed him for help understanding "all about me" and asked him if he could translate the dreams I was having about warfighting. I mentioned it seemed I had been in battle, forever fighting, and standing up for freedom.

As it usually was, Chief gave me his full attention and never interrupted me. He would wait, sometimes for a long while, as I chattered away. I filed his behavior away in my mind and decided I wanted to be able to do that when I conversed with others. It felt nice to have someone listen and not interrupt. He was showing me patience and acceptance of himself; he was demonstrating the true definition of love I had written down long ago.

> ***"Love is not an emotion. Love describes neutrality, the absence of judgement, censorship, desire, and worry."***

As I thought about this, I noticed my heart opening and felt a flood of joy wash over me. I had a sharp pain in my heart and, for a moment or two, thought I was having a real heart issue. I moved my hand to my heart and intentionally used Reiki to calm down.

Chief picked up on my dilemma and casually said it was time for my heart to be open, and to throw caution to the wind. He chuckled and said to not fight it by thinking crazy thoughts of actual physical harm. Many times, during his life, he had been aware of opportunities presented to him over and over again. They were perfect times to risk it all and let his guard down. I knew exactly what he meant and remembered the session in Chicago I had received many years before. I remembered the same pain and how I had felt physically ill when my heart protector was discovered and removed. I also remembered the words of my teacher and friend,

> ***"its risky business when a man shows his gentle side, and only a few see it."***
> *(Unknown source)*

Then, I saw the war face I wore to ward off anyone I felt threatened by. I immediately thought of my dreams and being a warrior and realized the real battle was going on inside of me. I was being shown the battles and the wars through my dreams. I was also understanding the triggers being pushed when I tuned into any injustice of any kind. I was being made privy to my lopsided views and belief systems. I was being made aware of how my programming and conditioning had influenced my lifelong struggle.

I told Chief about my discoveries, and he said, ***"In an instant, a life my turn around; a heart may open in a moment of grace. But, preparing for that moment can take a lifetime... Learning can happen quickly. Unlearning take longer."*** He laughed as he said, "Not my words," and mentioned, "The Journey of Socrates" written by Dan Millman.

I remember reading it and seeing what the young Socrates had endured in his life. He had trained under tremendous adversity to be a warrior and fight for the Czar. Although he was strong and powerful and could easily win most fights, he knew he had to seek out a "master" who could guide him. He was alone and had been on his search for many years before he was guided to a master who would teach him much more than just warfare.

It was then I spotted Chief smiling and seemingly to radiate. The sight was fuzzy, and I immediately thought I was seeing through tears. I looked around to see if anyone close by was seeing it also. Several folks had walked within feet of the bench, and when they looked our way, they seemed normal and not surprised. Maybe I was the only one seeing the glow that appeared around Chief. Again, like the last time, I wiped my eyes and there were tears this time. I felt very weird and was kind of uncomfortable gazing at him and apologized for gawking. We locked eyes and I immediately felt an energy surge envelope my whole being. As the powerful pulse slowly faded, I noticed Portia looking up and saw her eyes were filled with love. We sat for a long time in silence.

After a while, chief started the conversation while holding eye contact with me.

Chief volunteered information I would never dare ask of him. He filled me in on lots of detail about his two-month stay at the monastery. He laughed and said he was a lot like Dan Millman's *Socrates* in many ways. We were all a lot like him. He wasn't there to learn fighting, but to visit his "master".

I knew, beyond a shadow of doubt, chief had really changed as a result. I asked him about the "glow" I was seeing, and he dismissed it and laughed, saying I needed an eye exam. I then boldly asked him his age.

He chuckled and said, "I am one day old." He then roared his roar and laughed his great laugh. I joined in again not knowing the inside joke he appeared to know. It took a while for him to settle as I looked down at Portia, she too was smiling. Chief then explained his new philosophy to me. "Every day we awaken, it's a new beginning. We are born free each day, as we have always been. It is entirely up to us to use our day to gain as much awareness as we possibly can, and use our time to enjoy this very day in all its glory." He said, "We only have this day, yesterday is gone forever, and tomorrow is but a dream." He had gone to the monastery to learn just that. "To be grateful for living another day had to be forged in the fires of war and battle before it could be realized and understood. We had to learn the hard way to be grateful for our new opportunity to have another day and chance to win our battles of life. We only have 'a day at a time', and a chance to use the Serenity Prayer to ***'Grant us the serenity to accept the things we cannot change, courage to change the things we can, and the wisdom to know the difference.'"***

I knew that prayer very well and thought I knew what it meant. I tuned into **"serenity"** and already knew its definition. I actually looked it up when I sobered up many years ago. I remember it reading: *Serenity- calmness, tranquil, and peacefulness.* I understood it to mean, "A sense of well-being." It dawned on me then that calmness was very much needed in order to accept things, everything. That meant accepting things non-acceptable. Accepting "what is" instead of my emotions triggering overreaction. Instead of a knee-jerk, programmed reaction, peacefulness and a sense of well-being would guide me to act in an appropriate way.

Next came the **"courage"** needed to take the risk and stand up for truth and freedom. To be able to ***"change the things I can,"*** I have to have awareness to see what changes are necessary. That has to be done in serenity as well. Any other way would lead to possible altercations or possible harm. ***"To know the difference,"*** again requires the awareness to know right and wrong actions. ***"In awareness is healing; in awareness is truth; in awareness is salvation; in awareness is spirituality; in awareness is growth; in awareness is love; in awareness is awakening."*** *"Awareness" - (Anthony de Mello)*

My new definition of serenity has changed, as have I. I think serenity means love.

I ran all these new ideas by Chief, and he said, "Love makes the world go round," as he smiled. I was surprised when Chief kept talking. He, for some reason, only known to him, was sharing some of his personal history with me. He told me he had been a Navy Seabee, and he had spent several years in Vietnam. He was a steelworker and a trained and a certified Navy diver. He added that had done many hardhat dives and he had been an instructor in scuba. He then mentioned in almost a whisper he had gone through and completed Navy

Seal training. He had done many tours, doing missions in North Vietnam, Cambodia, and South Vietnam. His team operated out of Okinawa. Chief then stated, I now knew everything that needed to be known.

I agreed and knew Chief had been to hell and back many times during his Navy days. Suddenly, I felt gratitude pouring from my heart to my very soul. I was so, so, gratefully for the things, or situations, I didn't and don't have. I had thought my life had been difficult. That is until I remembered my military/Vietnam history, and knew Chief's personal history was much, much more of a challenge than most of mine had ever been.

Suddenly, I was jolted to my past and saw myself and the many times, and in certain circumstances, would find an excuse for sadness of my situation. I would feel sorry for myself and take on self-pity. I would then choose to sit on the "pity pot" for as long as I needed. Looking back with more clarity, I saw I was seeking pity from others. I wanted them to feel my sadness. I wanted attention and knew I could get it if everyone knew I was down. Funny, children will seek attention from wherever they can get it. Good acts received attention, fine. Bad acts drew attention, fine. Whatever it took to have the attention they were desperate to have. Already as a child, they felt the need for others to give them something they couldn't give themselves.

Imagine, a three or four-year-old child has been programmed to believe he needs approval from others. They already have self-worth beliefs, as well as conditioning that tells them not to love themselves. They also have at this young age, preconceived notions about success, and what is needed for happiness. Sadly, all of us, except a rare few, are in the same boat.

I looked over at Chief, and he smiled as I mentioned my thoughts. Chief said as we acquired more awareness, some of us are privy to streams of consciousness that provides us with information to help us to understand ourselves. It's universal knowledge, and at certain times, we can access. As our heart guard slowly falls away, we can receive the love always there to be had. Sometimes, during a deep meditation, we get a glimpse of truths and useful information that we need to make our gains. He looked at me and stated the streams of consciousness that we seem to be acquiring now and then, are similar to what we sometimes obtain during and after meditating. As we continue to boldly take the risk of letting our guard down, we begin to open ourselves more and more to information we were unable to obtain before. The information is out there, all we have to do is be aware of it.

Just then, Portia wheeled around and was on guard. Chief and I turned and looked for what had caught her attention and saw the figure of a woman walking toward us. Portia was wagging her stub of a tail, excited to see Freebird walking our way. The excitement was too much for her and she bolted over to greet her.

Chief stood and walked her way as I remained on the bench by myself. Portia was happy to see Freebird, and it appeared Chief was as well. I watched as Chief and Freebird embraced and kissed each other. I felt a little odd watching the scene unfolding and decided to greet Freebird. Chief and Freebird were holding hands and looked like they were more than just friends. They were both smiling, and as they got closer I saw the "glow" again. It surrounded them. I thought I could see Portia glowing as well.

Suddenly, I felt a joy in me beyond description. This joyous serenity was so overwhelming I had to turn back and sit on the bench before I fell. I felt light-headed and saw flashes in front of my eyes, and knew I was on the verge of passing out. It took a long while before I came around and noticed Freebird and Chief had joined me on the bench. Portia lay at our feet and looked to each of us for some kind of a que. It was then I noticed Chief and Freebird were still holding hands and beaming.

Chief spoke first and introduced Freebird as his long-time companion. He said they had met each other in college and had been together ever since. They had been together for over sixty years and Freebird had taught philosophy at a nearby university.

I was floored by all this news and in a state of mind where I was in total neutrality. Part of me wanted to know more, and another part of me was being a witness and accepting of all of it. Even though I felt a calmness, there was also a tension. I then remembered the battle I had going on inside.

Freebird said she and Chief had traveled together during his time in the Navy and had been fortunate to meet certain people who had helped them along the way. She proudly filled me in on some of the military decorations

Chief had received during his Navy tenure. Chief chirped in to clarify he had a few more, although they could never be officially presented.

Freebird and Chief looked at each other, and I could see the total respect and love they had. My eyes filled with tears as I felt their love for each other consuming me. I felt the slight pain in my heart return and observed my normal reaction of placing my palm on my chest.

Freebird sat between us, turned toward me, and put her hand over my heart as well. We sat like that for a few minutes, and as I started to calm, Freebird put her hands beside my face and kissed me on the forehead. With tears rolling down my face, and my nose running, I noticed then, I didn't care if anyone saw my tears. The *boys don't cry* belief system booted up and was immediately dismissed.

I lost track of time for a while and didn't care. I was in acceptance of what is, and totally in a neutral and non-judgmental frame of mind. Something in me had shifted. The committee in my head wasn't talking and I was carefree. I noticed myself smiling and on the verge of laughing out loud, I said, ***"Real men cry,"*** in a loud, almost yell, and it was my turn to roar with laughter.

We all had a good chuckle and a few more laughs with the extra funny comments added by Freebird and Chief. I knew they were trying to help me feel at ease for my crying jag and happy for me as well. I felt giddy and just a little confused at my own reactions and was glad for their comments to justify my statement. I learned a little more about their personal history as both Freebird and Chief volunteered information about themselves and each other. I felt honored as they brought me up to speed on their history before and after they met.

I asked them how they had managed to stay together for so long. Both said they were indeed lucky. Chief told of the many times he had wanted to end their relationship and call it quits. He said he didn't want to bring Freebird into his "military ways" and expose her to "his world" as a Seal and career Navy man.

Freebird stated she had been determined to keep the relationship alive and knew in her heart how it would benefit both of them if they worked together. I guess her education in philosophy and then her tenure as a professor had aided her on the decision. She exploded with laughter, although her look was serious at the same time, when she said, "I needed his masculinity, and he *definitely* needed my femininity." She said, "We were both way out of balance, especially Chief."

Chief chuckled and pounded his chest saying, "Me, Tarzan, you, Jane."

We all laughed at his antics. I said I was probably in the same boat.

Freebird bluntly, as usual said, "Yes, you are," and we continued our laughter.

It was then I noticed I was happy and enjoying myself immensely. I felt at home sitting there in the park with three great friends. A moment later, Freebird invited Portia and me to join her and Chief for a late lunch at their house. Chief and Freebird had purchased a historic, although run-down, house between the park and the common many years ago. Chief said it took him a hell of a long time to get it up to par, and he still had much work ahead of him yet to do.

My carefree mood continued as we all made our way up the sidewalk heading towards their home. Freebird and Chief were holding hands while they walked, and when anyone spoke, we all stopped to listen.

The house was enormous and a sight to behold. I immediately wondered why I hadn't ever noticed it in my travels. Chief pointed out the copper gutters and downspouts and said they were handcrafted by Freebird and him. It had taken them a long time to fabricate the sheets of copper in to the work of art I was seeing. They were indeed beautiful and the patina was awesome to see. We went through the side entrance and I noticed the intricate wood work on the heavy door. We walked into the kitchen area and sat at the antique looking table in the open area off the kitchen. Freebird removed the cover from a crockpot and the aroma of food filled the room. My stomach growled out loud and everyone laughed again. I felt carefree and noted I had been in that mood since seeing Freebird and Chief. I had happiness and felt light, as I watched Chief serve the divine looking and great smelling food to each of us. He even had a dish for Portia and set it aside to cool. Portia took a spot away from the table and rested her head on her paws and took turns looking at each of us through her loving eyes.

The meal was great as we ate in silence. Often, we would look at each other with ear to ear smiles. Everyone helped with the clean-up, and with dishes washed and in the rack, we all went to the living room and sat around the old coffee table.

I felt emotional again and was also feeling uncomfortable with my lack of discipline to control it. I asked Chief if he had any clues on this unusual (for me) behavior. He said, "Joy is impossible to contain when our hearts are beginning to finally open."

Freebird added when we take the risk of potential heartache, we have jumped the huge hurdle that has been in place keeping us closed off from each other. Fear of heartache and a broken heart are obstacles everyone has to overcome, and that only those few, who are willing to take the risk, will benefit from the reward of doing so.

Chief chirped in and said, "Surrender is not in my vocabulary," and laughed again.

I remembered how I had to finally surrender when it came to my alcoholism and knew I had surrendered to win the battle with booze. I also knew I had to surrender once again and give up protecting myself from those possibilities of headache and heartbreak.

I had lost track of time. Portia looked at me and I understood what she was telling me. It was time for her afternoon constitutional in the woods. I mentioned this to Freebird, and Chief volunteered to take her. Reluctantly, I agreed and he retrieved the lead I had used to walk her. Portia had other thoughts and refused to go without me. Another tear rolled down my cheek as I thought of her loyalty to me.

Freebird said she wanted to go with Portia and me on the walk and asked if it was alright. The dilemma was resolved as we left Chief to himself and walked our way to the park. Chief seemed happy to be alone for a while, and I understood completely. I loved my alone time also and found, I needed to be by myself sometimes to keep distractions at bay. Distractions gave me just the excuse I needed to put off or stop my progress.

"*Constant vigilance is the price I must pay*," and I understand sometimes I don't want to do the work. Most of the time, lately, I feel inspired, and in that mode constant vigilance doesn't seem hard, or even work.

As Freebird and I made our way to the park we walked in silence except when Freebird would stop and point out a particular flower or a cloud formation. I could see she was in *awareness* and enjoying everything it brought to her attention. It was like watching a child making first discoveries and the awe it brought about. I thought childlike, not childish, as I watched her gaze at length at a butterfly on a flower. She had no cares in the world and was taking in everything the universe had to offer. No fear, just total acceptance of all and everything.

We finally made it to the woods and the familiar old stopping grounds Portia and I walked and knew well. Although I felt in a fantastic mood, once in the woods my awareness opened and I was taken aback by the sight and sounds. I was seeing and hearing sights and sounds with a crispness I had never experienced before. My senses were alive, and I felt part of it all. Portia did her business well off the path and deep in the woods. She had lost track of Freebird and I as we found a fallen limb large enough for both of us. We were hidden from Portia's view, and as I chanced a look I noticed she seemed a little frantic. I stood and laughed as she made a beeline in my direction. Portia greeted me as if we had been parted for days as Freebird and I hugged her and played her game.

Freebird told me a little about her time on the reservation and went into more detail when she talked about her family's history. She told me of the history that had never made the books and how it had been passed down from generation to generation. The history was pure facts, and the truth was shocking. The history that had been passed down had not been embellished in any way.

When she went into detail, she painted a picture I could easily see. Everything was matter-of-fact and truthful, to say the least. Freebird said how lucky she had been to be spared the abuse most Native Americans had to endure, even today. The lack of jobs and the abundance of drugs and alcohol caused much difficulty for men and woman whose pride had been taken away. She was living in two separate worlds for a long time. Freebird had one foot in the "Indian" world, with all that came with it, and one foot in the "White man's" world, with all that came with that. She laughed; the war within her raged for years.

Because of her appearance, Freebird looked Scandinavian and was tall and full-figured. She reminded me of an aunt of mine who was also Swedish/Native American. I don't have "native" blood in me. I thought at one time I did. After years of research by my cousin, I was informed we had none. My cousin said many of our original family members had been killed by the "Indians", although we probably killed more of them than they did us. I didn't bother Freebird with those details though.

I asked Freebird about my inability to keep from tearing up at any given moment. She said, "The organs weep the tears the eyes refuse to shed – Unexpressed emotions are stored in the muscles of the body." While looking me in the eyes, she said I had a lifetime of not letting my tears flow, and now the tears were finding their way to the surface to finally be let go. Freebird informed me Chief had to endure the same condition, and it shouldn't last that long.

Relieved at that, I felt a little less anxious and had a seemingly legitimate excuse for my weeping. I then thought, why I thought I needed and excuse. On it goes and more questions popping up to be explored. I then ran the other question I had by Freebird. Why was I streaming so many thoughts, and was it normal?

Again, Freebird was quick with a possible reason. I was constantly getting detailed information about life events I thought I had accepted. She agreed with Chief's assessment and said, because of my willingness to "know myself" and my readiness to "find the truth at all costs", I was purposefully opening my heart and soul. Freebird said, knowing the risks involved and, in doing so, I was tapping into memories and events I had deeply buried and forgotten. Freebird said when our thoughts are overwhelming us, we need to remember being **present** is key to awareness. Freebird said, "Don't hang on to your moments too long or you'll get stuck in them and miss the next one." Our thoughts are past and future. We need to see this and return to now when observing ourselves.

Again, I felt her answers were factual. I actually felt good about myself, something I had been working on for years, and I was seeing the pay-off for my vigilance and treating myself much better. I also understood, I was choosing to visit the past and future instead of in the moment. Funny, how I made my own distractions to hinder progress. I thought, "Awareness is now, and now is where it will be found."

I then remembered something I had written down. I couldn't recollect exactly where I had read or heard it, although it seemed to be imprinted in my brain. ***"In happiness, mind and object are dissolved and we rest in the unity of self. Subject and object, mind and ego are all absent."*** *(Unknown Source)*

Freebird, Portia, and I decided it was time to head out and to return to see how Chief was doing. We again walked in silence; both of us looked around at the beauty availed to all who wanted to see it. I was feeling grateful, especially for the few great friends I had in my life. I was also feeling humbled by the few details Firebird had given me in regard to her heritage, ancestors' fate, as well as her own family's way of life. I could see I didn't have too far to look to see someone worse off than myself.

We continued and soon we were there at the house Chief and Freebird had restored. It was a beautiful home and captured the essence of those historic times of the past. Chief was there to greet and hug us all, including Portia.

Chief looked well rested as we sat in the living area. The furniture was overstuffed leather, and it was great looking and very comfortable. Seeing the couch, I wondered how it had fit through the door. Chief chirped up, "I'll bet you're wondering how they got it through the door, aren't you?"

I snipped back jokingly, asking him if he was clairvoyant and could read people's minds? Chief replied, "As a matter of fact, I can." He laughed his famous, by now, roar, although he kept it to a dull roar this time. We both laughed and Portia was excitedly wagging he stubby tail and laughing along as dogs do. Chief stated bluntly, Freebird and him had decided Portia and I would be their guests overnight. He went on to say my car was good where it was parked, and it would be a great opportunity for all of us to get to know each other a little more. A room upstairs was ready and available, and "no" wasn't an option.

I thought it over briefly, and said, sure, it would be great, and we would stay if I could treat them for dinner. Freebird asked if we could go downtown to the seafood place we had eaten at only a short while ago.

With that settled, we all sat and had great conversations on many topics. I noticed my mind wasn't racing and my emotional status was good as well. I was totally present and enjoying what being in awareness was all about. My senses were turned on high, and I was in awe of it all.

After a while, I asked to be excused and went upstairs to see the room Chief and Freebird had made available to me. The room was at the far end of the hallway and I noticed it had a full bathroom and furnished with very old, probably antique, furniture. The view was phenomenal as I gazed at the busy waterway with fishing boats dropping off their cargo of fish and lobsters. I decided then, at that very moment, lobster would be my choice for my meal later. Portia was sniffing around and looking to me for some kind of explanation. I laid down on the full-sized bed and Portia jumped up and nestled close to me looking as if she was happy with our accommodations. I had to get up after only moments. I was sleepy and knew if I stayed, I would nap.

As we descended the stairs, I noticed the beautiful hand-carved woodwork on the rails, spindles, and wooden steps. The carvings were nautical with detail you would see in good scrimshaw. I wondered how long the carving and finishing had taken to complete, and was curious who had done it all. I reached the landing and Freebird was sitting on the leather couch, eyes closed, and smiling. She looked over and mentioned Chief had carved all the woodwork in the house by hand. It must have taken years I thought when Freebird chirped, "It took four years for him to complete."

Hmmm, two questions answered and never asked.

Freebird must have picked up on my questions somehow, and it was a little unnerving. Again, Freebird replied, "The information is out there. All we have to do is listen."

This time, I asked my question verbally to please explain what was going on with her and Chief reading my thoughts. Freebird laughed softly and said it came with awareness, and not everyone is privy to it. She said, ***"Our journey consists not in seeing new landscapes, but in seeing through new eyes,"*** *(Unknown source)* She added, "In awareness, we have moments of clarity that offer us unlimited vision, which includes clarity in all of our senses. When we are inspired to be aware, instead of having the desire, we are able to access the consciousness of everything. This can only come about when the heart is open, and we are coming from love in all instances." Freebird was so sincere in her statements. I could feel the neutrality she was apparently coming from all the time. I felt humbled and was fully aware I was in the presence of a very wise lady.

Chief walked in and knelt so Portia could greet him properly. Of course, she responded and lapped his face as we all laughed. Freebird chuckled and brought him up-to-date with our latest conversation. I knew she said that out loud and was only doing it for me. I very well knew Chief was privy to our conversations, even though he wasn't present in the room. Although I had suspected him of having gained some kind of gifts because of his work, I still found it "out there" and hard to comprehend.

It dawned on me then all I needed to do was hang out with the two of them, and maybe I would be convinced. By seeing the "walk being walked" just might convince me if I worked hard I could have the same. I realized Freebird and Chief acted "normal" and, to all appearances, were average people like everyone else. They laughed and joked and played the games we all did. I saw they only *acted* hurt or disappointed, angry or sad, and, they were enjoying themselves immensely. They were master's acting their parts, as most of us were. Of course, I also knew they were showing me having fun with our humanness didn't end with "awakening". We still had our character and humor as we did before. Enlightenment wasn't the end of my personality or my ways. Instead, it was just the beginning of a world of constant blissfulness and being in total acceptance of what is.

I then became aware of the mirror. I was seeing my reflection and getting a glimpse of possibilities yet to come. I looked at Freebird and Chief sitting together and saw the love and full respect they had for one other. I was also conscious of the love both gave outward to everything. It was washing over everything around them like stage fog. I felt it engulf me like I was being swept away.

Portia nudged me, and I reached down for her come over. She sat between my legs, and I petted her chest and scratched the top of her head. Within seconds, she was resting her head on my leg. She was in another world and enjoying the atmosphere as well. I looked around for a clock to bring me up-to-date and noticed there were none to be found. I asked Chief if he knew what time it was.

He said, "Time to eat," and we all laughed.

With that said, we herded through the door and made our way to have seafood and be in good company.

Freebird and Chief walked ahead of Portia and me as we made our way to eat. It was a lot later than I usually feasted, and I was definitely hungry. I stopped with Portia to let them gain some distance and noticed they were holding hands. It was cute seeing them swinging their arms, hands interlocked and beaming. Yes, I saw a little glow around them if I squinted a certain way. Something else caught my attention as well. Both Freebird and Chief walked slowly, at a pace way too slow for me and Portia.

A thought flashed, and I saw how I had always moved fast. A motto I heard in the Navy was, "Hurry up and wait." I didn't need that training at all. As a child, I was nudged along and trained to walk at a good pace. Later, I saw I did the fast walking to look like a "man with a mission", someone important, and a person to respect.

I decided to slow my pace, and Portia was caught off-guard as we changed our usual ways. After a few minutes, we adjusted and fell in to a casual walk instead of looking for the finish line. Walking at this pace gave me an opportunity to look around and spot anything that drew my attention. Portia kept looking at me, and I saw she was a little confused by the change. We settled in on the new pace and soon it felt normal and instead of being vastly different. We were approaching my 4-Runner and I checked the back for an overnight bag I carried. It was a habit I got into when caring for family. I had a shaving kit, clean socks, and underwear, as well as a full change of slacks and a decent shirt. I felt I was living up to the Boy Scout motto of "Be Prepared", and had been that way long before I had ever heard the motto. My military bearing had been instilled by my father and had been developed over years and years.

We finally reached the seafood restaurant and took a seat outside so Portia could be with us. Within a few minutes, our server came over and took our order. Chief and I both asked for lobster, and Freebird ordered broiled bay scallops. We chatted while waiting and took in the sights along the waterway. Many folks were out that evening, and our meal took a while to be delivered. Once our food was on the table ready to eat, we feasted in silence and smiled and laughed at each other, especially Chief and myself as we devoured our lobsters.

I was glad they gave me a bib. Lobster juice was flying around and no one was sparred. That brought more laughs and a few odd looks from other patrons. We enjoyed our meals immensely and being in good company. I passed on dessert, although Freebird and Chief both had homemade apple pie.

With desert consumed and the meal paid for, we slowly walked our way back. Portia and I made a detour to the woods and then I retrieved the overnight bag from my car. Chief and Freebird continued. I thought for sure they would be back at the house when I caught a glimpse of a dull glow and knew they were just ahead of Portia and me. We caught up with them and continued our silence and the ultra-slow walk.

Once back, we settled in the living area while Freebird made coffee. I asked Chief about the slowness of their walking. He chuckled, saying, it had taken him several years to slow himself down. He had over twenty years of "hurry up and wait", and the habit of being early and having to wait was the price we pay for our military bearing. On the other hand, Freebird was taught as a child to be slow and deliberate in everything. Freebird said, "Nature works at a slow pace," and she mentioned the large animals move slowly and had slow heartbeats that added to their life expectancy. Elephants', whales', and turtles' heartrates were very low compared to ours, and they moved slowly and deliberately, and were in no hurry at all. She said all "nature's creatures" were always in the now, and fully engaged and present. It was a life and death matter for them, and used to be for us, long ago. I thought I saw a little sadness in Freebirds eyes, and felt a little down myself. She smiled and said it was sad to see, although "It is what it is!"

Accepting our plight as human beings and seeing most of us are "human-doings" is what I gained through self-observation. I knew then I would have to force myself to slow down and focus on "what is". I knew it would be a habit for a while and hoped inspiration would replace it.

I remembered a song from long ago" "Slow down, you're going to fast, you got to make this moment last..."

I caught myself smiling as I sang the song in my head and tapped my foot to the beat. Portia looked up, probably wondering what I was doing. We talked about our "human condition", and Chief blurted out a phrase he remembered from ***"Awareness":***

> ***"Humans love to be told what to do, but they love even more to fight and not do what they are told, and thus they get entangled in hating the one who told them in the first place."***
> *"Awareness"- (Anthony de Mello)*

He roared a laugh at what he had said. I totally understood. My memory flashed of the times I had behaved in this manner. I then thought of my son and knew he was "just like me". I realized we are all casted from the same mold; it's part of our human condition.

We talked into the night; the atmosphere was relaxing. I took Portia out, and she quickly peed. I slept soundly, and had a dreamless night. Portia jumped off the bed and made a beeline downstairs. I washed up and changed cloths with the ones I had in my bag. As I descended the stairs, I smelled bacon cooking. A thought entered, and I remembered Chief saying we had to eat right. *Is eating bacon eating right?* As I walked into the kitchen, I saw Portia under the table hoping for something to fall. She was a chow hound; I called her a "beggar" and she looked away. Portia was trained to not beg. I knew she was "all about food" and understood it was what dogs did. I also knew I could train her to not be obvious at least.

The food was cooked, and we served ourselves buffet style. I helped myself to a good portion of bacon, eggs, home fries, and toast. The coffee pot was on the table and the coffee itself was strong. I looked over at Freebird and Chief and noticed Chief's plate was very much like mine, while Freebirds was a smaller portion and had no bacon.

Before I started eating, I asked about eating right. Chief picked up a slice of bacon and said, "Anything that tastes this good has to be all right," and he laughed for a few seconds before eating it.

We ate in silence and Portia was rewarded for not begging. Freebird said eating right was much more than food. We must "take in everything, digest it, and let it go." This was eating right. Eating sattva food would be of great benefit as well, and she said our diets were all based on our upbringing and heritage.

I wanted to be clear on what she meant. Chief said even sattva food has all three gunas, and we should always try to eat good food when possible. I understood and was glad for the clarity.

Portia was anxious and needed a bathroom break. I excused myself and her and off to the park and woods we went. After returning, we said our good-byes and walked back down to the car. The drive was good, although traffic was heavy. I was in acceptance of what is and decided to take it all in.

We arrived home, safe and sound, and Portia and I were happy to be, "Home Sweet Home". I then thought, *Home is where the heart is,* and chuckled. I was glad I went over to see Freebird and Chief. They were the living example I needed to give me hope.

There are many folks like Freebird and Chief living among us all.

"When we are ready, the teacher will appear."

"When we are ready, the master will appear."

FINAL THOUGHTS

Now, with laundry running, I stretched out on my comfortable, well-worn couch and felt peace. Portia was looking out the back door at the wildlife that inhabited our backyard. Often, we would see deer, especially rabbits eating the sweet grass I offered. There were always birds, squirrels, and chipmunks to see and she enjoyed watching them, as did I. I was in my "sanctuary" and felt at home.

Freebird had said once when I asked her if she was looking forward to Chief's return, if she would be happy when he came home. She said, "Home is acceptance," and she knew Chief was always home, wherever he was. I saw in "accepting what is", there was a lot of barriers being dropped from around my heart. I then thought "surrender is acceptance" and realized how surrendering to my alcoholism wasn't an act of defeat, but instead, acceptance of what is and victory.

With the laundry washed, dried, folded, and put away, I looked outside and saw the light had faded and realized I hadn't taken Portia for her two-mile walk. She hadn't reminded me like she usually did. Instead, she was happy to relax just like I was. I opened the door and she jumped a bunny grazing on the clover. Wow, this time Portia almost got it. She was within striking distance when she stopped on a dime, only inches away from a dog feast. I smiled as I watched the show and thought she would maybe, this time, go in for the kill.

She didn't want that at all. The run was what she wanted, and why eat raw rabbit when she could eat human food? I laughed at the thought as she came bounding through the door. I gave her a piece of duck jerky and she happily devoured it with only one bite before swallowing it whole.

I was feeling so grateful as I looked out the glass door and tuned in to the sights and sounds I could hear through the door. I turned and looked over to my living area and noticed my bonsais. It was nice seeing them thriving and happy behind my new windows. I spotted a lot of dust on the laminate wood floors and made a note to vacuum (someday). I wasn't in a hurry to do stuff that could wait. I felt a slow motion feeling as I forced myself to not do. Instead, I focused on whatever caught my attention. I didn't need to be busy all the time, and funny, I wasn't feeling guilty for just *being*. Instead, I enjoyed the moments as they came and went. It dawned on me I was in acceptance and neutrality. I thought of Freebird and Chief and was grateful I had folks like them in my life. They were showing me how to walk the walk and fun can be had in awareness.

Weeks went by, and then a few months passed as well. I visited Chief and Firebird a couple times and they came to see me once. It was so nice to be in their company and see them in action. It was like watching a couple children oohing and aweing at almost everything. The childlike behavior in two adults was refreshing to see. They weren't trying to impress anyone or win approval. They were doing "their thing" and were in a world very much different from mine, although the same. They didn't care! Freebird and Chief were free of people pleasing, and self-importance wasn't needed. They didn't need others to tell them they were okay. Thinking how lucky they were, reminded me luck wasn't in the equation at all. Their years of self-exploration had paid off, and they were free.

I remembered reading a few pages from one of Castaneda's great books where Don Juan, the sorcerer (his word for enlightened being), was explaining self-importance. I had written it down and probably added a few of my own words. He wrote:

> ***"The burden of self-importance is a terrible encumbrance. If you're feeling depressed, disrupted, less than, and unno-***

ticed, or you are annoyed, bothered, or impatient, chances are it's a good sign that self-importance is at work. Through self-observation you will notice self-condemnation is always taking place and the only way out is through making ourselves important. Humans will go to any length to feel needed, to feel like they are important to someone. We sometimes dislike ourselves so much that we need others to like or love us, to tell us we're okay. Because, we don't feel okay."
(Dan Millman)

When I wrote this down, I paraphrased it for me to understand. The beliefs, conditioning, and programming we received had convinced us early on we needed people in our lives to be happy. We were sold a bill of goods that required our being successful in order to achieve worth, and success was without failures. Of course, we could never live up to these crazy expectations for ourselves or everyone else. So, we did fail, and in failing we ridiculed, condemned, and punished ourselves in some way.

> ***"Full awareness comes only after self-importance leaves. Only when you are nothing, do you become everything."***
> - *(Dan Millman)*

I decided it was imperative for me to slowly wean myself from needing people. I would instead try to enjoy their company without any demands. I had to maintain being true to myself by "keeping good company". I would continue making my gains of liking and loving myself instead of depending on others to fill that need.

Over the following months, I found a much slower pace than before. I'd catch myself getting ready to rush, and instead resorted to taking my time. I made way fewer mistakes and wasn't tripping at all. I found I could make a cup of coffee without making a mistake like usual when unfocused on the task at hand. I was conscious of what I was doing, instead of multi-tasking. "Drive when you drive, eat when you eat, walk when you walk," booted up, and I saw Freebird stop walking as she listened to a question I had asked. She then stopped and supplied me with her words of wisdom before resuming walking. Changes were coming about and I wasn't forcing myself to change. I was starting to become a "human being". Instead of doing, I was observing what was being done through me.

Although I'm not there yet, I am more focused on today and have used Chief's reply to his age of "one day" when someone asks my age. Maybe if I say it enough times, I'll believe it myself. I'm working on gratitude, and someday I'll be onboard with his philosophy. Until then, I continue to have my struggles in life. Family matters and just the hustle and bustle of living can distract and keep me from seeing reality. ***"Now, now, now"*** is the constant tool I use to reel myself back to the present in *awareness.* I know being present in all I do makes most of my tasks more enjoyable.

> ***"What you are aware of, you are in control of; what you're not aware of, is in control of you."***
> *"Awareness"- (Anthony de Mello)*

My whole idea of control is slowly fading as I acquire more evidence that I have little, if any. I have realized "being true to myself" is my only real control. Everything else is a tossup.

I must make better choices when it comes to ***"eating right"*** and appreciate it's more than just food I consume. My eating habits are lousy, and I know my health is important. I need to be mentally, physically, and spiritually healthy. The journey is hard on the body, and unless I have good health and stamina, I will not succeed. I must remember my body is a life support system for self, and unless I see myself as a temple, I'll likely not succeed. I should be devouring life itself and filling my belly with everything my senses are really offering me.

I must ***exercise,*** and I mustn't con myself saying, "I work hard and am physical, so that is *my* exercise." I have to purposefully take my walk and gain the benefit of exercise, while tuning into walking and the glory of my surroundings. I need to get my heartrate up, my lungs filled with fresh air, taking in everything being offered, and then letting go of everything. I try to walk every day and only skip it in very bad weather. I have foul weather gear for any condition, and no excuse. I hope to someday be inspired to exercise instead of it being routine. When it becomes a habit and a desire, inspiration isn't in the equation at all.

Meditation makes all the difference. It offers me an opportunity to justify sitting and not doing. I still revert sometimes and continue overreacting to my "keep busy" and do, do, doing, programming, although, much, much less than before. Years ago, when I practiced Kriya Yoga, my meditation took on a new dimension. Sadly, it fell by the wayside when people pleasing became more important than pleasing myself. I know I can come up with an excuse or a good reason to opt out of meditating. I also know my "me" doesn't want any part of it. My cunning ego will do what is needed to survive. I'll be bombarded by thoughts and distractions and give up.

I must try to remember: ***"Introspection must be treated cautiously, for it is already tainted by the very ignorance it seeks to dispel. We look at the world through our belief systems."*** *(Unknown source)*

Often, I am deliberate in my choice of the company I keep. ***"Being in good company"*** rather than needing company is part of being true to self.

I also know I can twist it around and be a hermit and avoid any company. I have to be in the heat of the battle and open to my lessons using the world as my mirror. "Smooth seas do not make a sailor." I must, however, protect myself from abuse from others, whether verbal or physical in nature. I won't let others cast their anger at me or blame me for the way they feel. It is their anger, worry, fear, grief, or sadness, not mine. Don't bombard me with your emotional turmoil.

In the book "*Awareness*", Anthony de Mello says, ***"Suffering exists in the 'me', so when you/me identify I with 'me', suffering begins. All suffering is caused by my identifying myself with something, whether that something is within me or outside of me."***

I'm so, so tired of suffering. My own, as well as almost everyone else. Sadly, I suffered at my own hand and through my ignorance of what really is. *I didn't know any better*, or *my programming was the cause*, are excuses I've used along the way. When I hold myself accountable, excuses don't count for much. I had great reasons for my failures and, of course, none of it was my fault. I would blame people, places, and things for my failures, knowing it was me who was the failure. Self-condemnation and self-hatred motivated punishing me, and again the lessons go unlearned.

I have learned over time I have to do the work of "knowing myself". I cannot take your word or anyone else's. Shamans, Guru's, and the enlightened may give us clues and point us in the right direction towards freedom, although I must take the plunge myself. I cannot ride on the coattails of others and expect results. To "know thyself" cannot be done by others and has to be my work and mine alone. Over the many years, I have read and heard the words of those who have the awareness and understanding I am seeking. These men and women who have done the inside job have finally circumvented the ego (me) and have accessed their true self. No one did it for them, and although they may have had guidance and help along the way, they all had to make the changes themselves. Change can only come about through awareness and understanding. We are shown the door to freedom from the ego, and it's up to me to go through that door alone.

Throughout my life, I have worked my butt off trying to gain respect from everyone I am in contact with. Respect was a high priority for me. If I felt disrespected in any way, I would go off. My emotional overreactions would boot up by beliefs, conditioning, and programming and I would be off and running. I would defend my beliefs and fight to the death to protect them at all costs. Only when I gained some awareness could I see I didn't respect myself! I wanted from others the very thing I refused to give myself. Over time, and through constant vigilance, I saw the error of my ways. Until I like myself and learn to love myself, I will be a prisoner of my conditioning and hardwired belief systems. My continuing need for people and my desire for positive feedback and respect will go on and on. No change will occur and my suffering will linger, maybe forever.

I have to admit, I don't always do what I know needs to be done. I still find myself unable to always be true to myself. I observe in myself thinking it is so much easier to "talk the talk" than "walk the walk". I am still bound by the ego and will be until I am free of it. All I can do is my best. Some days it isn't that great. Emotional turmoil still has its way with me at times, although I am not overreacting nearly as much as before. I am more apt to act accordingly, more often than not. If the inside job was easy and quick, what would I be gaining? Shortcuts will not work for me. I have to follow each thread as far as it goes. "Half measures avail us nothing," and I know this to be true. Only until I totally surrender will I be a winner. The battle that rages on in most of us will take its toll eventually. I truly believe awareness is my only real option. There is no turning back for me. My suffering is always an option; it's up to me to choose right and the way forward.

"One day at a time" and "keep it simple, stupid," (KISS) are banners I saw early on in my quest for sobriety. I had to finally throw in the towel when I saw my opponent (booze) was winning that battle. I luckily caught a glimpse of the truth and in a moment of clarity made my decision to admit defeat. Only then was I able to see, through awareness and understanding, the error of my ways.

> ***"Grant me the serenity to accept the things I cannot change, courage to change the things I can, and the wisdom to know the difference."***

The **"Serenity Prayer"** has been around for a while. I've repeated it thousands of times in my early recovery from alcoholism. Sadly, I didn't know how deep the words were or what they really meant then. I am slowly, very slowly, putting my human puzzle together, piece by piece. ***"From becoming, to being."*** *(Esther Veltheim)* The jigsaw puzzle I am had many, many pieces missing. I had to search and dig deep to get a glimpse of them and see where they fit.

Only until all the pieces are found and looked at, will I start to see the picture of me slowly coming into the light.

I must always remember and know, ***"Introspection must be treated cautiously, for it is already tainted by the very ignorance it seeks to dispel – We look at the world through our belief systems."*** *(Unknown source)*

I am trying to circumvent the ego with the ego. This is not easy to do as the ego becomes more and more cunning and sneaky. Funny or not, ***"The very***

mind with which you would affirm freedom is the very mind which is infected with desire and delusion." *(Anthony de Mello)*

As I continue doing the inside job, I find my ego is in service of the false me. When the ego is finally in service of myself, the battle will be over. Then I will be able to be myself instead of the many labels I took on or were placed on me. All the many roles and labels I have need to constantly be fed and nurtured and have to be fulfilled. The energy I waste on that can instead be used for awareness. I can imagine a time when I will be in awareness and acceptance 24/7. True to self and coming from love. I know it can be done, and through the "power of examples" Chief and Freebird have shown me, has convinced me of my own possibilities.

All my life I have lived within the limits set by others or myself. The limits I have are the very bonds that keep me chained to my ego. I am finding, through my readings and through human examples, we are limitless and can do and achieve a way of life that can open my heart to the permanent "bliss state". This is the reward for my vigilance and for "knowing myself".

WHAT ARE YOU WAITING FOR?